Proof Passionate

"Do you understand what's going to happen if you don't go?" Randall said hoarsely.

Rosalie managed to nod.

Suddenly Randall reached for her and enveloped her in his arms. As his kiss forced her head back, she opened her mouth under the pressure of his, allowing his arms to crush her against him. Rand's fingers tangled in her hair, caressing her head, as his tongue mated with hers.

Her breath came fast and shallow through her lips, mingling with his as he eased her gown down, then caressed her breasts through her light, filmy chemise. The night air struck her bare flesh with a gentle chill, and the warmth of his hands was splayed over her skin.

"You told me . . . it could be different from how it was before," Rosalie said breathlessly. "Prove it to me. . . ."

Ⓢ **SIGNET BOOKS**

SURRENDER TO LOVE

(0451)

☐ **WHERE PASSION LEADS by Lisa Kleypas.** Only the flames of love could melt the brrier between them. Beautiful Rosalie Belleau was swept up in the aristocratic world of luxury when handsome Lord Randall Berkely abducted her. Now, she was awakening into womanhood, as Sir Randall lit the flames of passion and sent her to dizzying heights of ecstasy. . . .
(400496—$3.95)

☐ **RENEGADE HEARTS by Peggy Hanchar.** Spirited Southern belle, Bree Riker had scorned all suitors, but when she unwittingly falls into the arms of bold Seminole, Shocaw, she is plunged to the depths of danger that only passion could conquer. . . .
(400208—$3.95)

☐ **JOURNEY TO DESIRE by Helen Thornton.** Delicate ambers and gold tinted Laurel's silky hair and sparkling eyes. Inflamed by the lovely innocence of this beautiful American flower, the debonair Englishman pursued her eagerly, first with camelias and kisses, then with a wild passion. His sensuous touch dared her to become wanton in his arms. (130480—$3.50)

☐ **DEVIL'S DAUGHTER by Catherine Coulter.** She had never dreamed that Kamal, the savage sultan who dared make her a harem slave, would look so like a blond Nordic god. . . . He was aflame with urgent desire, and he knew he would take by force what he longed to win by love.
(141997—$3.95)

☐ **TIDES OF PASSION by Sara Orwig.** Love sparked desire within Lianna as fierce as the stormy seas. Fleeing a forced marriage disguised as a maid, Lianna struggled against the notorious Captain Joshua Raven, a pirate who ravaged the Spanish main and claimed her for his own. But as his mouth came down on hers, the ocean's pounding roar she heard was really her hearts answer to his kiss. . . . (400356—$3.95)*

Prices slightly higher in Canada

WHERE PASSION LEADS

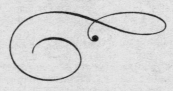

LISA KLEYPAS

AN ONYX BOOK

NEW AMERICAN LIBRARY

To Linda Kleypas with love . . .
Thanks for being my mother

NAL BOOKS ARE AVAILABLE AT QUANTITY DISCOUNTS
WHEN USED TO PROMOTE PRODUCTS OR SERVICES.
FOR INFORMATION PLEASE WRITE TO PREMIUM MARKETING DIVISION,
NEW AMERICAN LIBRARY, 1633 BROADWAY,
NEW YORK, NEW YORK 10019

 ONYX IS A TRADEMARK OF NEW AMERICAN LIBRARY.

SIGNET, SIGNET CLASSIC, MENTOR, ONYX, PLUME,
MERIDIAN and NAL BOOKS are published by NAL PENGUIN INC.,
1633 Broadway, New York, New York 10019

First Printing, September, 1987

1 2 3 4 5 6 7 8 9

PRINTED IN THE UNITED STATES OF AMERICA

One

All night by the rose, rose
All night by the rose I lay
Dared I not the rose steal
And yet I bear the flower away
                          —Anon.

To a young heart thirsting for passion, for adventure, it was not much of a life. The slow days of work and dullness were never broken for Rosalie Belleau, not by a lover's touch, not by a night of laughter and dancing, not by the taste of wine or the headiness of occasional freedom. She had no recourse from drudgery except for her dreams. More lamentably still, Rosalie was so unenlightened that she would scarcely have known what to dream of had it not been for Elaine Winthrop, who led the kind of existence that Rosalie could not help but envy. Elaine, only a year younger than Rosalie but far more advanced in experience, brought back gossip and lavish descriptions of the balls she attended, the glittering people she met, and the many delights that London held.

Although the season was closing and the summer was well on its way, London barely slowed its hectic pace and Rosalie burned with the fever of frustrated youth. She was helpless to change her situation and lacked the patience to bear her fate stoically. Slowly she simmered in the tepid, damp air of spring and buried herself in fantasies. Someday, Rosalie dreamed, she would wake up to a morning in which the gray and black that shaded her days would have burst into bright color. Someday the blood would sing through her veins with the sweetness of champagne. Someday she would escape her invisible prison and find someone to love, a man who would adore and cherish her. He would let her be a friend, a woman, a companion, a lover. He would share her dreams, arouse her most intense emotions, take her around the world to show her its wonders, absorbing every sight and sound. Someday everything would change.

When someday arrived, it was not at all what she had expected.

It was seldom that Rosalie found enough time to join her mother, Amille, in a private discussion. When such an opportunity arose it was appreciated and enjoyed by both of them. Theirs was an unusually close relationship, for they could speak to each other not only as mother and daughter but also as friends. Amille was the most important person in Rosalie's world, understanding the needs, questions, delights, and fears of her only child even though they were far removed from her own. Outwardly they were similar, two small, dark-haired women, but inwardly they were very different. Amille had a pragmatic view of life while Rosalie had an idealistic one, and as Rosalie reached the age of twenty she realized instinctively that the causes of this difference went deeper than age or experience.

Amille was rocklike in her stability and her love of order. She was well-read but unimaginative, whereas Rosalie's emotions and thoughts seemed forever soaring or plummeting. No matter how Rosalie tried to control her own unorthodox cravings, she knew that she was forever doomed to seek excitement and to give too free a rein to her feelings. She liked to laugh out loud instead of smiling politely, she loved to ferret out secrets and discoveries when she should have been reconciled to the way things were. Currently Rosalie's curiosity was focused on a subject that Amille did not want to discuss, but as they sat down to engage in needlework the younger woman plied her mother with persistent questions.

"Rosalie," Amille said evenly, a frown gathering between her attractive brown eyes as she took a careful stitch, "I have told you all that you need to know about your father. He was a confectioner near the East End. He was a kind, good man, and he died when you were a month old. Now, may we change the subject? It pains me to speak of him."

"I'm sorry," Rosalie said, feeling a twinge of guilt as she heard the unusually sharp note in her mother's tone. "I did not mean to bring up painful memories for you, *Maman.* I just wanted to know a little more about him."

"But why? Would it change anything about you or your circumstances to know more about him? . . . Of course it wouldn't."

"Perhaps it would," Rosalie replied, tilting her head to the side as she regarded her mother. "Sometimes I find it so hard to understand myself and my feelings . . . I wonder sometimes if I am more like you or him."

"You are like neither of us."

As Rosalie laughed, Amille shook her head and smiled at the picture her daughter made. Rosalie's blue eyes glowed with an almost violet light, and her lips were parted in one of those dazzling, abandoned smiles. She could appear almost angelic when she wished, but much of the time a hint of mischievousness glimmered in her expression, as if she were thinking of something naughty and inappropriate. At the beginning of each day her long sable-brown hair was pulled back and pinned into a thick coil, yet predictably it would be falling down her back around midafternoon. Her beauty, her eagerness, and her vibrant spirit were all enviable gifts, but often Amille wished that Rosalie had been less richly endowed. It would all lead to trouble one day.

"*Maman?* May I ask another question?"

Amille sighed.

"Yes."

"I've never met any of my relatives, because you've said that they are all in France——"

"Yes. A respectable French family, fallen on difficult times. That is why I had to take a position as governess here."

"Then surely you were higher-born than a confectioner? I am glad that you married my father, but . . . you are so beautiful! Why didn't you wait to see if you could have married a more influential man . . . perhaps a country squire who——"

"Ah, Rosalie, you worry me so often . . . tell me, please, what you desire from marriage."

"Well, affection, of course. And contentment with——"

"Contentment." Amille seized upon the word promptly. "That is exactly what you should strive for. And do you know what the true source of a woman's contentment is?"

Rosalie grinned wickedly. "A handsome husband?"

"No," Amille replied seriously, refusing to allow the intensity of her lecture to be diminished by any attempt at humor. "A woman is contented by the knowledge that she is needed by her husband. When he is exhausted and needs her to feed and comfort him. When he is dispirited and needs her to hold him. When he confides in her and places his trust in her. Give up your fantasies of a handsome, influential husband, for he would never need you as a poorer man will."

Blinking in surprise at Amille's vehemence, Rosalie looked down at her hands.

"But . . . a rich man would need someone just as much as a poor one——" she began, but Amille interrupted her.

"No. Not in the same way. To a rich man, a wife is a

possession. His fondness for her lasts until she bears him an heir, and then he tucks her away in the country to live by herself. He takes a mistress for his sexual needs and relies on his friends for companionship. I would not wish that for you, Rosalie."

Rosalie bit her lower lip, her eyes fairly dancing with rebellious lights. Certainly she did not want the kind of life that Amille had just described, but neither did she want to be burdened with more of the same drudgery that she longed to escape from right now!

"Do you know what I wish?" she asked impulsively. "That my father had been a . . . a duke! Or at the very least a baron, so that I could do all the things that . . ." Her voice trailed off into abashed silence near the end of the sentence, but not before Amille understood exactly what she had been about to say.

"All the things that Elaine does," her mother said quietly. Rosalie nodded slightly, ashamed at the covetous words. "All your life," Amille said with regret lacing through her voice, "I have wanted the best for you, more than what your station calls for. I have encouraged you to do what Elaine does, to learn what she learns, to have the same respect as I do for education. But I have omitted an important part of your education. I have not taught you to recognize what your place is, what *our* place is. You consider yourself her equal, and you are not. I'm afraid it will grow even more difficult for you to bear than it is now if you don't come to some understanding of it."

"I understand what my place is," Rosalie said matter-of-factly. "I am continually reminded of it. I am the daughter of the governess. I am Elaine Winthrop's occasional companion, more often her maid." She leaned over until her head rested on the fragrant cotton of Amille's apron front, her discontented heart suddenly aching. "But do you know what makes it hard to bear, *Maman?*" she whispered. "I have studied much more than Elaine ever has. History, art, literature . . . I can play the pianoforte and speak French, and I can even sing better. I could be just as successful a debutante as she is, but because of the circumstances of my birth—"

"Do not ever say that aloud again," Amille interrupted sharply, her cheeks flushed. "If someone overheard you . . ."

"But Elaine is going to be married soon," Rosalie said, her fingers twining together agitatedly. "What about my future? Will I continue to be her companion? And then nanny to her children?"

"There are worse situations to envision. You are not hungry. You have clothes and books, and little justification for such self-pity."

Rosalie sighed. "I know," she said apologetically. "It's just that I have the suspicion that I'll end up a spinster, and the thought makes me wild. I want to live! I want to dance and flirt—"

"Rosalie—"

"Toss my head until the pins fall out of my hair—"

"Shhh!"

"Make eyes at handsome men from behind my fan."

"*Chérie*, please."

"But despite my fantasies I know inside that no aristocrat would marry me. Do you know what they call it when a man marries beneath his station? 'Manuring the fields.' How I've been relegated to that status through no fault of my own escapes me."

"Of course you are resentful, but none of this can be helped," Amille soothed, the pace of her stitching increasing markedly.

"Sometimes I sit and read or copy verses in my album, and the room becomes so small I can hardly breathe. *Maman*, there must be some escape!"

"Rosalie, you must learn to be calm." Amille was becoming more than mildly disturbed. No properly reared girls spoke in such a manner, with wild eyes and passion trembling in their voices. How could she teach her daughter to reconcile herself to the course that life had set for her? "You have been inside too much, I think. Maybe a trip to the theater will be good for you." They had made such an excursion once before with the Winthrops, and Rosalie had been charmed by the gaudy Covent Garden production, a triple bill including a Shakespearean tragedy and a one-act farce. Amille was entirely aware of Rosalie's need for variety, and tried to provide it in harmless little ways, with books, new hair ribbons, and other fripperies that might ease her restlessness.

"That's a good idea," Rosalie agreed, subsiding a bit. She could not help remembering, however, how they had been required to sit with the other servants and the footmen in the gallery, looking at the upper classes preening in the box. It had been disconcerting to sit with what Elaine pointedly called "the rabble," especially considering the tendency of the lower classes to throw dried peas at the actors they disliked. "I need to do something new. Perhaps we could go walking down Pall Mall and bump into the prince during one of his elegant strolls. What do you say to that?"

Amille pursed her lips at the ironic note in her daughter's voice.

"According to Hume, each of us has a ruling passion, Rose. I hope that yours is not this restlessness. Some people can never be happy. I would not like to think that you have this affliction."

Rosalie also wondered if she would ever be completely happy. But surely she was not the only one to feel this way! How many women were like herself? How many fell so far short of the ideal?

The perfect woman was complacent, gentle, accepting of whatever her circumstances happened to be, nothing more than a pretty toy who would serve the convenience of the man she belonged to. And she was not to be loved too passionately, not in the way that Rosalie longed to be loved someday. *So divine, so noble a repast,* a well-known poem went, *I'd seldom, and with moderation taste. For highest cordials all their virtue lose by too frequent and too bold a use. . . .* In other words, she thought wryly, use a woman well and then put her up in the right place.

"I'll try to be more content," she said.

"And so you will be," Amille soothed, handling her needlework carefully to prevent a pinprick from staining the fine damask. "Your effort is all that is necessary. Remember, you must serve as a good influence on Elaine."

Slowly the young woman stood up, adjusting the pins in her hair as the heaviness of the tresses threatened to undo the simple coiffure.

"I should go now. Lady Winthrop wants me to read to her. She is in bed, feeling peaked."

"Probably the excitement of this morning. Did she decide to let Martha stay?"

"No. She said that any maid who had been caught with a man in her room would undoubtedly provide an unwholesome atmosphere for Elaine. And then Lady Winthrop looked at me significantly, as if she hoped that I would be next!"

Amille chuckled.

"Be kind to her, my good girl. She is not a happy woman. Bring her some tea, and those chocolate biscuits she has taken a fancy to."

"I would, *Maman,* but she needs slimming."

"Rosalie!"

The younger woman picked up her skirts with slender, well-kept hands and left the room as quickly as possible, endeavoring to avoid another lecture. They lived in a stucco terrace house, the Winthrops occupying the third floor while Rosalie and Amille stayed in a basement room next to the kitchen. It was a privileged position, for the rest of the servants slept in the attic, which was cold in the winter and stifling in the summer. Rosalie summoned all of her energy to climb the endless staircase, her breath quickening as she reached the top.

The book Lady Winthrop had requested, entitled *Avoid the Wayward Path,* absorbed much of the afternoon. Rosalie read in a clear and even voice, her eyes passing over the thick, small print until she could not stop from blinking sleepily as she turned each page.

"Stop that droning, child," Lady Winthrop finally said, leaning her head back until the pale gold of her curls rested against the pile of feather pillows on her bed. Her plump cheeks vibrated as she sighed and prepared to take a nap. "It's ghastly hot today."

Rosalie also sighed as she set the book aside, knowing that the chapters selected for today had most likely been intended for her own benefit. Quietly she stared down into the London street. Vendors walked up and down the pavement, crying their musical sounds to attract the attention of potential customers. "Cherrrries! Sweet cherrrrries!" "News in print! Neeeeews in print!" Crossing-sweepers of tender years swept the way across the street for well-dressed men and women, turning their palms up at the curbstone to receive a farthing or ha'penny for their service.

Twisting her hands in her lap, Rosalie allowed her mind to wander restlessly. There were so many places she was forbidden to go, so much that she could not do. Only a mile or two away were clustered the famous coffeehouses where the intellectuals read papers and conducted lively discussions on politics and theory. Further west was Hyde Park, Piccadilly, the Mall, Spring Gardens, and the Haymarket. She was not allowed the freedom to see these places by herself, a right which even the meanest street urchins possessed!

But it was dangerous for a woman to travel in London alone. The London police were poorly organized and underpaid and these conditions led to vast corruption within their numbers. It was up to private citizens' groups to look out for their own welfare. A harsh criminal code was the only deterrent to crime. Therefore Rosalie, Amille, and the rest of the servants traveled back and forth from Winthrop House in town to Robin's Threshold, the family seat in the country, without setting foot in the places in between.

"Rose!" came a whisper from the doorway. Rosalie automatically put a silencing finger to her lips as she turned to look at the visitor. It was Elaine, who had apparently recovered from the foul temper she had woken with that morning. It was difficult for Rosalie to bear a grudge toward her, because even at her worst Elaine possessed nothing of the nastiness that permeated Lady Winthrop's disposition. Elaine was basically a happy creature with the typical needs and desires of any well-bred English girl. She yearned for a handsome suitor, beautiful clothes, and adequate pocket money. There was no reason why she wouldn't be able to attain her goals. Elaine was gentle, pretty, well-dowried, and rather simple. This morning she was especially attractive in a powder-blue gown decorated with beaded flower appliqués. There was never anything to fault in her appearance, for Elaine took endless pains to ensure that her blond cornsilk hair was arranged as artfully as possible. She also cared for her skin with the same air of mission, guarding it zealously from the sun so that it shone like gleaming snow. As she peered into the room and took in the scene, the light, clear gray of her eyes glinted with a particularly gleeful expression.

"I have to tell you about last night," she whispered. "Come with me, Rosie."

Reluctantly Rosalie cast a glance toward the bed. A gentle snore rumbled from Lady Winthrop's direction.

"I can't risk leaving your mother—" she began, but Elaine shook her head impatiently.

"I'll tell her it's my fault if she wakes while you're gone. I want to gossip awhile and Mama won't need you for at least an hour or so."

Rosalie nodded and stood up carefully. Whether to stay or leave was not a difficult decision to make. The last thing she desired was to bring down the baroness's wrath on her unlucky head, but she was relieved to escape the stuffiness of the room. They tiptoed into Elaine's turquoise-shaded bedroom, done in the feminine style of Robert Adam, with festoons, white Grecian reliefs, and Venetian carpets, and they sat on the canopied bed. Eager to hear news, gossip, or descriptions of anything entertaining, Rosalie leaned forward to catch every word. "It must have been an exciting party. You slept very late this morning," she said, and Elaine grinned wickedly.

"Excuse my temper this morning . . . I was as cross as a bear when you came in with my tea. Last night was the longest party yet. I could hardly open my eyes today, after all of the dancing I've been through. Mama even let me *waltz*, can you imagine? And I met the *most* wonderful men last night, and the downstairs hall is already filled with flowers and calling cards for me." Dreamily she closed her eyes and fell back onto the goosedown mattress. "None from *him*, though, and that's what I would prefer. I must get him to notice me."

"Ah, him. And just who is 'him'?" Rosalie questioned with reluctant amusement. It was half-pain, half-pleasure to listen to Elaine's adventures when she wanted so badly to have one herself.

"Lord Randall Berkeley, the future earl. He and his friends attended the party last night. Every now and then one of them would dance . . . oh, you should see how Lord Berkeley dances! He approached Mary Leav-

enworth for a waltz and made the clumsy girl look
positively graceful! The rest of the time he and his
friends stood near the corner and talked mysteriously
among themselves, stopping occasionally to cast an eye
in the direction of the more popular debutantes."

"They sound rather arrogant to me." Rosalie could
picture the scene easily, especially the corner full of
young male peacocks, all strutting and preening because they were matrimonially eligible.

"Oh, but they looked so worldly and exciting, as if
there was nothing they hadn't seen or done before."

"Really?" Rosalie's interest was piqued even further.
"Do you think that's really true, or is this some grand
impression they seek to give?"

"From what I hear, Berkeley is very experienced and
utterly wicked. Mama told me that spending even one
minute alone with him would shred a girl's reputation."

"Take care that he's not a fortune-seeker."

Elaine suddenly broke into giggles.

"Haven't you ever heard of the Berkeleys? They own
a shipping company, Abbey House in Somerset, Devonshire House, a castle on the Severn . . . Heavens,
they own Berkeley Square!"

"That may all be true, but I've heard that some
London bucks are heavily into gaming, throwing away
hundreds of thousands of pounds in one night! They
give the appearance of wealth even while they are
deeply in debt."

Elaine ignored the remark, staring dreamily up at
the ceiling.

"He is attractive in a strange sort of way . . ."

"Lord Berkeley?" Rosalie questioned, and Elaine
nodded.

"Mmmmn. He is tall and I'll admit rather unfashionably dark, but his manner is quite fascinating. Most of
the time he wears a dreadfully bored expression—"

"Of course. Hence, everyone must seek to entertain him."

"—but occasionally he flashes the most charming smile you've ever seen. All he needs is a woman's gentle influence to moderate him."

"Is he a dandy?"

"He dresses well," Elaine conceded, "but I don't believe his cravat was as high as fashion demands. Why, some of the extracts last night wore them up to the ears!"

"Ridiculous," Rosalie pronounced, leaning forward in enjoyment. "I've heard them speak. Ridiculous creatures, lisping and playing with words until their speech is barely intelligible. Is he like that?"

"No, no, not at all. At least, I don't think so. I wasn't able to talk with him. But I'll attract his notice somehow. He's the catch of a lifetime."

"And so are you." Rosalie patted Elaine's pale, dainty hand. Suddenly she didn't wish to hear any more about people she would never meet or about balls the like of which she would never attend.

"And there's someone else I haven't mentioned yet, the most divine viscount from—"

"I would like to hear more about this," Rosalie interrupted, painting on a smile, ". . . later. For now, don't you think we should practice your French lesson?"

"Mercy, no."

"*Merci,*" Rosalie corrected, and Elaine moaned.

"I feel a distinct pain in my temples."

"You need a brisk walk and fresh air. I'll go with you."

"I need to rest. Bring me some orange-flower water and a handkerchief, please. And tell Cook I would like luncheon brought up in an hour. Oh, give my white slippers to Amille. The ribbons need repairing." A note of condescension had entered Elaine's tone as she spoke, reminding Rosalie momentarily of Lady Winthrop.

"Of course," Rosalie murmured in a voice so docile that her reply was a parody of submissiveness. The sarcasm was completely lost on Elaine. Rosalie gathered up the thin slippers and closed the door as she left.

Cautiously she glanced up and down the passageway, assuring herself that no one was nearby before she removed her own shoes and tried on the dainty white dancing slippers. Slowly she moved across the floor, gathering the excess of her skirt in one hand as she marveled at the feel of heelless silk shoes made especially for dancing. "No, thank you," she mimicked with the slightest touch of disinterest in her voice. "I've danced so much tonight that I could not possibly subject my toes to one more waltz. And the hour is quite late, you know. The monotony of these gatherings becomes quite dreadful, does it not?" In her mind the man she spoke to did not answer, merely looked at her with a smile tinged with mockery, and eyes filled with . . . Ah, what was the word in French? *Savoir-faire.* Directly translated, it meant "know-how-to-do." The question was, Rosalie pondered curiously, know-how-to-do what?

"Damn them all!" the aging Earl of Berkeley said in disgust. "We'll have another war with the French if this trade policy continues. The Berkeley affairs across the Channel are in a fine mess." His hawkish face was pale and lined heavily, his gnarled hands tapping impatiently on the desk. Similar to most of the furniture in the country house, the desk was unfashionably old, bracketed in a Chinese style with claw-and-ball feet. The massive furniture and the heavy-handed style in which the library was decorated suited the earl, who possessed an impressive and intimidating presence.

"I assumed as much. Otherwise you wouldn't have sent for me."

"All of your philanderings in London can wait until you return from France," the earl said, looking at his eldest grandson with exasperation that bordered on the extreme. For one reason or another, a conversation with Randall, as the earl was fond of saying, usually ruined one's digestion.

It was often said that they were two of a kind. Rand's face was a darker, smoother version of the Berkeley mold, and he seemed to have an innate callousness that was appropriate for a member of this particular family. He was certainly a legitimate Berkeley, being "a man of no mean parts, though very loose principles," a description commonly given to the men of the family. There was much to criticize about his upbringing, however, including the fact that Randall had never been taught the value of constancy. He had the reputation of being both reckless and heartless, and the earl had the justifiable suspicion that Randall had earned it well.

"I'll take care of everything," Rand said lightly, ignoring the earl's scowl.

"I have not told you the worst of our troubles yet."

"Oh?"

"It came out in the *Times* today. Berkeley Shipping recently delivered a cargo of cotton from New Orleans to France. A Mr. Graham at the port of Havre discovered that those blasted American merchants have been hiding stones in the cotton bales!"

Rand winced at the revelation. Practices such as concealing heavy articles in the cotton served to drive the weights and therefore the prices up, damaging the credibility of the company that delivered the shipment. Such a discovery could mean disaster for a highly profitable business.

"How bad is it?" he inquired, and the earl's answer came back like a shot.

"Over one thousand pounds of stones concealed in merely fifty bales!"

Suddenly Rand's eyes lit with amusement despite his efforts to remain serious. Of the Americans he had met so far, he liked them as a general matter of course, mainly because this sort of behavior was typical of them.

"Cheeky devils," he observed, and his grandfather glowered at him. "Don't worry, I'll handle it immediately."

"And not only will you persuade the port to let future shipments through, you will also find some way to assure that the bales are no longer fraudulent."

"If I have to pick the cotton myself," Rand said.

"A far more apt occupation for you than taking care of the family business," the earl remarked.

"I appreciate your confidence."

"Any other questions?"

Rand's face faded to implacability again. "No."

"Aren't you curious as to why I've entrusted this to you instead of Colin?"

Rand remained silent, but something in his expression flickered subtly at the mention of his younger brother.

"I see you are," the earl continued, and his lips twisted into a semblance of a smile. "Gad, it amazes me that your mother, that flighty bit of French nonsense, managed to produce two boys before she died. I see her in both of you . . . but especially in you. You look like a Berkeley, boy, but you were minted a d'Angoux. Same aversion to bearing the weight of any responsibility on your shoulders." He paused, and his expression sharpened. "It pains me that you are the firstborn heir. Colin is a fop, but I'd trust him with my last farthing. He understands money. Give him a penny, he'll make it a pound before the day is through."

"Most likely through ill-gotten means."

"You miss my point," the earl said sardonically. "According to common tradition, you will inherit everything save what is reserved for Colin. I must see if you are capable of handling it. If not, I will use what means I can to divide the estate between you, much as I would prefer to hand it over intact. But I am unable to picture you making weighty decisions with the proper care, and I cannot see the rest of the family looking up to you as the proper shepherd of the flock, not with that flippant attitude of yours. I must confess I do not believe you are remotely deserving of the entirety of the Berkeley holdings."

As always, Rand irritated the older man by treating a weighty matter as if it were nothing of much consequence. His attitude was careless, as if it didn't matter to him whether the Berkeleys doubled their fortune or went to hell in a hand basket.

"I am certain that I am not, sir," the younger man said wryly. "However, being deserving has no bearing on whether or not I am capable of handling it. You may rest secure on two points. I will keep the Berkeley fortune intact whenever it happens to be transferred to my care. And second, I don't foresee that such a situation will occur for a good many years. Your health, as always, is—"

"My health is failing. Haven't you seen that? The thing I desire most is the security of my lands and sundry possessions. And my demise is approaching all the quicker because of my fears about you." The earl's eyes narrowed as he regarded Rand with something akin to dislike. "What sort of bird are you?" he asked slowly. "You seem to care about nothing. What are your wants, your weaknesses? Women? Gaming? God knows it's not strong drink—"

"Thanks to my father's tender care, I've developed a ready caution for that."

Rand's general moderation in drink was well-known,

for as a boy his father had often forced red wine on him
as a preventive measure for gout. It had not taken long
for Rand to become an alcoholic. As a teenager he had
been in a lamentable condition even after the death of
his one remaining parent. Without the intervention of
his grandmother he would have drunk himself into the
grave by now.

"All I know is that I've done my best for you, boy,
and so far you've failed me. When are you going to get
married? When will I see an heir?"

"An heir," Rand repeated with weariness edging his
voice. "I suppose you'll see one when I discover a
woman I'd care to mix my blood with."

"Great Gad, boy, it's not as if there aren't hundreds
of prime candidates who would accept you! Have you
ever been attracted to a decent woman, the marrying
kind?" the earl pressed.

"I don't recall—"

"Damn, am I missing a discussion of Rand's romantic
activities?" Colin's smooth drawl disturbed the atmosphere. "Might liven up a dreadfully boring afternoon."
He sauntered into the room, conscious as always of his
appearance with every step he took. The thin tissue of
his slippers made no sound on the floor. He wore a rich
purple coat, the back divided into pleated tails that
fastened with hip buttons. A brilliant white vest and
canary-yellow trousers completed the outfit. Colin
raised his hand to his forehead, drawing attention to
the carefully tousled condition of his blond locks.

Though they were only two years apart it was
difficult to see the physical resemblance between Colin
and Rand. It was generally agreed that Colin had
inherited the looks in the family, for he was exquisitely
made in both face and form. His skin was pale and
polished, his eyes a remarkably pure green. Slim and
elegantly turned limbs were enhanced by his graceful,

catlike way of moving. The dandies he associated with were often moved to comment enviably on the bounty that nature had bestowed on Colin Berkeley, for every feature, every gesture, every accent of his words was nothing short of perfect. Rand, in contrast, had been cast in a different, rougher mold. His eyes were the murkier hue of hazel, the green often sullied by an indistinguishable shade of brown. He was much darker than Colin, his skin unfashionably dark and his hair a deep shade of amber rather than bright gold. Rand was also much taller, his body lean but built with solid muscles and powerful proportions. It was a body that was well-suited for physical labor, and as such it was inappropriate for an aristocrat, who was supposed to be as far removed from work as possible. Physical exertion was a burden for the lower classes to bear, not the nobility.

The brothers exchanged an assessing glance, and then Colin smiled slyly. "What is the most recent complaint?" he inquired with relish.

"He should be married," the earl replied, regarding Colin with disgust. "And you should have been a woman. You're too damned cattish and exquisite to be a grandson of mine. You and your friends usurp your manners, your costume, your values, from women. You have a woman's way about you, and I dislike it."

Unfazed by the words, Colin raised his nose slightly. "Grandfather, it is a privilege of aristocracy to be an exquisite. And if you care to discuss appearances, turn your attention to Rand. Hair cropped as short as a bruiser's, the language of a millworker. Not to mention skin as dark as a Gypsy's."

Rand's wide mouth quirked slightly. "At least I wear no dandy's corsets," he remarked, and Colin stared at him coolly, placing long white hands on his nipped-in waist.

There was no love lost between the brothers, perhaps because they were close in age and had fought bitterly in childhood. Still, Rand sometimes found in his heart an odd sort of affection for Colin, who was as harmless as he was effeminate. He let Colin's barbs bounce off him, for they did him no damage.

"Why have you left your pursuits in London?" Colin inquired.

"I'm off to France soon to settle a few business problems."

"Really." Colin viewed him through a quizzing glass with delicately arched fingers, frowning at first and then resorting to a snicker. "Dear me, how entertaining. I wish you good fortune." He walked across the room to a decanter of brandy and poured himself a glass. "What exactly are you going to take care of?" The earl handed him the paper and Colin scanned it idly as he spoke to Rand. "I caught word of your appearance at the gala last week. No tender morsel caught your interest?"

"White dresses, blond curls, hopeful girls with damp palms, scowling dowagers, simpering mamas. No, nothing caught my interest."

"Really," Colin said, addressing the earl, "one can hardly blame him."

"Someone can," Rand replied lazily, detaching himself from the scene and pausing at the doorway. "I have some affairs to take care of in London before I leave—"

"Why don't you begin to establish some court connections while you're there?" the earl suggested moodily.

"I'll leave Colin to court the prince. He has a far greater aptitude for humoring the royal inanities than I."

"Saint Lucifer!" Colin sputtered, brandy spraying over the paper. "Stones in the cotton?"

"*Au revoir,*" Rand said softly, grinning at his brother's discomfiture before he disappeared from sight.

"Your brother has quicksilver in his veins," the earl observed when he was gone. "No blood. No sense of family, no morals."

"He has morals," Colin corrected, lowering his quizzing glass and removing his attention from the empty doorway. His smile became tinged with saccharin, as if a sweet memory had suddenly turned sour. "His behavior is consistent with his own set of values, although from where he derived them I have no idea."

"I can enlighten you. He behaves exactly like the bucks he runs with. A spoiled lot of carousers."

"But they do have their own particular set of ethics," Colin said consideringly. "Ones I don't agree with, to be sure. Their object is to 'carouse,' as you put it, whereas mine is to achieve perfection in the subtle arts of life, in everything from manners to tying a cravat—"

"In short, you care about the insignificant and scorn what is meaningful, while Rand and his crowd make it a point to scorn everything in general." The earl harrumphed in displeasure before continuing. "Enjoy it while you may. When I go you won't be able to afford such dandified luxuries on the allowance Rand will make for you."

Colin lifted his eyebrows, peering down at his grandsire haughtily. "I have no doubt Rand will be generous."

"You will have to depend on that, won't you?" the earl remarked acidly, and wiped the slack corners of his mouth with a handkerchief.

"It is an ironic situation," Colin mused. "Considering that Rand cares not a whit for money—"

"And you worship it."

"And you expect," Colin said, "that when you pass on, your departed son's offspring will provide a fine show, scrabbling for your leavings as you watch from above"—he paused delicately—"or below. I pity us all." He pretended a yawn and left the room, searching in his sleeve for a snuffbox.

As soon as Rand arrived in London, he supped with his companions at the club, making last-minute plans to celebrate his journey to France. He relaxed in their company as he did at no other time, feeling free from constraints and cares, appearing almost boyish as he participated in the general merriment of the club. Every one of the aristocratic members of White's, originally White's Coffeehouse, were devoted to witticisms and gambling. The Earl of Chesterfield once wrote to his son that a member of a gaming club should be a cheat or he would soon be a beggar. Here at White's the statement was often proved to be prophetic.

Rand enjoyed plying his luck at the tables, yet there was a fine edge to his character that guarded him from making such a pursuit an ingrained habit. It was not the loss of money that made him cautious, but rather the prospect of losing his control, and so he played faro and hazard with the attitude of a man who mocked himself. What he forbore to mention to the rest of the Berkeleys was that Colin had no such self-restraint and that his gambling could someday become something dangerous. Even though Colin had always enjoyed stupendous luck, it could someday vanish with the flick of a card. Huge losses at the tables caused many a tragic end for those who frequented the most popular clubs. Families were bankrupted, lives were ruined and ended, all amid intoxication, excitement, and merriment. "White's," Rand had quipped once, "will be the undoing of the English nobility." His comment was still passed between the members of the club with delight.

On this particular night there was a mild commotion

inside the club, stemming from the collapse of a man just outside the door. They carried him in and laid him out on a mahogany-framed couch, wagers flying thick and furious.

"Fifty guineas he dies."

"A hundred he lives."

"A hundred he's only drunk."

"Don't call a physician—that will affect the odds!"

Rand shook his head in disgust and suggested laconically that more amusement was to be had in a disreputable tavern. Half-drunk already, a large group of club members offered to accompany him to the Rummer, once frequented by the recently self-exiled Beau Brummell, and they took off into the streets of London.

"I say, have you heard that your brother's luck is changing?" George Selwyn the Second remarked leisurely as they established a common pace.

Rand slid him a curious glance. "No, I hadn't," he replied with an offhandedness that contrasted greatly with the sudden narrowing of his eyes.

"He owes me close to a hundred pounds. Of course, I am not mentioning this as a point of concern, for it's obvious that the Berkeleys can make good on their debts. I am—"

"Just making conversation?" Rand inquired softly. He continued to lead the way to the tavern with a controlled stride and a mild frown. Colin's gambling was a developed habit. Winning constantly made it acceptable. Losing constantly was quite another thing.

Rosalie settled into her seat with excited anticipation, clasping the round shape of her embroidered stocking purse as her gaze flew around the Covent Garden theater.

"I can't believe we're here, *Maman*. You are so good to me," she said, looking upward to take in the

breathtaking appearances of the aristocrats in their
private boxes. Most of the women wore diamonds in
their hair, around their necks, on their wrists and
fingers. Their gowns for the most part were diaphanous, shaded in pastel or white, cut so low that Rosalie
wondered how they could wear the garments without
blushing. "How did you manage to get permission
from Lady Winthrop?" she asked, and Amille smiled
placidly.

"She is exacting but not an ogress, Rose."

Rosalie kept her opinion to herself, thinking that for
tonight she would say nothing derogatory about the
baroness. Escaping into another time and place, into
other people's lives for a few hours, was worth all of the
frustrations that Lady Winthrop was so fond of ladling
out. She sighed in pleasure as the play began.

From the moment that the actor Charles Kemble
stepped out onto the stage, the audience quieted and
watched him intently. Although he was reputed to be a
vain man, refusing to play Caesar because of the
knobby knees that a Roman toga would reveal, he was
also incredibly talented and chillingly dramatic. Othello was one of his finest roles, almost as good as the
legendary Garrick's Hamlet. His face was painted a
swarthy shade, his hair ebony black, his very stance
conveying both the bewilderment and murderous rage
of the character. He portrayed Othello in exactly the
way Rosalie had imagined when she had read the play.
She gripped Amille's arm tightly as Othello began to
suspect that the fair Desdemona had betrayed him with
another man. The entire audience witnessed his tortured countenance with horrified delight, already anticipating the fate of sweet, innocent Desdemona.

"Put out the light, and then put out the light,"
Othello rasped, declaring his intention to smother her,
and his wife pleaded for mercy.

"Oh, how could he?" Rosalie whispered, thinking in

frustration that the wretch had had no proof of her wrongdoing! Othello clutched a pillow.

"He loves her too much. He cannot see the truth," Amille whispered back, her dark brown eyes also riveted on the stage. Pitifully Desdemona struggled under Othello, her arms flailing helplessly. Suddenly a misguided movement sent the candle on the bedside table flying to the ground, rolling to a halt underneath one of the heavy velvet curtains that framed the stage. The action onstage did not cease even though the hem of the heavy drape began to smoke ominously. Uneasy murmurs filtered through the audience.

"*Maman—*"

"Wait. They will put it out," Amille reassured Rosalie as stagehands raced to the small fire with a pair of buckets. Kemble finished off Desdemona and began a lengthy speech, obviously endeavoring to turn his listeners' attention away from the growing blaze. The buckets, however, were fast proving useless, and the lifeless Desdemona suddenly gave a scream and ran offstage.

Immediately the entire theater burst into an uproar, men and women climbing over seats and shoving past each other to escape the building. Rosalie gripped Amille's hand tightly and pulled her out into the aisle.

"Don't let go!" Amille cried, but her voice was scarcely audible in the ruckus. The aisle was filled with the press of panicked masses, and Rosalie was pummeled with elbows and arms as people pushed their way toward the exits. The scent of smoke began to tease her nostrils. Rosalie was filled with congealing worry. The danger was not in being burned, but suffocated.

"*Maman!*" she cried, feeling their hands slip and separate, her fingers clutching in vain. Before she could find Amille again, several more people interceded between them. She was being carried by the crowd, jostled until her hair fell down, and it was all

Rosalie could do to keep herself upright. Her eyes were wide with horror as she saw people fall and become trampled by frantic feet.

Dimly she saw the doorway and by some miracle was pushed through it breathless but unharmed. The crowd was like an uncorked bottle of champagne forced through the small opening in an uncontrollable rush. Outside, however, the danger did not cease, for pickpockets and vagrants were already taking advantage of the mass confusion. Rosalie struck out blindly as she felt a brief tug at her waist, but it was too late. Her stocking purse had been cut neatly from her waistband. "Amille Belleau!" she shouted hoarsely at the hordes of people flying right and left. There was no sign of her mother. Unconsciously Rosalie clapped a hand to her mouth and tried to focus on her next step. It was impossible to return inside the theater.

Just then she felt a thick, brawny arm encircle her waist, and she screamed in reaction as she was lifted off her feet.

"Let me go!" she gasped, digging her nails into her captor's arm. As he cursed and dropped her, she caught the scent of a foul puff of breath. Rosalie was consumed with revulsion. It was the first time she had ever been held by a man. She fled down South Hampton Street and then took a quick left, ducking into one alley after another, all of them as rank as they were dark. When she no longer heard his footsteps she leaned against a damp wall and tried to subdue her breathing. Everything had taken the semblance of a disjointed nightmare. In the distance she could hear the screams of others who had not been as fortunate in escaping the vagrants and muggers. Tears filled her eyes as she thought of Amille, praying that she was all right. They had never been separated before; in fact, Rosalie had never been in a situation when no one knew of her whereabouts.

Suddenly a hand reached for her, and she gave a cry of terror, discovering that her pursuer had been only a few feet away around the corner. Her fear made her swift as he came after her. Desperately Rosalie acknowledged that the odds of escaping him were not in her favor. She was hampered by long skirts and light slippers that did little to protect her feet from the ground. Furthermore, she had no experience of these mustard-bricked London streets, which were becoming dirtier and shabbier as she ran. I must be heading toward the East End, Rosalie thought in panic, knowing that she was approaching the worst crime district in the world. There was a rotten smell in the air, of corners and ditches filled with foul matter, awaiting the long-overdue rain that would wash them clean. If she could only find a way to outmaneuver the man who chased her and somehow find her way back toward Westminster! Her side ached with cramps. She put a hand under her rib cage as she turned down yet another soot-dusted alley, and discovered with an inner quake that her luck had run out. It was a dead end, and by the time she swung around the man was at the entrance. His arms were brawny like those of a dockworker, his age probably advanced beyond his thirties.

"Leave me alone. I can get money for you," Rosalie breathed, trembling profusely.

He walked toward her without answering, his face blank of intelligence or mercy. Rosalie was afraid she would not be able to bear what seemed inevitable. She made one last desperate attempt to run. He caught her easily as she tried to slip past him, catching a handful of her hair. He was like an animal, unwashed, uncivilized, without any sort of human sensibilities. To survive in a world such as this it was necessary to brutalize those who were weaker. Rosalie cried out, fighting the hands that snatched at her gown.

Through the nightmarish haze she heard the sound

of loud and drunken voices near the entrance of the
alley. Her impression was a group of young blades,
their clothes a jumble of white, blue, yellow, and black,
idling through Fleet Street. Evidently they were cele-
brating something, for there was much laughter and
even snatches of song as they came from a nearby club
or tavern. Rosalie continued to scream, knowing that
they were her last chance of avoiding the violation of
her body and her life. As they became aware of the tiny
commotion in the dark alley, the man's grunts, the
woman's cries, and the swish of her skirts, they began
to laugh uproariously and made catcalls, continuing
their leisurely pace down the street. Rosalie used her
fingernails once more, aiming for her captor's eyes
with a viciousness she had never believed herself capable of. Although she didn't succeed in wounding him,
he dealt her an openhanded blow, sending her hurtling
through the alley opening. It was indeed a night of
firsts, for she had never been struck before. Rosalie fell
into the middle of the crowd of elegant extracts,
sinking into dark oblivion as she dropped to the
ground, her cheek coming to rest on the toe of a soft
leather boot.

"What have you done, that the Goddess of Chance
should cast such pearls in your path?" one of the bucks
asked the owner of the expensive boot, and a small
gathering formed around the crumpled figure on the
ground.

"A nice little piece," Rand commented, kneeling
down to lift the delicately curved face off his foot. She
was out cold. Her hair streamed everywhere in endless
swaths of silky brown, curling gently across the filthy
pavement. Thoughtfully he cupped her head in one
hand as he considered her features. Although somewhat sooty, her face was perfectly symmetrical, her
cheekbones high but not sharp, lips deeply curved. Her
body was clothed in the simple garb of a house servant,

yet the moderate swell of her breasts and the neat turn of her waist were discernible nonetheless. He found her figure fairly pleasing. Through the dirt it was obvious that her skin was as unblemished as a child's, and he felt an unexpected twinge of sympathy as he saw the tracks of tears on her cheeks. "Obviously overwhelmed by such gentle courting," he said, his tone indifferent and yet faintly acidic. Around him there was a predictable chorus of wagers.

"Twenty guineas he leaves her."

"Twenty-five that she warms the Berkeley damask tonight."

"Fifty that he won't be able to best her companion."

Protests and cheers emanated from the rakes as Rand grinned and hoisted her up over one shoulder. Chance had indeed thrown her at his feet tonight, and he saw no reason why he should refuse it. There was, however, still another matter to consider.

"You care to challenge me for the wench?" he inquired calmly of the lout in the alley entrance. He was answered by a bitter stare and a thick accent.

"She's mine. I chased her through 'alf of London."

"For your trouble, then," Rand said, and flipped a guinea to him. The dockworker caught the shining piece in one fist and remained where he was. "She's mine now," Rand pointed out softly, his dark hazel eyes resting steadily on the man, and after long hesitation the lout slunk away.

"You could get a good whore for half that," George Selwyn remarked, eyeing the trim backside of the body slung so snugly over Rand's shoulder.

"And you're not including the cost of cleaning the soot from my sheets," Rand added as he strode away, causing a general round of laughter.

"Berkeley," Selwyn said, walking hurriedly to keep pace with him, "you have little need of a woman in the midst of preparing to leave at dawn for France."

"Never fear, I'll fit her into my schedule somehow."

"Do me this favor . . . send her to my doorstep tomorrow morning, and I'll give you my new bays when you return. Perfectly matched, fifteen and a half hands high, not a white hair between them."

Rand slid him a skeptical look. "If she means that much to you, then throw in a cancellation of my brother's debt to you as well."

George Selwyn sighed and nodded reluctantly. "I only hope she's worth it."

"So do I," Rand said, flashing a wicked conspiratorial grin at his companion.

Transporting a limp form, no matter how light or small, was a nuisance, especially all the way back to his apartments in Berkeley Square. Rand laid her across the small seat of his one-horse, four-wheel chaise, a light vehicle that was suitable for driving pell-mell through the cobbled streets of London. She stirred not a whit even as he carried her through the door of his bedroom. Rand's first inclination was to have his valet clean up his new acquisition while he prepared for bed. This particular manservant was a valuable employee, accustomed to keeping his mouth closed no matter what the circumstances or provocation. But on second thought, Rand decided to perform the task himself. She was so small, so vulnerable, that he was oddly disinclined to let her out of his sight.

Gently he laid her on the fine Colerain linen bedspread, stripping her gown and stockings off efficiently and discovering that her underclothes were well-worn but scrupulously clean. Dampening a cloth with some water from a white porcelain pitcher, he wiped the soot from her face, revealing tender skin that shone like satin. Her features were a marvel to behold, even robbed as they were of expression or animation. Her body, divested of all but a chemise of thin cambric, was nothing short of magnificent. Slender, yes, but un-

doubtedly womanly. How had she come to be in the
situation he had witnessed tonight? he wondered, removing the grime from her arms and neck carefully.
She did not appear to be a whore, but neither was she a
member of the gentry. Her limbs were slim and
capable-looking, without the delicate roundness that
characterized ladies of nobility. She engaged in some
kind of labor, yet it was not overly exacting, judging
from the beauty of her hands. Absently he wound a
lock of her hair around his fingers. The mahogany
silkiness of it gleamed richly in the lamplight, as though
it had taken on its own life.

"Sweet angel," Rand murmured, "'tis a pity you're
unconscious."

Rosalie stirred slowly, her mind rising from the
incoherent darkness. There was a dull ache that spread
over her entire body, but most intense was the pain
that stretched from temple to temple. A soft exhalation
came from her mouth as she struggled to open her
eyes. She was laid out on a mattress of some sort, in a
room that was quietly lit, the yellow warmth of lamplight bathing the air. Painfully she tried to recall what
had happened, her last memory being the scene in the
alley, the echo of her own cries coming back to haunt
her. What had happened?

Giving a brief moan, she raised her fingertips to her
forehead, feeling stabs of pain rebound through her
skull. She must have been brought back home, Rosalie
thought, becoming aware that she was in a bedroom
and that there was a presence beside her.

"*Maman?*" she whispered, and ignored the sharp
throbbing of her head as she shifted slightly. Startled,
she encountered the sight of a man sitting on the edge
of the bed.

"So they're blue," he said huskily, looking at her
eyes, and she stared at him in wonder. She had never
seen anyone like him. About him there was a peculiar

appearance of vibrancy, of darkness overlaid with gold. Lurking behind the grave lines of his mouth was the possibility of tenderness, yet she was not certain of it. His features were not strictly handsome, being aggressively made and lacking delicacy, and his skin was too dark by far. As Rosalie looked at him she had the impression of a polished surface that concealed much, and it made her uneasy. Most remarkable were his eyes, dark-rimmed and brilliant gold, and somewhere in the gold was mixed a cool green. They were assessing eyes, she decided, and suddenly the effort of keeping awake became too taxing for her. It was a dream, she thought, feeling the softness of the bed engulf her exhausted body. Her fancy had been lent life and color in the imagination of sleep, and in her abstracted condition she was glad it was over.

Two

*If you would be, what I think you, some sweet
  dream,
I would but ask you to fulfill yourself.*
                                        —Tennyson

Pouring newly heated water from a silver
jug into a matching basin, Rand began his morning
ablutions. Slowly he became aware that his overnight
guest was awake, for he felt the touch of her gaze on his
back. He turned around to look at her. She was
regarding him with something far removed from the
calm curiosity of last night, her eyes a more brilliant
blue in the daylight than any he had ever seen. Her
breathing was quick and uneasy, her fingers tense as
they twined around the edge of the bed linens.

"Good morning," Rand said casually, but she remained mute. A woman's silence was a novelty to a man
of his experience. He soaked a facecloth in the water,
wrung it with a deft twist, and applied it to his night's
growth of beard, watching her all the while with cool
curiosity. Slowly the atmosphere began to take on the
nuances of a confrontation.

A thousand thoughts filled Rosalie's mind, and she
began to pull them out in twos and threes, frantically
searching for an explanation of how and why she had
come to be in a strange room with a man she had never
met before. She had been attacked near Covent Garden market last night and had run east, probably to the
vicinity of Fleet Ditch. She had cried for help to a
crowd of passing dandies, and as far as she knew, they
had afforded her none. Had this man been one of
them? Had he decided to intervene on her behalf? She

watched him intently, disregarding the fact that such a stare was usually considered extremely rude. He did not look like a Samaritan. He was a young man, probably in his late twenties, without a particularly kind appearance. She would have considered him handsome if his features had not been so aggressively formed. His cheekbones, for example, were blunt and strong when they should have been more delicately drawn, and his mouth was too wide. As he resumed the preparations for shaving, his very manner seemed to her rife with self-centeredness, for he asked no questions of concern as to her welfare and gave no genuine sign of interest in her condition.

But perhaps she owed him her gratitude. He must have helped her to escape the attacker, since she had no recollection of having been molested. Rosalie flushed hotly as she came to the discovery that her clothes were draped over a Trafalgar chair in the corner and that she was wearing nothing but her brief chemise. She had never even been alone with a man before, much less while tucked in his bed wearing skimpy undergarments! And this stranger was also clothed in precious little, although he wore the wine-hued robe as casually as if it were the most complete formal attire. It made her uncomfortable to realize how large, how very masculine his form was. Had he ever longed for the slender physique so prized by fashionable standards? Somehow she didn't think so.

Dazed, she cast her eyes around the room. It contained tortoiseshell cabinets, elegant Sheraton furniture and cerule chairs, and Grecian motifs that blended the whole with harmony. A glowing Brussels carpet adorned the floor, and a brilliant-cut chimney pier mirror gleamed above a table with cabriole legs. If he owned this, then he was a man of some means. It was richly furnished, more luxurious than even the Winthrops' residence . . .

Rosalie's blood ran like ice through her body as she dwelled on the subject of the Winthrops. No matter what the excuse or how extenuating the circumstances, Lady Winthrop would not tolerate the breaking of her rules. She would cheerfully throw Rosalie and Amille out into the streets right after poor Martha, quicker than a wink and with no afterthought. Rosalie realized that she had probably lost her job, her future, and every shred of security she had once possessed. She darted a glance to the window. It was barely daybreak, the sunlight just beginning to filter through the sky. Since the Winthrops slept until late morning, there was still a thin chance that she could get home before they awoke. But perhaps *Maman* had already alerted them of her disappearance? Only if Amille had made it home at all last night. Rosalie's heart pounded with worry. She had to get home as quickly as possible. But what of this man?

"Interesting," the stranger said, his voice pleasantly modulated, if cool. "With each new thought your eyes change a different hue."

"Where am I?" she asked, her voice coming out in a croak.

Ignoring her question for the moment, he brought her a cup of hot, fragrant tea from a tray on one of the Sheraton tables. She refused to move, eyeing him as if he were about to attack her. "Who are you?" she asked, her voice shaking. "Please tell me what happened last night."

"Why don't you take some tea first?" he suggested reasonably. "You look as though you need it." Rosalie hesitated and then accepted the heated china cup carefully, feeling trapped as she looked at him. The dark-ringed green of his gaze was peculiar, for it was lightened by several brilliant shades of topaz that made his eyes startling as they shone against the burnished tan of his skin. She wondered briefly at his obvious lack of care for the effects of the sun. Any darker and he would appear quite barbaric. Well-bred gentlemen kept their skin pale; even George IV, the prince regent, was known to apply leeches to divest his face of color. Perhaps this man was a naval officer or a port official.

"Where am I?"

"We're at my apartments in Berkeley Square," he informed her. Rosalie relaxed enough to take a sip of the strong, reviving tea. She was not too far from Bloomsbury, where the Winthrops resided.

Rand's eyes rested on her steadily as he became intrigued by the incongruity between her unfashionable clothing and her upper-class accent. "What is your name?" he asked, his mouth tilting slightly at the corners at the picture she made, her hair a silky tangle, her bearing demure, her grip on the teacup entirely proper.

Immediately alarmed, Rosalie shook her head. Her hands were still trembling from the shock of finding herself in such a predicament, causing a few drops of hot tea to spill on her arm. She could not begin to place any trust in this stranger, at least not until she found out who he was and how she had come to be here.

"I would rather not say," she said in a low voice.

"Then tell me where you come from."

"I . . . I would rather not tell you that either."

"Interesting," he remarked in a light, amused tone, his smile mocking. "To be strictly equal, I suppose I'm not obliged to reveal anything further. And yet I'd wager you have a few questions to ask."

"My name is Rosalie," she said in a small rush, knowing that as things stood she had to depend on what limited kindness he might possess. Better to try to oblige him if she could.

"Rosalie . . ." he repeated, turning toward the mirror of a mahogany shaving table and dampening a well-used cake of soap. The approaching sunlight gleamed in his hair, touching off cool gold tones in the closely scissored strands of brown. "No last name?"

"You have no need to know it."

"True enough," Rand drawled, unconcernedly lathering his face with the hard milled soap. "Well, since you've told me half your name, I'll be at least halfway obliging."

She started as he flipped open a long, well-sharpened razor. His expert manner with the instrument caused her no small amount of unease.

"Sir," she asked shakily, "how is it that I am here?" The razor made a smooth, careful path down his brown throat before he answered.

"My companions and I happened to pass by as you were accosted last night. Circumstances . . . made it impossible for me to ignore you."

"I am glad you didn't." That much was true. "I suppose I owe you a debt of gratitude, Mr. . . ."

"Lord Randall Berkeley, of Warwick."

No, he couldn't be. What an odd trick of chance. Of all men who might have rescued her . . . Rosalie set down the tea and raised her fingertips to her mouth, her eyes widening. Just as Elaine had described. Except that the romantic image Rosalie had conjured up had little to do with the Randall Berkeley she saw before her. In her imagination Lord Berkeley had been an audacious gentleman, perhaps roguishly charming, whereas in reality he was cool and rather haughty. A less charming man she would never hope to meet.

"I have heard of you," she admitted cautiously, and he wiped the last traces of soap off his face with the towel.

"No doubt."

A man full of his own importance, Rosalie surmised with distaste. An affliction common among the aristocracy. She rose from the bed cautiously, placing both feet on the floor and inching toward her clothes.

"Ready to leave so soon?"

"I must get back." Something in her tone must have indicated her budding disdain for him, for he pinned her with a stare of appraisal that seemed to reach inside her to the very bones. Her shoulders quivered slightly, her hair brushing her hips as she halted.

"Get back to where?" he inquired.

"I'd—"

"—rather not say," he finished for her sardonically. "You might as well sit down, for you're not leaving until I have some answers from you."

That sounded distinctly threatening. Rosalie remained where she was, wondering desperately what hour it was. Indecision gripped her—she had been trained by Amille all of her life to do the proper thing in any situation . . . but what in God's name was the proper thing in this instance? Should she run? Scream? Talk to him politely?

"Is this necessary?" she demanded.

"To satisfy my curiosity? Yes, it is."

"I don't have the time," she dared, and his response was uttered in the most cutting of tones.

"Neither do I, but sit down in spite of your overloaded schedule. We haven't yet discussed what you owe me."

Holding his eyes resolutely, Rosalie continued to move to the Trafalgar chair in the quest for her dress, stockings, and shoes. The only way to deal profitably with him, she sensed, was to conceal her uneasiness. He was bred of the same instinct as the creature she had tangled with the night before, quick to take advantage of weakness.

"Owe you? What do you think I owe you?"

"A few answers, for one thing."

"I owe you nothing," she said, her voice sharp in her eagerness to stand up to him.

"The hell you don't—your playmate of last night would have slit your pretty throat from ear to ear after your tête-à-tête." Rand neglected to add that even if that had not occurred, his own companions would most likely have offered to take the man's place on top of her. It was the wont of the younger bucks to treat life as if it were a selfish folly. They cared for no one, for nothing except pursuing pleasure and maintaining their reputations. A strange kind of honor it was, that required payment of gambling debts but made no quarter for simple compassion.

"You fought him?" Rosalie asked, a wealth of surprise coloring her expression. Had he been so compassionate that he would have seen fit to exert himself to rescue—

"I paid him a guinea for you."

"How pleasant," she said, unable to tame a wave of indignation at his casual manner, "to discover one's ultimate value. I'm overwhelmed by your generous expenditure on my behalf."

Inexplicably there appeared a gleam of approval in the strange depths of his eyes. She had spirit, he surmised, and her attractiveness was increased by the discovery.

"Rosalie . . . *petite fleur, vous devrez cacher les épines.*" Little flower, you should hide your thorns.

"*Un avertissement très appréciable, monsieur,*" she replied immediately, in an accent as pure as Amille's.

"You have French blood in you," Rand observed.

"Yes."

"Obviously not blue."

"Apparently not." Rosalie eyed him carefully, having been struck by the particular accent and intonation of his French. It was entirely too natural to have been learned solely in the schoolroom. Did he also have Gallic blood in him? No, he looked too much the part

of an Englishman, large, solid, and affluent, without
the slender agility or facile temperament typical of a
Frenchman.

"You also owe me for a night's rest," Rand remarked.

"What?" Rosalie questioned in a faint voice, realizing
just then that they had actually shared a bed last night.
She felt a leaden weight settle in her stomach. As far as
the rest of the world was concerned, her virtue was
ruined. She tampered down a burgeoning sense of
panic.

"Your tossing and turning kept me up until the sun
began to rise. You're hardly an ideal bedmate."

"You're hardly what I would choose either!" she
managed to retort, swallowing an unpleasant lump in
her throat. Perhaps none of this was real. Perhaps she
was having a dreadful nightmare. Surely she, Rosalie
Belleau, a girl with a tidy, orderly, and dull life, had not
been tossed into the worst imaginable scenario for an
unmarried woman to find herself in. Turning her face
away, she endeavored to conceal her confusion. It was
almost certain that by now her face was a shade of brick
red that would most likely remain permanent.

"Yes, I've seen the type of men you prefer to consort
with," Rand commented, his eyes taking in her every
move.

Silently daring him to object, she gathered the
somber material of her gown in her hands and thrust
one leg into it. She would not even take the trouble to
put on her stockings, as long as she could take her
shoes—

"I wouldn't bother with that just yet," he said calmly,
setting aside the shaving apparatus. Rosalie flinched.
Again, uneasiness clotted in her throat.

"I insist you turn around," she said, her tone cold. "I
am used to dressing in privacy."

His eyes traveled over the tangled waterfall of hair
that looked far too heavy for such a slender neck to

support, then touched on the trim, womanly proportions of her body before resting appreciatively on her legs. Her ankles and calves were slender but sturdy, their shape decidedly feminine. Rand smiled in an odd mixture of anticipation and self-contempt as he realized exactly where he desired those enticing legs to be. He was beginning to want her more each minute.

"Small rose, all blooms and claws, your vestments do you little justice. I prefer you just as you are. Put the garments down."

She began to understand what he intended to do, with or without her compliance.

"A gentleman would not press his advantage in such a situation," Rosalie breathed, every vessel in her body beginning to reverberate with the increased thumping of her heart.

"I agree. But I make it a habit to collect on my debts promptly," Rand assured her. Quickly she shimmied into her gown.

"I can return your guinea to you," Rosalie said in panic, backing away as he approached her. A mute plea shone in the sapphire depths of her eyes.

"But what of my time?"

"Make a *reasonable* request of payment!"

"A few minutes of your own in exchange," Rand suggested, grinning suddenly as Rosalie ducked under his arm and retreated to the other side of the room. "Come, there's no need to carry on like a bit player in a bad farce. I'm usually told that my company is quite pleasant."

"You're not going to bed me," Rosalie informed him grimly. "I'd be as well off with the monster you rescued me from."

She felt the edge of the shaving stand press against her back. A sudden idea lit through her mind. The razor . . . where was it? She would use it to threaten him and gain her escape.

"You would prefer to have taken your chances with your companion of last evening? I don't think so. Admittedly, he and I share the same sentiment with regard to you. But although the end will be the same, the means will be quite different . . . that is, if my lovemaking isn't grossly overrated."

"I have no doubt it is!"

"You can review my performance afterward," Rand said gently, and as she scuttled further away, Rosalie spied the shine of the razor out of the corner of her vision. Triumphantly she snatched it up before he could react.

"Not unless you care to be shaved a second time," she warned, excitement weaving through her tone like tightly drawn reeds. "And I must warn you, I am far less precise with this than you."

Rand halted in front of her, and Rosalie clutched the razor more tightly. It was terrifying to see his expression fade to metallic coolness, all hints of playfulness leaving his tone as he spoke.

"A threat which would be made all the more effective if you propositioned me with the sharp edge of the blade."

She glanced down at the weapon, and in that instant he caught her slim wrist easily in a light, steely grip, easily turning it until she felt the feathery press of the blade against her own throat.

"Oh! I loathe you—get away from me!" Rosalie hissed, furious that she had been tricked, dreading the consequences of her threats to him. He smiled with a faint bleakness, dragging her body so close to his that she was not able to move.

"No matter what value you place on my hide," he said softly, "I happen to cherish it. I don't wish to see if you feel similarly about your own. Let go of your prize."

She stared at him with hatred, refusing to loosen her

clutch on the instrument. It was her last hope of escape. "Let go," he repeated, and she moved slightly, causing a slip of the razor. Instantly it was lifted from her skin, but its mark had already been made. Gasping, she relinquished the weapon to him, and her eyes filled with unshed tears as she touched the smarting nick. A few drops of blood seeped to the surface, marring the pearllike whiteness. Never in her entire life had she been threatened in such a manner, and her rage was instantly diluted by surprise and fear.

"It's not often I meet someone so unreasonably determined," Rand remarked conversationally, placing the razor out of reach and whipping out a silk handkerchief.

"It's not often that I am held prisoner," Rosalie said, her voice quavering. "What are you going to do now? Strangle me?"

"If I were you, I would discard the practice of making such poorly timed and singularly appealing suggestions." He wound the cloth lightly around her throat, frowning in what might have been regret as his fingertips lingered against her delicate skin. The faintly gray shadow of a bruise marred the pale smoothness of her jaw.

"Don't fondle me! I will retch if you continue, God's truth!"

"Rosalie . . ." Rand discovered that he rather liked the feel of her name on his tongue. "Would it make this any easier to be assured I will treat you well?" Good Lord, he had no end of women, matrons and maids alike, all willing to share his bed. Why did the prospect seem so unappealing to this one? Was she playing some sort of game with him?

"I'd be a fool to believe you," Rosalie said, and as he brushed his fingers over the fabric at her shoulder, she struck him. The slap rang out like a shot through the room. Quick as a wasp, she drew back to hit again, and

this time his large fist covered hers to still the movement in midair. A spark of anger danced in his clear
hazel eyes before he seized her and pressed his mouth
to her tightly sealed lips. "Don't," she finally said in a
cry that sounded smothered under his mouth, aware
that the masculine body so close to hers was powerful
enough to break her in two. Inexorably he dragged her
to the bed and tossed his robe to the floor. She gave a
little squeak as she realized that he was naked. "I am
personal maid to Lady Winthrop, companion to her
daughter! I—"

"I don't care if you're *femme de chambre* to the
Princess of Wales," he muttered, flinging her across the
mattress and spreading her arms wide. Her wrists
strained against the confinement of his warm hands
until her fingers were numb. Rosalie could feel every
detail of him through the thin material of her underclothes. The solid heaviness of his chest and shoulders
was a burdensome weight on her breasts, and she
writhed in discomfort. Quaking, she shrank from the
taut pull of muscle across his waist and stomach, the
resilient strength of the legs that eased hers apart. Most
unfamiliar of all was the bold heat that branded her as
his hips pressed into the cradle of hers. Fear spread
through every pore like a delicate liquid, causing her
pulse to rocket, her thoughts to crash against each
other.

"Don't do this to me. You could have anyone,"
Rosalie panted, trying to escape the heat of him
between her legs. Rand responded by settling more
deeply against her, hard and impatient for the softness
of her body. The light feminine scent of her, the young
warmth of her flesh caused a hunger inside him that he
had not felt in a long time. It was unexpected, the
strength of this desire for a reluctant maid. "Please . . .
I've never been with a man," she whispered, pulling out
her last card, and he stilled. Hazel eyes met brilliant

blue in a split second of challenge. Momentarily Rand
allowed himself to wonder if what she claimed was true.
But it couldn't be. Someone in her position and with
her looks would have lost her innocence years ago.
Comely housemaids were readily accessible and very
desirable targets for men of almost any means and
station.

"I don't believe you," Rand replied flatly.

"It's true, *damn* you!"

Prompted by painful arousal and the inexplicable
necessity to have her, Rand closed his mind to the
possibility that she was not lying. It must be, he
reasoned, that she was afraid he would not recompense
her well for her favors, or perhaps she was merely
playing the tease to heighten his desire for her. He was
well used to that game.

"Then," he drawled insouciantly, "it seems I'm
called upon to find proof of your claim." He transferred both of her wrists into one hand. Her fingernails
curved into fragile, translucent claws. Desperately Rosalie fought, but even in her fury there was little she
could do to stop him. He stripped her garments off
easily, with an offhand attitude that was as much an
indignity as a physical violation. Her naked body quivered in reaction to the cool air and the unfamiliar
experience of being revealed completely in the daylight. Sickly Rosalie closed her eyes as Rand inhaled
slowly. He placed a warm, gentle hand on her finely
structured rib cage, his reverent touch drifting upward
along the velvet skin to the fullness of her breast. As he
took its weight in his palm, the expert caress of his
thumb brought the tender softness of her nipple to
complete arousal. At the same time he bent over her
other breast and took it into his mouth, the heated flick
of his tongue sweeping over her again and again. Her
soft skin, her quivering flesh . . . was so sweet . . .

As Rosalie struggled against him she realized he was

ten times stronger. His body was hard and invulnerable, built for aggression, so very different from her own. The hair on his chest brushed against her skin like rough silk, the abrasion feeling unutterably strange. I don't believe it is happening, Rosalie thought, frozen with shame as she pictured the scene from above. Herself, pale-skinned in the morning light, stretched out on the rumpled luxury of the bed, the man devoting his attention to the most private parts of her body as if he owned them. His dark amber hair gleaming immaculately, his large hands cupped around her, one of his legs insinuated between her tense and parted knees. She could barely hear through the labored rushing of her breathing and the drumming of her heart.

"This is disgusting," she choked, and he dragged his mouth up to the fragile line of her jaw, careful not to disarrange the silk kerchief around her neck.

"A wounding observation. Usually my services are more highly recommended," Rand said, his mouth curving in a momentary touch of humor. She turned her face away from him, clenching every muscle in rejection of what was occurring. She merely succeeded in imprisoning his leg more securely between hers. Then her breath caught in her throat as his hand stroked over the lowest part of her abdomen. "If you would relax, I believe this would all be more . . . tolerable to you," he suggested gently, and Rosalie thought she would die of shock as his fingertips drifted in an idle pattern through her soft, light curls. The world was spinning crazily, its humming whirl resonating in her head. The scents of bare masculine skin and sandalwood soap drifted seductively to her nostrils.

"Don't!" she choked, yet still the strange undreamed-of caress continued while she lay under him like a block of ice. It deepened, intensified until he was stroking the snug, shrinking tenderness of her virgin flesh, watching her stiff expression curiously. He continued until two wavering tears of humiliation wound their way down the sides of her face, yet still he did not appear satisfied with her response. "When are you going to stop?" The words fitfully issued from her lips, and Rand's mouth thinned. He discarded all efforts to make the act more pleasurable for her.

"You would prefer a fast-paced finale? I'll endeavor to oblige you," he said, and before she could take another breath he thrust into her, hard and demanding, rending her feminine softness without restraint. Rosalie cried out in surprise and pain, her body arching sharply into his in immediate reaction. The disembodied feeling returned as she realized that he had penetrated inside of her, that he remained there and was suddenly still as he stared into her dazed face. Rand whispered something, a trace of some undefinable emotion in his tone. He remained unmoving as Rosalie endured the uncomfortable sensation of being filled, too much and too deep. He held her face between his hands, but she would not meet his eyes or accept the touch of his mouth. She had not wanted to be possessed by him, neither did she want his consolation. Patiently he let her adjust to the feel of his body, allowing the first shock to wear off before he began to ease in and out of her with exquisite care.

As remorse mingled with his desire, Rand's manner changed entirely. He was extraordinarily gentle, trying to soften the stiffness of her body with his touch, brushing the lightest of kisses across her face. Although she lay underneath him like a stone, he continued to make love to her in a way that ordinarily would have given a woman unimaginable pleasure. But she was a virgin, and not only her body but also her spirit was wounded. She felt no gratification from his touch, only degradation.

Rosalie's arms, freed now, drifted down to her sides

as she felt the control and the power of his movements echo through her body. Each thrust aggravated the burning discomfort between her legs, and she felt as if she had been scorched by some inner fire. Now I know what it's like, she thought dully, her quivering thighs locked on either side of his. It was just what Amille had predicted it to be, full of pain, embarrassment, the baseness of physical desire. She had been told that women were created to serve man's needs, to give pleasure with their bodies. But how, Rosalie wondered miserably, did a man find pleasure in *this*? She doubted now that she would ever submit to someone voluntarily, not to this kind of invasion, this insult to her innocence, her dignity.

Finally, mercifully, he stopped, tensing as he pressed into the feminine sheath of her, then breathing out with a taut sigh. Exhausted, Rosalie lay beside him in misery, turning away as soon as he moved off her. She could feel rather than see the unnerving gaze that swept up and down her body. Rand glanced at the sheet, shaking his head slightly at the fresh stain of bright red. Even with such obvious proof, it was difficult to believe that she had been an innocent. He had never taken a woman's virginity until now. Baffled and disquieted, he rose on one elbow and contemplated her forlorn figure silently. At age twenty-eight Rand had known a considerable number of women, yet not one of them had provided such acute pleasure as he had just experienced. Somewhere in the midst of possessing her, his lusty enjoyment of her body had changed into awareness of her fragility. How vulnerable she was, how delicate the feel of her body clasping him, how crude his pleasure had been in comparison to her tender inexperience. She should not have been used so, and he felt a shame in the realization, a shame he covered up with his customary brusqueness.

"You were telling the truth," he admitted quietly,

and as Rosalie quivered with hatred, she refused to look at him.

"Let me go now," she said in a whisper compacted with emotion.

"Where exactly are you proposing I let you go to?" he questioned, wondering now about the situation she was in. Dammit, now he was uncomfortably aware of feeling responsible for her.

"To the residence of my employers, the Winthrops."

Rand frowned. He recalled having made the acquaintance of Lord and Lady Winthrop . . . miserly, overfed, patronizing, both of them sycophants to anyone of a higher station. It was doubtful that either the baron or his wife was magnanimous enough to extend any sort of mercy to a transgressing housemaid.

"I have had the opportunity to meet both of them," he said finally. "As well as their daughter, Elizabeth." He remembered her as a vapid creature, traditionally pretty, hardly interesting.

"Elaine," Rosalie corrected, feeling a sudden mad and illogical desire to snicker at his mistake. She had often wondered if others found Elaine as undistinctive and bland as she suspected. Now the truth was out.

"They did not strike me as being exceptionally understanding. You won't be welcomed back by them, not with the overabundance of women willing to take your place."

Rosalie did not know how to respond, acknowledging inwardly that he was right.

"I don't care where I go. I just want to get away from you," she said in a small, bitter voice. Suddenly Rand wanted nothing more than to be able to leave the scene, disliking the necessity of facing what he had done. But he could not wish her away, and if he simply cast her out, the memory of her would linger in his mind in the most tormenting way.

"Of all mornings to wake up with a conscience," he

muttered, "this is probably the most inconvenient." His straight brows drew together in an intimidating scowl. "I have no desire to see you further misused," he continued, "but I have no time to settle things here." As she turned toward him and opened her mouth, he cut her off. "Furthermore, I have no confidence in your ability to fend for yourself."

"I don't give——"

"I know. I understand your feelings. And believe what you may, I sympathize with them."

"Hardly," Rosalie said with accents of loathing, "unless you have a taste for suicide."

Suddenly Rand's white teeth flashed in a grin, a slight frisson of amusement at her testiness causing his remorse to subside. He didn't blame her for wanting to kill him. In fact, he was beginning to admire whatever it was that caused her spirit to rejuvenate so quickly instead of remaining humbled and crushed. Many women in her current situation would be flinging themselves out of the window, not eyeing him with a brilliant glare of hatred.

The thought crossed his mind: she would certainly enliven an unexciting trip. His first inclination had been to pay her off and let her make her own way in the world. But for some bewildering reason he did not want her to become a whore, and that was one of the few options that a ruined virgin of her status could contemplate. Perhaps the most convenient solution was to offer her his protection for a while, at least until he could set her on her feet again.

"It's obvious that what has already been done cannot be repaired," he said, his eyes measuring her reaction to his words. It was necessary to make her completely aware of what her circumstances were. "And unfortunately there are further consequences to the events of the past twenty-four hours—the loss of your employment, for example." As she made no response, he continued flatly. "I believe we can reasonably assume you will not be able to return to the Winthrops?"

"Yes," Rosalie said, her voice low. "I mean, no, I will not return."

"And the state of your finances is also apparent." She nodded slowly. She was utterly penniless.

"Any family?"

"My mother," she admitted, averting her gaze from his as she industriously gathered the sheet around her. "But she works for the Winthrops, and I will not compromise her position." Rosalie thought of Amille and covered her eyes with a hand in a weary gesture, unshed tears causing her head to ache. "I was separated from her last night when a fire broke out at the theater. I don't know what became of her. She might be out in the streets this very morning."

"You appear to be educated," Rand commented absently, ignoring the worry threaded through her voice. His concern was for her, not a mother who was most likely capable of taking care of herself. "It will be easy enough to find respectable employment for you, as a nanny if nothing else. The problem lies in that I have to leave this morning for France."

"I don't need your help to find employment—"

"Unless you want the events of last night and this morning to occur all over again, you need my protection until you are safely established somewhere," Rand said, rising from the bed and padding over to the pitcher and basin. He seemed unaware of the magnificence of his body, uncaring of his own nakedness. Quickly he scrubbed himself down with a square of damp linen. Then, as he brought the water to the bedside table, he saw Rosalie's red, flushed face and bowed head. A fleeting smile crossed Rand's lips as he pulled on his robe in consideration for her fierce

embarrassment, thinking that his past acquaintance
with such innocence had been limited.

"Your protection?" Rosalie murmured in a strangled
tone, making a useless effort to keep the sheet over her
body as he pulled it from her.

"I'll have to take you with me to France. It should be
nothing longer than a few weeks. When we return, I'll
settle you and your situation."

"No." Rosalie glared at him. What arrogance he
possessed! She would die before becoming his mistress,
allowing him to use her for his own pleasure. After
what he had done, how could he have the gall to
suggest it? Suddenly she gasped at the feel of the cold
wet cloth he applied to her body, and she made a feeble
attempt to escape the brutal intimacy of his eyes and
hands on her naked body. Washing every inch of her
skin industriously, Rand brought a rosy glow to the
surface. She shivered at the chilly friction of the
material, her flesh shrinking at yet another bout of
unwanted intimacy with him. Good God, did he have to
handle her as if she were a prostitute he had rented for
the night? "I can't believe you dare to propose it," she
said, her teeth chattering. "I would rather walk the
streets than submit to you even one night."

"I would not make any demands of you," he said,
plying the dampened cloth with strong brown hands.
"Inexperienced girls with sharp tongues are not usually
to my taste. Call this morning a . . . moment of weakness."

Rosalie snatched the cloth from him as she felt the
coldness of it between her legs.

"I can do *that* myself!" she snapped, waiting until he
turned his head before she completed the ablutions.
"Tell me . . . what would happen if your . . . desire
. . . was reawakened and I was the most easily available
woman? Would I still be so unpalatable to you? Exactly
how often do you have these 'moments of weakness'?"

Her tone made it clear that she considered him to possess all the discipline of a rutting dog.

"You will not be the only woman in France. When I feel the need for female companionship, I'll have plenty to choose from. So you may rely on my future discrimination." Rand was sincere in his pledge not to touch her again. His pleasure in her had not been inconsiderable, but it was completely marred by the guilt afterward. A willing whore was far preferable to an outraged virgin—that much he was certain of. Rand handed the chemise to her, and she slipped into it with fierce eagerness to cover herself.

"Rely on your discrimination?" she repeated skeptically. "When you have shown none so far? Do you think I'm an idiot?"

"Look, I would prefer not to think of you at all. And I would rather not waste more time talking, so make a decision. Walk out the door so I can be rid of you . . . or come with me, and I won't spare you a thought, much less try to crawl into your bed. Either way, I won't feel guilty, do you understand? But if you opt for the second choice, at least you have the certainty of being well-fed and lodged while you look for new employment."

"I . . . I don't know what to do," Rosalie whispered, her defenses crumbling in the face of his hard manner. "But I don't want to be with you."

Rand was almost startled at how young, how naive she sounded. It should have irritated him, yet somehow she had gently disarmed him. When, if ever, had he wanted to take a woman in his arms merely to comfort her? Rand was suddenly certain that he had become debauched, for not only did he want to cradle her as if she were a little girl, he also wanted to join her on the bed and show her what sexual pleasure was. His gaze moved over her face, her damp, smooth skin and rose-kissed mouth, the gentle curves of her cheekbones. Chafing at the unfamiliar nagging of remorse, Rand sighed heavily.

"Make the choice, little one," he said gruffly, knowing that if she decided to leave him he would take her with him anyway. It was clear that she had never been on her own before, clearer still that she would be forced to grow up fast if she hoped to survive. Even on his best behavior, he would not be a good influence on a sheltered girl . . . and no matter what he promised, he could not absolutely guarantee that he would not touch her again.

"I would expect nothing less than this from someone of your birth," Rosalie said bitterly. "You think that a few good meals and a few days of luxurious lodgings are going to pay for what you've done—I hope your conscience tortures you! You won't ever be able to repay what you owe me!"

No one had ever dared to speak to him in such a manner. Rand found himself enormously irritated by the imperiousness of her tone, and even more by the fact that a mere girl could affect him so.

"That I owe you anything is a debatable question," he said cuttingly. "The virginity of a woman of social consequence is a thing of some value. The virginity of a housemaid is usually dispensed of quite easily, and therefore of much less worth. If you have even a shred of common sense you'll accept my protection before I withdraw the offer."

"I suppose," Rosalie said, trembling with outrage, "that you think I should be prostrate with gratitude."

"I think," he replied levelly, his voice quiet, "that you are very young. And that you've been taken advantage of due to an unfortunate set of circumstances. And further, I think that if you don't accept my offer and you decide to try taking care of yourself, you'll end up flat on your back by nightfall, either in an alley or in a brothel. Now, for some reason that I don't understand and don't especially care to examine, I don't want that on my conscience. But if you refuse me I will consider myself absolved of all blame, whatever your fate happens to be."

"How convenient for you," Rosalie choked, bending her head in an effort to keep from breaking into violent tears. Again Rand felt that maddening twinge of guilt.

"Look . . . it is impossible to change what has happened," he said slowly. "But I'll try to make up for it by finding you a respectable position when I return from France. However, in the meanwhile I cannot leave you here alone. Come with me."

"I don't trust you," she said unsteadily.

"I'm afraid you'll have to."

Rosalie felt herself weakening. It was a temptation to relinquish herself to the situation. She was afraid of facing the world alone, especially in a city as dangerous as London. She did not want his protection, but she had to make the best of her present circumstances. The prospect of going to France with him actually began to seem like a sensible proposition. For one thing, he could do no further harm to her. In the eyes of society, the worst that could happen to a young woman had already taken place. People would probably be able to see that she was no longer unspoiled, for she was certain that it was branded on her for all the world to see. And she would be blamed for it, no matter what explanations she gave. What did she have to lose? What difference did it make if she went to France or starved in the streets of London? Nothing *Maman* could do would save her now. For the first time in her life, Rosalie was utterly aware of being alone.

"My mother does not know where I am," she said, her throat tight.

"Your mother . . ." he repeated, a furrow digging

into his forehead. He felt as if he had robbed a cradle. "God, how old are you?"

"Twenty," she said, and his expression became clearer, although there was still the residue of a frown in his strange-hued eyes. "But I must let my mother know——"

"Write a note," he said with flaring exasperation. "I'll have it sent to her."

She went to her clothes and slipped them on, feeling more like herself as she was enveloped in their protection. *Am I making the right decision?* she asked herself in consternation. It didn't really matter. There was nothing else she could do. Then Rosalie sat down at the mahogany French writing desk and accepted a sharp quill from him. Rand began to dress, sliding a perceptive glance at her stiff back. She was frozen in indecision.

"I have little experience with mothers," he remarked, "but I would suggest that you make it somewhat positive, unless you would like to severely upset what peace of mind she might have."

"Little experience with mothers?" she repeated. "I suppose your own refused to acknowledge you."

Rand grinned lazily, fastening the waist of his trousers and strapping them over his boots.

"It probably would have come to that, had she lived."

"Oh . . . I——"

"Hurry, we don't have much time."

Dearest Maman, Rosalie wrote, distractedly drawing the end of the soft feather quill across her nose as she thought. *Please be assured of my safety and well-being. This will shock you, but I am going to France with a man . . .* She glanced up at Rand Berkeley as he slid his arms into a well-cut coat of navy blue. He looked eminently more civilized in the conservative garb. A man like none she had ever seen or imagined, wry, violent, cool, passionate. He had been right: she detested him but was unafraid of him. He was a man, not a monster, and his treatment of her had been no different from what she would have received from any other. Something in her, perhaps the French part, caused her to look at the situation in terms of practicalities. What had been done was done, and now she intended to collect on the debt he owed to her. I'll find some way to make you pay, Rand Berkeley, she whispered inwardly. He would be sorry for what he had done. Then she lowered her eyes to the paper hastily, afraid he would see her thoughts. *I will see you when I return. I am not the same,* Maman, *but I will love you always. Rose.*

She addressed the note and handed it to him silently. Conscious of the soreness between her thighs as she approached the mirror, Rosalie regarded herself critically. There were dark smudges under her eyes and a faint shadow on her jaw where she had been struck the night before. Touching the place, she found that it was tender but not acutely so. It would heal soon. Frowning, Rosalie lifted her hair, which was a mass of tangles and snarls, and let it fall. It would take hours of work to repair the damage. Meanwhile, she had no pins or hats to confine it.

"I need a brush," she said, and Rand paused in the middle of tying his cravat. It was made of black silk, more informal and practical for daytime wear than starched white.

"The armoire," he directed, and she picked it up with determination, brushing at her hair until at least the surface was smooth. Somehow she managed to separate it into three tangled bunches and made a thick braid that fell over one shoulder and hung to her waist. Feeling his eyes on her, Rosalie glanced upward with vexation in her expression.

"I'll have to cut the snarls out," she said.

"You do and I'll lock you in a room until every strand grows back," Rand said tersely, folding his collar over the cravat and ushering her out of the room none too gently.

"A predictable reaction from you," Rosalie said, pulling at her imprisoned wrist as he dragged her through the door. She would learn soon that it was often difficult to tell when Randall Berkeley was serious or jesting.

Any other man would have expressed concern or regret at having taken her innocence, most likely with the bluntness that came with sincerely expressed emotion. But Rand had discussed her plight with mocking verbosity, as if he were conducting a teatime chat. He had a habit of mocking the trivial nature of most conversations by treating the banal with utter seriousness. He used intellectual words to discuss things of a highly *un*intellectual nature, and then utterly confused Rosalie by treating the most weighty subjects with irreverent lightness.

They left from Dover to cross the Channel in a forty-ton sloop. The sea was glassy and smooth on the first afternoon, and Rosalie slept with the deepness of exhaustion that night, curled up on a heavy chair in the compartment Rand had booked. The next morning, however, she woke up depressed and confused at the quickness with which her life had changed. The ocean was disturbed by huge swelling waves, enough to send Rosalie into the miserable state of seasickness. Rand forced her to come up from below to stand on deck for an hour with him, enduring her complaints until he could stand no more.

"If you stop badgering long enough to take a breath of fresh air, you might begin to feel better," he pointed out with irritation, and Rosalie lifted her pale face to him to deliver a cold blue stare. She envied his perfect health and composure. Her stomach had relieved itself of its contents several times over, and unbelievably the waves of nausea kept breaking over her.

"If it weren't for you—"

"You'd be rotting in an alley."

"Forgive my lack of gratitude—" Rosalie began acidly, but Rand cut her off sharply.

"For being a former companion, you lack the talent to provide tolerable companionship, *petite fleur*. All right, you can go back to the cabin. In fact, see if you can get as far away from my sight and hearing as possible on this unhappy little craft." He looked across the rolling water, his face turned away from her. Lord, it was tiring to have to worry about her comfort, her needs, when he was used to taking care of no one but himself. He was experiencing the beginnings of regret at the entire idea of enduring her for a few long weeks in France. What had possessed him to take her along?

Rosalie began to leave in relief, anticipating the prospect of lying down in privacy. When her hands left the railing, however, she realized with humiliation that she was not capable of walking by herself. She had never imagined it was possible to feel so sick and miserable, and it further galled her to ask him for anything. Reluctantly she placed a hand on his arm, her grip tighter than she knew as she fought off the throbs of pain in her head. Rand looked at the hand on his arm and then at her face, a question on his lips. She looked ghostly white.

"Please take me below," she muttered, and he knew it had cost her no small measure of pride to ask. Suddenly Rand felt a bewildering twinge of tenderness as he saw what was in her eyes. She was intimidated and a little afraid of him, trying to conceal it by arguing with him, finally driven to ask for his help even while hating him for what he had done to her. He knew of nothing to say that she would not take as condescending, and so he remained silent, brushing away the hair

that stuck to her damp forehead and sliding his cool
hand behind her neck. Rosalie sighed as the feel of it
momentarily eased her sickness a degree. Then his
hard arm slid behind her back, and Rand helped her to
the cabin with a consideration that most who knew him
would not have recognized.

The cliffs and receding hills of Havre rose before the
sloop like a massive gateway, white and brown and
green. At low tide the port was inaccessible to any kind
of naval craft, congealed with soft, heavy mud; however, now, in late morning, it was possible to enter the
lock. Havre was the seaport at the mouth of the Seine,
the wide river that narrowed at Quilleboeuf and continued to flow past Rouen until it reached the teeming
city of Paris. Paris, the capital of wine and silk, fashion
and fragrance, art and decadence, less than one hundred and ten miles away from Havre. The quay was
crowded with officials who boarded the boats before
anyone was allowed to disembark. The ship and its
passengers were checked for contraband and smuggled
goods, and only then were they free to enter the
country.

Rand watched the process of inspection with interest,
his hazel eyes taking in the various scenes being en-
acted in and around the customhouse. At a readily
visible distance were native coastal merchant ships
waiting for the signals from shore to bid them admit-
tance. Somewhere among them was a Berkeley frigate,
all eight hundred tons of her waiting with futile patience for permission to dock, her belly loaded with
English textiles and suspect American cotton.

"Welcome to France," Rand murmured to Rosalie,
who looked about with wide eyes, her ears pricking at
the fluid sounds of the Gallic language that came from
every direction. The quay was buzzing like a disorderly
hive, people quarreling, gesturing, waiting, moving. No

one seemed to be certain of what was going on. In a strange way Rosalie found the dirt, the color, and the action of the scene fascinating. Nearby a child waited on the dock with one hand clasped in her mother's, the other clutching a *brioche*. The sight of the soft sugar-glazed roll caused a distinct rumble of hunger in Rosalie's stomach. Feeling the excitement and unease of being in an unfamiliar place, she remained silent as they took a coach to the inn where they would stay. The vehicle bumped and jostled along the roughly paved roads, clattering past rows of stone buildings and open cafés.

The Lothaire, a small, elegant inn of two floors, displayed its name by means of a sign with small wrought-iron brackets, and a small porch settled beneath the entrance doorway was sided with more beautifully turned iron. The assembly room, or "long room," where political and social meetings were sometimes held, was located on the first floor, as was the newly installed coffee room. Flanking it was a corridor with a large window through which luggage was unloaded from the top of the coach. Rosalie was to find with delight later on that inside the inn reposed a tiny ballroom, shaded in white, pink, and gold, with a marble fireplace and a musicians' gallery. Beyond the yard was a small walkway lined with colored sand and porcelain ornaments, and a small kitchen garden from which the warm breeze brought hints of mint and thyme, dill, and ripening vegetables. "You'll like it," Rand said, helping her from the coach, her elbow caught firmly in his hand. "It's as much English as French. Every convenience is available."

"I'm certain it will be fine," Rosalie answered, thankful for any place in which she could find a bed and a bath. "But didn't you mention yesterday that we were going to the Hotel d'Angleterre?"

"I was given a tip on board the ship that they've been having a few problems."

"Poor service?"

"Bugs," he said, devilry sparkling in his eyes as he watched for her reaction of consternation. Although Rosalie shuddered inwardly, she refused to gratify him by allowing any dismay to show on her face.

They were to occupy a suite, two bedchambers flanking a central room. It was fit for a husband and wife on familiar and unromantic terms with one another. Rosalie supposed it would also be suitable for two strangers who wished to keep their lives and their beds separate.

The rococo style, of short-lived popularity in England, had enjoyed a much healthier and fruitful existence in the architecture and the furniture of France. It was predominant in their suite, its main characteristics being those of baroque curves, gaudiness, a voluptuous sense of movement, and a peculiar lack of symmetry. All of the pieces, even the gold-framed fire screen, contained designs of shells or birds, leaves, flowers, wings. The carpets beneath Rosalie's feet were of the finest Venetian make, the windows adorned with delicately sculptured grating. The beds were covered with soft down mattresses, icy linen sheets, and Marseilles quilts and counterpanes. Rosalie had never slept in such an elaborate place. She hoped suddenly that it was not something one could become accustomed to easily, for it was unlikely that she would ever have such an opportunity again.

"I assume you're in the habit of bathing regularly?" Rand inquired, having ordered a high-sided tub brought up to the suite.

"Frequently," Rosalie answered immediately, having always had the desire if not the opportunity to develop such a habit. For the servants in the Winthrops' employ, soap was expensive, time was rare, and heating enough water was a difficult process. She was by nature, however, a fastidious woman.

"Good. I don't mind perfumes or sweet waters unless they are intended to camouflage a stronger scent." Rand strode over to the window and crushed out the musk and civet pastilles that had been recently lit in order to fill the suite with their odor. They were intended to ease the unpleasant fragrance of unwashed bodies. "I also don't like the rooms I frequent to smell like a harem." Although Rosalie agreed with him, she disliked his high-handed manner.

"Then would you mind locating a place where I can have my clothes washed?" she asked, picking up her soiled skirts and displaying them in all their disreputable glory. "Else I will undoubtedly drive you to check into the Hôtel d'Angleterre."

Rand half-smiled at her impudence.

"It seems that we'll have to purchase something for you to wear during our stay here."

She didn't like the idea of him buying the clothes she would wear. It was far too personal, and she realized that she was dependent on him in a way that only a kept woman should have been. But it wasn't my choice to be kept, she reminded herself.

Rand sensed the course of her inner debate with unnerving acuteness. "Think of it as part of the reparation I owe to you," he said. "And if it's still unpalatable, content yourself with the reasoning that you can hardly go about naked . . . unless you'd like to, of course," he tacked on with perfect politeness.

Suddenly Rosalie could not resist smiling back at him. "You'll dress me like a whore, no doubt."

"Like a butterfly," he corrected gravely, and slowly her amusement faded.

"I am no butterfly, Lord Berkeley. Not a whore, nor

a lady . . . not a wife, nor a maiden. I wonder that we'll have me dressed suitably at all, for I have no idea how to explain myself."

Rand looked at her with a sort of baffled irritation. "Then I'll leave you to reflect on the matter," he said, and scowled for good measure before he left to prowl around the inn.

As the bath was being prepared, steaming buckets laboriously emptied into a porcelain tub in the central room by two chambermaids, Rand encountered her in his bedchamber. She had procured his brush from the dresser and sat on the bed while working vigorously at her tangled mane. Her face was flushed from the tugging of the hairbrush, her eyes smarting with tears from the painful exertion. Unaware that he watched, she took the most obstinate snarl between her fingers and lifted a pair of scissors to it.

"Don't!" his voice suddenly cut through the air.

Rosalie glanced at him in surprise, the scissors remaining in her grasp.

"I can't get them out," she explained impatiently. "Tangles the size of mice . . . I've tried for *hours*. It won't show if I—"

"Not one hair," Rand warned, walking over to the bed and sitting on the edge next to her. The scissors were removed unceremoniously from her fingers.

"Try if you like," she said with resignation, holding still as he lifted a lock from her shoulder. A few moments later, detecting no sign of progress, she made a timid move toward engaging him in conversation.

"I've been wondering what to call you, my lord."

"No inoffensive names have yet come to mind?" he inquired with suave politeness.

Rosalie flushed and smiled slightly. "Something like that. Would you care to make a suggestion?"

It was a delicate point to consider. It was not often that Christian names were used, even between the closest of friends. Among the higher-bred classes, husband and wife properly called each other "Mr." and "Mrs.," while one addressed a father as "sir" and a mother as "madam." Undoubtedly they should have referred to each other as "Lord Berkeley" and "Miss Belleau." However, in this peculiar situation, such formality seemed excessive.

"My dear Miss Belleau . . ." Rand drawled, completely aware of the multitude of distinctions between one form of address and another. He paused as if testing the sound of it, and then shook his head in negation. "No, that doesn't feel right. You're 'Rosalie' to me, and there's no help for it. I'll have to use your first name."

"Why not?" she responded dryly. "You've taken worse liberties."

"I assure you my preference doesn't imply a lack of respect—" he began mockingly.

"I'm certain it doesn't . . . Randall."

"Rand."

She nodded at his correction, deciding that she liked the shortened version of his name. Brusque, masculine —it suited him far more than the elegant "Randall." She half-smiled with the novelty of being able to call a man by his given name. It felt odd to address someone, especially him, so casually. "Why did you decide to come to France?"

Rand hesitated before replying, reflecting ironically on the fact that he rarely bothered to acquaint himself with a woman on any terms except sexual. This woman, this *girl* who lacked so much in sophistication, was the last sort he would turn to as a source of conversation, yet she was not silly or giggly as most of the debutantes her age were. Probably she had never had the freedom to talk alone with a man. Lord, what different worlds they came from.

"Have you come up with any theories on the matter?" Rand inquired, deftly untwisting several silken skeins.

"It's not for social reasons, or you wouldn't have brought me along with you."

"It's for business," Rand began, and then he sighed. "Well, for personal reasons as well, I suppose." As she remained silent, he persisted in the task of unbinding her hair, becoming absorbed in the methodical process. Her quietness encouraged him to continue. "The Berkeleys have many sources of income, but the most well-known besides Berkeley Square is the shipping company. We are trying to cut into the business done by the East Indiamen, now that Europe is recovering from the economic havoc of Napoleon's rule. According to my grandfather the earl, managing it all requires a staunchness of character and an affinity for responsibility that I've shown no sign of possessing so far. And unfortunately the earl is quite old."

"You'll inherit everything?" Rosalie could not help but be impressed by the immense power and the weighty obligations that would eventually be passed on to him. How could he speak of it so casually?

"If I am not capable of resolving the shipping problems that have sprung up between Boston and Havre, he'll find some way of giving a large portion of the estate to my younger brother." Rand suddenly gave a soft, dry laugh that rasped pleasantly along her nerves. "If he has to bury me alive, he'll do it to keep as much as possible of the Berkeley fortune intact."

"And your brother has this . . . staunch character and responsible nature that your grandfather desires for you?"

"No. But he has talent with money." Rand had a head for facts and figures, but he had never shared an affinity with Colin in the way he regarded currency. Colin prized money not for what it could buy or accomplish, but for itself. He worshiped a metallic goddess, constantly seeking ways to make the coins multiply.

Rosalie absorbed the information silently. Something in Rand's voice indicated that his was more of a personal quest than he wanted her to believe. Perhaps he was trying to prove something to his grandfather. She wondered what kind of man his brother was, and why he spoke of him with such an odd, sardonic note in his voice.

Slowly the strands of sable were freed from their woven prison, two or three at a time, until finally he was satisfied that they were all gone. Rosalie sighed in gratitude, and then she felt his fingers slide under the hair to her scalp, massaging away the soreness and tension that had built up. Hardly daring to move, she allowed his strong hands to ease away her weariness, wondering guiltily if she should be enjoying it, unwilling to stop him.

Rand felt himself pulled into the curiously erotic sensation of liquid silk flowing through his fingers. When he realized the effect it was having on him, he stopped abruptly and let his hands fall from their task. "I think the bath is ready," he said. "You can use the water first."

As if coming awake from a brief dream, Rosalie blinked a few times and then stood up, throwing him an uneasy glance before she left the bedchamber. Rand closed his eyes until the quickly awakened and slow-to-die fire left his body. He had been wrong: he hadn't been sated by her. He wanted her still, wanted her even more than he had a few mornings ago. A wave of something between surprise and dread swept over him as he recalled that she was the one woman in the world he had promised not to touch. "Rand, you fool," he muttered, wiping damp palms against his hard thighs and wondering if there was anything else he could do to further complicate his life. Unwittingly he had set himself up in his own particular hell, in which he was left with the thirst of Tantalus. Worse than the desire to take her again for his own pleasure was the knowledge that he'd left her unawakened, afraid of a man's desire, empty of the anticipation of love. And he had promised to leave her so, and so he would. He had a debt to face, the price of his passion.

Three

He that hath no mistress,
must not wear a favour,
He that woos a mistress,
must serve before he have her.
                              —Anon.

The innkeeper's talkative wife, Marie
Queneau, had been adamant about recommending
Madame Mirabeau's as the only draper's shop worth
mention in Havre. Rand had deposited Rosalie there
after putting in a perfunctory appearance as her bene-
factor. *"Tout ce qu'elle veut,"* he had said. As the words
"all she wants" danced through her mind, Rosalie had
smiled at him wickedly, endeavoring to cause him as
much unease as possible about what she would spend.

Rosalie did not relish playing the role of his mistress,
but she found that the unspoken title had given her a
certain status, even though the clothes she wore had
become filthy and ragged. It seemed that the mistress
of a wealthy man had more influence and importance
than even his wife, at least in Madame's viewpoint.
Madame attended to Rosalie personally, strewing designs, "fashion babies," and samples of cloth and lace in
front of her. After years of conservative clothes and
serviceable colors, Rosalie found herself in the midst of
a minor predicament. Trying on Elaine's castoffs was
one thing but actually purchasing such high fashion for
herself was both unnecessary and pretentious. Pastels
were the rage, delectable shades of carnation, coral,
cucumber, powder blue, and lavender. They were
colors that would be quite useless for a servant who

73

came into occasional contact with soot and dust. There was no need for her to order a ball gown, since Rand would obviously not have the time or desire to take her dancing, even though balls were held frequently in celebration of Napoleon's defeat. And the delicate, mouth-watering laces and frills, the ruching and edged scallops . . . on her, they would be like peacock's feathers on a pigeon. *Don't dress yourself like a maid*, Rand had warned her mockingly, and his words remained in her ears as she looked uncertainly at one sketch after another. But that's what I am, she thought despairingly, a maid and a companion. She should select things that would last long after Rand Berkeley had faded from her life.

I want to live!

Her own words came back to haunt her.

I want to dance and flirt—

She could almost hear Amille's reply: *Rosalie!*

Toss my head . . . make eyes at handsome men . . .

Don't dress yourself like a maid.

Rosalie, a voice said in warning.

"Madamoiselle Belleau," Madame Mirabeau inquired with exquisite tact, "would you like me to 'elp you choose?"

"Oui," Rosalie said, her brow furrowed in concentration. "Make me . . . as elegant as you can. *S'il vous plaît."*

They spent all morning and part of the afternoon choosing, discussing, measuring, fitting a simple gown that had been stitched quickly by many pairs of hands for her to wear until the rest of the lot was finished. The total order included scandalously fine underwear, stockings, slippers, bonnets trimmed with feathers, gloves, two pelisses, one with sleeves, one without, and some chemise dresses, light and closely fitting, trimmed with wide bands of embroidery around the bodice and hem, or pleated frills and ruching, with deeply scooped necklines. Rosalie wondered at the differences between the French and English versions of the classical style.

"It seems to me that the French make much more of a production out of the . . . breasts than the English," she remarked, looking uneasily at the display of cleavage one of the gowns would reveal, and for some reason Madame Mirabeau burst out into gales of laughter. By the end of the session Rosalie was feeling daring enough to ask for the formal-wear designs, and she found her interest caught immediately.

"The Valois," Madame explained, her voice faintly excited. "No longer the cool, pure lines of the classical style. This is more for a *woman*, do you see?"

"I see," Rosalie said, peering at the sketches curiously. There were puffs and slashes in the sleeves and skirts, longer waists that were nipped in to small proportions, wider shoulders, fuller skirts. Some of the sleeves were gathered several times down the arm, finished at each gather with bows or tassels. "I gather corsets are coming back?"

"Pah!" Madame exclaimed. "They would have come back years ago, had it not been for the war! Women have been letting great rolls settle on their stomachs without the laces."

They've also been more comfortable, Rosalie wanted to point out, but she was not experienced enough to be a critic of fashion.

"Then make this one for me," she said, indicating a design with a peculiarly shaped neckline, a V that reached down to between the breasts.

"In silver-blue?"

"*Justement*," Rosalie agreed, and they grinned at each other. "But, Madame, tell me, is this an extraordinarily expensive order?"

Madame Mirabeau picked up a bolt of silk and fingered it idly as she fastened Rosalie with a speculative look.

"*Monsieur* seems to be a generous man, yes?"

Rosalie nodded doubtfully. Rand was generous, perhaps. But philanthropic? No. She would not dare complain if he decided to cancel half the order, for she and Madame Mirabeau had most definitely picked out more than she had need of.

It took most of the day for Rand to convince the customs officials at the port to allow *Lady Cat* to dock. They were convinced that the cotton shipment she carried was fraudulent, and none wanted the responsibility for it. The close-minded attitude they all shared was a result of the trade barriers Napoleon had established during the worst of English and French hostilities. In order to defeat the British, Bonaparte had banished all trade with England by setting up a formidable customs network. The plan had backfired, nearly ruining the French merchant class and agricultural system. Without a sympathetic French minister of the interior to ease the bans, it would have been an even greater disaster. Even though the former emperor was now languishing on a small island in exile, there was still a residue of hostility toward the British on the part of the customs officials.

The captain of *Lady Cat,* a weathered man in his mid-forties who went by the name of Willy Jasper, assisted Rand in checking the first few bales of cotton as the customs officials watched. Jasper ran his ship like a man-o'-war, with discipline and efficiency. He was dependable and self-assured, for the job he held was equal to a similar position in the Royal Navy and he possessed a large amount of pride in what he did. In return for his excellent service he was granted several tons of the ship's total weight capacity to use for private trade. It was no secret that he intended one day to retire and use the money to buy his own ship. Jasper and Rand worked their hands into the fragrant Geor-

gia fleece, and predictably the bales were rife with
stones. A flurry of conversation ensued among the
Frenchmen, so fast that Rand could understand only
one word in ten.

"Sorry about this," Jasper apologized in a low mono-
tone. "The bloody American buggers swore they
weren't cheating anymore. What do they think we are,
bloody idiots?"

"It would seem so," Rand replied, his face carefully
neutral as he flickered a glance toward the customs
agents.

"Send it back?"

"No. Despite the extra weight, there's still some
valuable cotton here. Send back a message instead:
'Cargo lost at sea. Too heavy to float.' "

Jasper chuckled suddenly.

"Aye, sir."

"I doubt our position could be much clearer. The
problem is in getting the next shipment through."
Rand turned to the chattering officials and tried to
clear the situation with his laborious French. He had
little doubt of his ability to persuade them to see
reason, for postwar France was not in much of a
position to upset the fragile, newly established trade
channels with England. Slowly the French market was
beginning to recover and they had need of both raw
and manufactured cotton, guns, wool, leather and
saddlery, and especially coffee and sugar. The best and
most luxurious goods in the world came from England
at a massive volume as steam power was being developed and made use of in the tide of Britain's industrial-
ization. Rand intended to take as much advantage as
possible of France's hunger and England's overabundance.

Much later in the day as the sun was beginning to
lose its tenuous grip on the darkening sky, Rand pulled
the smart, fast curricle-hung gig to a halt in front of

Madame Mirabeau's shop. Impatiently he entered the small building and stood near the doorway, wondering how his one-time mistress had fared. Madame Mirabeau peered at him from a curtained-off room.

"One moment, *monsieur*," she said, and there were muffled sounds of giggling as her head disappeared. Obviously they intended to stage some sort of production for his benefit. He could hear Rosalie's voice, although it sounded as if they were trying to keep her quiet.

"He won't care which slippers! Yes, I know he's paying, but you don't understand . . ."

In another few minutes Madame came out and flung open the red curtain dramatically, gesturing for Rosalie to follow. Rand smiled slowly as an elapse of several seconds occurred. When she finally emerged the smile left his face, the color of his eyes changed from tiger-gold to green. Rosalie stopped in front of him, feeling unaccountably bashful as he viewed the results of their day-long handiwork. She waited in vain for him to speak. Did he like it? It doesn't matter what he thinks, she told herself. As he said nothing and continued to stare, Rosalie lifted her chin slightly, her attitude becoming faintly regal as she gathered pride around her like a mantle.

The gown was of the softest, palest pink imaginable, glimmering like the inside of a shell. Small puffed sleeves caressed the tops of her arms and the neckline plunged so deeply that it merely clung to the tips of her breasts before cupping them underneath and falling in thin folds to the floor. Her figure was youthful and slim but the full curves of a woman were undeniably there, enhanced by the soft, clinging material. The only jewelry she wore was a small gold pin which gleamed and winked from the pale velvet ribbon fastened around her neck. Rosalie's skin flushed slightly at Rand's intent perusal, her eyes shining a clear daylight blue. They had trimmed her hair in the front so that what had formerly been wisps were now fashionably curled bangs, but the rest was pinned in a heavy, gleaming mass at the back of her head.

"I hardly recognize you," Rand said huskily. The sight of her had hit him like a blow, leaving him unprepared, defenseless. He looked at her as he wavered between desire and resentment. She wasn't covered enough, he thought, relentlessly tearing his fascinated gaze from her breasts . . . yet the rational part of his mind insisted that she wore no less than any other fashionable women. A question stung him suddenly with painful accuracy: was he going to be able to bear keeping his hands off her? His pride, his word, was involved in the matter, for he had promised not to take her again. Good Lord, how had he devised such a trap for himself? I didn't know, he thought with hungry discontentment, I didn't know then that I would want her so much.

"You look very nice," he mumbled, aware that an approving statement was expected of him from the women. Although Madame Mirabeau had apparently expected a more flamboyant compliment, Rosalie appeared to be satisfied with it. She gave him a small smile and looked down at herself, and in that moment Rand saw the actions of someone else, a moment of startling clarity, too brief to grasp. Immediately his physical craving subsided as he focused on the surprising realization. Somewhere, somehow . . . he had seen her before.

"Where did you get the pin?" he asked, his gaze thoughtful as it rested on the small circlet of gold. The initial B was carved in the center, surrounded by tiny etched leaves. It was a gentleman's stock pin intended to anchor the intricate folds of a cravat.

"It belonged to my father, Georges Belleau," Rosalie replied, fingering the circlet absently. "It was given to

me by my mother on my eighteenth birthday." Why in
the world had he asked about her pin? she wondered
with vague irritation. Had he even looked at her dress,
her face, her figure? Was he so unaffected by her? Not
that she cared a whit for his blasted opinion, but after
spending all day . . .

"You are pleased with the gown?" Madame Mirabeau
inquired coyly, and Rand's green-gold gaze swerved to
her.

"Madame," he said slowly, "your artistry is equaled
only by the materials you were initially given to enhance." They were polite words of admiration, spoken
so perfunctorily that they were meaningless. Rosalie
was annoyed more by them than if he had kept his
mouth shut.

"Ah, somehow I think you do not speak of the
cloth," Madame Mirabeau simpered, hedging for further snippets of praise in a manner that only a French-
woman could. Rand adroitly cut short the exchange by
alluding tactfully to the bill.

"Such a transformation is of course worth any price,
chère Madame . . ."

"Ah, yes," she said instantly. "You will notice at first
glance the economy of my work, *monsieur*. You are a
foreigner, but I do not take you for a fool. I charge you
only the bare minimum . . ."

Now feeling uncomfortable at the prospect of having
a man pay for the clothes, the slippers, even the
chemise she wore, Rosalie remained silent until they
left an eminently pleased Madame Mirabeau in the
shop. He owes it to me, she told herself over and over.
Because of Rand Berkeley she had lost her innocence,
her employment, her home. A few clothes were the
least he could offer. Still the sensation of unpleasantness remained with her, as if the exchange of money
between the man and the dressmaker had somehow

labeled her as his possession. As they drove home, Rand was the first to speak.

"So you've had a profitable day," he remarked. Rosalie nodded, reaching an experimental hand to touch the newly shorn curls at her forehead. "I see they cut your hair." The displeasure in his voice was heartening. At least he had noticed something about her that aroused more than polite blandness!

"Just the front," Rosalie replied casually.

"No more decisions without consulting me first."

"I'm not your servant, Lord Berkeley. I take no orders from you."

"No orders, just my money?"

"You were the one who suggested the clothes in the first place!"

"I suggested clothes, not cutting your damned hair!"

"It's my hair. I belong to myself, not to you. And snapping at me isn't going to bring those few little snippets of hair back. And why do you care any—"

"I don't care," he interrupted sharply, gritting his teeth in an effort to control his temper.

They said nothing for a few minutes as the horse's hooves and the cabriolet wheels rattled over the uneven road, and then Rand sighed in an effort to release some of his pent-up frustration.

"We can't live like this for the next few weeks. We'll end up killing each other."

"As far as I can tell, our differences are uncompromising," Rosalie said flatly. She also had no idea of how they would be able to survive the stay in Havre.

Rand's disturbed expression was suddenly lightened by a wry and fleeting smile.

"If France and England can make an effort at coexistence, I think you and I can work something out."

"What exactly do you suggest?" she inquired warily.

"What would you say to calling a truce?"

A truce. Rosalie toyed with the smooth fabric of her new gown as a debate raged in her mind. A truce, a cessation of hostility. But it would be dishonest to agree to something like that while she still felt hostile toward him. It couldn't be changed easily. At times she merely had to look at him to feel the same anger and helplessness that had filled her as he had stripped off her clothes and taken her. He was the only man who had ever had intimate knowledge of her, and she hated the fact that while there might be others in the future, he would always be the first. She would never be able to forget that sunlit room at Berkeley Square and what had happened there, and that alone was reason to despise him. Possibly he saw her now as a person with feelings, but once he had looked on her as only a body from which he was entitled to steal his pleasure.

"It would be pointless to try," she said in a low voice, looking out at the rows of dirty houses they passed. She felt a weight settle on her shoulders, and she continued while feeling horribly guilty at refusing his overture. "I wish I had a more forgiving nature, but I don't. It wouldn't work."

Rand nodded slightly, his face implacable, his mouth grim as he clicked to the horse and increased their pace. Obviously the thought had not occurred to her that the situation was glued together only by his often-neglected sense of honor—he could leave her on any street corner and never be bothered with the sight of her again! Then he discarded the thought of pointing that out, disgusted with himself. Frightening a defenseless woman gave him no pleasure. In the ensuing moments of silence he was free to analyze his odd mixture of reactions to her words. He was offended at her refusal to cry truce. The worst part of him suggested rather snidely that, considering who was who

and what was what, she had no right to refuse his
tentative offer of friendship. Another part of him was
vaguely hurt, as if he had extended a hand to a fluffy
kitten and received a scratch for his trouble. And yet
overall his regard for her had increased, for she had
made it clear that she would play neither the saint nor
the martyr by mouthing words of forgiveness that she
did not feel.

He wondered how to deal with her. The only solution to the problem seemed to lie in staying as far away
from her as possible.

From then on it seemed that the lines were drawn,
for Rand made no more approaches and Rosalie made
no concessions. A day passed, and then another, and
their pattern was repeated until a week was behind
them. Despite the brief snaps and arguments, the long
silences and oddly tense, watchful conversations, Rosalie knew that she would remember those days at the
Lothaire as being idyllic. She slipped into the French
language as if it were a fitted glove, the lilting accents
often reminding her of Amille. Rand left her alone a
large part of the time as he went either to the docks or
to check on properties that the Berkeleys owned, and
she nestled in the cozy haven of the inn with contentment.

Rosalie had never experienced this kind of leisure
time, in which she could choose whatever she wanted
to do and know that there would be no interruption.
She practiced her music, sat in a velvet nook reading
novels by Jane Austen, wandered through the kitchen
garden and chewed sun-warmed mint leaves, sat in the
meeting-room and chatted idly about the contents of
the thrice-weekly Continental newspapers with the
other guests of the inn, two of whom were girls from
the American colonies touring Europe with their parents.

The only time that she shared regularly with Rand was when they breakfasted in the coffee room on hot *café au lait* and flaky rolls, and once again in the evening when they shared dinner with the Queneau family and the other guests of the inn. They all sat in the *salle à manger* and ate huge meals that included fresh herbs and vegetables from the garden. After the main course the top tablecloth was removed to reveal an even finer one beneath, and then decanters of claret, port, and sherry were set out for them to imbibe as they partook of the hothouse fruits for dessert. Rosalie never dared to ask Rand why he never took more than a sip of wine, but she watched him every night and found his lack of taste for it very curious indeed.

Slowly the choice food, the cider from Normandy, the fresh air and sun, the leisure, the freedom, caused her pale skin to bloom with color and health. Rand said nothing about the change that was taking place, but at times he would look at her with eyes containing a bewildering mixture of craving and bleakness.

Although Rosalie continued to avow that she disliked him, she found that he aroused a great deal of curiosity in her. She began to know exactly when he had been brawling, gaming, or engaging in some adventure, because sometimes he would walk in with a reckless and irresponsible gleam in his eyes. It seemed that he enjoyed himself only when he was doing something that the rest of the Berkeleys would undoubtedly have disapproved of. It was difficult to understand him, however, because he was more complex than a typical amusement-seeker. The more she became acquainted with him, the more surprised Rosalie was by the fact that he had bothered to rescue her from her attacker on the night of the Covent Garden fire. Although he could occasionally be kind when the moment suited him, Rand was certainly not a humanitarian. Often he was given to mocking and heartless moods that both awed and dismayed Rosalie.

One night he came back to the inn unusually late after spending the day journeying to Louviers and back. Having made up his mind to forage out additional trade partners, Rand had engaged in negotiations and obstacle-ridden conversations the entire day, with a fair measure of success. He wanted a piece of the French wool business and he was also willing to take the risk of investing in what promised to be an explosion of development in the silk industry. Now that Napoleon was rotting in St. Helena, industries that rested on the whims of the upper classes would undoubtedly flourish.

He strode into the suite wearily and was confronted with the sight of Rosalie submerged in the high-sided tub in the center of the room. Candlelight played over her features, causing delicate shadows to lurk deliciously behind her earlobes and in the gentle hollows under her cheekbones. Wisps of steam curled around her neck, wafting around her head and floating toward the ceiling. Working soap into her hair, Rosalie looked toward the intruder calmly. When she saw that it was Rand, her eyes widened slightly. He had always remained in his room while she took her bath, not having once seen her unclothed since that morning in London.

"I thought you were the maid," she said, her voice higher than normal. "She's gone to get some towels." Don't be an idiot, she told herself instantly, it's not as if he hasn't seen you before! A powerful tension immediately filled the room and shimmered almost visibly in the air. Rosalie had not been this aware of him as a man since that morning in London, and she sank a few inches lower in the water as unwanted memories tormented her. Rand stood as if nailed to that one spot on the floor, his mouth having gone dry, his bright greenish eyes unblinking. With a superhuman effort he tore his attention away from her and regarded his nails intently.

"Sorry. I spent longer in Caen than I thought I would—"

"Did you get many things accomplished?" It took much contrivance to keep her voice casual.

"I . . . Yes."

"Well . . . I'll be finished with the water soon," Rosalie said, and Rand took a step or two backward until he felt the carved door against his shoulders. His pulse picked up speed until its rapidity caused every inch of his skin to prickle in awareness of the fact that her naked body was only a few feet away.

"Don't hurry," he said, finding it a miracle that he hadn't choked on the words. "I'm heading out again— more business to take care of."

"What about dinner?" Rosalie inquired, frowning, and he shook his head hastily.

"I'm not hungry. I'll be back later . . . lock the door behind me."

Disgruntled, Rosalie watched him leave and then she slumped against the back of the tub in relief. After finishing her bath she ate alone and went to bed early, her ears pricked for the sound of a key turning in the main door of the suite. It seemed that for most of the night she remained in a semiwakeful state, waiting for the release of knowing he had returned. He finally arrived when the morning did.

Groggy, her eyes puffy from lack of sleep, Rosalie awakened to the muffled sounds of someone entering the apartments, and she pulled on the pelisse that matched her white nightgown before opening her door. Rand had just come into the suite. She looked at him first in surprise and concern, then in disgust. She could smell some cheap harlot's overly sweet perfume, its scent distilling through the entire room. His clothes were disheveled, his face as haggard, his eyes as blood-shot as Rosalie's. His condition hinted more of exhaustion than drunkenness, as if he had been awake most of the night. Rosalie could not help picturing him rolling and rutting in bed with another woman, and she felt indignation catch in her throat. Promiscuous wretch!

"Well. We make a pair this morning, don't we?" he said, his words overly soft and carefully enunciated.

"You are appalling," Rosalie stated in a low, taut voice, and he focused an unsteady golden gaze upon her.

"Why, pray tell?"

"You look and smell as if you have slept with every prost . . . *whore* on the western coast."

"Very possibly," Rand agreed, pulling his coat off and letting it drop to the floor. "But if you'll remember, that was part of our little understanding. If I feel the need, I find some other outlet for my attentions. Or would you rather I had shared your bed after all?"

Rosalie could feel an unbecoming sneer form on her face. She was powerless to remove it. "You're revolting."

"I'm an unmarried man with no commitment to any woman. What in hell is so revolting about it?"

"That your wandering lust, troubadour that it is, will apparently perform for any female capable of lifting her own skirts."

Growling, Rand made a move as if to shake her, but she stood her ground even as his large hands closed over her fine-boned shoulders. His mouth twisted in self-contempt. What was wrong with him? What had caused such inexplicable desire that could not be satisfied by any other woman's touch or talent? He could not allow this to continue, or he would become as mad as King George.

"I wonder why you lead me on in fruitless bickering," he questioned softly, his fingers curling slightly into the softness of her upper arms. Rosalie flinched at the bite of his grip. "Could it be that you remember how easily I am led from words to action?"

"If you are implying that I am trying to provoke you," Rosalie said unsteadily, her blue eyes blazing, "you are mistaken. I was moved to speak only because living in such close quarters makes it difficult to hide my disgust at your promiscuity."

"Hide it," Rand advised, jerking her an inch closer so that their bodies were almost touching. She was so small that her head didn't even reach his chin. "Or I could be tempted to forgo my attempts to satisfy myself discreetly . . . and focus my attentions on the nearest reasonably palatable wench around—which, most of the time, happens to be you."

Reasonably palatable! Rosalie wanted to slap him across the face as hard as she was able—but she remembered what had ensued the last time she had done it. She held herself stiffly, her hands clenched.

"Then force me again," she said between her teeth. "It won't be anything out of the ordinary."

Abruptly he let go of her shoulders and framed her face with his palms, holding her head in an unbreakable clasp.

"Tell me what appeal you could have for me," he invited gently. "A woman who offers all the warm comfort of a crusty winter snow. Tempting and haughty in manner, every impulse to draw away from me as if the merest touch is loathsome. You've been content in your solitude . . . but I am not so self-sufficient. I was imprisoned for years in such a wintry abode until finally all that made me human drove me to seek warmth. You, however, are the first that I've hurt in the quest."

"What are you talking about?" Rosalie whispered, but he continued as if he hadn't heard her.

"My attraction to you is ironic . . . a mad desire it is, to sweep away the snow and melt the ice with my hands.

And yet I dare not, for it seems that there is nothing underneath the crust, and you would melt away to nothing."

"You're mad," Rosalie breathed, finding that she was trembling as he brought her closer, her breasts quivering against the solid hardness of his chest. As he saw the flicker of dread in her eyes, Rand swore and let her go with a groan.

"Out of my head," he agreed. "Would to God I didn't want you." Abruptly he disappeared into the bedroom and slammed the door. Shocked and amazed, Rosalie discovered that she had lost her tongue. How safe was she from him? Exactly how much self-control was he prepared to employ—could she count on him to keep his promise?

They met each other warily that night before dinner, silently, tacitly agreeing to forget the past twenty-four hours. Rand approached Rosalie as she sat in a corner of the main room, her hair shining in the lamplight while she bent her head to read. Slowly she looked up, ready to resume the careful antipathy they had shared during the past several days. The sight of him caused a sudden fluttering in her stomach. Hunger pains, she assured herself.

He wore a navy coat and a shirt and pantaloons of pristine white, his long legs encased in black Hessian boots, a starched white cravat gleaming immacuately at his throat. Somehow Rosalie had become accustomed to the dark golden hue of his skin, for it no longer struck her as odd or unattractive. Although he was not handsome, she knew now with utter certainty why many women would want him. There was something peculiarly magnetic about him, the faint roughness, the vibrancy, the lavish masculinity of him, that made a woman sharply aware of her own femininity. His unpredictability only served to make him more intriguing. His dark-rimmed eyes would change so quickly, from coldness to laughter, and then to shining opaqueness that dared her to guess what he was feeling. Rosalie knew that most women must have been sorely tempted to try to tame him, to coax him to place his trust in them, yet she knew also that not one of them had succeeded.

"You've been kept in this place like a little bird in a cage," he said quietly, and Rosalie stood up as she answered him.

"It was not your responsibility to provide entertainment."

His eyes swept over her, seeming to catch and retain the glow of the lamp as he surveyed her slender figure in an eggshell-shaded gown trimmed with an intricate leaf pattern.

"This small corner is all you've seen of France. I'd like to show you more of it." His attitude was matter-of-fact, but somewhere in his tone was a touch of apology. Rosalie regarded him uncertainly. Why would he care if she were enjoying herself or not? Her presence here was merely for convenience.

"You planned to begin tonight?" she questioned, indicating his clothes with a nod of her head.

"That depends on whether or not you'd like to go out for supper. There is a place—"

"First I'd like to ask you something," Rosalie said, her even teeth catching at her full bottom lip as she contemplated him. She had decided in his absence that she would be better off as Rand's friend. She was not strong enough to last as his enemy. "Is your offer of a truce still open?" Rosalie held out her hand as she spoke. After hesitating, he did the same. But instead of shaking her hand, Rand held it for a long moment, his eyes narrowing as he tried to read her thoughts. Rosalie was deeply surprised at the warmth, the security, the satisfaction she experienced at the simple clasp. What disturbed her was that she did not want him to let her go, and that when he did, she could barely restrain herself from continuing to hold on to him. Her fingers still retained the warmth of his.

"I have some free time in the next few days," Rand remarked, helping her to slide her arms through the long sleeves of the pelisse. "I thought we might pay a visit to an old acquaintance of mine." As he pulled free a straying curl that was caught under the pelisse, he smiled down at her with blinding charm.

"Oh?" Rosalie had difficulty in focusing on what he was saying, so enmeshed was she in the sense of well-being that began to wash over her. Rand, she was beginning to discover, could be very nice when he wanted to. "Who?"

"Some call him the King of Calais."

"Who is that?"

"Beau Brummell, of course."

Rosalie doubted that much of what Rand told her of Beau Brummell was true. She quizzed him the next two days during the coach ride to Calais, her expression full of delight and incredulity as Rand regaled her with colorful stories that seemed to have been spun by an active mind and fertile imagination. She began to suspect the gleam in Rand's eyes that belied his perfectly grave countenance, but he assured her repeatedly that everything he had said comprised merely the bare facts of Brummell's existence. There were some things Rosalie could not dispute: the fact that Brummell had fled London amid scandal and a tremendous debt was well-known, for his Sèvres porcelain, his library of fine books, furniture, wine collection, and works of art had all been auctioned off by Christie in a very public manner. His friendship with George IV, the prince regent, was also famous, for his highness and the most elegant members of the *beau monde* had often visited Brummell at number four Chesterfield Street, begging for his opinion as to their apparel and their style.

Brummell, or the Beau, as he was most well-known, had a legendary way with a cravat, having invented the method of starching the neckcloth in order to make it gleaming and immaculately shaped.

"It is rumored," Rand told her, "that he has three people make his gloves, one for the thumb, one for the fingers, one for the palm—"

"I don't believe it!" Rosalie exclaimed, and she leaned a fraction closer, her eyes fixed on his. "Did you meet him often?" she inquired. It was all Rand could do not to plant a kiss on her soft mouth. He smiled, his dark brown lashes lowering slightly as his gaze flickered unnoticeably to her mouth.

"A few times. He would not deign to walk anywhere with me, however. He said that it was obvious by my stride that I would undoubtedly splash his boots."

Rosalie grinned.

"He didn't want to get his boots dirty?"

"He had the soles of them polished, as well as the tops and sides."

"Such a man must have a very inflated opinion of himself."

"For eighteen years he's been the Prince of England, much more so than the fourth George. I imagine his fall from grace has had a humbling effect on him. But I wouldn't be surprised if it hasn't."

"Are you certain he'll welcome visitors?"

"You don't think he moved to Calais for no reason, do you? He has strategically located himself to receive all the English visitors to the Continent as they cross the Strait of Dover. Anyone coming to or from Paris practically trips over his doorstep."

The Beau lived near the Hôtel de Ville, the center of town, at the home of a French printer named Leleux. As was proper etiquette, Rand had previously sent a messenger with a calling card to inform Brummell of the visit. To express the greatest amount of consideration and attention to the nicety, it was customary to write E.P. *(en personne)* at the bottom of the card.

It had not occurred to Rosalie until near the end of their journey that there existed no proper or acceptable explanation for her relationship with Rand. Brummell would conclude that she was Rand's mistress, since she was obviously not his wife or his sister, and the lack of a chaperon indicated that she was not of a respectable family. Many would regard her as a creature of weak morals, without respect for the sensibilities of decent people. It did not matter that those who condemned her hid equal if not worse vices behind the privacy of their doors, in the concealment of impressive titles and polished reputations. Appearance was all that mattered, and if casting stones was in order, she stood in plain view of those hypocritical eyes. She worried silently about the situation, hoping that Brummell would not hold such a thing against her.

She need not have worried. Rosalie would never again meet someone with manners as exquisite as Brummell's. He ushered them into his apartment as soon as they arrived, as if there was not a moment to lose in making them comfortable. His present home consisted of three perfectly decorated rooms, one for conversation, one for dining, one for sleeping, furnished in a manner that was not at all what Rosalie had expected from a man heavily in debt. As Rand explained later, the Beau was an expert at borrowing from Peter to pay Paul. He procured almost limitless credit by employing his bountiful charm. A valet named Selegue was his only servant, a quiet little man who bustled about unobtrusively as Brummell welcomed them in.

"I am rejoiced that you have made it here!" he exclaimed, his eyes on Rand. "My apartment is humble, nothing like what I'm accustomed to, but in such a crude setting one must shine all the brighter, eh?"

Rosalie stared at him in fascination, having never seen a man more carefully attired. She could well believe that it took him two hours each day to tie his cravat, for each blinding white fold, each tiny crease, was a detail that bespoke care and consideration. He wore a blue coat with a velvet collar and a buff waistcoat, black trousers and matching black shoes that were polished until they reflected his stock. Brummell was thirty-eight, exactly ten years older than Rand, yet he looked so much older and so different that it was impossible to compare the two.

"It frizzles the mind," the Beau said pointedly to Rand, "how brown you've become. Have you no care for your complexion? Skin as dark as a peasant's—and judging from your brother's fairness, you cannot use the excuse of heredity . . ."

As Rand murmured something apologetically, Rosalie smiled, knowing full well that her erstwhile lover had no intention of staying indoors to hide from the sun. She observed Brummell's white, clear complexion admiringly. She could well believe the rumors that he buffed his skin carefully each day with a flesh-brush and rinsed with milk and water.

He had a pleasant round face and bright blue eyes, a face reflecting a wealth of vanity and innocence, charm and entreaty. He loved beauty and simplicity; he believed that those two virtues were embodied in himself, and it was said that he tried to encourage them in others. So this was the man who had humbled a prince and presided over English society for so long.

"I had found the most charming Chinese cabinet for over there . . ." he was explaining to Rand, and as he spoke, those bright eyes turned in her direction. Rosalie felt an odd quake as Brummell stared at her in silence. For several long seconds blue eyes met blue, caught, holding, wondering. Then Rosalie smiled hesitantly.

"I think your apartments are beautiful," she said simply.

Rand cleared his throat. "George Brummell, let me introduce you to Miss Rosalie—"

"—Belleau," she interceded.

"Miss Belleau . . ." Brummell spoke in a moved tone, bowing deeply. "I speak in humblest sincerity in saying that I have seen few that have ever come close to your beauty, none that have ever excelled it. The angels must look down as you pass by and weep in envy."

"Kind sir," Rosalie replied, smiling at his verbal flamboyance, "surely your precious words are wasted on one so undeserving of them." Unknowingly she had tilted her head in a halfway flirtatious manner as she spoke, and as she stood before him, Brummell suddenly wrinkled his brow in confusion.

"Jeremy!" he called, his voice impatient and anxious, and as the valet shuffled hurriedly into the room, he caught sight of Rosalie and stopped completely. Feeling herself the object of two shocked and intent stares, Rosalie moved closer to Rand. Protectively he let his fingertips rest lightly on her back.

"Is something amiss, Brummell?"

"No, no, my good man, no." The Beau recovered himself quickly and patted his valet on the shoulder. "Fetch it, Jeremy. Dear Miss Belleau, please excuse my taxing rudeness, but I hope to explain my actions to you momentarily. I have never seen such a likeness, not in all my born days."

"A likeness?" Rosalie questioned, her curiosity aroused. As she became aware of Rand's hand on her back, she tried to keep from moving or changing position, oddly aware that it was a pleasant sensation.

"Before your arrival," the Beau replied, "she was the fairest woman I had ever been blessed to meet." His pleasant face became gradually doleful as he continued. "My heart belonged to her as the stars do to heaven

. . . surely they all faded a bit when she and I parted."
He sighed. "The saddest tale in the history of love, if
not one of the better-known."

Rand smothered the smile that twitched the corners
of his lips as he saw the pity and interest leaping in
Rosalie's expression. She was not aware that Brummell
had a warehouse of tales and fabrications, of love,
adventure, scandal, tragedy, all of which were carefully
preserved and frequently pulled out to entertain his
guests. It was one of the marvels of Brummell, that he
could find a story to absorb the interest of any listener.

"Shall I continue over refreshments?" Brummell
inquired, and solicitously led Rosalie to a small damask-
covered table on which reposed a silver tea service.
Without interrupting his monologue, he assisted her
into a small Windsor chair and indicated that Rosalie
pour the tea. By the teapot there was a small platter of
red-currant cakes, gingerbread, gooseberry tarts,
scones with Corinth raisins, and *biscuits de Rheims,*
expensive almond-flavored cookies. "Her name was
Lucy Doncaster," Brummell began the tale. "Her
appearance startlingly close to yours, except that her
eyes were the blue of the mist on an English morning.
Her hair was the same hue as yours, and it . . ." He
cleared his throat meaningfully. "I had the occasion of
discovering that it reached nearly down to her waist."
Which was a polite way of saying, Rosalie recognized,
that he had been very intimate with Lucy Doncaster.
What a charming way to reveal the character of their
relationship. "She had the gentlest nature of any
woman before or since—she would never contradict,
never complain, never reveal a shred of
impatience . . ."

As the Beau continued, Rosalie turned to her left
and met Rand's eyes, which held a fair amount of
wicked amusement. ". . . and it was not possible for our

hearts to resist the silent importunings of love. At sixteen I made the acquaintance of the prince regent, was given a cornet's commission in the tenth regiment, and thus began a celebrated and regrettable friendship that has lasted the past two decades or so. As you are aware, I have recently lifted the blinders of this friendship with Prinny and seen that his shortcomings are too unbearable for a man of my ilk to tolerate . . . but getting back to the story. We met at Brighton, as Prinny was in the habit of ordering our regiment, the Hussars, back and forth from the Pavilion to London. She and her parents were guests at one of many splendid balls at the Pavilion—"

"And it was love at first glance," Rosalie said with certainty, her young heart feeling as if it had expanded two or three times over. She could hardly believe that here she sat, being entertained by the flattered companion of royalty as he sought to entertain her. Brummell spoke in an extravagant, leisurely manner, as if the world had stopped to allow him as much time as he desired to weave his romantic story.

"Love! What a trifling word that is for what I felt! I was born anew the first time our eyes met. She was . . . innocence itself, come to life in human form." The Beau picked up an almond biscuit and nibbled it carefully, seemingly lost in his reflections. Rosalie watched him silently, not daring to speak a word. But having discoursed with Brummell before, Rand knew that he was waiting for the prompt of another question.

"Your sentiments were mutual?" he inquired dryly, and the cue was picked up instantly.

"I had her kind assurances that they were. But alas, there were obstacles before us that no mere man could overcome."

"Suddenly I sense an overbearing father entering the scene," Rand said. Rosalie sent him a quelling look, which he managed to ignore. He knew she disliked his tendency toward irreverence, but at times it was impossible for him to resist.

"How perceptive," the Beau commented, accepting a cup of tea from Rosalie with gratitude. "I hope you were liberal with the sugar . . . ? Bless you, m'dear. You are as gracious as the Duchess of Devonshire herself, another good friend of mine. Now, to continue with my recounting . . . Ah, yes, the father. Sir Reginald Doncaster, a well-meaning but misdirected man, who had ruled beloved Lucy with exacting discipline all of her life. Doncaster felt that no man was fit to husband his daughter, and while I agreed, I also felt that I came as close to being worthy of the honor as any other. Despite my petitions, her hand was eventually promised to the Earl of Rotherham. At the same time, the regiment was sent back to London, and during our enforced separation, disaster occurred."

"She committed suicide," Rand guessed.

"No, what a silly idea!" Rosalie exclaimed. "Not when she had everything to live for—she was young, she was in love . . . I know what I would do. I would pack my belongings and leave—"

"Which is precisely what she did," the Beau affirmed, his attitude becoming sad and puzzled. "Except that she did not run to me. She virtually disappeared with her governess. No one knew where she went. There were rumors that she had gone to France, but no one knew for certain. The days, the weeks, the months marched onward, and in the blackness of my despair I sensed that I would never see her again. The story ends a year later. She was found here in France." Shaking his head, he reached for another almond biscuit.

"What happened?" Rosalie asked urgently, and as the Beau chewed and swallowed the confection, Rand answered for him.

"She committed suicide."

"No!" she contradicted.

"Yes," Brummell said, reaching out a hand to receive a small ivory box from his valet. "Drowned in the Seine."

"It doesn't make sense that she would just give up hope," Rosalie said, feeling tremendous pity for the unknown Lucy Doncaster. She herself had never experienced the pain of star-crossed love, yet she knew it must have been unbearable.

"Ah, for you, perhaps not," the Beau said, withdrawing a miniature from the gleaming box and staring at it reflectively. "To understand, you would have to have made the acquaintance of my beloved. So fragile, so in need of protection. She was strong enough only to flee, not to fight."

"I'm afraid Rosalie would not understand such a reaction," Rand said, his voice shadowed with laughter, and he stood up from the table to peer over Rosalie's shoulder as Brummell handed her the likeness.

At first glance Lucy Doncaster appeared to be very young, a quaint child, her face rounded sweetly with youth, her hair powdered with pale gold-white and pulled up into an elaborately curled, immensely tall heap on her head. Her skin was fair and almost translucent, a tiny black heart-shaped patch applied near the corner of her mouth. Her lips were quirked with a delicious hint of a smile. The delicately etched face, the pert nose, the eyes as dark and clear as fine sapphires, caused Rand to whisper something in amazement, his breath gently stirring Rosalie's hair. She shivered, having no idea if the chills in her spine were because of the picture or his presence behind her.

"It's Rosalie," Rand said, and the Beau chuckled triumphantly.

"I told you the similarity was remarkable."

"Yes, it is," Rand agreed slowly, his tawny eyes fixed

on Rosalie as he returned to his chair. Were it not for
the previous existence of Georges Belleau he would
had sworn she was a Doncaster by-blow. As if she knew
what he was thinking, she met his gaze defiantly. Just
imply that I'm some nobleman's bastard child, she
thought while clutching the miniature, and I'll make
you sorry!

"What a kind twist of fate it was that you decided to
visit Calais," Brummell commented, breaking the
heavy silence, and Rosalie turned to him with the
determination to enjoy herself.

"And how kind of you to receive us," she said.

"I felt assured that any company Rand Berkeley
brought with him would be enjoyable. As usual, I was
correct."

"Thank you," Rosalie replied. "Ran . . . he . . .
Lord Berkeley . . ." Suddenly unable to decide how to
refer to Rand in front of Brummell, she hesitated in
confusion. Both men were silent, one of them out of
politeness, the other out of some inscrutable, mocking
impulse to let her flounder on her own. "He mentioned to me," she continued with a spark of anger
toward Rand, "that you had previously made acquaintance."

"Yes," the Beau said, an ironic smile crossing his
face. "The first time that we met, I was obliged to
thank him."

"Thank him?" Rosalie glanced toward Rand skeptically. "Whatever for?"

"It was on Berkeley Street that I found my lucky
sixpence. I picked it up from the gutter—with a
handkerchief, of course—and ascertained that it had a
hole in the middle. A battered token, but worth
Aladdin's lamp. From then on I had the most unremit-
ting luck a man has ever dreamed of—"

"Hardly because of any contribution *he* made," Rosalie pointed out, indicating Rand with a movement of her head. He smiled innocently at her.

"I take credit whenever possible."

"—and I lost the coin," Brummell continued, oblivious of the exchange, "when I inadvertently paid it to a hackney coachman. Hackneys! I've always harbored a distaste for them. From then on my life plunged on a downward course, until I came to the straits in which you see me now. Before my move to France, however, I had had the occasion to attend a hunt or two at Berkeley Castle. Rand, how goes the present earl?"

"My grandfather is sickly." There was a flash of bitterness in Rand's eyes, so lightning quick that Rosalie might have imagined it. "I spoke with his physician before we left London. There is doubt as to whether he'll last another year."

"A pity," Brummell murmured, yet there was no regret in his voice. Aside from Rand, he had always disliked the Berkeleys. A solemn and pretentious lot, prone to value their money and possessions above everything else. A miserly lot, a cold family . . . basically an *unsociable* family, which was to the Beau unpardonable. "Then you will assume the earldom soon."

"An unappetizing prospect," Rand stated, swirling his cooling tea in the bottom of his cup, his eyes absorbed in the motion of the liquid.

"Yes." Brummell looked at him with a trace of sympathy. "I would not welcome the responsibility."

"I don't mind the responsibility. But it is a title with many deep and unattended stains."

"Surely not beyond your capability to wipe clean."

Rand smiled suddenly, looking at Rosalie's uncomprehending expression. All she had were kitten's claws, sharp enough to dissuade but useless for real self-defense. She was indeed an innocent, one in dire straits if all she had to protect her from the civilized, savage world was him. His gaze did not swerve from her as he spoke.

"Unfortunately," he drawled, "I tend to follow in the well-worn tracks laid out by my family. And the sins of a Berkeley are sometimes impossible to make adequate reparation for."

Rosalie tried to steel herself against the faint curl of feeling that had begun to insinuate itself into her heart. Alarmed by it, she lifted the teacup to her lips, nearly choking on the smooth sweetness of her next sip. She mulled over her distressing reaction to him in silence.

Rand Berkeley was a man who did what he pleased regardless of the consequences. That was not unusual for someone in his position. But Rosalie was becoming aware of the surprising fact that he had some sort of conscience. From the way he sometimes looked at her, she had the feeling that his mockery and sarcasm concealed a wealth of far gentler emotions. And when his hard, handsome face contained that peculiar mixture of bleakness and amusement, as it did now, Rosalie wished that she could reach out to that deeply buried part of him that was still young and vulnerable. What is happening to me? she wondered, and, mildly panicked, she took another swallow of tea.

Four

Lovers they knew they were, but why unclasped,
*   unkissed?*
Why should two lovers be frozen apart in fear?
And yet they were, they were.
                              —John Crowe Ransom

They arrived at the Lothaire at such a late hour the next night that Rosalie did not stir from her bed until midmorning. She was lifted out of slumber by the heat of the sunshine that gleamed through the windows of her bedroom, and the muffled sounds of knocking, low voices, and the closing of a door. Sliding into a light robe, Rosalie opened her chamber door and rubbed her eyes as she regarded the scene before her. She was quiet, uncertain of whether or not to interrupt Rand's thoughts. Unaware of her presence, he sat at the Sheraton table with his broad, firmly tapered back toward her. He opened a note and scanned it quickly. Then his shoulders sagged slightly, as if in relief. Rosalie tilted her head in sleepy curiosity, for she seldom caught him in an unguarded moment. He whispered something to himself, the words indistinguishable as they were borne to her ears on a warm breeze from the window.

"Rand?" Immediately his head turned, dark amber hair seeming to come alive and then settle back into place as he stared at her. Wariness flashed in his hazel eyes, and then was replaced by a smoky look of rapidly deepening interest. Following his gaze, Rosalie stared down at herself and then hastily jerked her robe around her body, realizing that the pink-hued peaks of her breasts shone through the silk of her nightgown in

the brightness of the morning light. In silence she sat
down at the table, folding her hands primly in front of
her body. Rosalie could not help turning red in consciousness of her reaction to him, for she had found
lately that she was spending a great deal of time
thinking about the occasions when he had touched
her . . . about how warm his skin was, how large and
firm his hands were. And when the light shone on his
hair, illuminating the golden streaks in the dark amber
mass, she wondered what it would be like to let her
fingers play through the well-cropped thickness of it,
for his hair shone like satin and would surely be a
delight to the touch. At first Rosalie had been horrified
at her own thoughts, but after having lived with them
for weeks, she was becoming accustomed to her own
insatiable curiosity about him.

"Bad news?" she asked as his fingers half-crumpled
the letter.

"No, not at all." Although his words were positively
spoken, something in Rand's manner revealed an opposite emotion as he threw a quick glance down at the
paper in his hand. "Very good news, courtesy of this
morning's packet ship. I've received authorization from
the earl to take care of something I've wanted to do for
a long time."

"Oh?" Her one word was loaded with encouragement for him to continue.

Rand smiled reluctantly at Rosalie's expectant expression.

"You're obviously determined to find out everything." His voice was softer now, curling at the edges
with the beginnings of wry amusement.

"I'm interested," she acknowledged. "Or do you
have a monopoly on the enjoyment of good news?" She
continued to stare at him in silent entreaty until he
relented.

"I've wanted to sell off some family property here in

France. The d'Angoux estate. Most of the land has been divided and leased to tenant farmers. I want to sell it to them. It's of little use to the earl, but it's been a battle to obtain his consent to break up the holdings."

"Why? If the earl doesn't need it—"

"Because it belonged to my mother, Hélène Marguerite. She was the daughter of the Marquis d'Angoux, the last of the line. The Berkeleys, the earl in particular, have certain notions of family obligation . . . of continuity. Now that my mother is no longer alive, we have no ties to the d'Angouxs, but Grandfather has insisted for years on keeping the d'Angoux estate." Rand smiled rather grimly. "Since I am the eldest grandson, it's been dangled in front of me for years."

"But you don't want it?"

"I'd rather have a ball and chain manacled to my neck."

"Oh." Rosalie frowned as she considered his darkening expression, and decided to pursue another subject. "So . . . you are half-French?" When he nodded, she smiled with a hint of self-satisfaction. "I knew you must be partly French. Your accent is so clear . . ."

"My mother spoke French more often than English."

Rosalie hesitated for several seconds as she contemplated him. How bewildering his manner was—one moment ago he had been amused; now suddenly he was preoccupied and distant. Although it was not unlike him to sometimes jump from mood to mood in the manner of a foraging honeybee, he was unquestionably disturbed about something, and she wondered why the subject of his mother's estate would have this effect on him.

"You were fond of your mother?" she asked daringly.

Rand shrugged. "I don't remember much about her."

"She passed away when you were very young?"

"I wasn't that young." He sighed and absently

dropped the note onto the floor. "She didn't have much to do with Colin and me. She and my father, Robert, lived in London while we were raised in Warwick by a staff of servants." One side of his mouth lifted in self-mocking humor. "Colin and I ran wild in the country, barely fit to be seen by anyone in polite society."

"So that's where you learned your manners," Rosalie said gravely. Rand glanced upward with quick suspicion, and then he smiled lazily as he realized that she was teasing him.

Rosalie was so entranced by his slow smile, the sunlit twinkle in his hazel eyes, that her breath caught in her throat. If given the option, she would have sat there all day merely looking at him with a new sense of feminine appreciation. It was an effort for her to continue the conversation.

"And your mother, she liked to be in London more than with you?" she asked. The concept was not an unusual one, but Rosalie felt that it was unnatural for a woman not to want to be with her children. It was more common among the upper classes to have their offspring raised by servants and strangers than the lower classes.

"It was better with her there," Rand assured her, and then the sketching of humor left his face. "For that matter, it was better with my father in London as well. But he moved to Warwick permanently when I was in my early teens."

"He wanted to be with—"

"He had gout. Severe gout. He was in agony most of the time, in so much pain that a mere sheet over his leg would make him howl. Understandably, that made him unfit to stay in London. He became a drunkard because of it."

"Is that why you don't drink often?" Rosalie asked, wondering why his face was becoming shuttered as she delved further into the subject. "I've never seen you take anything but a sip of wine—"

"Do you know what I find interesting?" Rand parried, his eyes looking more green than usual in the morning light. "You're unusually direct for a woman. I've never met one that dares to look a man straight in the face quite like you do." In his experience, a gaze of uncompromising straightforwardness came only from whores who eyed a man with brassy promise or from little girls who had not yet learned the artifice of flirtation.

Rosalie's cheeks colored and her glance flickered away to focus on the window. "I know. It's unladylike."

"Yes, it is." It was impossible to discern whether he approved or disapproved of her directness.

"Why are you trying to change the subject?" she persisted.

Their eyes met in challenge, hers questioning, his unfathomable.

Suddenly Rosalie felt like a bumbling detective who had stumbled onto a significant clue. Something was important about her question; there was something he was reluctant for her to know about. It became immediately imperative for her to discover what it was.

"It's nothing you would care to hear about," Rand said dismissively.

"You care so much about my opinion of you?" Rosalie inquired, her soft words taunting. She knew that he rarely, if ever, explained himself or his actions to anyone, but perhaps she could gain what she sought if she provoked him enough.

"You expect a Brummellian tale," Rand said with a grim smile. "All I have to offer is a mundane recollection of childhood, sordid enough in its own way. No, I don't think you would be interested."

"Sordid backgrounds come by the baker's dozen, anywhere you'd care to look."

As Rand heard the hint of challenge in her tone, he suddenly felt the inexplicable need to shock her, to peel away the covering from his wounds and witness her disgust.

"You wonder why I never drink?" he asked, his tone light and honed, like the blade of a steel knife. "I used to. Quite a lot. Like a swine at a trough, as the earl so tactfully puts it. When I was younger, my father was told by a quack that red wine would cure his gout and prevent the affliction in someone who hadn't developed it yet. He needed little encouragement to develop an already established habit of drinking constantly. And then Father affected a sudden concern for me, although I suspect he was mainly looking for some activity to ease his boredom. The gout would come and go, and when the pain had eased, he would become restless. I remember the first night it happened . . . he cornered me in the library with a wine bottle in his hand." Rand looked down at his hands and unclenched them as he continued. "I took a swallow to placate him, and found to my immediate discomfort that he intended to pour half the bottle down my throat. I struggled, but he was a large man. Being of smaller stature, I wasn't in much of a position to disagree with him. The same thing happened daily, as long as his gout wasn't with him. I used to thank God when his pain would start again. Colin was next in line, but most of the time he managed to hide as I was getting my share of Father's . . . attention." Rosalie flinched at the way he spoke, his voice self-mocking, his face blunted with a mixture of emotions too complex to untangle. The awful, wrenching pity of it trickled steadily through her veins.

"Your mother," she asked in a voice as raspy as aging leaves, "did she know?"

"She knew. She didn't take it upon herself to say anything. As I said, she preferred not to become too involved with us. She refused to leave London except for her occasional trips to her family château in France."

"Your grandparents—"

"Only suspected. They lived on the Severn, at Berkeley Castle. Not at Warwick."

"How long did he . . . how long did this last?"

Rand smiled, his expression tainted with the poison of memories that were never far from the surface.

"Until I stopped resisting. And then . . . then I began to drink without hesitation. I drank freely. I wandered through the next two or three years in a sodden haze. You can imagine the types of situations I was in and out of. Then in eighty-nine, the first year of the French revolution, my mother died at Château d'Angoux in childbirth, taking the baby with her. My father might have mourned her more deeply had the child she carried been his."

"And you?" Rosalie questioned softly. No wonder, she thought with compassion, no wonder that his eyes were sometimes so bleak. No wonder he had cut such a reckless swath through London. Some memories left no quarter for anything but the need to escape.

"I drank myself into a two-day stupor as all the relatives gathered together at Warwick for the funeral. When I woke up, I was with my grandparents on the way to the castle. They attributed my . . . problem to the liberal amount of French blood in my veins. As soon as I dried out I was sent to school, while Colin stayed with the earl. A year later my father was gone." Rand sent her a look filled with self-disgust. "I was born to follow in such a lofty tradition. I'm sure you agree I've shown the potential of living up to it."

They were silent for a few minutes. In an effort to subdue the compassionate ache in her chest, Rosalie breathed in and out in a regular pattern. Frozen to her chair, she sifted rapidly through ideas of what to say to him. She didn't know how to respond, how to act. The realization pounded through her head that he had trusted her enough to have confided in her, and the knowledge made her exultant and afraid. Rand, she cried silently, how can I help you? They both waited in the tense stillness for someone to make the first move. Gradually Rosalie came to the conclusion that any offering of sympathy on her part would be disastrous. He was a proud man, and in this moment he could be humiliated. In her confusion and concern, it didn't occur to Rosalie that now was the perfect moment for revenge, that one cutting remark could scar him deeply.

"I can understand a little of why you would be glad to get rid of the d'Angoux estates," she said carefully. "It will be good to cast off reminders." She had the impression that there was much that he had kept back from her, but Rosalie did not want to risk anything more by prying. Slowly Rand raised his head, and she saw the trace of relief in his gaze at her matter-of-factness, her lack of pity.

"I'd like to leave today and get it over with."

"Of course," Rosalie agreed instantly, her voice betraying none of her inner turmoil.

"You'll be safe here for a few days while I make some arrangements."

"I'll be perfectly content." *Take me with you,* she wanted to beg, and she bit her lip to keep the plea unheard.

Rand took a deep breath and stood up from the table, drawing his shoulders back to stretch them.

"Do you want me to order coffee or chocolate for you?"

"No. Please go on ahead. I have some things to do." Smiling slightly, Rosalie waved him out of the suite, toying with the end of her long braid. When she was certain he was gone, she went into her bedchamber,

releasing the emotion that had been trapped so tightly
in her chest. Her heart was trembling with anguish, her
cheeks becoming wet even before she closed the door
behind her. As soon as the latch clicked, a sob broke
from deep inside. How can you weep for him? she
berated herself, wiping the tears from her face with
one hand, sitting on the edge of the canopied bed. She
tried to remember all he had done to her. Rand would
not allow himself to feel the same for her or anyone
else; she wondered if he had the capacity for tears.
Furthermore, he would be repelled by her sympathy.
But still the unwanted tenderness seeped through her
veins like a drug, diffusing gently, softening the thick
barriers by which she had sought to hold him away
from her.

The farewell they exchanged was a hasty thing. They
mouthed conventional words and exchanged brief,
unconcerned smiles, and as the coach left the inn
Rosalie felt immediate dejection. I feel like a sea wife,
she thought morosely. I bid him hello and good-bye,
without knowing him . . . and he leaves so easily. But
why shouldn't he? I am not his wife, she reminded
herself, not even a mistress. I have no right to feel
empty, no claim to force him to keep me.

She had no right to feel as though she belonged by
his side.

Château d'Angoux was the former home of Hélène
Marguerite d'Angoux, although Rand would readily
have argued that the term "home" had little to do with
such a structure. It had ruled the landscape with stern
simplicity for four centuries, built on the ruins of a
castle that had challenged many an invader as far back
as the tenth century. Careful efforts to soften the harsh
gray of its countenance had been made. The lush
ground had been allowed to produce flowers and vines
of ivy that clung protectively to the edges of the bare,

cone-topped towers, and small streams lined with trees wound in a seemingly artless pattern around the château. The gardens were splendorous, filled with rose beds that connected in intricate figures and thickets of brilliant blossoms. Yet the building still gave the appearance of a warrior waiting patiently for the battle.

A small staff of servants had been retained to look after the château, and Rand alerted them to his presence before he prowled in the house and around the grounds. The panicked alarm that the master had come to stay was whispered rapidly from ear to ear, and from time to time Rand heard various scufflings of feet as they sought to prepare for him. Château d'Angoux had been beautifully kept. Still, merely being in the place where his mother had been born, courted, and married left a sour taste in his mouth, and he could not appreciate the beauty so lavishly presented.

He walked up the marble staircase, trailing his fingertips curiously along the gilded-bronze railing. The Renaissance tapestries of wine-red, ocher, black, green, and blue were of such immense proportions that Rand felt dwarfed by them. Having been here once before, he had a sudden flashback of how it had felt to look at them with the eyes of a child, and the result added to his unease. Then in one of the upstairs rooms he discovered a portrait hung precisely between two heavily framed mirrors. From the canvas Hélène d'Angoux stared out into the room with an aristocratic tilt to her head, her golden hair soft and gleaming, her eyes glowing a cool, unearthly shade of green. Her lips were thin and finely drawn, stretched in a smile so soft that it looked as if the artist had caught only the premonition of humor in her expression. The house was filled with her presence, and as he strove to ignore a sense of smoldering airlessness, vague snatches of memory assailed him.

Closing his eyes, Rand could almost smell the violet

scent he had always associated with her. His recollections were those of a boy—Hélène, a beautiful, elusive creature, a woman full-grown with the soul of a deceitful child. She had possessed a spirit of mercury, enchanting one moment and poisonous the next. No matter how fierce his efforts to win her affection, she never stayed, she touched but never embraced, she gave enough to make what she withheld more painful.

Rand opened his eyes once more, and as he stared at her face, it was the same as always. She smiled but did not speak, she looked at him and seemed to recognize the darkness that seethed inside of him. She was dead, and yet her spirit filled the house like an invisible web, catching at him, binding until he could not move. Château d'Angoux had been her sanctuary—she had come back here periodically to hide from the consequences of the mischief she had wrought—and for that reason alone Rand disliked the place.

He swerved his gaze away from her and flinched as he felt the protections he'd built around himself tear like old parchment. In all those years between her death and now, he thought he had succeeded in destroying the fruitless need of love. It was still there, stronger than before.

Wryly he thought that those who enjoyed life had somehow managed to circumvent the workings of the heart. What had happened to the man he had been only a month ago? He remembered how orderly, superficial, and *amusing* life had been. He had once been forced to seek out feelings when the pattern of his days became too dull: he would find a new woman, spend the night gambling, roam around the city with his companions. It had been an empty life, one which had left him unable to recognize innocence when he had seen it.

But somehow, unwittingly he had stumbled onto his salvation the moment he had encountered a hapless housemaid in a London alley. Rosalie . . . who had survived the careless crush of his touch and the trial of being forcibly transplanted. He thought of her at the little country inn and wondered how she fared without him.

"Rose," he sighed, doggedly trying to ignore a persistent yearning as he turned from the portrait. "Reveling in my absence, no doubt. Enjoy it, for I won't leave you again."

Rosalie had never dreamed that time could drag so slowly. She did not know why or how everything had changed. All that was obvious to her was that each minute of solitude had once been a treasure. Now she bade the minutes fly, her heart full of impatience, her mind in need of something more stimulating than ink and paper or serene landscapes. The guest list at the inn changed at a laconic pace, and when the colonial girls and their parents left, there were no more prospects of even mildly entertaining conversation. The Lothaire was as quiet as the green, slumbering fields nearby. Safe? Rosalie fumed occasionally, remembering what Rand had said to her. She couldn't have been safer if he had hidden her in a monastery.

She read over the few books he had brought to France——a few volumes of Shakespeare, some political analyses, an album of poems inscribed in a female hand. It was obvious from the inscription on the inside of the morocco cover that the snatches of sonnets and Byronic verse had been collected for Rand by a former mistress. At some point the giver's name had been blotted out, whether by accident or intention it was not clear.

One day passed, two days, three days . . . It could not be much longer, could it? She pored over the French newspapers, which came out only three times a week, unlike the English ones, which were printed in daily editions. Taking pity on her boredom, the innkeeper's wife, Madame Queneau, took Rosalie out on her daily excursion to the marketplace. Shopping began quite early in the morning, and they took a break from purchasing vegetables, ripe fruit, eggs, and meat in order to have breakfast at nine o'clock. As they sat in an open-air café and ate *pain au chocolat,* chocolate-filled bread dusted with sugar, they watched the activities of the inhabitants of Havre. The retail stores, which had opened at six in the morning, were beginning to swarm with customers. The streets were filled with peasant-driven carts, housewives, and housemaids, all engaging in the sharp, fluid bickering of buying and selling. There was even a fortune-teller on the street corner, doing profitable business as a result of the current popularity of Spiritualism.

"You would like to have your fortune told?" Madame Queneau inquired in friendly curiosity, noticing Rosalie's eyes on the woman. Rosalie laughed and shook her head. Since Madame Queneau could not speak English well, they carried on a conversation entirely in French. For a few minutes it almost seemed to Rosalie that she was speaking to Amille, so familiar were the wise eyes of the older woman and the perfectly intoned language.

"No . . . I do not have the money, and even if I did, I don't believe she knows my future."

"How can one be certain?" Madame Queneau asked prosaically, her delightfully round face wearing a whimsical expression.

"Because men . . . and women . . . choose their own fate." Rosalie smiled a little sadly. "Because I have made choices that have changed the direction of my entire life from what it was supposed to be. It was not my original destiny to be here in France, *madame,* nor to be with . . ."

As Rosalie's voice trailed away to nothing, Madame

Queneau's delicately set wrinkles deepened in curiosity, then lightened in sudden understanding.

"No matter what brought you together, I do not believe *monsieur* regrets it."

"I don't know what he feels," Rosalie admitted. "It is not easy to read him."

"This I agree with," Madame Queneau said, taking a deep sip of *café au lait*. "He does not play the fashionable man."

It was in style for the French bucks to imitate Byron, to sigh constantly with passion and disappointment, to go about with long hair, pale skin, to hint of longings and of weary souls. Rosalie almost smiled at the thought of Rand compared with them. He had no patience for such affectations.

"*Madame* . . . I would be frank if it pleases you—"

"*Certainement!* I enjoy frankness most of the time."

"You have not remarked upon my relationship with Monsieur de Berkeley. Do you think very badly of me for the kind of woman I appear to be?"

"*Mais, non!*" Madame Queneau appeared to be surprised. "Not at all. In France, the aristocrats like him cannot find love in anything besides the kind of arrangement you two have."

"But even knowing he won't marry me—"

"Here, young men have *mariages de covenance* all the time. After the first year, the husband and wife spend little or no time together. They have different friends, different activities, sometimes different homes. No, your kind of love is respected by most, and cherished, for the human needs are met not in the exchanging of rings, but of hearts."

Rosalie absorbed the statement in silence, and then she could not resist a question.

"But what of morality?"

"Morality . . ." Madame Queneau mused out loud.

"I make a pact with morality, *mademoiselle:* I never take it to bed with me."

What she said made sense. But, Rosalie wondered unhappily, is that all I'll ever be able to expect of love? Am I destined to be the third in a triangle, kept by a man, hated by his wife, sneered at by his friends? She wanted her own husband, her own life . . . but what kind of man would settle for a ruined housemaid?

Five

You have been mine before
How long ago I may not know:
But just when at that swallow's soar
Your neck turned so,
Some veil did fall,—I knew it all of you . . .
                    —Dante Gabriel Rossetti

*I*t was three o'clock in the afternoon, and Annette Queneau had arrived home from school only a few minutes before. Annette was a quiet child, not given at all to her parents' assertive pragmatism. She appeared to daydream often, especially as she played music. Rosalie did not wish to interrupt the child's reverie, and so she enjoyed the light, rhythmic music of the polonaise and the waltz while sitting in the tiny ballroom nearby, perched on the railing of the musicians' platform with her eyes closed as the pianoforte rang with music.

The ballroom, with its ornamental pink and gold, seemed like something out of a fairy tale to Rosalie. It had not been an unexpected find at the inn, for there were ballrooms everywhere in France, reportedly more than seven hundred in Paris alone. Dancing had never been so popular or so necessary to the morale of the public. Rosalie imagined what the room would look like filled with dancing and music. The accented strains of a romantic, bittersweet melody floated into the room, trembling in the chandeliers, falling through the air like invisible rain until Rosalie could resist its call no more. She stood up and whirled to the center of the floor, her slender arms and filmy blue-and-white skirts wrapping around her body gracefully, her hair coming

118

loose, the pins flying in every direction. Then amid the
blur and the freedom of her private rapture, she sensed
someone's eyes upon her.

Rand stood in the doorway, his throat strangely
tight. He had never seen anything so lovely as she was
in that moment, pirouetting like an exuberant spirit,
her dark hair tumbling down to her slender waist. She
came to an immediate halt as she saw him, her eyes so
bright and vivid a blue that their color shamed the sky.
Her heart clenched in resistance to a great pull of
longing.

"Rand!"

Rosalie picked up her light muslin skirts and rushed
to him impulsively; for a moment they both thought
that she would fling herself at him, but she stopped a
few inches away from him, her cheeks flushed a bright
pink. Rand felt curiously bereft as he looked down into
her face, realizing that for a split second he had
anticipated the feel of her in his arms. Faintly dismayed
that the time away from her had not lessened his need
of her, he gave in at last to the undeniable truth of his
desire. He would want her until he lived and breathed
no longer.

"Hello," he said, his voice soft with some emotion
Rosalie could not identify, and she let her eyes travel
over him hungrily. His tall, powerful frame was shown
to advantage in top boots, buckskin breeches, a brilliant
white shirt, and well-cut coat. How impossibly vibrant
he appeared, as if he were prepared to meet the
relentless world with sword drawn. It was good to see
him again, so good that as Rosalie looked over him she
had the sensation of being nourished after a long time
of fasting.

"Did everything turn out the way you wanted?" she
asked, and he smiled down at her.

"For the most part. The land has been sold to the
tenant farmers at a fair price. There's still the château

and the parcel it rests on, but there are prospective buyers for it."

"I'm glad."

He looked different, Rosalie decided slowly. Open, less guarded, less troubled. The magnetic quality about him had increased many times over, or perhaps it was just that she was more attracted to him than ever.

"Dancing to a waltz," Rand said as they stared at each other, his mind sifting busily through ideas to find any excuse to hold her. "Scandalous behavior."

"I hadn't anticipated the existence of a witness."

"What about an accomplice?"

Before she could utter a word, he caught her hand irretrievably in his and coaxed her out onto the floor. The music drifted around them, enticing, urging, drifting in a tempting pattern.

"We can't," Rosalie protested, laughing and pulling ineffectively at her hand.

"Why not? You can't deny you're in the mood to dance."

"Because." A nervous expectation filled her as his hand settled at the small of her back, beneath the wondrous curtain of hair. "Because it would be dangerous for your toes. I've never danced with a man before. I practiced with *Maman,* and she always let me lead."

Rand laughed softly, amused but not dissuaded. He held her with a proper distance set between their bodies.

"If the attempt becomes too abusive on my toes, we'll abandon it," he said, and turned her very slowly.

The waltz was circumspect and leisurely, their feet moving at an indolent pace. He was a marvelous dancer, guiding her so firmly that there was no chance of a misstep, and Rosalie dreamily followed his smooth movements while gradually relinquishing all control to him. His eyes contained the myriad hues of an autumn forest—green, gold, amber—so intense that they seemed to glow. She could not break her gaze from his.

"All right?" he questioned huskily, and Rosalie nodded mutely. Dancing with him was the most seductive experience she had ever encountered. An embrace . . . almost. An excuse for holding each other, a socially sanctioned reason to clasp hands and entwine fingers. Their bodies were close enough to brush together occasionally, and each time they drifted toward each other unconsciously, Rosalie felt as if fire had flickered over her skin.

"I'm surprised your mother let you learn how to waltz," Rand said, one corner of his mouth lifting in a half-smile. Although the dance had become the rage in France at the end of the previous century, it had been acceptable in England for only a year or two. The intimacy it allowed between two partners had originally shocked most of English society, which had decried the waltz as vulgar and demoralizing.

"She didn't think I would ever have the occasion to practice the knowledge."

"Not even when the Winthrops gave a ball?" Rand questioned, his eyes alight with an odd tenderness.

"Well . . . even *Maman* agreed with Lady Winthrop that it was not suitable for me to dance with any of the young men there. It might have encouraged them to . . . well, it might have encouraged *me* . . . so I stayed by Lady Winthrop and the dowagers who . . ." As she trailed off uncomfortably, it seemed to her that his hold on her tightened, and that during the next turn he urged her the slightest bit closer to him. "Imagine," Rosalie resumed a trifle breathlessly, unable to keep from chattering, "if I had never gone to the theater with *Maman* that night, and you had attended one of the Winthrops' balls, and I had seen you from afar, dancing with Elaine. We never would have met, but Elaine would have told me everything about you . . ."

Silly as her prattle was, he appeared to consider it thoughtfully.

"I would not have been dancing with Elaine," Rand said. "And I wouldn't have let you sit with the dowagers."

"Oh?"

"I would have found someone to make the necessary introductions and then made you waltz with me until your slippers were worn through."

Rosalie giggled at the thought. "You wouldn't have given me a second look," she accused.

"Taking into consideration the fact that I avoid a gaggle of dowagers whenever possible, I might have taken an hour or two to notice you. But eventually I would have seen you in their midst from far across the room . . . and in one glance I would have drowned in a pair of great blue eyes," Rand murmured. The low huskiness of his tone flustered her to no small degree, and Rosalie stared up at him, spellbound.

"I . . . I might have danced the quadrille with you," she said, perhaps a little wistfully. Swallowing, she suddenly realized that it was imperative for her to break the mood before she melted in his arms, and her voice became brisker. "But I wouldn't have waltzed with you, no matter how often you asked—"

"Wise girl."

"—although I think all the criticism of such a harmless little dance is hardly well-deserved," she finished in a sensible tone.

"Obviously you've never read Salamo Wolf."

"Who?"

"A German writer. Two years ago he published a best-selling pamphlet . . . the title was something like 'Discussion of the Most Important Causes of the Weakness of Our Generation in Regard to the Waltz.'"

Rosalie laughed up at him. "You're not serious."

"The sequel was even worse."

"I fail to see what's wrong with waltzing."

"Ah, now you're daring me to show you."

"Show me," she repeated in a challenging way.

With a dazzling smile Rand accepted, for he was never above playing the rogue.

"The trick of it is all in the timing," he said, his hand drawing slowly across her back and pulling her inexorably nearer. "This pace is slow, sedate . . . appropriate for when dowagers and chaperons lend a watchful eye to the activity of their charges. But this . . . this is the French waltz." Their steps became more theatrical, the half-turns became deep circles. Expertly Rand turned her in a pirouette with one hand, and Rosalie's eyes widened slightly as he caught her again in his arms, this time so closely that she could feel the hard, smooth coordination of his thighs against her own, her soft breasts pressing against his chest. She dared not say a word, for their mouths were almost touching, and she felt the warm caress of his breath against her cheek. The dance echoed some ancient impulse buried deep within . . . the man to guide, the woman to follow, to submit. The momentum and the circles forced their bodies together, and as they moved together Rosalie felt herself become pliant and responsive to him, her insides tightening in an unfamiliar pulsing which she would recognize later as the beginning of desire.

Rand closed his eyes briefly, his control undermined by the clean, feminine scent of her skin, the waterfall of wondrous satin hair that flew around them, her soft body brushing against his, the closeness of a delicate earlobe which he longed to nip lightly with his teeth. "And this," he said with difficulty against her temple, letting his lips press there almost unnoticeably, "is the Viennese waltz, the worst of them all." He whirled her around the room so quickly that Rosalie had no time to breathe or think, crushed against him in an undignified but exhilarating madness, her skirts wrapping around his legs during each turn and then falling, clinging, falling, clinging . . . She began to giggle in dizzy jubilation, her very soul on fire as he laughed huskily in her ear, his arms firm around her. She was on the edge of a spiry precipice, yet he would not let her go. Finally he began to slow down and Rosalie clutched at his shoulders unsteadily, feeling as if she were drunk.

"Rand," she said in the midst of her merriment, gasping for breath, "I'm going to fall—"

"I'll catch you."

He looked down at her in a way that he never had before. Rosalie's smile vanished slowly as she realized that they were not dancing any longer and that he was still holding her. Carefully Rand stroked the curls away from her face, and with butterfly lightness brushed a kiss on her forehead. She stared at him in shock and extreme awareness. It had been a brotherly gesture, but he stared down at her not with the eyes of a family member, but of a lover.

"Why . . . why did you do that?" she whispered, and Rand blinked as if he did not know the answer. He resorted to quoting a well-known writer.

"How was it once said . . . ? 'I were unmannerly, to take you out, and not to kiss you.'"

"Shakespeare," Rosalie guessed, following his cue and making light of the kiss. "King Henry IV."

"King Henry VIII," Rand corrected, and let go of her with reluctance. "I see you've been doing some reading."

"I've been quite busy between Shakespeare, Hume, and sordid love poems of dubious origin."

"Oh, those." Rand flashed her a grin, turning and wiping the sheen of dampness from his forehead with a sleeve. "I hope you didn't place any significant meaning on any of them."

"At one point, someone obviously did."

"'I barely knew her—'"

"'His face is fair and heav'n,'" Rosalie recited wickedly, "'When springing buds unfold, Oh why to him was't giv'n, Whose heart is wintry cold?'"

Rand smiled slightly as he beheld her, wondering suddenly at the bright, inquiring gaze fixed so intently on him. He would have sworn in that moment that Rosalie was curious about his past romantic involvements. It was an auspicious sign.

"This isn't the kind of discussion appropriate for you to engage in," he said. As he had intended, Rosalie's curiosity deepened to a conspicuous level.

"Appropriate?" she repeated. Was he seriously suggesting that her maidenly modesty would be offended by such a subject? "Heavens above, you sound as if I've just arrived straight from the convent."

"Ah, yes, forgive me," Rand said, and abruptly his mood changed from subtle amusement to caustic mockery. "You know all about matters of passion, don't you?"

Rosalie knew that he was thinking about that morning in London, and suddenly she felt hot and uncomfortable. Backing away a step from him, she lifted a hand to smooth her hair, trying to think of another direction to steer the alarming turn of the conversation. The music slowed, stumbled, halted as Annette Queneau ended her practicing.

"Rand?"

"Yes?"

She swallowed painfully before broaching a question. "Are we going back to England soon?"

"I . . . No, not yet. Not until the next shipment from New Orleans is delivered here. And I want to pursue the matter of a contract with a local silk manufacturer. Why do you ask?"

"I know that we're not going to stay here forever. I just wondered when we were leaving."

"A few more weeks."

Rosalie nodded, her expression becoming pinched. "It makes no difference to me. I have no . . . pressing need to get back immediately."

Rand wished he had not let go of her.

"Are you unhappy here?" he asked hoarsely, and a thousand answers came to the tip of Rosalie's tongue.

No. Yes. I was happy a few minutes ago. I'm happy when you smile at me, and when I first see you in the morning after a long night apart, and when you look at me and try to guess what I'm thinking. I'm happy being this near to you, I'm unhappy knowing we're so far apart in every sense. And realizing all of that makes me miserable.

Rosalie kept silent, looking down at the floor. Then with a short sigh she left him. He raked a hand through his hair and walked over to lean against the baroque door frame, staring vacantly down the hallway.

The next morning Rand mentioned to Rosalie the possibility of calling on Brummell in Calais. As he had hoped, the suggestion revived her good humor. Despite the inconveniences of the long journey, she looked forward to the lazy, comfortable hours they would spend with the Beau, hours spiced with targeted gossip and delightful stories. Wanting to look her very best, for she knew that Brummell paid meticulous attention to his visitors' attire, Rosalie dressed her hair carefully and pulled out a dusty-blue gown. All of the clothes made by Madame Mirabeau were impeccably styled and perfectly fitted, but this one was especially fine, covered with ornate scrollwork in silver and gold at the sleeves and hem. The skirt was also trimmed with satin ribbon and flounces of satin and muslin. The problem that Rosalie encountered in dressing herself was that the gown had been fitted to her as she had worn a tightly laced corset of dimity and whalebone, hence it was now necessary to wear one.

She ventured out into the central room of the suite, the dress gaping widely in the back as she held it up to her shoulders.

"Rand?"

Immediately his head appeared from behind his bedchamber door. "What . . . . ?" Rand's eyes flickered over her silver-and-blue-clad form intently. Finally he brought his gaze to her face. "That's a beautiful gown," he said after a few moments' silence.

"I know," Rosalie said, irritated at her own reaction to the way his eyes had seemed to strip her bare. "I can't fasten it."

A slow smile pulled at his mouth. "Have I been feeding you too much?"

"No, I can't lace this bloody corset tight enough!"

Rand continued to smile. "How can I help?"

Silently she presented her back to him to display the crisscrossed lacings. She heard his soft footsteps, then felt the light tug as he took hold of the cords.

Rosalie held on to a doorframe and gasped as the whalebone prison cinched more securely around her ribs and waist.

"I think that's enough," Rand said doubtfully.

She shook her head. "I'll never get the gown fastened if it isn't tighter. Go on, pull."

He hesitated, aware of a vague unpleasantness in his stomach at the thought of compressing her body with the laces any more. Due to the sensibly styled empire gowns, corsets hadn't been necessary for more than a decade. Binding a woman's figure in the contraptions seemed like an unnecessary form of torture.

"Why don't you wear another gown?" he suggested.

"Am I going to have to call for one of the maids to do it?"

Muttering under his breath, Rand pulled the cords again, watching her waist diminish another inch to an unbelievably tiny size. Rosalie took several shallow breaths and held a hand to her midriff.

"Can you—?" she began to ask, but he cut her off sharply.

"No. No more. I'm already battling an urge to look for a pair of scissors." He pulled the back of the dress together and fastened the buttons efficiently as he spoke. "Why you women insist on bringing back a fashion that should have been outlawed in the last century—"

"I've heard some men are doing it. Even the prince regent supposedly—"

"Yes, the ones who frequently overindulge their taste for wine and food. But you don't need it, Rosalie."

"How can you be a judge of—?"

"I've seen you," Rand reminded her, and as she stiffened he lingered over the last three buttons. "It's a crime to alter your shape."

Rosalie closed her eyes, heat rushing to her face as she felt the warm, sensitive touch of his fingers at her neck. Suddenly it seemed as if he had just touched her for the first time. The memory of their naked bodies entwined was distant and no longer clear. Sometimes she could recall briefly the hardness of his body over hers, the flexing of heavy muscles, the deep shudder that had racked his limbs as he had thrust into her. But strangely, it seemed that two other people had been joined in that bed, that she had never met Rand until they had arrived in France. In self-protection, Rosalie dragged herself to the present and hunted for a way to break the intimate silence.

"Coming from a connoisseur, I suppose I should be pleased at the compliment," she said.

"I'm not a connoisseur," he said quietly, looking down at the top of her head.

"You're right. The term 'connoisseur' implies a certain respect for the subject of your interest. A hobbyist, then."

Rand stifled an urge to close his hands around her throat and throttle her, wondering grimly why she was determined to antagonize him. "If you're a hobby of mine, I must have a peculiarly masochistic idea of enjoyment."

She turned around to face him. "I have only my experiences with you to examine—and the obvious conclusion is that you have no respect either for me or for women in general."

"If that were true," he said in a dangerous tone, "we'd be in that bed right now, regardless of your prickly little thorns, Rose. I do respect you."

"Then I don't understand . . ." she began, and her voice diminished to nothing as she stared at him. The shape of his mouth, a touch too wide, finely made, expressive, had altered slightly with his irritation. A flash of memory curled insidiously through her mind; how hard his lips had once felt as they had demanded access to hers, how soft and tender as he had brushed her forehead with a kiss after their dance together. I'm lost, she thought, realizing in that moment that she was beginning to care for him.

"You don't understand what?"

"Why you did . . . what you did . . . in London," Rosalie muttered, desolation encasing her heart like hardening plaster.

Rand's irritation evaporated immediately. Bleakly he searched for an answer and found it impossible to speak. How could he explain it to her? The world he had been raised in had been one without compassion, without patience. He had learned his lessons well, the main one being that pleasure was something taken, not given. It was a conditioned reflex that when he discovered a need he satisfied it without considering the consequences. And how could he further explain that because of her he was beginning to change, that he had learned to feel regret?

"I didn't know you then," he said slowly. "All I knew was that . . . Oh, hell, Rosalie, you were beautiful and you were there at a time when I wanted a woman."

He expected her to fly at him in anger, and he would not have blamed her for reacting in such a way. But instead her expression twisted in bewilderment, her voice became quieter.

"I don't understand you," she whispered. "Why are you so kind sometimes, and then so . . ." She could not find the appropriate word to use; how could mere words describe his changeable nature? And how could she ever hope to trust someone who was cold, sweet, gentle, selfish, without explanation, without warning, without consistency?

They were both subdued as the carriage rattled on its way to Calais, avoiding each other's eyes as they were jostled along the poorly constructed roads. Their stops for food and rest were too infrequent to break the tension or relieve their growing weariness of travel. The atmosphere inside the vehicle was so stifling, watchful and restless that Rosalie almost leapt out of it when they reached Brummel's residence. It was all she could do to accept Rand's assistance docilely. Visiting Brummell again, however, was well worth the trip, especially when Rosalie detected a shadow of loneliness leaving his face as they crossed the threshold. Despite the constant flow through his door of the best of English society, including the Duke of Argyll, the Duke of Gloucester, the Duke of Beaufort, Rutland, the Duchess of Devonshire, the Lords Alvanley, Craven, Bedford, Westmoreland, and d'Eresby, Brummell's social life was a mere fraction of what it had once been. He could not help but sorely miss the popularity and the activity he had until recently enjoyed.

"*Ça fait une éternité qu'on ne vous a pas vu,*" he exclaimed, beaming at them, and Rosalie felt an answering smile curve her lips.

"It *has* been a long time," she agreed, allowing him to help her off with the pelisse and lifting her skirts slightly as she walked to an armless upholstered chair. "Have you received many guests since the last time we met?"

"Dozens, m'dear, all bringing the latest news from London. I'm afraid, however, that the quantity of visitors exceeds the quality."

"They brought pleasant news, I hope."

"Some of it was. It is always pleasant to be missed, and I gather Prinny's unpopularity has been on the rise since I took my leave of England. What is your opinion, Berkeley?"

Rand somehow refrained from observing that Prinny's unpopularity was due to more than the end of his friendship with Brummell. The prince regent was a notoriously corrupt individual, a spendthrift of horrible proportions, an inept politician who was often given to drunkenness.

"He is indeed an unpopular individual."

"Just as I thought," Brummell said in a self-satisfied way. "Without my advice, his extravagance will lead to disaster. I've heard that he's already taken to wearing pink satin and jeweled shoe buckles." He shuddered delicately at the thought. "Good taste is understatement—don't forget it. A good cut and fit, cleanliness, dignity, changing the gloves at least six times a day . . ."

Eager to prevent a long discourse on the Beau's principles of style, Rand sought to interrupt him with tact and haste. "News of the Pavilion has been in the

English papers of late, also stirring up public displeasure. Since John Nash was hired to work on it last year, many costly additions have been built. Oriental rooms, cast-iron towers, steam-heated kitchens——"

"The Pavilion . . . a tasteless toy. But to give Prinny his credit, quite impressive in a vulgar way."

"Mr. Brummell," Rosalie inquired, her forehead creasing in a frown, "is there a chance that you will ever reconcile with the regent?"

"I doubt it," the Beau replied stalwartly. "As they say, too much water has gone under the bridge. I believe the dissolution of a spectacular association——my wit and his title——began when his weight almost doubled."

"I've heard he's something of a stout fellow," Rosalie said, and Brummell nodded emphatically.

"The last time I saw him, he was well over three hundred pounds. It took a platform, a ramp, and a chair fitted with rollers merely to get him into the saddle to take some exercise."

"Oh, my."

"It was shocking, without a doubt. So much so that Prinny reminded me of a huge, ungainly porter at Carlton House, whom we all nicknamed Big Ben. Since Mistress Maria Fitzherbert, the celebrated . . . associate of the regent was also stout of girth, I naturally began to refer to her and Prinny as 'Our Ben and Benina.' " He paused as a smothered laugh was heard from Rand's direction. "It was not well-received, though my jest was delivered in an affectionate manner."

Rosalie looked at Rand and they exchanged a fleeting smile. Charming though George Brummell was, he did not possess a considerable amount of tact.

"The next wedge," the Beau continued, "was hammered into place when Prinny exhibited the grossest piece of rudeness I have ever witnessed—ignoring me completely at the Dandy Club masquerade. The final blow occurred as I was walking down Bond Street with Lord Alvanley. We happened to accidentally meet the prince and Earl Moira, and after a few minutes' conversation during which the regent again ignored me, I quipped to Alvanley, 'Who's your fat friend?' "

"Oh, my," Rosalie gasped again, wondering how anyone could possess such daring and audacity to say something like that in the hearing of the ruler of England.

"It was merely a poorly timed jest. But eventually a few debts forced me to quit England before the breach had healed."

"I see," Rosalie murmured, concealing her sympathy behind a polite nod. The great Beau Brummell was impressive and entertaining, but there was something about him that aroused a strangely protective feeling inside her. He was like a child whose vanity made him excessively naive. She wondered what would become of him, for it was obvious that he had no source of income that was great enough to support the style in which he lived. There was no trace of worry or caution in his face, nothing to indicate that he was aware of his unstable position.

"Miss Belleau," Brummell said, unfolding his moderately sized form from an upholstered chair, "would you care to see the album I have put together? It is quite sizable, having contributions from many of my present and former acquaintances. There is a verse in particular I would like you to see, penned by that marvelous woman, the Duchess of Devonshire. It begins with the line. 'I have valued the charms of the rose, as I plucked it all fresh from the tree . . .' I do not remember the rest."

"I would be honored to see it," Rosalie said gravely,

and he muttered something in satisfaction before going to a built-in bookcase and hunting for the album.

"Selegue!" Brummell called imperiously, and the little valet came scurrying. "I can't find my album," he explained, and Selegue nodded vigorously before waving him back to his chair.

"I'll fetch it, Mr. Brummell."

"If it's too much trouble . . ." Rosalie began.

"No, no, not at all, m'dear. It is a very special album, with unique verses that only my favored guests are invited to regard."

"We're very flattered," Rosalie said.

As she and Brummell smiled at each other with the same degree of beguiling charm, Rand suddenly froze, the idle tapping of his fingers on a hard thigh stilling. He looked at the pair of them and leaned forward, his eyes flickering from one to the other and then widening in astonishment. Nothing in the world could have induced him to say a blessed word in that moment, for his mind was spinning with suspicion, wonder, curiosity, disbelief.

Brummell must have regarded himself in the mirror often enough to recognize the vague echo of his own expression, for his smile dimmed in puzzlement as he walked toward Rosalie. The album was forgotten. Then he turned pale and his gaze focused on her throat. Uneasily Rosalie remained where she was sitting.

"Mr. Brummell?" she said hesitantly, and he appeared overcome.

"Where . . . did you get . . . that pin?" he finally was able to stammer.

Her fingers flew protectively to the small gold ornament that was attached to the ribbon fastened around her neck.

"It was my father's stock pin. He died when I was

young. My mother gave it to me so that I would have something of his."

"May I see it?" The words were taut, brittle, almost breaking in the complete silence.

Confused, Rosalie untied the ribbon and handed it to him, the tiny gold cirlet dangling from it like a teardrop. She was amazed to see that his hand was shaking. Darting a glance at Rand, she saw that his gaze was focused completely on Brummell. After she had relinquished the stock pin, the men seemed to have forgotten her very existence.

"What is the matter?" she asked. No answer was immediately forthcoming. Brummell walked over to the window and held the pin up in the sunlight to examine it closely.

"Selegue!" he shouted strainedly, and the wiry little valet came running back into the room.

"Here is the . . ." Selegue began, stopping as he saw the oddly stooped posture twisting Brummell's normally upright frame. "What happened?" he asked, and Brummell handed him the pin wordlessly. A minute of silence ensued as the valet scrutinized the object with care.

"Tell them," the Beau muttered, as if the effort of speaking were too great to allow more than those two words.

"It is the stock pin your father, William, had commissioned for your sixteenth birthday," Selegue said matter-of-factly. "The same pin that you gave to Lucy Doncaster before you were parted from her. The B stands for Brummell, the leaves patterned after those that adorn the walls of your family estate, the Grove—"

"The B stands for Belleau!" Rosalie interrupted, smiling although her voice was slightly shrill. "I told you, this is my father's pin . . . Georges Belleau."

"Georges Belleau," Rand repeated softly. "George Brummell. A strange coincidence that the initials are the same."

"Stop it!" Rosalie snapped, her chest rising and falling rapidly.

"Please, Miss Belleau," Brummell said, making an effort at calmness. "I am sorry to distress you. Let us clear this matter immediately."

"At once," she agreed sharply.

"Then would you relate to us the circumstances of your birth?"

"Certainly. I was born in 1796—"

"The year I was eighteen," Brummell interjected.

"—in France. My mother and father moved to London soon afterward. According to *Maman*, my father was a confectioner. He was killed by a stage-coach as he crossed the street from his store."

"You have been brought up solely by your mother?"

"Yes. I have lived with her all of my life until . . . until I made the acquaintance of Lord Berkeley."

"Your mother's occupation?" the Beau pressed.

"She is governess to a respectable—"

"Her name. Her *name*."

Rosalie stared at him, transfixed by the urgency in his face. Unreasonably frightened, she stood up from the chair and backed away a step. She could hardly speak. "Amille Belleau," she said, her throat dry.

"Before she was married."

Silently Rosalie shook her head. She had the premonition that he already knew the answer. Somehow she forced out the name. "Amille Courtois."

A deathlike pall fell over the room, for so long that Rosalie thought she would cry out from the tension. Then Selegue broke the stillness.

"That was the name of Lucy Doncaster's governess."

"What are you saying?" Rosalie demanded unsteadily.

"She must have . . . Lucy Doncaster might have born you in Europe after she fled England," the valet replied gently. "It is quite likely that you are a product of the relationship of George Brummell and Lucy Doncaster. There is not only the pin to consider, but also the amazing likeness between you and her."

Brummell clutched the pin in his fist, bending over and pressing it to his chest.

"No!" Rosalie felt indignant tears well up in her eyes. "My mother is Amille Courtois Belleau. My father was Georges Belleau. You're mistaken, you're terribly wrong!" She stumbled backward, everything in the room looming toward her at odd angles. "Give me my pin," she sobbed, and as she turned blindly she felt hard arms close securely around her. "Rand," she wept, pressing her face into his shoulder. "Rand, tell them . . ."

"This cannot be possible," Brummell rasped, hiding his face. "I cannot think, I cannot . . . For God's sake, let me alone to think!"

Six

I speak not, I trace not, I breathe not thy name,
There is grief in the sound, there is guilt in the
fame . . .

—Lord Byron

Although there were only four people in the room, it was crowded with confusion, tears, and panic. Quickly, efficiently, Rand and Selegue worked to dispose of the situation, since father and daughter were both unable. The valet guided the distraught Brummell to a chair, speaking in a soft undertone. Rand held Rosalie's trembling form against his, letting her draw from his strength and stability. His sensitive fingers curved around the vulnerable back of her neck in a calming touch.

"Rose. There's no need for this," he said, sounding so utterly practical and in control that it helped to dispel the queer aura of unreality clouding her mind. "Take a few deep breaths and relax." Rosalie listened to him and obeyed automatically, forcing deep gulps of air in and out of her mouth as she stared at Brummell's hunched figure. As soon as her trembling lessened, Rand dragged her from the room, pausing only a moment at the door to deliver a low-voiced comment.

"I'll be back to straighten out this mess in a day or two. If you two have distressed her unnecessarily—"

"I assure you, this was entirely unexpected," Selegue interrupted apologetically before bending to speak to the Beau. Brummell was muttering brokenly about Lucy, lost in his own world. His head was clasped in his hands, his elbows braced on his knees as he stared at

the floor and began to weep. Rand cast the pair of
them a dark look before pulling Rosalie's arm through
his. She followed him blindly, stumbling a little over the
hem of her skirts. She was dazed at what had just taken
place, her mind completely occupied with replaying the
scene over and over again. Everything she had taken
for granted, the person she was and the background
she had come from, had suddenly been wrenched away
from her. It could not be true . . . none of it could, for
Amille would surely have told her about it! How could
Amille not be her mother? How could George Brummell be her father? It was all some trick of coincidence!

The carriage that would take them to a local inn was
outside the building, the French driver leaning against
the vehicle as he turned the page of a daily periodical.
"Allons," Rand said tersely, and the man looked at
Rosalie with vague alarm before leaping to his seat with
alacrity. Inside the carriage, Rosalie felt a wave of
sickness lurch through her body. She held a hand to
her middle and closed her eyes, her lungs feeling as if
they had shrunk to a condition of airlessness. As she
fought to draw a breath, her chest tightening, she
looked at Rand in panic. She was being methodically
crushed to death by the garments that bound her.
Muttering a curse, he drew her halfway onto his lap
and worked at the tiny fastenings of her gown.
"Damned corset," he said, buttons flying as a result of
his efforts. "The last time, the very last, that I ever let
you wear one." As the cords loosened and her waist
expanded, Rosalie inhaled with relief, her head swimming dizzily. Rand also took a breath, realizing that he
had unconsciously held it until she had been freed from
the laces. Gently his fingers slipped under her chemise
and stroked the red-scored flesh of her back, soothing
the delicate and ravaged skin. Gradually her illness
began to subside.

"Thank you," she whispered, and then burst into fresh tears when she had garnered the strength. Clutching the sleeve of his coat in a death grip, she stared at him with a tormented expression, her eyes brilliant and wet. "They think . . . that *Maman* isn't my . . . real mother—"

"I know," he murmured soothingly. "Breathe deeply—"

"Listen to me—it's not true! He is *not* my father! I'm Rosalie Belleau . . . you believe it, don't you?"

As her words broke into sobs, Rand hesitated uncomfortably and then cradled her against his chest, his mouth tender with sympathy. He felt peculiarly helpless. The other times he had been faced with women's tears, they had been an artifice and not the product of genuine misery. No woman had ever needed him simply for comfort, and he was not used to such a demand being made of him.

Rosalie pressed her wet face to his shoulder, her nails curling into the lapels of his coat like kitten claws. As Rand held her small form against his, he felt part of her pain, an odd tugging at his heart. This wish to soothe, to offer refuge, was brand new, gleaming brightly as a candle flame, and without questioning it further, he sought to warm her.

"It's all right," he whispered, his hand stroking her back in a gentle, repetitive motion. "I'm here. It's all right."

"Rand, what am I going to do?"

"Relax for now. We'll talk about it later," he said, and she subsided against him, accepting his touch as if it were her due.

As time spun on steadily and her weeping faded, Rosalie felt a fragile trust crystallize between them. An invisible web clung tenuously from one heart to another, a bond so frail that it could be destroyed with one

WHERE PASSION LEADS   141

easy blow. Rosalie came to her senses gradually, becoming conscious of how intimately he held her, how the warm strength of his body enveloped her, his masculine scent pleasant to inhale, his breathing even and steady as it disturbed the curls at her forehead. She knew that she should move away from him. Surely by now Rand knew that she had recovered herself enough to move to the other seat. But Rosalie did not want to move at all. His body was solid and hard, yet strangely comfortable. Don't let go, she pleaded silently, closing her eyes tightly.

He did not say a word during the short journey to the inn, allowing her to remain in his lap. Both of them were fully conscious, wondering what the other thought, sharing in the mystery of an attraction that neither of them understood.

I swore I wouldn't touch her.

I wish he would kiss me.

I wish I didn't want her.

Then, as they both had dreaded, the carriage swayed to a halt. Avoiding his eyes, Rosalie unpeeled herself from the warmth of his body slowly, her limbs stiff.

"My dress . . ." she said, and he handed her his coat.

Wearily Rosalie trod through the front door and up the narrow stairs that led to the suite, pausing as Rand unlocked the door.

"Get into a robe," he said, pushing her inside. "I'll order up a bath and some dinner."

"I'm not hungry—"

"Lock the door behind me."

"All right," she said, her voice nearly inaudible. "Whatever you say."

"You don't have to be so agreeable," Rand said, amused, in spite of the situation, at her uncharacteristic docility.

Although her eyes were still lowered to the floor,

Rosalie managed to summon a brief and tremulous smile. She felt unbearably alone. This was her problem; this entanglement was centered around her. It had nothing to do with Rand, and she could not allow him to assume all of her burdens.

Rand's gaze was caressing as it rested on her down-bent head. "Close the door, *rose épineuse,*" he said, and was gone.

Thorny rose. His voice, the softness of his accent, had fallen on her ears like a slow stroke.

Bewildered, she slipped his coat from her shoulders. It was scented of him, and she inhaled the subtle male fragrance of sandalwood as she carried it to his bed-chamber. Had she imagined the possessiveness in his manner, the caress of his voice? Was she so unnerved that her imagination was coloring everything in deceptive hues?

When Rand returned he bullied her into downing a glass of cherry brandy, which burned pleasantly as it filled her with false courage. Her energy depleted, Rosalie found that she was ravenous at the sight of the simple fare set before them: thick-crusted bread, the soft sweetness of Camembert cheese, succulent fruit, and a bottle of wine. As she ate, she felt Rand's approving eyes rest on her, and as soon as her initial hunger passed, Rosalie set down a piece of bread and met his gaze squarely.

"Better?" he inquired, ascertaining that her strength had returned.

"Much better."

Rand's attention flickered to the chambermaid, who was in the midst of emptying the last bucket of scalding water into the metal tub. It would take some time to cool enough to bathe in. Hurriedly the woman finished her task and fled from the room, reading the impatience in his tawny eyes. Rosalie's heart began to pound nervously as she realized that they were about to discuss what had happened, and all that she had eaten seemed to rise threateningly to the base of her throat.

"I don't think I'm ready for this," she said, and an agitated laugh stuck in her throat. "I don't think I'll ever be."

"All we have in front of us," Rand replied reassuringly, "are a few pieces of circumstantial evidence. Nothing's been proven—"

"But what about the pin?"

"It's not all that distinctive. The initial B and the motif of a leaf pattern are nothing unusual. It could be pure coincidence."

"And my . . . my mother's name? What if she really had been Lucy Doncaster's governess?"

"That doesn't necessarily mean you were Lucy's illegitimate daughter, no matter how much of a resemblance there might be. It's possible that this whole situation is a Brummellian tale that has gotten out of hand. As you've already gathered, the Beau is not the most reliable source of information. He is romantic, he's fanciful. He's been weakened by a recent ordeal. I would sooner trust a London wine merchant not to water the claret than to take Brummell's word for anything."

Rosalie sighed, at once grateful for his rational skepticism and unconvinced by it. "Besides," Rand continued, "there is no motive for keeping your . . . the existence of such a child secret. Lucy Doncaster had several options more feasible than giving this hypothetical baby to her governess to raise. Her first reaction, I suspect, would have been to approach Brummell with the news and garner his support. Failing that, she could have married the Earl of Rotherham and pretended the infant was premature."

"Why do you seem to know so much about it?" Rosalie could not resist asking dryly, and Rand smiled at her.

"Not from personal experience. But it is hardly an unprecedented dilemma."

She nodded and chewed on a crust of bread meditatively, finally shaking her head and frowning. "I have a bad feeling about all of it," she said.

"The only way to refute or prove anything is through Amille Courtois Belleau."

"No." Before Rand could say anything, Rosalie spoke in a vehement rush. "She has been my mother for the past twenty years. If any of this were true, she had her reasons for keeping it from me, and I'll abide by them. If I can't trust her judgment, the judgment of a woman who has fed and clothed and cared for me my entire life, then I can't believe in anyone or anything."

He stared at her in a perplexed manner.

"But how could you not want to know? What if Brummell were your father—"

"I would gain nothing, and think of what it would do to Amille. Don't you see? George Brummell is incapable and, I suspect, unwilling to be a father to anyone." Her expression darkened with hurt. "He didn't exactly open his arms to me this afternoon."

Rand bit off an agreeing reply and searched for something to offer in solace. "He was shocked."

"He is too vain to want a child. He is a dandy, and it's common knowledge that men like him resent growing old. They don't want reminders of their age." Rosalie's expression became haunted as she continued. "And as for Lucy . . . if she was my natural mother, I don't know or care why . . . why she wouldn't want me. Amille did, and that's what matters."

Rand nodded slowly, sensing that now was not the time to try to change Rosalie's mind. She was tired and she was not ready to be honest with herself. He knew her well enough to be certain that she did care about her past and that she wanted desperately to know more about Lucy Doncaster. But Rosalie was afraid of the secrets that the past held, and it would take time to build her courage.

"Then we'll let the subject rest for now."

"You don't agree with my decision," Rosalie said, her eyes questioning as they searched his face. She couldn't tell what he thought. He lifted his shoulders in a slight shrug.

"It's not my right to tell you what to do." It was her right, Rand mused, to approach her past in any manner she cared to. God knew that *he* hadn't been eager to deal with his own!

His comment suddenly amused Rosalie.

"May I ask what prompted this change of policy?"

Deciding not to reply, Rand smiled, looking lazy and oddly content. The sky was dark outside but the room was filled with hazy candlelight. The glow of the flames picked up the gold in his tousled hair and his eyes, and gleamed across the darkness of his face with a metallic sheen. Rosalie was momentarily engrossed in his movements as he stretched his arms back and locked them behind his head, his muscles swelling and then smoothing under the whiteness of his shirt. What a strange sight he was with his gentleman's attire and his swarthy skin. It was an incongruous combination, but oddly attractive nevertheless.

As Rosalie looked at him with inquiring sweetness, Rand felt an aching hollowness gather in the pit of his stomach. He wanted to hold her again, he wanted to taste and touch her, and he realized that he had run out of pretenses to lure her into his arms. What recourse was left? He looked at her in hungry contemplation and felt some part of himself give way to a stronger demand.

"Rose . . . what would you do if I asked you to come over here?" he asked quietly, his intent stare urging her to trust him.

Rosalie blinked in immediate confusion, wondering

if she had heard him correctly. "I . . . I don't know,"
she said, her forehead creasing. "I suppose it would
depend on why—"

"You know why." His voice was softer now, more
coaxing. A long pause ensued before he spoke again.
"Come here."

It was impossible not to obey. As if she were being
drawn by an invisible rope, Rosalie stood up and walked
around the table to him, stopping as she reached his
chair. He wants to kiss me, she thought distractedly,
and the delight and dismay of it tumbled inside her
chest like a pair of hard-thrown dice.

They stared at each other, hypnotized.

"Why do you have to be so beautiful?" Rand whispered. Her blue eyes were dark with wonder and
disquiet as they met his. Still she stood by him, every
instinct clamoring for her to stay.

"Don't give me a reason to—" she began to warn,
but Rand interrupted her huskily.

"I will never hurt you again, Rose. I will never do
anything you don't want. You must know by now that
my word is good."

She nodded slowly, suppressing a tiny shiver at the
honey-soft way he spoke.

"I believe you."

"Then come closer."

The air was fraught with suspense. After several
moments of inner debate she moved hesitantly to sit
down on his thigh, feeling the hard muscles flex
beneath her as he shifted to accommodate her. His
hands settled at her waist, their pressure light and firm,
a steady influence that served to keep her secure, still,
close. Suddenly trembling with the awareness of what
she was doing, Rosalie extended her hands and placed
them on his shoulders. Her fingers spread over their
breadth and strength, her thumbs detecting a strong

pulse through the thin material of his shirt as they
pressed into the shallow hollows beneath his collarbone. She was nervous. A quick impulse to pull away
from him seized her, but something caused her to
remain. Perhaps it was the curiosity that pulsed inside
of her, or the odd, waiting look in his gold-green
eyes . . . perhaps the insane feeling that he deserved
the right to hold her in this way. His fingertips rested
on her body with gentle lightness, promising magic.

"I've tried to take kisses from you before," Rand said
huskily, drawing her further between his spread knees,
"but you would not yield to me."

"You were different then," she whispered, thinking
of how his mouth had crushed hers. "I remember—"

"Don't." Rand's gaze was edged with bleakness.
"Don't remember anymore. Let me replace your memories."

The stillness stretched between them, surrounded
them, seemed to press her slowly toward him. His
words, his gaze, the strange new leniency about his
mouth, all of it tempted her beyond reason.

Slowly Rosalie lowered her head, finding his mouth
with her own, shivering slightly as they first touched.
His lips were warm, firm, undemanding. She knew that
it was an inexpert kiss, for she did not know what to do
except to press her mouth against his . . . surely a man
of his experience would not be satisfied by her un-
worldliness. But when she lifted her head with a shaky
breath, Rosalie saw that Rand had also been affected.
His gaze was soft and hot with desire, his chest rising
and falling a degree more quickly than before. Underneath her hands, his pulse had increased in strength.

The silence was broken only by the faint sputter of a
candle flame.

Rand was unaccountably touched by the innocence
of the chaste caress. As Rosalie watched him with the

wary courage of a kitten, he fought hard to tamp down
the violent strength of his response to her, and he won
the inner battle by only a hair.

"Is that what you . . . ?" she breathed, her hands
tightening an inch or two closer around his neck, her
body tingling as the tender surface of her inner arms
brushed his skin. "Was that all right?"

Rand longed wildly in that moment to drag her into
his bedroom. The feel of her as she perched on his lap
was unbearably tempting, like a kitten begging to be
cuddled. She was so soft and feminine, so easy to
hold . . . The insistent pressure of need in his body
increased, and he lashed down his impatience ruthlessly.

"Yes," he rasped, a sultry glow emphasizing the gold
in his eyes. Then he smiled, his teeth a brilliant white
against the copper of his skin. "But too fast."

Rosalie smiled as well, shaking her head slightly as
she looked at him. Leaning forward until their noses
nearly touched, she felt his muscles tighten into unyielding hardness.

"Let me try again," she offered, and tentatively she
sought the tender fire of his lips once more. Now Rand
allowed himself to respond with careful eagerness.

"Open your mouth," he murmured, his large hands
coming up to frame her face. Uncertainly she obeyed,
finding that as her lips parted they were held open by
the increasing pressure of his kiss. His tongue touched
hers; in confusion she tried to jerk her head back, and
he followed her movement, their lips still fused. Slowly
Rosalie subsided, an incredible, yearning heat suffusing
her body as his mouth slanted over hers, demanding
access, finding it, rewarding her with undreamed-of
pleasure. She felt marauded and cherished at the same
time. Rosalie sank down into his lap, her body becoming boneless, sinuous, pressing against him of its own
accord. The boldness of his masculinity throbbed

against her, and she felt an answering pulse in her midriff as she yielded to his embrace. In Rand's arms was a world of luxurious sensation that she had never dreamed of. Here was safety . . . here were warmth, light, and color . . . here was enchantment that nothing could dispel. Their mouths moved together deeply, and a tremor flitted through Rosalie's veins in response to the barely restrained urgency of his kiss. Rand cradled her head in one large hand, his other fumbling blindly with the belt of her robe. As she felt the slight tugging, Rosalie stiffened and turned her face away from his.

"Stop," she gasped, her senses groggy with arousal, blinking as if she had just risen from a deep slumber. She could hardly remember who she was. "I've no wish to lead you on a fruitless . . . Rand, I don't want . . ."

There was not one trace of apology in the fever-bright green of his eyes, only a wealth of need.

"I understand," Rand said hoarsely, and then he couldn't help but smile wryly at the strained sound of his own voice.

"I'm sorry," she said, making a move to get off his lap, and he kept her there by tightening the circle of his arms.

"Rosalie . . ." The way he said her name caused her ears to burn. "Little siren, you've lured me between Scylla and Charybdis. It doesn't matter if I crash against the sharp rocks or sink into a bottomless whirlpool. Either way, my fate is sealed. I want you. And the curse of it is that I only want you if you're willing."

She moistened her lips nervously, feeling restless and empty, rather as if she were the one being drawn into a whirlpool. Reluctantly she searched for an alternative to offer him. "Maybe someone else—"

"There could be no one else," Rand said honestly, flatly. Their encounter in London had been an equal exchange. He had taken her virginity, she had taken his freedom. He had no desire for any other woman.

Rosalie stared at him unhappily. Although she was relieved by his refusal to go to another woman to ease his needs, she was conscious of her own limitations. She couldn't help thinking suddenly of the discomfort, the fear she had experienced in his bed.

His mouth became twisted with a bitter wistfulness. "Do you think I don't understand how it was for you?" he asked in a haunted voice. "Don't let the memory rule you, Rosalie. You have no idea of what it could be like."

"Please," she moaned, her eyes becoming damp, "it's not a question of what I fear or remember. It's a question of independence. I don't want to need you. Please let me go."

Instantly he let go of her as the last glow of arousal faded reluctantly from his loins. Rand walked over to the bathwater and tested it with his fingers. "Go ahead with your bath," he said, sounding vaguely weary. "Call me when you're out."

"Rand . . . we can't leave it like this. Aren't we going to talk about—"

"Not now," Rand said tersely, walking toward his bedroom door. His unsatisfied desire was slowly transforming into a deep-rooted frustration that nothing could ease. One more minute around her, and he would undoubtedly regret what it would prompt him to say and do.

"He's not feeling well," Selegue offered apologetically.

"Because of him," Rand said softly, "I've never had a worse night's sleep. I'm not feeling well myself. Let me in."

The door to Brummell's apartments was swung

wide, and Rand strode into the drawing room. The Beau reclined in a built-in cushioned nook, fingering an object which Rand instantly recognized as the gold pin, still fastened onto Rosalie's velvet ribbon. He didn't appear to be surprised at Rand's presence.

"Amazing," Brummell murmured dolefully. "Prinny and I each sired a daughter in 1796. His Charlotte and my Rosalie would most likely have been fast friends, had my own relationship been—"

"If Rosalie is your daughter," Rand interrupted sharply, "I'd say she's been far better off away from the lot of you."

"There's no doubt that she is mine. She's the living image of Lucy, and I fancy I saw a little of myself in her."

"Not much."

"Enough," Brummell insisted, and Rand became increasingly annoyed as the other man continued to stake a claim to Rosalie. For now, whether she wanted to or not, Rosalie belonged to Rand himself, not to an aging fop whose name spelled certain trouble for her.

"Aren't you going to ask how she is?" Rand inquired with unnatural calm.

The romantic aura of loneliness dropped from the Beau's facade as he smiled with anticipation. "Yes, do tell. Come to think of it, why didn't you bring her?"

"She's confused. She's unhappy. She doesn't know who she is, and she's afraid to find out. And if you care a whit for anything besides the condition of your cravat, Brummell, you'll erase every trace of yesterday afternoon from your mind."

"Dear man, have you gone spoony? She's my *daughter!* I have no family, Berkeley, at least none that will admit connection to me. She's all I have. And there is an entire heritage I must tell her about, the legends I have left behind, the—"

"Accepting your name would ruin her," Rand said bluntly. "You left England with scores of creditors snapping and sniffing over the pittance you left behind. What would she inherit from you?—a legendary debt and a lengthy sojourn in debtors' prison while you cool your immaculately polished heels in France."

"I suppose it is far better for me to leave her in your hands, sir! Far better for her to be your hummingbird, and then to be cast off to some other pup when you've tired of her. You forget that I have previous knowledge of your reputation, Berkeley. You use the ladies lightly, and then you cast them aside like soiled gloves."

"I wouldn't call them ladies," Rand replied, and his expression became inscrutable. "And I would not cast a waif out into the street. I'll take care of Miss Belleau—"

"Brummell."

"Belleau," Rand stressed gently, meaningfully, "if your neck means anything to you. For her sake, not yours or mine. I know about the flood of visitors you receive, and moreover, about your fondness for gossip and sad tales. But this will be a secret you carry to your grave, or else I will consider your loose tongue an invitation to hasten your demise."

For a moment Brummell appeared to be suitably impressed by the words, for he was one to religiously avoid the threat of physical confrontation. Then he managed to put on a show of unconcern.

"Picturesque words," he scoffed.

A dangerous gleam shone in Rand's eyes. "Don't forget a single one of them."

"Does my daughter agree with you?" the Beau inquired stiffly.

"She doesn't know I'm here." Rand began to leave, and then stopped as if remembering something. "As of now, only four people know of the possibility of her connection to you. If the rumor ever gets out, it will spread like wildfire, and I'll know that it wasn't started by me or my . . . hummingbird." He emphasized the last word with light sarcasm. "I would advise both you and your valet to hold your tongues."

"Selegue, show our visitor out," Brummell commanded, striving to attain an imperious tone.

"I know the way," Rand assured him, but hesitated before he left. "One more thing, Brummell. The pin. I want it back, in the event that Miss Belleau decides she would like to have it."

The Beau suddenly flushed in distress, shaking his head and meeting Rand's eyes directly. "I can't give it to you."

"It's not yours to withhold. The pin was given to her by her mother."

"My God, man . . ." Brummell said slowly, the first real traces of emotion lacing through his voice, ". . . are you really as heartless as your reputation would indicate? She's my daughter. I'll go to my grave believing it, and from all appearances I'll go without ever having known her. The pin is the only proof, the only sign that I have of her existence."

Rand went through a brief inner debate before nodding reluctantly.

Once they had returned to Lothaire, Rosalie found her dilemma growing worse daily, for she was trapped in a situation that she had never anticipated. Confronted with two unacceptable alternatives, either to have Rand or not to have him, she tried instead to find a middle ground. That proved to be impossible.

She had decided at first to treat him with casual friendliness, studiedly ignoring any spark of the sexual awareness between them. The ploy failed because any hint of amiability between them seemed destined to turn rapidly into intimacy. A simple exchange of smiles turned into a long look of shared desire; a touch of the hands threatened to become a much warmer embrace. She thought all of the time about kissing him, and wound up blushing guiltily whenever their eyes met. Finally Rosalie resorted to her old antagonism, which was an even worse tactic. The arguments, the sharp, fast exchanges they engaged in so readily, held a powerful undercurrent of excitement. In those moments they wanted each other the most, and so Rosalie began to feel helpless against the oncoming tide of her feelings for him.

But what would happen after she gave herself to him? Rosalie was afraid that the old saying was true, that what attracted a man in a woman rarely bound him to her. She did not want to touch heaven and then settle for less; much better never to know what she could not have. Rand did not make the situation any easier. At times he looked at her so intently that she flushed in pleasure and confusion; how heady it was to be desired by such a man. She had not allowed herself the right to feel possessive toward him, but when they walked down the streets of Havre, pausing to look at the gaudy merchandise displayed in the store windows, Rosalie was aware that many envious eyes were on her. Rand, with his tall, well-built form and exotic coloring, was a highly visible prize.

Helpfully Rand left the Lothaire during the moments when the closeness became unbearable. Rosalie made the disagreeable discovery that she spent most of the time that they were apart wondering when he would return. Steadfastly she refused to mention their oncoming departure from France, even though it was obvious that his business affairs would be resolved soon. A new life in London, new employment, being able to see and talk to Amille when she returned—these things should have given Rosalie pleasure to think about. She knew that Rand cared enough for her in his own way to see that she would be established in a good situation, perhaps as companion to a kindly widow, or nanny to young children of an agreeable family.

But Rosalie found no gladness in anticipating the end of their stay in France. To be strictly truthful, she wondered how she would bear never seeing Rand again. When she was old and gray-haired she would still be able to cast her mind back to the time when the not-yet Earl of Berkeley had wanted her passionately, had danced alone with her in a little ballroom and kissed her once with the warmth of a blazing noontime sun. She would live the memories over and over, keeping them worn bright with use.

On the dreaded day when the American cotton finally arrived at port, Rosalie sipped her chocolate and watched Rand shave. After becoming accustomed to the small intimacies of living together, such as helping with dress fastenings and the tying of cravats, Rosalie's habit of creeping into his room to watch him perform the morning ritual of shaving caused little comment from Rand. After their first week in Havre, Rosalie had admitted to herself that she enjoyed looking at him so casually dressed in the wine-shaded robe: the long, powerful muscles of his calves, the light golden skin at the back of his neck, the sparse, glinting fur visible at the part of his chest that the robe didn't cover. She had never had the occasion to persue the body of a man with such leisure before, and Rand was undoubtedly a prime example of what was most desirable in a man. He did not have the slender, elegant physique of many of the admired and celebrated bucks; instead, he was tall and substantially built, well-conditioned from riding and hunting. His body was hard, muscular and compact, unaltered by pads or stays. Rosalie had come to find his lack of artifice attractive, more so than the carefully curled locks, the reedlike slimness, and the refined shapes of more fashionable men. Surely, she thought, no woman in her right mind would disagree.

"Rand?" she questioned as he scraped the last trace of soap from his face.

"Yes?"

"What happens if the shipment is good?"

"Berkeley Shipping will probably win the silk-manufacturing contract over East India, giving us a good portion of a valuable market. What else? You and I go home. From my grandfather I receive praise for a job well done, for proving myself capable of handling the family affairs, and my share of the inheritance will be declared secure."

"What if it isn't?"

"I engage in an ignominious battle, pointing fingers and resorting to pleading and threats, developing tremendous headaches, and losing my appetite. And you and I remain here until the problem is resolved."

Rosalie squelched the traitorous hope that she would be given a few weeks' reprieve. For Rand's sake she would hope that the cotton bales were without flaw.

As he hunted on the washstand for a fresh towel, Rosalie stood up from the chair she had been leaning against and walked over to him. Seeing her approach from the vantage of the mirror, Rand turned around and looked down at her with a question in his hazel eyes. Without her slippers on, her head came to a spot well below his chin. It always surprised him, when they were close, how small she was. His heart skipped a beat as she reached up to his face with her fingertips. Gently Rosalie wiped away a smudge of soap from the underside of his jaw with her thumb and smiled at him.

"You missed it," she stated unnecessarily, and then she stood on her toes to press a lightning-quick kiss to his smooth-shaven cheek. He was utterly still, his ex-

pression unfathomable. "Good luck, Monsieur Berkeley. Don't let a few *américains* get the better of you."

"My problem isn't an *américain*," Rand said, and his
mouth turned up at the corners in a smile that would
have enchanted a heart of stone. "It's a little *anglaise*
who shouldn't come into gentlemen's bedrooms to
watch them shave."

"What gentleman?" Rosalie inquired, her smile almost saucy, and Rand reluctantly grinned as he motioned her out of the room with a nod of his head.

The early-morning commotion had begun at the
dock, but this time Rand's attitude was unconcerned.
"It's fine," were the first words Captain Jasper had
uttered upon their meeting. As the cotton and other
goods were being inspected by customs agents, Rand
thrust his hands in his pockets and watched the process
with something close to nonchalance. His eyes followed
the stout and active form of Willy Jasper as the older
man gave brief directions to the crew of *Lady Cat*
during unloading. The men worked together like a
well-oiled machine, so accustomed was each to his
function in the procedure of docking and unloading.
As Jasper felt the touch of Rand's gaze, he turned
around and looked at him thoughtfully, as if he were in
the midst of making a decision about a particular
matter.

"Captain," Rand said, inquiry threading his tone,
and Jasper walked toward him with a slow seaman's
stride.

"If you have a minute, I'd like to speak with you, sir,"
the captain said, his gray eyes matching the soft steel
color of his hair. Rand inclined his head curiously and
Jasper hesitated once more. "It's none of my concern,"
he said, "except that you are a good employer and a
fair man . . . and I suspect we'll be doing business

together well on into the future. You do not strike me as the sort who likes to hear only tidings of—"

"Jasper," Rand interrupted, his white teeth flashing in a quick smile of amusement, "you don't have to beat around it. Is there something you want to say?"

Silently the older man nodded and reached inside his coat to pull out a folded sheet of newspaper. It was a section from a recent issue of the *Times,* the largest and most widely read of all the London papers. It was advanced far beyond its European contemporaries, its only equal being the *Messenger,* an English paper produced in Paris. Rand scanned it absently, one large hand reaching up to rub the back of his neck to ease the tautness of the muscles there. Then, under the column labeled "France," the words leapt out at him:

> An astonishing rumor has come to our attention concerning George Brummell, Esq., currently residing in Calais. The recent report involves the existence in France of a young Miss Belleau who claims to be the illegitimate daughter of the former resident of London. Curiosity is rampant concerning the possibility of this famed gentleman's offspring. Our sources cannot be confirmed.

Rand felt his belly tighten with anger. Slowly he raised a carefully blank expression to meet Jasper's scrutiny. "Interesting," he commented. "What has it to do with me?"

"What the paper didn't state," Jasper said cautiously, "is that the prevalent rumors link your name with this woman. They say that the reason for your sojourn in France is not business, but the fact that she is your . . . your . . ." It was not necessary to finish the sentence. Rand knew that Jasper traveled in high enough circles so that his information was probably accurate. And if so, Rosalie's name was being bandied about at every ball, every breakfast, every hunt, every street corner in England.

He swore fluently, the string of soft curses heard every day in a London street but uttered with such an intensity of feeling that Jasper fairly blushed.

"Brummell," Rand muttered, "when I get to you I'll gag you with your own cravat."

"You don't deny it, then?" the captain asked.

Rand's mouth twisted in disgust. "Does it matter? The damnable thing about rumors is that whether they're confirmed or denied, they proliferate like weeds."

"True." Jasper was about to add something when he spied a fraying hemp rope being used to lower one of the small, heavy crates of porcelain. "Excuse me, I must attend to something."

Rand barely acknowledged the captain's departure as he scowled at the dock. He would be damned if he would take Rosalie home before he knew what kind of reception she would have. The thought of what she could be subjected to made his hair curl.

Brummell's daughter. To the sophisticated set of London she would be a wonder, a novelty, a curiosity, a prize. She would become a celebrity among the wilder circles of London, toasted and feted, exposed to all the seaminess the jaded elite had to offer. To the elite, the art of corrupting the spirit was not only a game but also a subtle art. They would all want her, they would try to lure or steal her away from him, tempting, taunting, breaking the thin silken bonds that Rand had so carefully tied around her. She would be wooed and courted by every buck in sight, who would desire her as a mistress because of her beauty and her famed father. The thought of her being drawn away from him so insidiously made Rand's jaw harden in anger, aroused an instinct to protect what was his. He would not allow them to touch her.

A previously unconsidered thought raced across his mind. What if he gave her his name?

People would be more loath to take advantage of a woman under the shield of the Berkeley name and power, no matter who her father was. And if Brummell's angry creditors dared to approach her, Rand would have a legitimate claim and legal means to deal with them himself. Marriage. The thought had never appealed to him before now, but it suddenly presented itself as the perfect solution to his problems. He had always scorned the idea of being confined by the matrimonial bond, but the prospect of being tied to Rosalie held a certain appeal. He knew far more about her than he could ever have the opportunity to discover about some simpering debutante during a carefully supervised courtship. Although Rosalie was a lively woman with a marked willingness to argue with him, she could also be very companionable. She was young and beautiful, and there was no question as to her innocence. Before they had met she had been untouched by any other man—that much had been proved.

And most important, if she were his wife, he could have her anytime he wanted.

Putting the shoe on the other foot, Rand considered what her life would be like as Lady Berkeley. He knew he was one of the most desired matrimonial catches in London because of his title and wealth. Surely Rosalie could have no objection to the home and the living he would provide for her. But aside from that, could she learn to be happy with him as a husband? He had started their relationship off in the worst imaginable way, yet he would not demand any forgiveness that she could not give, only try to make amends. Disgruntled, he stared distantly into the sky, wondering exactly how she felt about him. It was fairly obvious that on some level she had developed a kind of fondness for him. It seemed to Rand that that was enough to begin a marriage with. Rosalie could learn to be happy with him, especially during the endless hours they would spend in his bed. Although she did not know it yet, Rosalie was a woman who needed to be loved long and well, and Rand had no doubt that he could satisfy her in that respect if not in any other.

Rosalie flew to the door as soon as she heard the key turn in the lock.

"What happened?" she demanded, flinging the door wide, and Rand caught it deftly with one hand. There was a vaguely triumphant air about him as he looked down at her with an intricately blended gaze of gold and jade.

"You can offer me your congratulations," he said, and Rosalie laughed in delight. Before she had the opportunity to say a word, Rand closed the door and pulled her into his arms to kiss her. Rosalie was immediately paralyzed, her lips soft with astonishment, and he took advantage of her vulnerability without hesitation. His mouth was searching, urgent, knowing, even more intoxicating than she had remembered. As the warmth of his touch suffused her, Rosalie stumbled closer, to meld herself against his hard body. Fire licked smoothly along her nerves in instant reaction to him, and a soft sound came from Rand's throat as he sensed her surrender.

Rosalie became oblivious of everything but the searing contact between their bodies, the hungry clasp of flesh to flesh. She was consumed like tinder fed to a flame, feeling hot and light, weightless. Their passion was new, desperate, too long denied. His hand slid upward along her side, searching for her body through the fine material of her gown, cupping her breast delicately. Her knees weakened at the sensation and she leaned against him, letting the hard muscles of his legs take her weight. Somewhere in the back of Rand's quickly evaporating mind the thought intruded that he was not going to be able to stop. He had to get control of himself. He lifted his head, his breath quick, and she made a slight gasp of protest as the loss of his mouth.

"We have to talk," Rand said thickly, his thumb making a regretfully brief search of a tender nipple. Rosalie shivered and then nodded, her face flushed and her body aching for more of his touch. He let her rest against him until her legs had strengthened, and then she moved away to sit down, feeling peculiarly languid and confused.

"About going home?" she asked.

"Precisely. There is something I'd like to do first." He paused before asking slowly, "Would you mind it if our return was delayed another week?"

Rosalie took an uneven breath and lowered her eyes so that he would not see the transparent gleam of relief. Another week, she thought with an overload of thankfulness. Another week with Rand.

"That depends," she said carefully. "Why do you want to delay it?"

Rand paused in a split second of indecision, feeling a quick sting of guilt. He had already decided not to tell her about the report in the *Times* until he could make the most use of it. He would buy enough time to beguile her into accepting his proposal. If she proved to be particularly obstinate, he would use the newspaper article to convince her that she needed the protection of his name.

"I was speaking this morning with a French naval architect about the *Prinzessin Charlotte*, a double-hulled steamboat which carries passengers on the Elbe in Germany."

"A steamboat? Why would you be interested—?"

"Right now steam is used only as auxiliary power for passenger vessels like the *Charlotte*. Only for short inland runs. But when they are developed more, it's going to change the entire shipping business. They'll take the place of cargo freighters, and they'll cut the time from trade routes significantly."

"And you want to talk more about it with this naval architect?"

"I want to talk more about it with someone in Paris, a former apprentice of Robert Fulton. When Fulton lived in Paris he built a steamboat that went up the Seine, and he left behind a few burgeoning experts in steam navigation."

Rosalie frowned. She was hardly concerned about Fulton, steamships, or trade. What occupied her thoughts was the prospect of Rand leaving her alone for a week while he went to Paris.

"How soon are you going to leave?" she managed to ask quietly.

Rand smiled at her. "That depends on how much you intend to pack."

"How much *I* . . ." she repeated, dumbfounded, and his smile deepened.

"Unless you don't want to go."

Rosalie recovered quickly and masked her elation by adopting an undecided expression. "Will it be very boring, talking to some old man about ships?"

She looked so much like a little French coquette that Rand had to smother an impulse to snatch her up and kiss her until she was senseless.

"Boring?" he questioned thoughtfully. "Have you ever sailed up the Seine in a full-rigged freighter? Have you ever gone to the Maison d'Or and whispered behind your fan as the dandies strolled by? Seen a play at the Comédie Française? Have you ever gone dancing in Paris until the night ends and dawn begins?"

"No." Her gaze was filled with excitement and longing.

"Then you won't be bored. Go and pack."

Rand grinned as she scampered off to her room. He was beginning to understand how to deal with Rosalie Belleau-Brummell. A good thing that she was proving to be so temptable.

Paris was unimaginable to someone like Rosalie, who had been sheltered all of her life from the kinds of sights and activities that proliferated there. Every narrow, poorly paved street seemed to run riot with energy and glee, with the colors and shapes of fantastic art, with the music from the theaters and the loud talk of the radical intellectuals who frequented the cafés. To those who wished to act and speak as they pleased, Paris was the City of Light. For twenty-four francs Rand had hired a carriage to take them to the Hôtel de Ville, a noble structure that had stood on the Right Bank since the sixteenth century.

Rosalie tried to prevent herself from hanging out of the carriage window in an unseemly way as Rand pointed out the strange and delightful scenes they passed: the open-air summer restaurants, the huge mass of the uncompleted Arc de Triomphe, the Tuileries Gardens, and the Palais Royal, where numerous small shops beckoned to the passing tourists. Across the Seine reposed the dwellings of the secluded aristocracy along the Right Bank. Every part of the city was filled with the delicious smells of a multitude of the finest restaurants.

The first night in Paris, Rand took Rosalie dancing as he had promised, to a public ball that was crowded with the most varied assemblage conceivable. It was filled with gamblers, prostitutes, aristocrats, and elegant ladies, who intermingled as if the sharp class distinctions they usually sought to protect did not exist. There was an orchestra at either end of the dance hall. The music of the fiddle, clarinet and the *cornet à piston* floated out of the huge Gothic doors to the small garden walkways that were lit with colored paper lanterns. Inside, Rosalie went to the refreshment table after the first quadrille and eyed the drinks with dismay.

"Warm March beer," she commented, and out of nowhere Rand managed to produce a cup of tart lemonade. "You're a magician," she accused, laughing up at him and then downing half the drink in a few rapid swallows. She was careful not to let the pink liquid spot either her long gloves or the immaculate high-waisted, puff-sleeved gown she wore. The daylight-blue gown was at first glance demure, but the neckline was cut so deeply that it riveted the attention of all who saw her. The fragile inset of Valenciennes lace did nothing to camouflage the alluring vale between her breasts.

"Be careful," Rand said, picking up a fresh three-cornered puff and eyeing it with interest. "You might come to find me indispensable."

"Tonight I do," Rosalie said, biting off the corner of the puff and allowing him to finish the rest of it. "You're a better dancer than anyone else here." She felt like she was flying when they moved together. She had felt the stares of many people on them as Rand had whirled her around the ballroom, and strangely she had not minded being regarded as his woman.

Rand smiled at her, wondering at her relaxed openness with him. It was a new attitude, one which interested him greatly. It seemed that there had been a few changes in Rosalie since he had first brought her to France.

"A dancer is only as good as his partner."

"Not true," she corrected, taking another refreshing swallow of the sugar-fruit-and-water concoction. "I know the extent of my capabilities. You enhance them greatly."

"False modesty. Are you looking for more compli-

ments from me?" Rand accused softly. Their gazes
caught and melded together in an electric completeness, and then they became aware that the orchestras
were playing the unmistakable accented rhythm of a
waltz. "The first waltz," he said, and took the lemonade from her to set it down on the table. "We're
obligated to dance again."

"Really," Rosalie responded dryly, and she allowed
him to pull her into the center of the crush of couples
before it became any more crowded.

"I must speak with Madame Mirabeau about your
clothes," Rand remarked, sliding an arm around her
waist with the caution of utter propriety.

"My clothes?" Rosalie repeated, wrinkling her nose
at him in a flirtatious manner that was utterly unlike
herself.

"You're only a fraction of an inch away from being
underdressed," he said, and as his gaze flickered to the
plunging neckline of her gown it was obvious as to
where he would have added the extra inch of material.

"If you'd bother to look around, you'd see I'm the
most overdressed woman here."

Rand made some noncommittal sound, having no
desire to look at any other women. As he stared down
at her and smiled, Rosalie was suddenly consumed with
a rush of feelings that threatened to suffocate her. Why
did this night ever have to end? she thought, caught in
an indescribably painful moment of realization that no
hour, no minute of her life would ever be this perfect
again.

It seemed that they danced the entire night without
stopping. Rosalie clung to each moment until it was
wrenched from her, reveling in the cloud-woven hours
as Rand turned the considerable amount of charm at
his disposal completely toward her. One minute he
would entice her into laughing out loud, and in the
next he would look into her eyes with an enigmatic and

steady gaze as he swept her around in wide, circling steps. Their clasped hands, the music, the privacy of an intimate glance—it was a sweet flash of fulfillment, too brief, elusive. She was caught between night and day in an insubstantial dream, able to do nothing except follow where he led.

I've allowed it to happen, she thought, and her breath caught in her throat. I've brought it on myself. She had fallen in love with him. She loved a man she could never, never have, someone that perhaps no one could ever have. And worse yet was the knowledge that if it had happened despite her best efforts to resist, her flourishing love for Lord Randall Berkeley would likewise be impossible to dispel.

Seven

Come to me in the silence of the night;
Come in the speaking silence of a dream;
Come with soft rounded cheeks and eyes as
    bright
As sunlight on a stream
Come back in tears,
O memory, hope, love of finished years.
                                —Christina Rossetti

A breeze flew across Rosalie's skin as the carriage door was opened, a cool brush of gossamer that sent soft chills chasing through her body. The faltering moonlight barely illuminated Rand's set features as he helped her out of the vehicle. His eyes flickered with a brief smile, but the set of his mouth was inscrutable, the expression of his features almost emotionless. Rosalie accepted his hand as she descended to the ground, wondering why her fingers were cold when his were so warm.

"You must be tired," Rand said, and Rosalie nodded automatically, although she was not tired at all. She had no idea of what hour it was, but the sky was as dark as velvet and there was no promise of daybreak in sight. She could find no explanation for the excitement and apprehension richocheting through her stomach, except that somewhere inside burned a premonition of what would happen soon. The dance was over, the night fertile and young, the air seasoned with the intoxicating flavor of romance.

Silently they entered the quiet, dimly lit hotel and proceeded up the long, straight flights and landings of a deep-welled staircase. Rosalie could detect an odd blend of fragrances that mingled in the hotel: tobacco smoke, hot candle wax, strong tea, ladies' cologne. The treads of each step were finished with brackets that pressed into the sensitive soles of Rosalie's slippers. Finally they reached a hallway off which branched several rooms.

"It's so quiet," Rosalie whispered. "The guests must all be asleep."

"More likely they're all out dancing," Rand said, ushering her inside a room with studied aplomb. They shared two chambers that were connected by a gilt-framed door, rooms that were decorated in only a degree or two less luxury than the Lothaire. The gold-draped windows opened out onto small balconies, and Rosalie went over to peer out through a thin glass pane.

"What a beautiful view," she remarked in a small voice, and Rand frowned quizzically. Beautiful view? He knew that she could hardly see more than the dark outlines of the street. Was she uneasy because she didn't trust him? He didn't blame her; he hardly trusted himself around her. Sighing, he walked over to the connecting door and opened it gingerly.

"Your bags and trunks are all next door," he said. "Call for me if you have any difficulties."

Rosalie stared at him, making no move to leave. As she thought of what she wanted, of what was in her power to bring about, her heart pounded so heavily that she wondered if her pulse were visible. Jerkily she clasped her hands before her and ignored the faint tugs of panic along her veins. A quick glint of memory appeared before her eyes . . . the image of Rand as he had possessed her, his eyes hot with desire, his body tense with need of her, his skin and hair damp with the exertion of striving for the pleasure that she had brought him. I want him to hold me again, she thought, and her cheeks flamed. I want him to need me desperately, whisper my name, press me tightly against his body. And what of the pain the joining had brought her? Would it occur again? It did not matter anymore. She remembered how he had seemed to forget everything in the world except for her during those minutes of passion.

"Actually . . . I do have a small difficulty," she murmured, and turned partially away from him. "I . . . need help with my gown."

For a split second Rand remained rooted to the floor. Her words hung in the air, soft sounds that his tortured imagination had twisted into tones of enticement. Wanting her desperately and reminding himself that he had sworn not to take her again, he swallowed painfully before moving toward her. What had he done, he wondered miserably, to deserve this kind of torture? Tonight he did not have the patience to resist his own clamorings of need for her. Helplessly he drew near her, all of his renowned skill at unfastening women's apparel fleeing in a hazy instant. Rand took special care not to let his fingers brush against her back as he fumbled with the miniature buttons of her gown, muttering something about needing a lamp, his senses soaking up the details of her nearness, the feminine scent of her, the sleekness of her pinned-up hair. Then the job was done, and he caught a glimpse of her brief white chemise before she turned around quickly.

"Thank you," Rosalie said, her eyes huge as she turned her face upward.

"Good night," he said curtly, praying for her to leave before he could no longer keep a rein on his raging impulse to scoop her up, carry her to the bed, and drive into her greedily. To his confusion, she didn't move away from him, and Rand's every muscle protested against the tight control he exercised to keep still.

"Rose, you'd better leave," he said, his voice harsher than he had intended.

"Rand . . ." She withheld the other words she wanted to say, wondering wildly how to continue. She had no experience at seducing a man. How could she please him? What if she disappointed him? This is a terrible idea, she thought, and yet she stood there mutely as she met his eyes.

Rand took one, two, three even breaths as he tried to read her thoughts. "Do you understand what you're doing?" he finally asked hoarsely. "Rose, do you understand what I'm thinking, and what's going to happen if you don't go?"

She managed to nod jerkily.

Suddenly Rand reached for her with a smothered curse and enveloped her in his arms, his hands sliding inside the gaping back of her gown. His mouth sought hers and found it instantly, tasting, devouring. Rosalie closed her eyes, wrapping her arms around him loosely. As the kiss forced her head back, she opened her mouth under the pressure of his, allowing the steel bands of his arms to crush her against him. Her nostrils were filled with the fresh, intoxicating scent of him, a pleasant masculine distillation that had a peculiarly seductive effect on her. A strange warmth seeped lazily through her body, and Rosalie discovered that her knees had suddenly turned to rubber. Rand's fingers tangled in her hair, anchoring her in one position as his head moved slowly over hers, his tongue mating with hers and then exploring the deepest recesses of her mouth.

Heady desire pounded through her relentlessly, a delicious excitement that overwhelmed every inch of her body. She had dreamed of a lover who would be tender and gentle, but Rand was impatient, insistent, voracious, kissing her as if he were a starving man partaking of life-giving sustenance. She didn't mind his roughness, she welcomed it as the hard, unyielding masculinity of him provided relief for the hunger of her aroused flesh.

He lifted his mouth from hers, and Rosalie heard with shock the sound of her own voice as the cool air robbed the moistness from her lips. Don't stop, she seemed to be pleading, and he pulled her up against him as the scorching heat of his mouth slid along her fragile neck. She felt the bold hardness of him between her legs, the strident masculinity of his body both threatening and arousing, and she shuddered in rapidly awakening anticipation of what was yet to happen.

"Rose . . ." he rasped, his arms tightening around her as his hands wandered fervently over her slender form, "I've wanted you more every day. I've tried to forget what it was like to hold you . . . it's no use, you're *mine,* and I can't last one more night without you."

Recklessly she pressed closer, her mind clouded with misty excitement.

"You told me . . . it could be different from how it was before," Rosalie said breathlessly. "Prove it to me."

Rand stared down at her with eyes that had darkened to velvet green, focusing on the swollen curve of her lips.

"It will be different," he said thickly, and his thumbs caressed the exquisite line of her jaw. Burying his mouth in the curve of her neck and shoulder, Rand stilled himself for a moment as he fought for self-possession. He could so easily be overcome by the urgency of his own passion, but that was not what he wanted. He intended to make Rosalie as drunk with desire as he was, and that would take much more time. Painstakingly Rand pulled the pins from her hair, his heartbeat seeming to triple as the heavy mass of satin fell down her back. Heady thoughts surged through his mind: she was more beautiful to him than any woman he had ever seen, she was everything he wanted, she was here in his arms. He felt her stir against him with the beginnings of arousal, and as painful as it was, Rand forced himself to go slowly.

The sleeves of Rosalie's gown were halfway down her arms. Easing the garment down, Rand pulled her hands free and bade her to lock them around his neck. Her breath came fast and shallow through her lips, mingling with his as he caressed her breasts through the light, filmy chemise. Light-headed and filled with an unfamiliar languor, Rosalie made no protest as he eased the undergarment down to her waist. The night air struck her bare flesh with a gentle chill, and then the warmth of his hands was splayed over her skin. An odd quake shook her as she stood half-naked before him, realizing that he was still fully dressed. Rand took the weight of her breast in his hand and stroked the soft nipple with his thumb until it contracted from the vibrant sensation. She started in surprise as hunger tightened inside her abdomen, her first impulse to shrink away.

"Love, be still," he whispered, and slipped his other arm around her back as he wonderingly stroked her yielding flesh, arousing her with the sensitive brush of his fingers. "You're perfect . . ."

Rosalie clung to him with love and bewildered desire, her hands slipping up his neck to caress the cool silk of his hair. "Rand," she finally moaned, recoiling from the lightning that gnawed at her vitals. Blindly he lowered his mouth to hers, seeking the fullness of her response until she hardly noticed as her chemise and gown dropped to the floor. When she was naked Rand lifted her and carried her to the bed, her satin-skinned body fragile and supple in his arms.

"Before we go any further," he said, shrugging out of his coat in one lithe, efficient movement, "you should understand something. This won't be the last time. And after tonight I won't wait for any more shy advances." His voice was heavy with desire. It was difficult for him to say the words, for he doubted that he would ever want anything as much as he wanted in this moment to possess her—yet he intended that there would be no surprises on the morrow.

Rosalie lay before him and shivered slightly, her pale form startlingly lovely, the shine of her eyes visible even in the darkness of the room. Her hands closed and unclosed in a restlessness she had never experienced before, her body seeming to throb with fever, her very skin fervid and bereft without his soothing touch.

"Please come to me," she gasped fitfully, unaware of anything but a distress that only he could ease. "Please."

His passion raged, and Rand knew that he could not stop himself from taking her, any more than he could hold back the tide. Impatiently he stripped off the rest of his clothing and dragged the covers away from the place where Rosalie lay. She was still and quiescent as he moved to reclaim her, his arm sliding beneath her neck to elevate her head, and one hand coming to rest lightly on her flat stomach. Curiously attuned to her, Rand sensed the innocent shyness she felt at the intimate warmth of his hands, and his heart contracted in silent empathy. He forced himself to wait until her hands lifted to his back in a delicate, questing touch, her fingertips examining the hard, deep solidity of his muscles, the burnished smoothness of his shoulders, the masculine furring over his chest.

"Rand?" she questioned faintly, and he looked down at her in the darkness.

"What?" he murmured, his skin burning as she tentatively acquainted herself with the long, sloping firmness of his back.

"Did you feel . . . nervous your first time?"

He chuckled huskily at her question, his voice catching as he replied, "No. No, never until now."

Rand whispered something unintelligible, his mouth touching hers in the most tempting of kisses. Her arms curved eagerly around his neck to pull his head closer, but still he resisted the deeper joining of their lips, preferring instead to tease and torment until she thought he was trying to drive her mad. Her fingers sank into the thickness of his hair as his head moved lower, down her neck, along the frail ridge of her collarbone. Suddenly she arched upward as his mouth possessed the sensitive peak of her breast, a sweet cry escaping her throat. Straining toward him, Rosalie held his dark head to her breast with shaking hands, searching for a way to reciprocate and yet unable to do anything but cling to him and feel what he was doing to her. After several long, lazy moments he moved to her other breast and courted it with the same attention, his hand stroking the curve of her waist as if to calm the shocked trembles that racked her.

"Rand . . . oh, that feels so . . ." she said unsteadily, trying to find words to describe the incredible rapture. Slowly he moved back upward, seeking her mouth. Heat flowed and swirled over her body like a timeless river, and Rosalie subsided beneath him with drugged satisfaction, her lips moving under his, searching for even sweeter and more thorough pleasure. Her nerves ceased their alarmed jangling and ached instead with a steady, surging rhythm. Rand's voice floated to her ears in smoky whispers, in snatches of praise, of desire, of guidance. She obeyed him without question, moving instinctively in any way he desired, anxious to fulfill his every whim, just so long as he would not withhold this seductive rapture.

She had never known him before now, not this tender, urgent man who was a partner, a lover. He was a dream to her, a golden vision, an erotic apparition that would disappear with the first cruel light of morning. He answered her curious whispers with half-smiles and lingering kisses, creating a world that was made of nothing but blind sensation. As she clung to him tightly, his hand stroked over her stomach and down to the softness between her legs. His head lowered to hers to catch her trembling sighs in his mouth, his fingers gently searching, moving, finding out which caresses pleased her the most.

Leisurely he sought for and discovered the well-hidden entrance to her body, and Rosalie's eyes flew open in stunned wonder as his fingers slid inside her. She stared directly into the intentness of his green-gold gaze, her body helplessly clamping in response to the unfamiliar invasion. Then his artful and sensitive touch altered slightly. He flexed his fingers in a way that caused her entire body to gather in unbearable tension. "I'm going to faint," she gasped, and still he would not stop, the intimate plundering becoming more intense. Shaking, Rand lowered his mouth to the warm fragrance of her neck and tested the smoothness of her skin with the feathery brush of his tongue. Finally, light-headed with the agony of extreme arousal, Rosalie sobbed that she could stand no more. Rand's face was taut and damp with torment as he looked down at her. Spreading apart her paralyzed limbs, he settled between her legs and pressed slowly into her.

Rosalie cried out, and immediately he stopped, full and heavy inside her.

"Hurt?" he asked against her lips, and her arms locked around his solid torso.

"No," she breathed, lifting her hips against his as she experienced the wonder of knowing that he was a part of her. "No . . ."

Rand felt all coherence, all consciousness fade away as he eased deeper within her. He, as well as Rosalie, was a stranger to this kind of passion, for it was different from, it was more than anything he had ever experienced. They had become one body, one being that could not endure separation. Caught in the storm of passion, Rand forgot to take her slowly, and his gentleness disappeared as he thrust into her with rough desperation. A low, keening sound vibrated in Rosalie's throat, and she moved unconsciously to make his possession more complete, instinct taking the place of what experience would have taught her. Greedily she welcomed him back to her again and again, her hips rising in answer to his, her arms wrapping around the powerful, flexing surface of his back. She wanted to touch him everywhere, wanted to stroke and explore, yet the slight fear of doing something forbidden caused her hands to be still. She would not risk displeasing him, for if he stopped, it would be impossible for her to bear.

Suddenly Rosalie was suspended in a hot, nebulous cloud, unable to move at all as violent contractions of pleasure shook her body. She caught her breath and surrendered helplessly to the tide, the undertow, the bright and smooth eddies of a sensation she had never imagined. Clinging to Rand's hard, bare shoulders, she was only vaguely aware of the light tracing of his hands along the trim curves of her hips. Rand pushed deeper inside her, prolonging the sweet agony until the last shudders left her, and only then did he allow the powerful convulsions of fire to blot out everything else.

They drifted back to sanity with the greatest reluctance, their limbs still fitted together in startling harmony. Exhausted and replete, Rand lifted his heavy lashes and stared gravely at Rosalie. For once, he was left stunned and wordless by something that had once been commonplace to him. For a man of his experience, a woman's body was an easily accessible commodity, the act of love merely a form of entertainment, the heart unaffected by a simple physical joining. What trick, what magic did she possess to make it all so different? Was it because he had waited so long for her? Was it because of her innocence? Was it a coincidence of time and place?

Rand discarded the disturbing thoughts as soon as Rosalie shivered. He pulled the covers over them as the night air chilled the dampness of her skin.

Rosalie was amazed, shocked, profoundly worried by what had happened. He has more power over me, she thought, than I do over myself. Two tears slipped from the corners of her closed eyes, and Rand kissed them away, his mouth lingering over her satiny skin and delicate eyelids. Blindly she turned her face toward him, and he kissed her in an unhurried manner, as if he were wooing her still. Gradually he lifted his head and looked down into her midnight-blue gaze.

"Any regrets?" he asked quietly, and she shook her head.

"Only that the first time wasn't—"

"I know."

He strained a lock of her hair through his fingers, letting it curl and wind around his hand until she was bound to him by that one skein of sable.

"Someday," Rand said, his voice threaded with a hint of steel, "that will be such a distant memory that you won't believe it happened." She shook her head to deny what he said, and his jaw firmed. "I'll make sure of it," he asserted, and pressed a hard kiss on her mouth before she could speak. Rosalie slipped a cool hand behind his neck and parted her lips to allow him access, gentling his sudden aggression back into sated laziness.

Several minutes later, as she began to drift to sleep, Rosalie felt his hands travel over her body intimately, reawakening the tightness of desire in her abdomen and the trembling of excitement along her nerves. She murmured in drowsy protest, trying to sink back to sleep, but finally she gave up and opened her eyes.

"How much sleep," she asked breathlessly, her body beginning to crave him with the alarming desperation of before, "are you planning to allow me tonight?"

Rand's gaze was filled with a mixture of amusement and impatience as he wedged a knee between her legs. "Not much," he admitted, his voice sounding like a heavy purr, and lowered his body to hers as she gasped his name and writhed in the throes of potent desire.

When dawn began, Rosalie opened her eyes to stare at the window through the mists of groggy wakefulness. Beside her Rand slumbered deeply, sprawled on his stomach with his head half-buried in a pillow. Turning her head to look at him, she was oddly stricken by how young he appeared in sleep. His face was shaded a burnished gold and was unlined by worries or cares, his firmly held mouth softened with the gentleness of slumber. Lashes several shades darker than his amber-streaked hair curled slightly at the tips, a trace of vulnerability not usually detectable when he was awake. A lock of her hair was caught possessively between his fingers.

What am I now to you? she asked him silently, her lips curving in a smile that was both wry and wistful. Am I your woman, am I your new toy? Am I a habit that can be discarded as easily as it was assumed?

Randall Berkeley was most definitely not a boy, but a man full-grown, accustomed to taking care of himself. Rosalie knew, however, that he had never before assumed the responsibility of looking after anyone else, and therefore it was up to her to protect her own welfare. Could she entrust him with her heart? Miserably she admitted that the answer was no. After his initial hunger for her was sated, Rand would treat her carelessly. Aside from her form and face, both of which she considered to be pleasant but unspectacular, Rand had no need of anything she had to offer.

Slowly she detached her hair from his grasp and eased herself from the bed. All of her muscles were sore, as if she had run from one end of Paris to the other. Wincing, Rosalie bent to pick up her chemise and slipped it on before walking into the adjoining bedchamber. It was upholstered in soft green and brilliant gold. All of the silkwood and mahogany furniture was elaborate, especially the lacquered armoire where her clothes had been neatly hung. She caught a brief glimpse of her reflection as she passed by an upright gilt wall mirror of silvered glass, with colored and painted glass panels above the central plate. The design was of a garland of yellow and pink flowers, a note of cheeriness that did not complement her mood of this morning.

Wishing she had a cup of *café au lait*, Rosalie fumbled through her garments until she found a melon-colored robe of silk, and she pulled it on gratefully. What am I going to say when I face Rand? she asked herself numbly. She loved him. She had loved him even before he had led her through the brilliant terrain of passion. And with the strength of such love came anger, bliss, torment, fear, and the knowledge that she would slit her own wrists before telling him how she felt about him. He would only pity her, and the thought of that was revolting.

It was just then that she heard a sound at the doorway. Rand stood there with his hair ruffled over his forehead and faintly shadowed eyes, looking so sleepy and masculine that she wanted to rush to him and bury herself in his arms.

"Good morning," he said cautiously, and Rosalie wrapped the robe more tightly around herself.

"Good morning," she replied, and distractedly she

realized that her voice had sounded as chilling as a winter snowfall. Slowly his expression changed from wariness to blankness, and Rosalie saw that he was retreating behind a familiar wall. They might have been two strangers standing there regarding each other with polite curiosity.

Eight

During his relatively short lifetime Rand had had limitless experience with the fickle nature of women. Hélène, his capricious mother, had developed the art of taunting those who loved her by giving them only sporadic affection. Rand's only form of self-protection had been to adopt a facade of indifference, and now he was powerless to prevent the automatic defense from establishing itself as he met the coolness in Rosalie's cerulean eyes. He could not guess what had brought about the change in her manner, but as an inner voice urged him to hold Rosalie tenderly and coax her to confide in him, his overwhelming impulse was to stare at her with a blank sort of civility. The barricades were there again.

"Have you been up long?" he asked.

Rosalie blinked, startled by his casual attitude. "No. Just a few minutes," she replied, wondering uneasily what inward emotions moved him. It was chilling to suspect that perhaps his words of the night before had been merely a common form of love play. Did he whisper such things to the women he slept with as a matter of routine? Ask him how he feels, a voice from her heart intruded on her racing thoughts. Tell him how you feel.

I wouldn't dare, Rosalie told herself immediately, and she stared at him with a mute, poorly disguised appeal.

Rand's expression held an element of the same uneasiness. He could not risk saying anything that would earn her scorn, and he certainly would not throw out a declaration or proposal without being far more certain of the reception he would receive.

"Does the idea of breakfast appeal to you?" he inquired.

Rosalie nodded unhappily. "Yes. I'm . . . a little hungry."

Suddenly Rand's lips twitched with amusement, his tension breaking as they found a relatively normal footing to meet on. "That's understandable," he said. "You've earned the right to a decent meal."

"Don't joke about it," Rosalie said, scowling in quick response to his comment.

He frowned curiously, finding that for some odd reason he was reassured by her sharpness. Perhaps her willingness to share his bed the night before had surprised her as much as him. If so, she was probably uncomfortable with the knowledge that for the first time she had approached a man with desire. Uncomfortable, but not necessarily regretful.

"Conscience-stricken?" he inquired mockingly, and she wiped the betraying scowl from her expression.

"No," Rosalie replied, thinking that it probably would have reflected more highly on her character had she been attacked by pangs of conscience. But instead, she reluctantly realized, she was not at all sorry they had made love, just that she had chosen the worst man possible to fall in love with.

"Good." Rand looked at her for another long moment and then turned around to go back into his room. "I'll ring for the maid," he said over his shoulder.

"Fine," Rosalie replied, fighting a mad urge to cry, or shout, or do anything that would relieve the gathering heaviness inside her chest. The power he had over her filled her with dread, for although she had fought to keep her independence, her struggles had been for naught. She could refuse him nothing, for now she owned only half of herself. The other half was his.

Rosalie could only guess at what game Rand had decided to play. After breakfast in a small café he took her shopping, brushing aside all of her hastily conceived objections. Momentarily it seemed that he had discarded all considerations of business, contracts, steamboats, and trade in order to show her the sights and amusements of Paris. Apparently sensitive to the fact that she would balk at any signs of possessiveness from him, Rand kept the attitude of the day on an undemanding level. His manner was light, casual, and considerate, and helplessly she succumbed to the delight of being with him, unable to resist his smile, his gentleness. Occasionally she would catch a glimpse of their reflection in the shop windows, and it seemed each time that the image changed: bashful strangers . . . a lover and his mistress. He purchased countless gifts for her—soft ribbons of satin and velvet, a flask of scent, embroidered gloves, a corded-silk bonnet trimmed with feathers, and other sundry articles— until Rosalie began to laugh despite herself and begged him to stop.

When early evening approached he took her to the grand opera house of Paris, the Italian Theater. Rosalie was dazzled by the huge building of marble, gold, glass, and light. A huge chandelier hung from the center of the building, its heavy, glittering mass seeming to be suspended in midair. As they sat in a conservatively located box, Rosalie was absorbed in the rich, swelling strains of *Don Juan* and *William Tell*, and in the ballet *danseurs* who performed the story of Sleeping Beauty with such magical precision that she held her breath as they flew through the air. She exclaimed over their grace and ephemeral qualities even after the dance was over, until Rand wryly informed her that those selfsame ethereal creatures were at that very moment in the theater green room to greet the wealthier spectators who wished to spend the night with them.

Sometimes Rosalie bewildered him, for he had never met a woman of her tender years who was as outspoken, as spirited and pragmatic . . . and yet she had been sheltered to such a degree that she knew little of things that he had assumed were common knowledge. Her lack of worldliness charmed and at the same time bothered him greatly. Why had Amille Courtois chosen to raise her in such manner? What could she have been thinking of? Perhaps knowing that Rosalie was not born to be a servant, she had encouraged the girl to escape the dreariness of her life through dreams, novels, flights of fancy. As events had proved, it had been a disastrous decision, for there had been no one to protect Rosalie from the hazards of a greedy world that she knew too little about. Rand frowned as he watched Rosalie's absorption in the artful presentations onstage. She was too tempting, too vulnerable to men like him.

At the first intermission Rosalie turned to speak to him, her sapphire eyes extraordinarily beautiful as they gleamed with an odd light. He would never know what she had intended to say, for in that moment two women approached their box, one of them so beautiful that Rosalie could hardly keep from staring at her in amazement. She appeared to be about the same age as Rand, her confidence and self-possession seeming to be

quite remarkably well-developed. Her mouth was
etched and shaded in soft red, her cheeks glowing with
the same vibrant hue. Her hair was such a pale gold
that it shone like a moonbeam, her eyes a delicate
eggshell blue. Most remarkable of all was a magnificent
bosom which nearly swelled out of her gleaming white
gown, further emphasized by a necklace thickly en-
crusted with diamonds.

"Colette, what a find we have made," the woman
addressed her companion, and both of them stared at
Rosalie in a way that made her wonder what was wrong
with her appearance. Rand stiffened at the sound of the
woman's bell-like voice. Slowly he turned around with
grimness darkening his face, his expressive mouth
tightening as she addressed him. "Lord Berkeley, how
pleasant to see you again."

The way she emphasized the word "pleasant," Rosalie noticed with annoyance, implied that it was far more
of a pleasure to see Rand than was proper to admit in
public.

"Lady Ellesmere and Madame Duprin," Rand acknowledged them both reluctantly, standing to greet
them. Lady Ellesmere, Rosalie gathered, was the beautiful gilt-haired woman. Her friend was not as attractive
but matched her in sophistication.

"London has been languishing without you," Lady
Ellesmere said to Rand, her tone indescribably sweet
and her eyes intent as they met his. She stood very close
to him, her slim height making it easy for the pair to
stand face-to-face. As she regarded him with familiarity, her gaze touched caressingly on his beautiful hair,
his well-hewn features, his wide, firm mouth. Rosalie
remained silent and plucked unconsciously at the gold
banding on the sleeves of her apricot velvet gown, pain
constricting her heart as she watched them together.
She felt some of her naiveté crumbling rapidly as she

realized that there was a certain way in which two people who had once been intimate looked at each other. It was evident to anyone who cared to look beneath the surface of banal conversation and urbane facades that Rand and Lady Ellesmere had been lovers in the past.

It was no surprise that Rand was a man of experience. But to look upon the lovely face of someone he had known just as he had known Rosalie herself, brought a killing sense of dejection to her soul. The thought of him holding this woman, kissing her, entwining with her, was much more than unpleasant. It was degrading, as if the sophisticated blond had somehow managed to taint every sweet memory that Rosalie had shared with Rand. You fool, she sneered at herself. You've come to think of yourself as the only woman in his life. But just as this woman shows that you are not the first, she also proves that you won't be the last. If his desire for Lady Ellesmere had eventually abated, there was no shadow of a doubt in Rosalie's mind that he would tire of her as well.

Suddenly the next few words the woman spoke abolished Rosalie's misery, drenching her with shock.

"Ah," Lady Ellesmere drawled, focusing a light blue gaze on her, "so this is the famous Miss Belleau." Rosalie went still, her eyes widening. Rand shot Lady Ellesmere a killing glance, which the woman blithely ignored.

"Famous?" Rosalie repeated faintly.

"Why, yes! You're all over the *Times,* my dear woman! Why, everyone in the civilized world knows that you claim to be the daughter of Beau Brummell." Lady Ellesmere turned to Madame Duprin. "I must say, she doesn't look like an adventuress. Perhaps her claim is true."

Rosalie felt her face turn white and numb. She had

neither the coordination nor the energy to look at
Rand, focusing all of her efforts on subduing a surge of
panic.

"It is neither my intention nor my desire to claim
George Brummell as my father," she managed to
murmur quietly, pride enabling her to meet the woman's gaze directly.

"I can't quite see the resemblance," Lady Ellesmere
remarked thoughtfully, regarding Rosalie as if she
were inspecting the work of a second-rate artist. "But
perhaps you share more of an inward similarity. Do you
find that you are excessively fastidious, as the Beau is?
Or irreverent? Or—"

"Or fond of overspending?" Madame Duprin added,
and giggled at the weak sally.

"When did you first discover . . . . ?" The pair of
women seemed to have taken a smooth and savage
delight in plying her with pointed questions. Rosalie
switched her gaze to Rand's face, and what she saw
there made it an effort not to burst into tears. *He had
known.* He was not surprised at the information that
she was in the papers. Somewhere deep in his clear
hazel gaze was a plea for her not to abandon her trust
in him, but she was too hurt to heed the silent words.

"When will you be coming back to London, Lord
Berkeley?" Lady Ellesmere inquired, her eyes still
fastened on Rosalie's pale face.

"When Paris becomes tiring," Rand gritted.

"I do hope you'll bring your . . . Miss Belleau when
you return. She would enjoy so many of our haunts—"

Rand smiled grimly. "Clara," he interrupted her
prattle with unnatural softness, "I would take Miss
Belleau straight to hell before giving her into the care
of London society."

Lady Ellesmere seemed not in the least upset by the
profanity as she smiled with catlike contentment. "Are

you certain that hell is more amusing than London, my lord?"

"I only know which one possesses a more wholesome atmosphere. Good night . . . ladies." He stressed the last word lightly and proffered an arm for Rosalie to take. "I believe, Miss Belleau, that the performance is over." Her hand was shaking as it slipped through the crook of his elbow, yet Rosalie managed to give both of the obnoxious women a polite nod before leaving. Her voice was surprisingly steady as they made their way outside to the waiting barouche cabriolet.

"You had no right to keep it from me," she murmured in a low tone.

"Rose, I was going to tell you—"

"Don't bother to finish!" she whispered vehemently. "I know when you were going to tell me. At your own convenience. For your own advantage—"

"Rose—"

"I'm beginning to feel like the pawn in a game that everyone else is playing! No, don't look at me like that. I don't want to be coaxed into a good humor. I don't want to cry or argue, or talk about it at all—I just want to be left alone to think!"

"And stew about it until it's out of proportion."

"That's my right. Just as it was my right to be told about something that affected me so directly!" She groaned in escalating fury. "But to find out from one of your former . . . from a *lightskirt* who doesn't even—"

"My former what?" he asked ominously. "She's a lightskirt, I'll grant, but she's not a former anything of mine."

"I saw the way she—"

"Clara Ellesmere behaves that way with anyone fit to wear breeches."

"And just how familiar is she with the contents of yours?"

Rosalie surprised even herself with the crude question. There was silence in the cabriolet as Rand stared at her and arched a dark eyebrow. Her cheeks burned as he began to smile slowly.

"There's no need to be jealous, Rose."

"I'm not jealous!" she snapped, but still the insufferably conceited smile remained on his face.

"To be strictly truthful, over the past few years I've had no lack of invitations to Clara's bed. Unfortunately, of late I seem to have become rather discriminating."

Rosalie looked down at her tightly clasped hands, part of her anger transforming into embarrassment, frustration, and yes, undeniable jealousy. Rand continued in a gentle, no-nonsense voice as she kept her eyes averted from him. "*Petite,* we're going to have to get something straight. I'm not an inexperienced man, much as I would like to say you've been the only one. There's a likely chance, a probability, that you'll hear gossip . . . or perhaps you'll even make the acquaintance of someone I've been intimate with. Not one of them ever meant anything to me beyond an hour or two of pleasure, superficial pleasure at that. But you might as well tell me now if you plan to squabble about every one of them."

"I hardly plan to squabble about women I never intend to meet," Rosalie said frostily, slightly mollified by the way he referred to his former lovers as "them," as if they were an indistinct group that had nothing to do with her. But then she wondered how soon she would be relegated to the category of "them," and she asked herself for the thousandth time how she had been foolish enough to fall in love with him. "I don't want to talk anymore," she said stiffly. "Would you please allow me a few minutes of silence?"

"Only until we get back to the hotel," he said, a scowl

gathering on his handsome face as he contemplated the satisfaction he would get out of shaking her stubborn little body until her teeth rattled. "And only because it's a matter not meant for the ears of curious coachmen."

"Your discretion astounds me," Rosalie muttered, clamping her lips together and folding her arms as she settled down into the carriage seat. The vehicle rolled and bounced through the uneven streets of the city as she sifted through her tumbled emotions.

After collecting her thoughts somewhat, Rosalie decided in a flash of complete honesty that she could not blame Rand entirely for keeping the newspaper article a secret. With her silent and unconscious encouragement he had styled himself her protector, and as such he felt responsible for everything that affected her. In a way, she had almost given him the right to take such an action. But his protectiveness could not continue, that was obvious. He would not be there to shield her forever.

Grimacing slightly, she risked a quick glance at him. Every tautly drawn line of his posture betrayed his impatience. Rosalie had to suppress a small and unwanted smile from settling on her lips, knowing that he was annoyed with her for refusing to talk to him. But she needed time to puzzle out what she was going to say to him, what stance she was going to take, before he had a chance to twist everything around to suit his own purposes. It was far too easy for Rand to convince her of anything he wanted to. Sighing, Rosalie returned her gaze to the slender hands clasped in her lap. How much worse all of this would be if she had confessed her love for him: Rand was far too capable of using it to manipulate her.

The sunset was in full bloom as they walked into Rand's room. After he helped her off with her pelisse and began to remove his own coat, Rosalie strode over to the window and looked outside at the sky.

"You knew I would want to know that the news was out," she said, her gaze moving from one side of the street to the other.

"I had planned to tell you soon."

"It is not up to you to shield me from things like this. I'm not a child"—her voice lowered in self-disgust—"although I've acted like one."

"No—"

"Yes, I have," Rosalie asserted, flushing with shame and self-reproach. "I've given all responsibility for my own well-being into your hands, when you already had enough to worry about. I came to France with you in order to avoid having to make difficult decisions . . . and worse, to take advantage of your remorse. I shouldn't have come with you. I was perfectly capable of finding a job on my own. I didn't need your help or your protection—"

"I wouldn't have let you go off by yourself," Rand interrupted. "Blame yourself if you like, Rose, but it's a man's world."

"Nevertheless, I could have done it on my own instead of taking advantage of you," she insisted stubbornly. "But it was far easier to tell myself I hated you and let you take care of things."

"And do you hate me now?" Rand asked, watching her turn and pace across the room in a distracted manner. Suddenly Rosalie halted, surprised at the question. So her feelings weren't as transparent to him as she had feared. She met his eyes, finding in them a hard, watchful expression.

"Now?" she asked blankly. "No, of course not. There's a difference between being angry with someone and . . ." She paused by a small table and trailed her fingers across the smooth surface, refusing to look at him. "Of course not. How can you even ask that?" she mumbled.

Rand took a few steps closer to her.

"But what about when I . . . what about the first time? Have you forgotten what I did?" It seemed almost as if he were trying to reawaken her old animosity toward him.

Rosalie swallowed hard before answering. "I prefer . . . to think of last night as the first time."

In the small fragment of time it had taken to utter the words, Rosalie unknowingly slipped past his inner barriers to a place no one had ever reached before. Rand's heavy lashes lowered over soft hazel eyes as he struggled to subdue the sudden emotions that battered him. He could not remember a time when anyone had forgiven him for the wrongs he'd done, no matter how great or small the transgression. The general assumption had always been that he would not have cared a whit for anyone's forgiveness, and he had reinforced the attitude by being too proud to ask for it.

"Rand?" Rosalie asked, keeping her face averted from him.

"What?" he responded evenly, endeavoring to reassemble his faltering control.

"What did you mean in the cabriolet . . . about wanting to say that I had been the only one?"

There was a long silence, during which Rosalie waited for his answer and fidgeted with the tassel that pulled back the window draperies.

"You deserve someone with an irreproachable past," he finally replied curtly. "Someone . . . untainted."

Her fingers ceased their restless twining in the tassel cords, stilling as she was suffused with slow, tender warmth. She had once dreamed of a chivalrous knight, a man without flaws who could bring her steadfast and perfect love. And now all she wanted was Rand, with his tarnished past, his easy charm, his strength, his flashing moments of bitter despair and elemental passion. She would prefer him over anyone else—especially over some unfledged boy.

"A callow youth," she mused out loud, and then smiled. "Innocent, graceless with immaturity. Perhaps I should long for his ill-executed caresses, his awkward kisses, but surprisingly I don't." She turned around to face him. "And for that matter, I doubt the irreproachable lad would care to taint himself with the bastard daughter of—"

"Shut up." Rand's chest rose and fell unsteadily as he looked at her in the newborn twilight. The weak rays of the dying sun touched feebly on her glossy sable hair, the sweet curve of her lips, the vibrant beauty of a face that would haunt his dreams forever, no matter what fate befell his future. "Any man would want you," he said thickly. "Any man sane or raving, green as a pasture or wizened with age."

"Don't . . ." Rosalie breathed, her heartbeat doubling as she saw the look in his eyes. Then she smiled self-consciously and strove for a more normal tone. "Don't even try to pacify me. I'm still furious with you. And . . . you might as well know that I'm sleeping in my room tonight." She had to start thinking of some way to break the hold he had on her.

"Do you think you can run away from me?"

"No, I'm not running away." She gave a determined shake of her head to emphasize her words. "Not any longer. I'm going to find out if the rumors are true, Rand—I have to know who I am, and if he really is my father. I should have written to *Maman* . . . to Amille . . . the moment George Brummell started all of this."

"We'll be back in England soon. I'll take you to see her as soon as we arrive."

"I'm going to find a position as soon as we arrive," Rosalie corrected. "And then I'll go to see her alone."

His jaw was set with resolution as their gazes locked together.

"I hadn't planned to have this discussion now," Rand said, his voice taking on an uncompromising edge. "But I doubt we'll find an appropriate time in any case."

"A discussion about what?"

"Rose, why don't you sit down?" Rand suddenly looked self-mocking as he continued. "Having no experience with this sort of thing, I have little idea of how long it will take."

"I don't want to sit down."

Her eyes widened as he walked toward her, taking her cool hands into his large warm ones and drawing her close to his body. The crisp, masculine fragrance of sandalwood soap caressed her senses as she looked up at him with rapidly growing uncertainty.

"Rosalie." He stared down at her with translucent gold-and-green eyes. As if tempted beyond his ability to resist, he lifted a hand to stroke the soft smoothness of her cheek with long fingers. "I know you value your independence. I know you've had precious little of it. But there are other needs of yours, just as there are needs of mine that . . . that are more important than independence."

"What are you trying to say?" she asked carefully. He took a deep breath, his expression containing an odd, hungry quality.

"I can't let you live alone in London."

Instinctively she placed a restraining hand on his chest, her palm curving to the solid, muscled surface.

"I know you must feel an obligation to protect me," she said softly, "but I can deal with everything by myself. I have a fair idea of what to expect—"

"You have *no* idea of what to expect! My God, Rosalie, leaving aside all of the idiocy engendered by the rumors about Brummell, do you know what you would face? Do you realize the kind of men, the *quantity* of men who will come sniffing after you like dogs in July? Do you know—?"

"What exactly is the point of this?" Rosalie interrupted, her cheeks burning at his words.

"The point," Rand said slowly, "is that I want you to be my wife."

She couldn't believe he had said it. Her heart began to thud heavily, her mouth going dry with shock. She wanted to fall to his feet and weep with the agony of wanting him but not being able to accept him. Letting out a wavering breath, she cast her eyes downward as tears threatened to overflow onto her cheeks. She could not allow herself even to contemplate marriage to a man who might want her now but would surely scorn her later. For the moment, he found her entertaining, but what guarantee was there that he would not tire of her? At her silence Rand frowned, seeming to feel called upon to list more reasons why the union was a desirable one, not admitting even to himself why he truly wanted her.

"It's obvious that we're not incompatible. And I've decided that I've waited long enough to marry. It's time I took a wife and produced some heirs . . . you and I would have attractive children—"

"We agreed," she said, her voice shuddering with unspent emotion, "that you would help me find employment after you accomplished what you set out to do in France."

"That was a lifetime ago. That was two different people ago. And besides, I've just offered you a position."

"You said you would help me find something acceptable."

As it became obvious that she was not going to accept his proposal easily, Rand's tension wound like tight springs in his body. By God, if she had decided to

meet him with unreasonable stubbornness, she had no
idea of what lengths he would go to in order to make
her marry him!

"What is so unacceptable to you about becoming my
wife?" he demanded. "God knows enough women have
vied for the position—why is it my lot that the first one
I offer for finds it so distasteful?"

"I don't find it distasteful," she said, her eyes down-
cast. "If you continue to desire me even after we
return, then . . . then perhaps we can arrange to see
each other until you no longer want to . . . but I won't
be your wife, and I won't be kept by you."

"Oh, wonderful," Rand interrupted savagely, now
wanting to choke her. "You're offering to meet me on
the sly, possibly on your days off, or, God help me, on
Sundays. And what do you plan for me to do after
you're set up as some brat's governess or old woman's
companion? Leave a note at the back door of the
kitchen when I want to spend some time with you?
Exchange pleasantries with the footmen in the servants' hallway while I wait for you? Like you were some
servant—"

"I am a servant," Rosalie said with artificial calmness.

"You aren't. You were not meant for that."

"Stop it!" she said, and then pulled a hand free to
cover her eyes with trembling fingers, knowing that she
could never be happy again. Love had trapped her. She
could hardly bear the thought of living without him,
but it would be equally impossible for her to marry him
and then watch his interest dwindle. Any affection
Rand had for her would not come close to matching
the measure of her feelings for him, and such an
unbalanced situation would lead to his becoming bored
with her. The picture that thought presented, of being
lodged in a lonely country house while Rand amused
himself in the city, left her appalled. And being his
mistress was hardly preferable, for after he tired of her

she would have little choice but to find another man to
support her in a similar fashion. "Just let me go," she
whispered.

The four words were all that was necessary to cause
Rand's temper to explode. Somewhere inside flickered
the ugly thought that she was taunting him with his
own need of her. The more he had of her, the more he
wanted . . . and the more he wanted, the less she was
willing to give. She stood before him, within reach and
maddeningly unattainable, and he could not stand it
any longer.

"Look at me, damn you," he rasped, pulling her
hands down by her sides and jerking her up against his
body until they were nearly nose to nose. He glared
down into her reddening eyes as if he could see into her
soul. "I don't care why you don't want to be my wife. It
doesn't matter, because you know inside that you're
mine, and no matter how you try, you can't change it."
His large hands were tight around her wrists, and she
could feel the anger in him coursing like a violent river.

"Rand, stop!" For the first time since they had met,
Rosalie was almost frightened by him, for he seemed to
have let go of his control. Her heart began to patter in
an erratic tempo.

"I don't think you really give a damn about the
money," he continued hoarsely, "or even the security I
could give you . . . but I do know one thing you want
from me." His hands slid down to her buttocks and
urged her firmly against his hips, not allowing her to
wriggle free. She gasped as the hard, powerful outline
of his manhood pressed insistently between her legs. "I
heard you cry out my name last night," he said, his
breath filling her mouth with delicious heat. The
warmth, the potency of his aroused flesh struck her
with the force of lightning. "I remember every little
sound you made," Rand said huskily. "The first time,
when you discovered what it was like to be pleasured by

a man . . . the second time, when you learned how to move underneath me . . . the third . . ." Weakly she shook her head, and he bent to kiss her with deceptive leisure, forcing her lips apart to allow the erotic stroke of his tongue. "You'll marry me if I have to tempt, bully, and seduce you into it. You can't pretend you don't want me, not when your needs are so obvious. Say you're mine . . . *say it.*"

"You don't understand—" she began, and her words were muffled as he kissed her again, more thoroughly, more desperately. Her entire body started to glow with an unquenchable fire, but still she tried to strain away from him. She gasped for air as Rand lifted his head and stared down at her, his dark face unreadable except for the desire that burned so brightly in his topaz eyes.

"Tell me," he said huskily, and lowered his mouth to hers once more, craving the softness of her lips as if he were addicted to her. This kiss was gentle, sensitive, allowing her to respond to the artful coaxing. Rosalie's world was cloudy and blurred, everything fading away except his mouth, his hands, the large strong body that offered all the shelter, all the pleasure that she could ever want. Her body was charged with an unfamiliar energy, her response to him quick and surging, her nerves dancing as if her entire system had gone berserk. She was consumed with love and the insanity of her passion for him . . . oh, how she wanted him, how she longed for him. Avidly his hand trailed up her body to the swell of flesh at the top of her bodice, and with a quick, savage motion he pulled down the top of her gown. Rosalie's moan was muffled under his mouth as he pushed aside her chemise, as his hand curved around a warm, naked breast and effortlessly wrought a response from her traitorous body. His fingers played delicately with the tender peaks of her breasts, teasing, searching, encouraging her flesh to waken to his touch

until she felt it down to her toes. Her response to him
was as undeflectable as a bolt of lightning, for in his
arms she was a stranger to herself. Suddenly she was no
longer fighting to pull away from him, but to free her
hands from the offending sleeves of her gown.

Rand felt the crackling heat of her immediate arousal and he broke the kiss reluctantly, his breath coming
hard and fast as he pulled one of her hands and then
the other from the soft velvet material. His fingertips
traced upward to her bare shoulders as he felt her press
against him, yet he held his mouth out of reach from
hers. His face looked in the gathering darkness like it
had been molded out of copper.

"Rand," she whispered, trembling with the knowledge that she could not withstand him. "I'm yours . . ."
She flushed and then ignored all the promptings of
reason as she held on to him, suddenly weak with need.
"I want you. I *am* yours."

Although her words caused his desire to reach
feverish proportions, Rand seemed to relax slightly.

"You'll be my wife?" he demanded unsteadily, and
her eyes met his directly. Rosalie could not answer. She
would not be coerced into agreeing, no matter what
kind of temptation he offered. "Rose?" he prompted in
a hard voice.

"I do want to make love with you," she said, letting
his question remain unanswered as she sought to draw
his attention to other matters. As her blue-prismed
gaze fused with his, Rosalie tentatively began to explore the splendidly masculine body, her fingers sliding
over the steely surface of his chest, the hard, tapering
line of his waist. He was magnificent, the kind of man
that all women secretly dreamed of being possessed by.
"You make me feel things I've never even imagined,"
Rosalie said, the sound of her voice silky as it rippled
against his ears. "I want to give you the same pleasure.
Tell me . . . is what we share special? Is it common to

feel like this? And if it isn't, how long will it hold you to me?"

Rand's belly tightened as he stood there quietly, a self-restrained captive under her hands. *No, it isn't common—it's something out of my wildest dreams,* he thought. But the words dissolved somewhere in the pit of his stomach. The painful mixture of emotions— hurt, desperation, aggression—began to crumble as she touched him. The thought of a small woman holding such power over him caused him to flinch in denial, but as always, his need of her overcame everything else.

Slowly her hand drifted over his aroused manhood, delicately examining, her fingers tingling as she succumbed to the heady experience of touching him so intimately. Her fingertips stroked lightly over the bold, burgeoning shape of him, and then rested there for a moment as she tested the masculine firmness and scorching heat that burned through the barrier of his trousers. In wonder Rosalie looked up at him, seeing his eyes darken to velvet green, his jaw clench as if she inflicted a pain too great to bear. Then Rand could no longer endure the touch of the shy temptress. Gripping her wrist with a smothered sound, he held it away from his body, his eyes closing briefly. "God, tonight won't be enough," he said, and his voice was threaded with desire and despair. "It will never be enough."

Scooping her up easily in his arms, he carried Rosalie to the bed as she fumbled helplessly with the clothes that bound him . . . the cravat, the buttons, the coat. After settling her on the mattress, Rand pulled the crumpled gown and chemise over her hips and tossed them to the floor. Every nerve in Rosalie's body rioted with excitement as he removed her thin slippers and rolled down the fragile net of her stockings, his warm fingers lingering on the tender flesh behind her knees, along the inner curves of her thighs. She breathed his

name with a shivering sigh as his cravat loosened
beneath the eager questing of her hands, and then one
by one she clumsily undid the buttons of his snowy
white shirt. Rand remained still, allowing her to perform the small tasks, though it would have been much
faster if he undressed himself. Nothing mattered but
this moment . . . the privacy, the intimacy of discovering each other, the suspense and the fear of last-minute
denial.

Slowly Rosalie spread the edges of his shirt apart, her
fingertips drifting across the wide expanse of his chest
and leaving trails of exquisite sensation wherever they
touched. Intrigued by the silky, crisp fleece that was
revealed as the shirt gaped open, she leaned closer and
splayed her hands across the hard, sculptured contours
of his chest, her palms absorbing the heavy thud of his
heartbeat. Rand caught his breath and then pulled his
shirt off with increasing haste, the deeply toned proportions of his shoulders flexing as he moved. Her eyes
flickered over his large half-naked form as he bent to
unstrap the legs of his trousers and pull off his boots.
He was so beautiful, so tawny and male and perfectly
made, that Rosalie suddenly experienced a flash of
uncertainty. Instantly aware of her small movement to
draw her knees up protectively and shield her unclothed body, Rand paused in the act of unfastening his
trousers and leaned over her with a low murmur.

"Last night seems like a century ago."

"Yes." She stared up into the golden glimmer of his
eyes as he pressed her back against the pillows. Rand
braced his forearms on either side of her head, the
solid network of muscle and sinew effectively caging
her. How could they have known each other for such a
short time? she wondered giddily. How could he have
taken over her life so easily, plundered her emotions so
effortlessly?

"You think I've waited for you only a few weeks,"

Rand said, as if he had read her mind. His lips brushed against hers with the lightest of touches, savoring the taste of her, "but you're wrong. I've waited years for you." A small gasp left her lips as she felt the electric shock of his chest and steely midriff pressing into the bare tenderness of her breasts. He could easily have crushed her, yet he took care to make certain that he gave her nothing more than a satisfying weight to bear. "Before this night is over you're going to know exactly how much I want you," Rand murmured, fully aware of how the light furring of his chest caused the soft peaks of her breasts to contract in tingling arousal. "And you're going to wear the mark of my ownership, just as I wear yours . . ." Rosalie closed her eyes, floating in a mist of voluptuous sensation as his soft, erotic purr continued to caress her ears. ". . . so that whenever our eyes meet, even in the most staid and proper of circumstances, you'll remember the things we've done, the things I can make you feel, and you'll despair of the few hours we'll have to wait before we're in bed again." Before she could utter even a word, he sought her lips passionately, urging her mouth to open to his so that any thought of protest or apprehension flew dizzily from her head. The stunning wonder of the kiss flowed over her in a sleek, roaring current, and she lifted her arms around his neck, craving the damp heat of his mouth, seeking his nearness as if he were her only salvation.

She would forever remember that night of lovemaking as one of the most tormenting experiences of pleasure she would ever endure. It gradually became clear that he intended not to satisfy her desires quickly but to arouse them to an excruciating pitch, to leave her suspended in a state of eager frustration and then to drive her even higher. As she whispered his name pleadingly, she felt the faint brush of his teeth against the tautness of her breast, and though the light nip seemed to be accidental, her entire body jerked in reaction. Farther down on her midriff she felt his teeth catch oh-so-gently at her skin again, and this time his hands were there to restrain her startled quiver.

"What are you trying to do to me?" she moaned, and was met only with his silence as he let his mouth drift across the softness of her stomach. His tongue dipped into the shallow depression of her navel, causing her to draw her knees up slightly in a response of self-protection. Suddenly his hands were parting her thighs, his warm, silken mouth beginning to travel below her navel, and as Rosalie realized what he intended to do, she began to struggle in alarm, a queer shock running through her.

"Rand, don't! You can't possibly mean to . . . oh, *Rand* . . ."

Immediately he perceived the cause of her distress. Lifting his head from her abdomen, Rand gathered her into his arms to subdue her agitation, his mouth suddenly curving with a mixture of dismay and tender amusement.

"Rosalie," he said, his mouth searching gently through the curls that lay damply on her forehead, "you're so lovely . . . I didn't mean to frighten you. *Petite fleur,* I only want to give you pleasure. Let me—"

"No," she said in a sobbing breath.

"Sweet, there's nothing wrong about—"

"Rand, I wouldn't be able to face you afterward . . . knowing that you had . . ." Her face flamed with embarrassment, and Rand chuckled softly.

"What an innocent you are, Rose." His hand traveled down the smooth line of her thigh to her buttocks, and he hesitated before relenting unwillingly. "For now you win . . . but someday there won't be an inch of your body that I haven't tasted." His voice was smothered as he kissed her throat, his hands wandering

possessively over her skin. As Rosalie became aware of
their naked flesh pressing together, it seemed that she
was bathed in fire. She lifted her lips to his, blindly
seeking until she felt the velvet press of his kiss once
more. Their mouths moved together differently than
before, in a faint but unmistakable rhythm. "Little
witch," Rand muttered, his voice muffled against her
lips, "let's see how curious you are now." He took her
hand and pulled it down to his hips, placing her fingers
against his toughly muscled abdomen in an invitation to
explore.

Quivering, Rosalie took up the challenge and let her
fingers slip from his smooth, flat stomach to his manhood. She felt awkward, clumsy, and shy, but overwhelming curiosity prompted her to explore him as
intimately as he had touched her. He was full and hot,
and surprisingly silky, and gradually her hesitancy
disappeared as she stroked the demanding hardness
and heard his breathing rasp in his chest.

"Rand?" she whispered, in wonder that her touch
could affect him so, and he shook his head slightly.

"I want you too much. No more," he groaned, and
then her knees separated to accommodate his large
body as he settled between her legs. A dizzying, pro-
found gratification surged through her as he entered
her slowly, the compacted muscles of his arms flexing.
Rosalie felt a slight strain as her body stretched to
welcome him, and then she shuddered with the overwhelming sense of completeness that they had shared
once before. He thrust into her with a low growl of
need, his movements urgent, the rhythm of wings
beating on warm air, sweeping her aloft until the
culmination of their passion became a resplendent
moment of perfection, too pure, too stark to bear for
longer than a moment. Then, as she fell, his arms were
there to hold her, his body there to shelter her from all

that dared to encroach upon the fantasies that saturated the ebony night.

Rand was gone when she woke the next morning, and Rosalie found the tersely worded note that he had left on the table as she went to ring for the chambermaid to bring a small breakfast. His absence drew out until early afternoon as he attended to various business matters, leaving her to read and amuse herself in the hotel room. After a few hours Rosalie began to regard her luxurious surroundings with distaste, feeling like a bird imprisoned in an attractive but small cage.

My life is fast becoming structured around him, she told herself grimly, and then she wondered what she was going to do when he was no longer there for her to dote on.

Rand returned much later with a weary scowl gracing his features, and Rosalie managed to surmount her preoccupation with the personal issues that faced them in order to ask how his meetings had fared.

"I've spent the entire day negotiating with idiots," he informed her, dropping into a chair with a sigh of relief. "Quotas, embargoes, restrictions . . . Don't ask me about the future of Anglo-French trade, because if it depends on men of the ilk I've just associated with, the outlook is gloomy."

"But don't the French want to build back the economy by trading with the English?"

"They're in a vulnerable position due to Napoleon's previous policies. They don't want to become indebted to England, and they resent us for all that happened during the war—to the point of refusing any sort of compromise."

"Do you really blame them?" Rosalie asked, and he smiled lazily.

"No. Their attitude is entirely understandable—just not convenient for me. What's that on the table?"

"Cold meat, sandwiches, cake, fruit, and wine. Out of a lack of anything else to do, I ordered lunch."

"I regret having to leave you here, but the parts of Paris I had to visit today weren't places for a woman to frequent."

"I understand," she said, and as they looked at each other, a long and intimate silence filled the room. Rosalie blushed deeply as she met his gaze, knowing that he was thinking of the night before, and she had a fairly good idea of which moments in particular were foremost in his mind.

"Bread, wine, and Rose," Rand commented, the shadowed look in his eyes replaced by the twinkle of a smile. "Dare I hope for this kind of welcome even after the marriage?"

Rosalie did not return the smile. She caught at her bottom lip with even white teeth, hesitating several seconds before plunging into the matter that had to be discussed.

"Rand," she said, finding it an effort to drag the words up from her heart and through her lips, "I didn't agree to anything last night."

"Except that you're mine," he reminded her steadily, his gaze unflinching.

"I said that in a very . . . emotional moment. But even so, what I said did not constitute an acceptance of your idea."

"It was not an idea," Rand said, the warmth leaving his eyes rapidly, to be replaced by wariness. "It was a proposal. You didn't accept it outright, true. But you implied acceptance, and I'm willing to take that as a binding promise."

"Why?" she asked desperately. "If it's just a matter of convenience, I guarantee you can find someone in a quarter of an hour who would be willing to marry you, probably someone of higher birth and more suitable temperament. If it's because of any sense of duty on your part to save me from having a poor reputation, I need not point out that it's a hopeless cause."

"God in heaven, why are you so eager to run from me?" Rand demanded, his voice tautly laced with impatience. "You have no employment, no money, no references, no family, no fiancé, no friends who are in any position to help you. I spent the majority of last night demonstrating some of the more attractive benefits of a marriage between us, and still you shrink from it . . . from *me* . . . as if I had made you the basest offer. Are you still bent on wringing remorse from me for having forced your virginity? Are you——?"

"No! That has no part in anything between us now," Rosalie said, her eyes bright and so dark a blue that they shone with almost violet light. Finally she found the impetus to speak freely, and her words tumbled over themselves. "I don't deny our physical compatibility—but even in my admitted inexperience I know that marriages crumble on so small and flimsy a foundation. Do you really think a marriage between you and me would bring any lasting happiness? Are you prepared to keep a vow of fidelity to me? I don't think so. So far, your commitment to me has lasted for a few weeks, but I have no proof that you will not find someone you prefer over me tomorrow. I can't predict what kind of father you would be, but I do know the kind of examples that were set for you when you were younger, and I doubt that you——"

"You bitch," Rand whispered, his eyes going cold, and Rosalie's voice faltered a little before she spoke again. The words had to be said, for this was the only way she could think of to put him off.

"You're starting to assume responsibility for your actions, for the interests of your family, the shipping company, the Berkeley properties. You've made a good beginning, but how far will it extend? What will happen on the morning when you wake up next to your wife

and decide that all of your responsibilities weigh too
heavily on your shoulders and that you would prefer to
game and roam through London and make love to a
pretty stage actress?"

"So you think you know what kind of man I am,"
Rand said, and Rosalie was suddenly chilled to the bone
at his icy expression. He looked like a stranger. "As well
as believing in my eventual infidelity, you've also implied that I'm a likely candidate for abusing my children, and predicted that I'll let my inheritance and
family go to the devil."

"Don't put it like that."

"In this case the burden of proof would seem to rest
on the passage of time, but unfortunately, time is the
missing element, isn't it? I want you now or not at all.
My loss, I suppose, that you don't consider me a risk
worth taking."

"I can't. It's a matter of survival," she said quietly,
beseechingly, and he stood up as if he couldn't stand to
be in the same room with her.

"Then so be it. You won't have to tolerate my
proposals or my touch any longer. I'll stick to our
original agreement. I'll recommend you for a respectable position, and then you can rejoice in never having
to see me again. In the meantime, I'm going to be out
for a while." He strode to the doorway and paused to
rake his eyes up and down her slender, straight form.
"Something tells me you'll adapt very well to the art of
surviving alone in London," he said silkily, each word
driving into her like a sharp arrow. "If you find that
wiping children's noses or reading to old crones is not
to your taste, you have one particular talent that is
guaranteed to earn you a fortune."

As the door closed, Rosalie clenched her fists and
held them up to her mouth. She was frozen in place for
several minutes, her mind racing and her heart throbbing with regret. Her ploy had worked only too well.

She had hurt Rand terribly, but she could not allow
herself to be sorry for what she had said.

Needing something to settle her nerves, Rosalie went
to the small table which bore the weight of an untouched lunch and an octagonal wine cooler. Uncork-
ing the bottle of wine with an easy twist of her wrist, she
poured a hefty amount of it into a crystal glass. Raising
the sparkling crystal in a mocking gesture, she made a
toast. "To the future," she said sardonically, and swallowed the wine with her unshed tears. The unsettled
jangling of her nerves began to calm down after several
more swallows, the shaking of her hands easing even if
the aching of her heart did not. Giving in to the
weakness of her knees, Rosalie sat down in an embroidered chair and poured more wine into her glass. If
only the sweet distillation could bring permanent for-
getfulness, she mused, grateful for the temporary
peace it provided.

How much better off she had been with her wistful
dreams of youth. Now she would have to live with
bittersweet memories that would cause her to die a
little each time she relived them. Was it preferable to be
ignorant of what she could never have, or to have had a
few bright, painfully clear moments of it? Sighing,
Rosalie tilted her head and drained the last measure of
liquid in her glass before filling it one final time.
Wearily she loosened the tiny ruff at the neck of her
gown and then relaxed in the chair with the sorrowful
resignation of a condemned woman. Reflectively she
stared around the room as the glowing afternoon
sunlight painted the walls. She loved France . . . she
had known the greatest happiness of her life in this
country, a place where all that was turbulent, peaceful,
sophisticated, and simple, somehow fit together in an
understandable scheme. And she could never forget
the weeks of paradise at the Lothaire or drive them out
of her thoughts. Numbly Rosalie set down the half-

empty glass as she contemplated her return to England. How was she going to endure hearing the gossip about Rand, wondering how he was, wanting to be close to him, remembering his passion, his smiles, his pain?

She shuddered and moved to the window, her feet dragging across the carpet. The day was cooling rapidly, and a thin, icy draft of air curled around her body in a serpentine pattern. Vaguely surprised at the swift arrival of lassitude, she closed the window and then shut her eyes for a moment, all of her energy expended after the simple action. Then she raised a hand to her midriff as she became aware that her stomach was churning.

"Rosalie . . . you idiot," she scolded herself, thinking miserably that almost three glasses of red wine had been two too many. Staggering over to the chamber pot, she opened the cabinet that housed it and waited only a few seconds before nausea took hold of her and her body purged itself of the vile fluid. She had never felt so cold, so tired, so incredibly ill. The water from the porcelain pitcher on the silkwood stand tasted sweet and blessedly clean as she rinsed her mouth out, but it did nothing to alleviate the sensation that her blood had been frozen in her veins. It was becoming immediately clear that this was no simple case of overindulgence. Something was terribly wrong. She had to get help. Staggering over to the maid's bell, Rosalie pulled on it three times before she was forced to stop and clasp her head. It was sheer luck that a young chambermaid was passing by at that moment, for almost immediately a light rap sounded at the door.

"Come in," Rosalie said weakly, leaning against a damask-covered wall. "I mean, *entrez* . . ." She squinted at the maid, who kept lurching in and out of focus. "Listen here," she said desperately, "something is wrong with me. I've had some bad wine, or . . ." Oh, God, hadn't she read countless stories in the newspapers about thieves drugging hotel guests before robbing them clean? "The wine . . ." she murmured again, and then realized that the tiny maid did not understand English. *"Aidez-moi,"* she managed to say, and the young dark-haired girl began to chatter excessively as she gestured toward the bed and took Rosalie's arm. "Don't leave me," Rosalie managed to gasp, afraid that if she had been drugged, someone was waiting for her to fall unconscious. She did not know which language she had spoken in, but she tried to say it again and failed.

Rapidly an opaque cloud was rolling over her; with each second it obscured a larger portion of her vision, until she was blinded. She thought of Rand and tried to form his name, and failing that, she submitted to the suffocating cloud. As the maid urged her gently away from the wall, Rosalie felt the floor dissolve beneath her feet, and with a moan she fell helplessly into a bottomless hole. In the blackness she continued to sink, the ice that collected on her arms and legs serving as added weight to make the pace of her endless descent faster. Only one thought occupied her mind before the darkness swallowed her whole, and it was that she had plummeted too deeply ever to reach the surface again.

Nine

I will not let thee go
I hold thee by too many bands;
Thou say'st farewell, and lo!
I have thee by the hands
And will not let thee go.
                    —Robert Bridges

The chambermaid tugged in frustration at the crumpled body on the floor, finding that it was nearly impossible to move the limp weight. Although Rosalie was not by any means a large woman, the little maid was of extremely small, fine proportions. Her large dark eyes, the color of dark pekoe tea, flickered from Rosalie to the bed, and then she ran to ring the bell violently.

Suddenly the room seemed to burst into commotion, for not only did three other maids and a small group of curious hotel guests gather inside the doorway, but the *maître d'hôtel* himself stormed in, asking jumbled questions and then berating her for not knowing the answers. His fine black mustache quivered in distress at the sight of the unconscious woman. After he sent for a physician he occupied himself with shooing everyone out of the room while assuring them that the young woman had merely fainted. However, no one appeared particularly convinced that it was a mere faint. Rosalie's skin was the blank white of bleached parchment, her slender form utterly limp.

Hesitantly the chambermaid picked up her dustcloth and began to leave, casting an anxious eye at *mademoiselle* but knowing that she would lose her job if she did not resume her duties.

"*Non!*" the *maître d'hôtel* said sharply, grabbing her by the collar of her shabby but pristine dress and dragging her back into the room. He spoke to her in rapid and excited French, the syllables melting into each other like sizzling pats of butter in an omelet pan. "You will remain here to explain what happened and how you found her! It will be on your head alone—I had nothing to do with this!"

Silently the maid nodded, not daring to protest, and after he released her she went to stand by the bed in quiet and frozen terror. The room became as still as a tomb, for the *maître d'hôtel* had retreated to the doorway and stared pensively down the hallway in expectation of the physician's arrival. The maid looked down at the prone figure on the bed, lacing her fingers together tightly as she remembered her struggle to help the panic-stricken woman to the bed. Then, darting a cautious glance to the *maître d'hôtel* and finding his attention focused elsewhere, she dared to reach down and pull away the few strands of hair that were caught between Rosalie's pale lips.

As the minutes ticked by, the chambermaid began to develop a vaguely protective attitude toward the unconscious woman, for *mademoiselle* was so extraordinarily lovely that she presented an intriguing mystery. "*Comment vous appellez-vous?*" she questioned softly, the lively curiosity of a child taking precedence over her wariness. "My name is Mireille. Mireille Germain. Whom will we have to tell? Your brother? Your parents? Your *mari* . . ." No, on closer inspection it was evident that the woman wore no ring. "You are an *anglaise* . . ." Mireille's dark brown eyes flickered around the room in search of clues that would explain what had happened. She tried to remember some of the foreign-sounding words the woman had flung at her. "*Monsieur?*" she questioned, raising her voice so that the *maître d'hôtel* would hear. "*Qu'est-ce que c'est* 'wine'?"

"*Vin,*" he said sharply, sparing her only an exasperated glance, and she looked at the half-empty bottle on the table in dawning realization that this was what the woman had referred to. *Mademoiselle* had been drugged, or perhaps even poisoned.

"*Monsieur!*" she said insistently, the expression on her small face becoming even more anxious than before. "I think—"

"*Tais-toi,*" he interrupted, sighing with relief. "Shut up. The physician is here."

A stout, elderly gentleman carrying a leather bag entered the room, his thick glasses shining opaquely as he introduced himself and approached the bed. He made a clicking sound with his tongue, picking up Rosalie's slim wrist and checking her pulse. It was weak and hardly stable enough to reassure him that she would live much longer. After a brief examination of her condition, he nodded in an assured manner that dared anyone to contradict his conclusion.

"Some sort of opiate," he said. "An overdose. Is there a laudanum bottle around—?"

"What in hell is going on?" A new voice filled the room, charged with angered demand, and the three of them stared at the doorway.

Rand could not believe his eyes as he took in the scene. He spared the three strangers only a glance before his eyes fastened on Rosalie. Her head was turned to the side, her face obscured by the loops and curls of hair that had escaped its confinement. He would never forget the sight of her white, lifeless hands, the fingers curled like half-open blossoms.

Mireille quivered with fear as Rand paused only a split second and then reached the bed in three long strides. She shrank against the brocade-covered wall as he brushed by her and the physician, bending over the prostrate form of the woman. Mireille had seldom seen a man of aristocratic bearing as large and dark-visaged as this one. To one as small as she, he seemed vaguely barbaric. He muttered something under his breath and then turned his head to look at them one by one, his light-colored hazel eyes contrasting startlingly with the burnished hue of his skin. He asked something in English, his words foreign but his low, threatening tone unmistakable.

"*Le vin* . . ." Mireille quavered immediately in French, unable to keep the supposition to herself any longer. "I found her, *monsieur*—she rang the bell . . . she was holding her head in her hands *comme ça* . . . and then she fell to the floor. The drink made her sick."

"You're suggesting the wine was laced with the drug?" the physician asked, recovering himself sufficiently to look at her and then the *maître d'hôtel* with accusation. "There has been a rash of such crimes lately in Paris . . . a ring of thieves . . . but usually their victims are not drugged to this excess. Still, none of the various tinctures of opium are distilled with precision, and if administered with a heavy hand . . ."

"Opium," Rand repeated, switching from English to French. His eyes darkened with a peculiar pain, much deeper, more insidious than anything he had ever felt before. Suddenly he gathered the woman's limp body in his arms, looking as though he would murder the nearest person within reach. He cursed with a hissing sound as he felt the soft, helpless weight of her in his arms.

The other occupants of the room backed away a step or two, watching him as he sat down on the bed and made an effort to waken her. As it became obvious that his attempt to rouse her was useless, he glared at the stout man. "Who in God's name are you?" he demanded, and the physician drew his heavyset form up a little straighter.

"Je m'appelle M. André Goujon . . . et vous?"

"Lord Randall Berkeley," he supplied curtly. Mireille's fear of him did not lessen as she regarded his overpowering form, but suddenly she felt a twinge of pity when the woman's head fell against his arms as if there were no bones in her neck. For a moment something had flickered in his eyes that echoed of harsh anguish.

"How long will it take to wear off?" Rand asked abruptly, his arms tightening around Rosalie's body.

"Monsieur de Berkeley . . ." Goujon said with a great deal of hesitancy, "it is a classic case of opium poisoning . . . pinpoint pupils, shallow breathing, slow, weak pulse . . . but it is difficult to predict the extent of the overdose. I've seen similar cases in which the victims continue to sleep into death, unable to take in water or nourishment. Or her heart may suddenly stop beating—"

Rand interrupted him brusquely, speaking to the *maître d'hôtel.* "Get another physician. Immediately."

"Monsieur!" Goujon bristled. "I assure you any qualified man will tell you the same—"

"Get someone else," Rand repeated darkly, and the *maître d'hôtel* scurried off in fright. Goujon stormed out of the room, muttering under his breath, and Rand gently laid Rosalie back down on the bed, his hands framing her face as his thumbs skimmed the round softness of her cheekbones. "Rose," he breathed, unable to believe how white and cold her skin was, and the seething anger in him drained rapidly as an unfamiliar fear took its place. She seemed like nothing more than a fragile shell, deeply entombed within her own subconscious. It seemed that she had fallen even beyond the realm of dreams. "Rose, don't do this to me," he said desperately, as if she were merely playing a trick on him, but her face was utterly still.

"Rose?" He heard a tiny voice repeat behind him, and Rand turned with a start to find the little chambermaid still huddling against the wall. He had forgotten that she was still there. She said the name as if marveling at its sound.

"You can go now," Rand said, and at her uncomprehending expression he repeated the words in French. Immediately her face fell, and she shook her head slightly before regarding him with the darkest, most beseeching brown eyes he had ever seen. Swearing softly, Rand returned his attention to Rosalie, and as it became apparent that he did not intend to shoo Mireille out, the chambermaid leaned her thin back against the wall. She remained unmoving for more than an hour, watching solemnly as another physician was brought in, a tall, thin one this time. His prescription was to bleed the unconscious woman in order to drain out the poison and allow her depleted bloodstream to renew itself. Envisioning the large wooden bowls, the lancet that would open the veins, the gruesome trickle of precious fluid from *mademoiselle*'s slender neck, Mireille gathered up the courage to protest, but there was no need. Rand received the suggestion with cold disgust, his language both colorful and effective as he ordered the man to leave at once.

"The perfect example," Rand commented to no one in particular as the physician departed hastily, "of why most people fear the members of the medical profession more than illness itself. God knows how the human race has survived them so far." Unfortunately, most physicians relied less on scientific methods than on superstition and tradition when treating a patient.

"Monsieur de Berkeley," the *maître d'hôtel* asked, clearly bothered by the black sarcasm and the expression on Rand's set face, "what are you planning to do now?"

"I want to question the person who received the order for the food and wine, those who prepared the meal, and whoever brought it up here. As far as retributive action against the hotel . . . perhaps I'll consider it again tomorrow with less gratification . . ." He paused, his eyes flickering to the figure of the small chambermaid, who had forgone her silent vigil in order to straighten up the room. ". . . if you'll free the girl from her other duties in order to watch over *mademoiselle* until she wakes up."

"Until she . . . Certainly," the *maître d'hôtel* said, looking doubtfully at Rosalie and then issuing a small rush of orders to Mireille. As she nodded vigorously, even more dark curls fell to join the profusion of ebony hair that had already escaped her white mobcap.

"Bring the employees I mentioned into the next room," Rand said, turning from the sight of the bed, his face turning into an inscrutable mask. He spoke in French so that Mireille would understand as well as the hotel manager. "I don't want anyone in here except for the maid, and I want to be told immediately if someone attempts to set a foot beyond the doorway."

"Yes, *monsieur,*" the *maître d'hôtel* murmured dutifully. "I will find the people you wish to speak to in a matter of minutes."

Rand watched the wiry little man depart with alacrity. Releasing a long taut breath, he raked a hand through his hair, unconsciously disheveling it into thick amber waves. A potent sense of unreality nagged at him, as if this were some nightmare.

He discounted the theory that it had been the handiwork of clumsy burglars, even though similar occurrences involving petty thievery had been reported recently. It was too coincidental that this had occurred so soon after the news concerning Rosalie and Brum-

mell had been released. Would Rose have been held for
ransom? Or simply taken by one of Brummell's more
vengeful creditors in exchange for a large debt? It
definitely had the earmarks of a botched kidnapping
attempt, thwarted by Rosalie's presence of mind to call
for help and the fortunate timing of a small chambermaid. Rand's mouth twisted as he thought of someone
planning to come into the hotel room to find him and
Rosalie unconscious from the tainted wine.

"Why don't you change her clothes?" he said abruptly to the maid, motioning to the armoire with a nod of
his head. "Her nightgowns are there." Blushing at his
casually revealed knowledge of where Rosalie's intimate apparel was kept, Mireille jumped to the task like
a startled rabbit as he left the room.

Rand was to realize soon with mild irritation that
Mireille was genuinely afraid of him. She was so small
and delicately made that perhaps she harbored the
inner suspicion that he would crush her with a booted
foot if she displeased him. He was kind to her when he
remembered to be, but most of the time his attention
was absorbed by Rosalie. He came into the room to
begin the grim vigil by her bedside after conducting a
fruitless interrogation into how the drugging had happened. The information he had elicited seemed to
indicate that the wine could have been altered at any
one of countless points before it had arrived at the
room, and there was no way he could pinpoint suspects,
method, or motive.

The first twenty-four hours brought about no
change at all in Rosalie's condition. Although Rand
stayed by her, dozing in a chair or staring blankly at her
by turns, she gave no sign of returning consciousness
and remained in a chillingly waxlike state. Frequently
he gave in to brief urges to check her pulse and breath,
for there were moments when he thought he could see
the life ebb from her still body. Even after the flashes of

fear were extinguished he was tortured by anxiety, for he did not know if she would soon take a turn for the worse or the better. Mireille hovered nearby, her little face solemn, her eyes quietly anxious as she pretended not to hear Rand's orders for her to go to her own bed and come back in the morning.

At one point Rand left the bedside in order to stretch and walk over to the window, and he stared broodingly outside into the darkness for several long minutes. The crush of guilt weighed heavily on him, making it nearly impossible to bear the gnawing memory of the things Rosalie had said to him, of the things he had said to her before storming out of the room. He had come back to apologize, to shake and kiss her, to tell her with his usual arrogance that he wouldn't let her go. Dammit, she had a way of driving him beyond all reason, and he should not have let her affect him so profoundly. Not when her safety and welfare depended on him.

His thoughts wandered briefly to the crowd of London bucks he had kept company with the past few years. Would any of them understand the fix he was in? Probably not. They prided themselves on being carefree; they would not understand the need, the sense of responsibility, the remorse that plagued him. Until now he had conducted himself exactly as they would have, handling his obligations with negligence. Finally it seemed that he was reaping the rewards of his carelessness. Suddenly all the lectures and recriminations of his grandfather began to hit hard.

He had treated Rosalie as though she were a posy he had plucked by the wayside, not admitting how rare she was, that she was as fragile and in need of protection as the most valuable of blossoms. Selfishly he had played games with her, games of desire and indifference, seducing her until she had finally made the first move to his bed, when he should have dealt with her in a

straightforward fashion. Knowing what darkness was
hidden in his own heart, how had he come by the
temerity to demand her hand in marriage with such
high-handedness? He smiled bitterly before turning
back to the bed.

A few times the next day Rand wondered what had
caused Mireille's fascination with Rosalie. It hardly
made sense, since as far as he knew they had never met
before. The little chambermaid scurried back and
forth in the process of sponge-bathing Rosalie, brushing the long sable hair and braiding it neatly, changing
the sheets and making certain that the room was free
from dust and clutter. She chattered in French to
herself, hummed snatches of folk tunes, and more
perplexing still, her pockets were occasionally weighted
with a small book or leaflet. It was clear that she had
received some sort of education, a peculiar quality in a
French servant. She seemed to be an unusually imagi-
native child.

Mireille's devotion to Rosalie did not stem from any
sort of desire to attract Rand's notice. She was distinctly
uneasy around him and ran like a fleet-footed deer
whenever he issued even the mildest request. The
thought did not enter his mind that she might have
pitied him, for he did not know that desolation shone
in his eyes with a cold and unmistakable light.

As night approached and Rosalie still lay in her
endless sleep, Rand felt the last of his patience drain
away. He left the hoop-backed chair at her bedside to
flex his aching muscles and then strode over to the
small satinwood writing desk. He wrote a precisely
detailed letter to M. Bonchamps, the manager he had
appointed in Havre, concerning the credit affairs of
one M. George Brummell. As far as Rand was concerned, Brummell's loose tongue had contributed
greatly to the circumstances that had led to this situa-

tion, and he would not let the Beau's part in it go unrevenged.

Rand instructed Bonchamps to travel to Calais and personally make visits to all of those who conducted any sort of transactions with Brummell, systematically ensuring that credit for all except the most essential services would be cut off. Brummell would receive only the minimum of coal and food needed to stay alive, no matter how he wheedled or cajoled. No more freshly laundered cravats or champagne and japan-blacking for boots, no more tailoring services, hair oils, almond biscuits, or expensive snuff, no more elegant dinners or leisurely promenades down the boulevard, for Brummell would be reduced to such a state that he would not want himself to be viewed by the public.

Savagely Rand wished that he had a heartless enough disposition to request Brummell's complete starvation, but the mere possibility that the Beau was Rosalie's father checked him from taking that drastic action. Rosalie would probably be aghast and incensed if she knew what Rand was doing, but it was either that or go mad from an unsatisfied lust for vengeance. And, Rand promised himself as he succumbed to bleak moroseness, if Rosalie should die of malnourishment, he would personally guarantee that Brummell suffered a far more painful fate.

As he sat at the desk and brooded, Rand was oblivious of the supper that Mireille herself had undertaken to prepare down in the kitchens. For obvious reasons she did not trust anyone else to handle his food, and so she had supervised the arrangement of cold meats, fruit, and bread with quite an air of authority for a fifteen-year-old girl. As the platter went untouched, however, she began tentatively to draw his attention to it.

"Vous n'avez mangé rien, monsieur."

Rand looked at her blankly, and then his gaze flickered to the food. "I'm not hungry," he said, and folded the letter neatly before reaching for a stick of sealing wax. "You may have it." He spared not a glance as Mireille approached the food with barely restrained eagerness, for she needed little encouragement to partake of the tempting array. The quality and quantity of nourishments was far superior to the scraps she was usually accustomed to. After Rand had settled down in the chair by the bedside again, he braced his elbows on his knees and stared at Rosalie steadily. In the corner of his field of vision the sight of a tactfully proffered sandwich held in a napkin cloth appeared. Mireille had tucked a slice of peppered roast into an *echaudée*, a round, gold-crusted roll. She regarded him entreatingly as she raised his eyes to her.

"You haven't eaten anything," she repeated in French with a slight quaver in her voice, and to her relief Rand wryly reached to take the food.

"I suppose you think it will improve my disposition," he questioned, and his eyes remained on her as his strong white teeth bit into the crackling crust.

"Yes, *monsieur*," she agreed gravely, and Rand suddenly chuckled. After she brought him strong tea to wash the food down with, he looked at her in a kinder fashion, wondering at the hard life she seemed to lead. She worked hard in an uncomplaining manner, her attitude servile, but she appeared to be far more quick-minded than the usual servant.

"Do your parents work in the hotel, child?"

"I have no parents, *monsieur*."

Rand frowned. She was extremely young to be married, but perhaps . . .

"A husband?"

She smiled at the thought, shaking her head vigorously. "No, *monsieur*. I have a brother who takes care of me. We have traveled all over France, and whenever he finds a job, we stay there until . . . until—"

"He is fired?" Rand guessed, and she nodded.

"There are always more jobs. He can do anything," she said prosaically. Remembering her shyness, she lowered her eyes as she picked up the tray to take it from the room. *"Monsieur?"* she questioned. From the way she spoke, Rand guessed that she was nearly consumed with curiosity about Rosalie. "Is *mademoiselle* your . . . sister?"

Rand was silent for a moment. His eyes flickered to Rosalie, containing a bleak gleam. "No," he said huskily. "She's not my sister."

"Ah." Mireille ducked her head in a nervous bob and scurried away as he continued to stare at the bed.

The sky darkened, night fell, and slowly the hours crawled by. As Mireille dozed lightly in the next room, Rand searched in vain for any sign that Rosalie would wake. The entire world seemed to have shrunk to the proportions of the small room, and nothing outside of it was of any consequence. For long stretches of time he held her hands in his, curling and uncurling her lax fingers, warming them with his palms. Finally weariness swept over him in a relentless wave, and he leaned forward to pillow his head in his arms, his hands tangling in the edge of the bedclothes.

"Rose," he whispered huskily, the cotton sheet blotting the dampness of his lashes, "come back to me."

It seemed like something out of a dream when he woke much later in the dead of night to the tiny clicking sound of the door latch. Blinking sleepily, Rand looked toward the subtle noise and saw a thin wire inserted at the edge of the door, sliding upward to lift the latch easily. In less than a moment Rand silently moved from the bed to the wall by the door, flattening himself against the brocaded surface just as the portal opened smoothly. A slim dark shape glided into the room, and Rand's eyes narrowed as he tried to make out the figure in the darkness. The intruder moved with lanky grace and an assured step, approaching Rosalie and staring down at her before reaching to find a pulse in her neck.

Rand felt a protective rage sear through him like a bullet, and with swiftness he crossed the floor in two noiseless strides. Hooking a steel-banded arm around the stranger's neck, he jerked the man backward and began systematically to exert the pressure necessary to cut off his windpipe.

"I think," Rand snarled, "that introductions are in order."

With a smothered sound, the intruder burst into immediate action, and Rand flinched at the crushing blow of an elbow in his ribs. He cursed as his hold on his opponent was broken, and without a split second of delay he launched himself at the wiry figure, intending to break every bone in that hapless one's body. The scuffle lasted during a lightning-quick succession of movements, both of them hampered by the darkness. It was immensely satisfying on some primitive level for Rand to have a tangible opponent to fight. All of his building frustration finally had a release, and he thirsted to draw the other man's blood. He grabbed the first opportunity to fasten his hands around the intruder's throat and began to squeeze unmercifully, his lips parted in the imitation of a smile.

"By God," he rasped, his fingers tightening, "if you're the one who did this to her, I'll pop your head off like the cork of a bottle."

Rand's satisfaction, however, proved to be short-lived as he felt a quick, searing strip of pain along his right side. Somehow the man had managed to produce a short, gleaming blade in his left hand. As Rand was forced to avoid another quick jab of the knife, he found that the wall was against his back, preventing further retreat as the stranger dealt him a stunning blow to the jaw.

Several seconds afterward Rand shook his head and realized to his disgust that he was sitting on the floor, his back braced against the wall. The intruder was long gone, but Rosalie was still there, untouched. Wincing, Rand clasped a hand to his burning side and stood up, feeling the dampness of blood on his shirt. The connecting door to the next room opened just then. Mireille peeped around the corner with a lit candle in her hand, her rumpled clothes looking as though they had been hastily donned.

"*Monsieur,* did you call for . . . ?" she began, and her eyes widened as she took in the scene. Quickly she approached him, holding the candle up to view his condition. Rand smiled grimly as he saw her face blanch in the sputtering candlelight. Her huge brown eyes were so dark that they appeared to be black.

"We received an unexpected caller," he murmured. Suddenly he swayed.

"*Monsieur,* please sit down," Mireille muttered, rushing to the washstand and setting the candle down. "I will make a pad for the wound, and then the physician—"

"No physician," Rand interrupted sharply, half-sprawling in a hoop-backed chair. Any report of this on top of all that had already happened would stir up a tidal wave of controversy and interest that would make the situation even more precarious. "It's not deep, it's just a scratch."

"But you should—"

"Promise that you'll keep your little mouth shut," he said roughly, feeling fire seep from the wound to deep within his gut, "or I'll find a way to—"

"*Oui, monsieur,*" Mireille cut in hurriedly, bringing a bowl of water and a small heap of linen to him. "Open

your shirt, please." As he regarded her dubiously and
opened his mouth to question what effect it would have
on her maidenly modesty, she threw him an uncharac-
teristically stern frown. "I will not faint, *monsieur.*"

Rand's lips quirked, and then he shrugged out of the
rent, bloodstained garment with difficulty. His compact
brown torso gleamed in the weak candlelight.

"No, but you'll blush to death, from the look of it,"
he murmured, stifling a colorful oath as she firmly
pressed a cool, soaking cloth to the well-separated flesh
left in the wake of the knife. The cut ached like the
devil.

"Would you like a drink, *monsieur?* There is some
whiskey in—"

"No."

After a momentary pause Mireille could not resist
asking another question.

"Someone came to rob you?"

As Rand nodded, thick brown hair ruffled over his
forehead in a damp swath.

"Someone came to rob me of *mademoiselle,*" he
clarified, his voice as dry as fire. Mireille's eyebrows
knit together in perplexity, but wisely she refrained
from making any more inquiries and lifted the cloth to
look at the wound. Her unaffected, businesslike manner interested Rand, for it occurred to him that she was
not unused to the sight of blood . . . or a man's bare
chest. Several questions were on the tip of his tongue,
but since she respected his privacy, he would respect
hers. His eyes flickering with gratitude, he accepted a
thick square of dry linen to hold against his side.

"Before we make a bandage, I will run for some
salve," Mireille said, and stood up to leave.

"If you mention this to anyone downstairs," Rand
said slowly, meaningfully, "you will have cause to regret
it." His eyes were hypnotic, gleaming through the

darkness like golden coins set in a face that was harshly lined with pain and exhaustion.

"I promise to keep silent," Mireille replied gravely, and her small figure appeared almost ghostly as she glided quickly out of the room.

The wound was indeed only a superficial one, and it showed every sign of healing with miraculous speed. Rand barely gave it a second thought, becoming enmeshed in sober, weary vigilance as he watched over Rosalie. He became convinced during the next two days that every sin he had ever committed had been carefully tallied and that his penance was now being visited upon him. He did not know if Rosalie suffered in the confinement of her unconsciousness, but he did every time he looked at her, each time he noticed how dry and cracked her lips were or how prominent her finely structured bones were becoming. He could not bear to look at her and yet could not take his eyes away from the sight of her. He became aware of little else but the slight, motionless form on the bed, and it was only because of Mireille's insistence that he ate anything at all. Sleep was elusive except for the short periods of time when exhaustion overwhelmed him. For the most part, he could only stare and wait.

Mireille approached him on the third day as sunset began, her dark, clear brown eyes gleaming with compassion as she regarded him with a little less nervousness than usual.

"*Monsieur?*" she inquired softly. "Would you like for me to order something for you?" He raised his head to look at her, his skin pale underneath the coppery tan, his eyes cold. "You will make yourself ill," she continued, wringing her thin hands together. The subject of his wound was unmentioned but hung between them palpably. "Perhaps you should take a walk in the fresh air? . . . Or would you like me to order a bath?"

"A bath," Rand said, rubbing his eyes and smiling slightly, his expression lacking any sort of genuine humor. "Doubtless I need one. And coffee."

"*Monsieur* . . . you would not wish to worry *mademoiselle* with your appearance when she wakes, no? You must sleep, you must eat—"

"When she wakes," he repeated, and his lips curved in that same frighteningly humorless smile. "Is she going to wake, Mireille?"

Obviously wishing she could say yes but unwilling to lie, the chambermaid began to stutter. Finally she fell silent, her palms upturned in a gesture of helplessness, and Rand sighed grimly.

"You should see her eyes . . ." he murmured absently as he returned his attention to Rosalie. "The darkest blue you can imagine. At night they shine like sapphires. She can't hide a single emotion with those eyes . . . you can read her every thought."

"This is inconvenient for her?" Mireille questioned, tilting her head slightly as she watched him. She was beginning to lose her fear of him, for any man who cared for someone with such tenderness was surely not as dangerous as he had first seemed.

"For her. But damned convenient for me."

She smiled at him for the first time, her entire face seeming to glow for just an instant, and she slipped out of the room to fetch the coffee.

Slowly Rand moved to sit on the edge of the bed, his hand coming to rest on Rosalie's finely turned hip, his gaze moving over her features possessively.

"*Petite fleur,*" he said, and a peculiar, pained half-smile curved his mouth. "I never thought a woman would have the power to break me. But you've been my undoing." He bent his head, his voice becoming thick and unsteady. "Don't leave me here alone," he whispered.

He thought he saw her eyelids twitch. Frozen and

still, he watched her face, the steady beat of his heart escalating to a rapid pounding. Miraculously the satin gleam of her eyelashes fluttered and a small sigh escaped her lips. Rand caught his breath, leaning closer. Softly he murmured to her, stroking her skin with fingers that shook slightly, and the waxen stillness fell away from her. Wakefulness spread through her like a gentle balm, warming her veins, bringing her sluggish pulse back to life. As if the effort cost her agony, Rosalie moaned and opened her eyes, protective tears coming to ease their dryness. Bewildered, she squinted up at Rand, endeavoring to moisten the coarsened surface of her lips, trying to speak but finding it impossible. "It's all right," he said, reaching for a pillow to prop under her head as his eyes devoured her hungrily. His hand supported the back of her neck, his touch firm, tender, possessive. "Everything's going to be fine."

Mireille returned with a small tray several minutes after she had left, artfully endeavoring to turn the knob without the use of her hands. Suddenly the door was flung open, and she stared up at Rand in surprise. The harshness of his face had relaxed into a strange sort of calmness, and his weariness seemed to have disappeared.

"She's awake," he said as if reveling in the sound of the words, and her lips parted in a brilliant smile.

"Oh! I'm so glad! I'm so . . ." She trailed off, searching for words, making an instinctive move in her excitement to clasp his hands and then stopping in confusion as she gripped the tray. Rand flashed an exuberant grin, suddenly bending his head to her upturned face, and he brushed a hard, warm kiss of thanks on her cheek.

"Take the coffee back. Bring some broth and some fresh water. And be quick." With that he disappeared into the room again.

Mireille's eyes were round with shock as she turned away and hurried down the hallway. The kiss had been one of gratitude, not passion, yet still she could feel the tingle of his mouth against her skin. It was a wonder she had not dropped dead on the spot. Although Mireille was not a high-strung girl, Rand filled her with agitation. An aristocrat was supposed to be aloof and idle, yet there was a physical, earthy quality about him, a drive that contrasted oddly with his station and position. Compared with her brother, Guillaume, and the other men she knew, he was exotic and rather overwhelming, handsome in a certain way but disturbingly unpredictable . . . a man she would not want to cross in a thousand years. It was for his sake that she had wanted Rosalie to recover, because he looked at *mademoiselle* as if she were the reason why the sun rose and fell. And Mireille was not too young to appreciate love when she saw it, for love was a meager commodity in her world.

Listlessly Rosalie sipped from a glass of water and handed it back to Mireille, her face whitening as she leaned back against the pillow.

"I do not think you will be able to get out of bed today," Mireille announced, her voice laced with the infinite practicality that sometimes seemed comical coming out of the mouth of a young girl.

"I think you're right," Rosalie said, sighing and then closing her eyes. Her limbs felt heavy and flaccid, and she wondered if she would ever have the energy to get up. She seemed to be able to do nothing but sleep.

"Don't relax yet," Rand said in an impersonal voice, and she heard the clink of dishes near the bed. "You need to eat more."

"No," Rosalie replied with weak stubbornness, managing to lift her eyelids and regard him with revulsion. She would gag if she had to go through another session in which he relentlessly and dispassionately ladled soup down her throat, paying no attention to her lack of appetite. "No more juice, broth, or soup."

"Then what will you have?" he persisted, seeming to lose patience with her. As she refused to reply, feeling sick at the thought of food, Rand turned to Mireille. "Maybe an egg and some dry toast—" he began, but Rosalie interrupted him peevishly, lifting her head with effort.

"Don't talk about me as if I'm not here! Why don't you eat something yourself? You need it more than I do!" He was a more starkly authoritative figure than before, slightly thinner than she remembered, his skin lighter by several shades, his face haggard. Suddenly he scowled at her, feeling caged by the small room and the pall of sickness that was threaded through the very air. In the few days since she had woken up, Rosalie had been curiously listless, not even asking what had happened to her. He missed the old Rosalie desperately, wanted to hold her, wanted her to laugh and press a warm kiss against his lips, and instead he was confronted with a shadow of the woman he longed for. Rand, who had once been the most self-sufficient bachelor in London, found for the first time in his adult life that he was lonely. Though he struggled to maintain his calm, he felt something inside snap.

"*I* need to eat?" he repeated in a dangerously low tone, striding over to the washstand and picking up a small lacquered hand mirror. "At least I don't look like a damned skeleton! Are you trying to starve yourself into the grave? Do you think that somehow I'll manage to feel even guiltier then? Look at yourself!" He thrust the mirror at her, and Rosalie stopped breathing as she saw her own reflection for the first time since her illness. She was as white as chalk, her skin splotchy, deep circles carved underneath her eyes. Her hair was lank and dark, pulled away from her face for the sake of

neatness, with none of the sprightly curl or shine that
she was accustomed to seeing. The only sign of color in
her face was her eyes, and they appeared startlingly
huge and blue above the fragile, sharply carved lines of
her cheeks. To her blurring gaze, the vision appeared
to be that of an old woman.

"Take it away and leave me alone," Rosalie said
throatily, and as her initial shock wore off, misery
threatened to overpower her completely. "I can't bear
for you to be around me anymore—you're overbearing
and unfeeling, and I can't . . . I don't . . ." Trailing off
in a tiny voice, she looked up into Rand's unreadable
face and then burst into tears, unable to think of
anything else to do. Swearing vividly, Rand dropped
the mirror onto the carpeting and sat on the bed,
pulling her into his arms to cradle her. Her body shook
with sobs as he rocked her gently, and his exasperation
fled as he felt her hot tears dampen his shirt.

"Rose, hush. I didn't intend for you to cry," he
murmured against her ear. "But you're not going to
ruin yourself through your own stubbornness. I intend
to take care of you, *petite*, and that includes keeping you
from starvation." Rosalie's noisy weeping continued
while he tried to soothe her with indulgent words, and
Rand's heart ached at the woeful sounds she made.
Unexpectedly he was all velvet charm and tender
warmth, the transformation quite startling from the
harsh stranger of a minute before.

Unfortunately it seemed that unhappiness was infectious. As soon as the commotion began, Mireille stared
at Rosalie with round eyes, and inexplicably she jerked
her hands over her own face as tears blurred her vision.
Now she stood in the corner of the room like a tired,
punished child, sobbing just as loudly as Rosalie. Either
the girl was profoundly affected by Rosalie's condition,
or the crying had reminded her of some past tragedy,
but in any event a storm had been unleashed that

showed no signs of abating. "Mireille, why . . . ? Oh, hell," Rand muttered, near his wits' end as he was confronted with two weeping females in a room of tiny and stuffy proportions. He almost had to smile at the ridiculous situation he found himself in. His mind cast about for the best course of action to take.

It was clear that they could no longer stay in the hotel. It was dangerous for two reasons: Rosalie was easily accessible to anyone who wished her harm, and second, anyone in a physically weakened condition was prey to the multitude of fevers that constantly circulated through the city, fevers that struck at any time and could cause a variety of damage to the victims. And putting all that aside, Rand was beginning to loathe the place. The city was beginning to press in on them, bricks and buildings blocking out air and light, relentless sounds of the street abusing the ear with a myriad of shouts and clatterings. A deep and basic urge suddenly possessed him, to retreat, to find the shelter and comfort of a protected home, a sanctuary. It was the same urge that his ancestors had felt after surviving the taxing clashes with the outside world, when they had finally sought relief within the walls of the Château d'Angoux.

A corner of his mind immediately protested the thought of returning to the château, but he countered it with clear and rational reasoning. The château was an ancient fortress, strong and protected, surrounded by miles of land through which it would be difficult for trespassers to travel undetected. It was clean and luxurious, although it was staffed lightly, and it was situated in the country, the ideal place for Rosalie to recover. There were fresh food, sunny gardens that made for pleasant and leisurely walks, and an abundance of grateful tenants who would most likely tend toward minding their own business during the harvest season.

"It seems we're in something of an untenable situation," Rand said dryly, and Rosalie nodded as she hiccuped against his shoulder. She felt weak and fretful, completely unlike herself. Lightly Rand pressed his lips to her hair and shifted her in his arms. His touch was comforting, his cool hard strength a blessed relief to her. "Mireille, get out of the corner, *s'il te plaît.* There are some handkerchiefs in the armoire in the second drawer—get one for Rose and one for you." As Mireille hesitated at the unorthodox breach of protocol, he sighed impatiently. "Yes, one for you also." Rosalie suddenly giggled through her tears as she listened to his overpatient tone, and unceremoniously Rand clamped the fresh white cloth to her nose. "We'll leave tomorrow morning for the château in Brittany. It's peaceful there and it will provide a welcome change of scenery. I want all of *mademoiselle*'s belongings packed tonight, Mireille." The tiny chambermaid nodded, mopping her face solemnly with a handkerchief.

"What about Mireille?" Rosalie questioned in a small voice. "Are we just going to leave her here?"

Thoughtfully Rand regarded the girl, who was caught in an immediate agony of suspense. Her wet eyes were dark and hopeful.

"Are you capable of being a companion to *mademoiselle?*" he asked. "Helping her dress, doing whatever she wants done without question?"

Mireille nodded violently. *"Oui, monsieur!* I will even learn to speak English!"

"A sacrifice that would be greatly appreciated," Rand commented, suddenly grinning.

"Then she can come with us to the château?" Rosalie asked.

Suddenly Rand's pulse leapt at the eager note in her voice. He would have given her the moon to keep it there. Smiling down at her, he tucked a lock of hair behind her ear, and then he raised his head to fix Mireille with a meaningful stare. "Only if she is the kind who keeps a promise," he replied enigmatically, a hint of steel edging his voice, and he and Mireille exchanged a somber glance that utterly confused Rosalie. In order to keep her from worrying, Rand had decided not to tell Rosalie about the intruder in her room, or about the scuffle that had taken place there. Concerning the matter of the opium-tainted wine, he had told her succinctly that it had been the work of inept thieves who had wanted to steal their valuables after drugging their victims into unconsciousness. It was a common ploy of burglars, and Rosalie had not questioned Rand further on the subject.

"*Oui, monsieur,*" the little maid murmured dutifully.

"Then be ready to leave tomorrow morning."

Mireille gave a little shriek of happiness and ran from the room.

"Thank you," Rosalie said, looking up at Rand in a grateful, wondering manner. "But what was that all ab—?"

"You'd better try to get some sleep," he interrupted, plying the handkerchief to her face again. "You're going to rest and eat like a country maid until you can barely fit into your clothes."

Rosalie smiled faintly. "Do you like the look of a voluptuous woman?" she murmured.

His fingertips traced gently over the overdefined edge of her cheekbone. "I like the way you looked before," Rand replied, and wiped her face with the handkerchief once more.

After the last of the tears had been blotted, Rosalie snuggled against him in search of further comfort, pressing the softness of her face against his rough, unshaven jaw. To her surprise, his arms loosened, and he unloaded her carefully from his lap.

Had Rand refused her advance because he was annoyed with her? Rosalie stared apprehensively at him, but his face was impassive. It was then that she

reflected on the fact that his behavior toward her ever
since she had woken from her drugged slumber had
been exactly like that of a brother—kind but completely platonic. Could it be that after the ravages she had
been through he found her too unattractive to kiss? She
could not blame him if that were so. Or perhaps he had
finally lost his desire for her—perhaps upon reflection
he had decided that she was no longer a novelty.
Confused, she lowered her lashes and obediently settled under the covers.

"Are you going to mind going to the château?" she
asked. "I know that you dislike—"

"I'll mind staying here one more day," Rand said,
deftly arranging the pillows behind her head. "I'm
tired of inns and hotels. I've forgotten what it's like to
live in more than one or two rooms at a time. I also
haven't been riding in weeks—"

"What about your business concerns?"

"I have appointed an efficient manager to handle
them for a while, and I'll be able to get in touch with
him without difficulty."

"And the meetings in Paris?" Rosalie questioned
sleepily.

"They can wait."

"And Brum—"

"He can wait too."

"Rand . . . when are we going back to England?" she
whispered, closing her eyes, afraid of what she might
see in his face.

"When I decide we will," he said in a hard manner
that squashed any inclination she might have had to
question him further. The prospect of returning to
England was loaded with too many indefinites. It was
unpredictable as to how their relationship would
change when they reached London. But in France he
knew how things stood: she was his without question,
and there was no way she could alter the fact.

Ten

Prithee, say aye or no;
If thou'lt not have me, tell me so;
I cannot stay,
Nor will I wait upon
A smile or frown.
If thou wilt have me, say;
Then I am thine, or else I am mine own.
—Thomas Shipman

"I've never seen anything so peaceful," Rosalie said, staring out of the carriage window at the wide slate-blue expanse of the Loire River. "From what I remember of my geography lessons, I expected it to be fiercer, more turbulent." Underneath her head she felt Rand's shoulder flex as he leaned to get a closer look of the scene.

"The Loire varies from place to place," he said, his eyes turning a bright shade of gold as the rich light of the sun crossed his face. "In Nantes it's as congested with traffic as the Seine . . . at Orléans it's a docile stream barely a few feet deep. Just when you're convinced the Loire is tame and gentle, it begins to rage." Rand's mouth twitched as he added, "As unpredictable as a woman."

"As fickle as a man, you mean," she rejoined immediately, uncertain as to whether or not he was making jest of her. Rand laughed, enjoying the signs of her returning temper. Lately he had taken an apparent delight in baiting her, in the manner of one who provokes a kitten to take tiny-clawed swipes at him. Mireille, who was sitting on the seat opposite them, spoke as she peered out of her window. Wisely she had pretended ignorance of the mildly testy exchanges that had been going on ever since they had left Paris.

"*Vraiment,*" Mireille said, "the Loire is unpredictable —sometimes it floods the vineyards, the valleys . . . some of the more stupid peasants think it is a punishment from God. Nearer the ocean the river becomes big and deep, and I do not like it so much there. But at Touraine it is regal, it is aristocratic—*avec les châteaux,* and the trees . . . It looks rather dry for this time of year, don't you . . . ?" Quickly the girl's words trailed off as she discovered that Rand was eyeing her in a speculative manner. Rosalie merely appeared to be surprised.

"Mireille," Rand said slowly, "appears to be exceptionally well-traveled for a chambermaid."

Flustered, the girl turned away from the window and stared down at her hands. "I have been all over France with Guillaume."

Rosalie felt a mixture of protectiveness and compassion for the small girl, for she knew exactly how it felt to be alone. Mireille had no parents and no one to take care of her. All that she had said about her brother was that he was away on a new job and that she had left a note at the *hôtel* in Paris concerning her plans. When they had pressed her for more information about him, her expression had become guarded, almost as if she were bent on forgetting all about him. Mireille was certainly an interesting puzzle, for she had talents and capabilities far above those of any average girl of her age and position. Not only could she read and write, but also she had a lightning-quick mind and had picked up an unconventional mixture of knowledge during her short lifetime.

"Mireille, where are you from? Where were you born?" Rosalie asked.

The girl shook her head. "I don't know. And

Guillaume says he does not remember anything about it. One year we spent a long time in Touraine, though, so I suppose you could say I'm from Touraine."

"And what did you do there?" Rosalie questioned further, smiling gently as the girl adopted a whimsical expression and shrugged.

"Anything, *mademoiselle*. I can do anything." Mireille suddenly beamed at them both, a wide smile that indicated supreme pleasure with the world in general, and then she looked out the window again.

"I have no doubt of it," Rosalie said in an aside to Rand, and he grinned in agreement.

"As long as she pleases you, love."

The endearment was meaningless, offhand. It wrung a response from her receptive nerves effortlessly. Love. The only other time he had called her that had been during a moment of passion, and she felt startled at the intimacy it recalled. The word sounded soft coming from his lips, slipping through the pores of her skin like an airy caress. Quietly Rosalie eased herself into the crook of his arm, soaking up the nearness of him as the carriage rolled past the Loire.

How much simpler her life would have been if she had been able to choose whom and when she would love. She could have picked a kind, uncomplicated man, someone who would have fit easily into the pattern of her life—perhaps a junior clerk at a bank, or a baker or tailor. Someone whose kisses were agreeable, not devastating . . . someone who would beg instead of bully . . . someone whose looks were pleasant rather than sensually disturbing. She had never bothered to imagine the problems of loving someone like Rand Berkeley. How much better it would have been to set her sights on a man who would make life steady, not mixed-up and painful, wild and sweet. She would not have chosen someone who would have turned her world upside down. Rand was the stuff of which her

dreams had once been made, but how wrong she had
been to dream with such ambition!

Slowly her mind wandered to the subject of the
Château d'Angoux as she realized that they would
reach it in an hour or two. Somewhere in the jumble of
sleepiness and troubled thoughts was a twinge of
excitement at the prospect of seeing the château, for it
might provide a few more revelations about Rand's
past. Once she recovered her health completely, Rosalie was determined to find out more about Hélène
d'Angoux and Rand's heritage, about the recent and
far-reaching histories of the people who had lived
there. She did not know how things stood between her
and Rand now, for the former pattern of their relationship seemed to have dissolved in the past two days. So
far it had not been reassembled. Perhaps at the château
she would be able to discover what remained and what
was gone, and how the two of them would go on from
there.

As they drew closer and closer to the d'Angoux
estate, the fertile green land became gently sloped, and
the road pulled away from its parallel course with the
Loire. Languidly a dark shape broke through the
horizon, causing Rand to tense slightly.

"That's it," he said, and Mireille jumped to the
window, her tiny fingers curling around the edges.
Huge walls and cylindrical towers surrounded the
château, as well as a shallow moat that had been
partially filled in and bridged over, now serving an
ornamental rather than useful function. Treetops,
flowering ivy, and fluffy pale roses swayed lazily over
the edges of the walls.

"*Sang,* how many towers are there?" Rosalie asked,
unable to see the mass of them clearly through the
half-open iron gate.

"Eight," Rand said, bracing an arm against the
windowframe to prevent her from pitching forward as

the hired carriage jolted to a halt in front of the gate. Mireille was thrown backward against the velvet-upholstered seat. Undaunted, she glued herself to the window once more.

"*Mademoiselle,* look at the gate!" she exclaimed, and Rosalie leaned forward. As Rand withdrew his arm from in front of her the back of his hand brushed accidentally against her breast. They both froze instantly. The immediacy of Rand's desire washed over him without mercy. He inhaled sharply, wanting her uncontrollably, images filling his mind: the pliant firmness of her flesh in his hands, in his mouth, anywhere, everywhere. The inward rush of air dried his lips of their moisture.

Rosalie could feel her nipple contract immediately, suddenly aching, tingling in unquenchable arousal. Every nerve was thrown into instant confusion, her pulse heavy and rapid as if her blood had thickened into melted silver. She knew that her body's reaction to him was unconcealed by the thin cambric of her dress. Cheeks flaming in embarassment, Rosalie blindly focused on the sight outside the carriage.

"Look at what, Mireille?" she murmured.

"At the d'Angoux coat-of-arms," the young girl replied in fascination. "Engraved on the gate—a young man holding a shield . . . and a rose."

"A rose?" Rosalie repeated, swallowing hard as she became aware that Rand was staring at her intensely. "But isn't that a sign of royalty?"

"The d'Angouxs have a few ties with royalty," he answered in a carefully casual way, "albeit in the distant past. In the twelfth century Geoffrey of Anjou married the daughter of England's Henry I, and later their son became Henry II. In the 1400's the daughter of René d'Anjou joined Henry VI in marriage—"

Gratefully Rosalie seized on the subject, eager to set her mind on something besides her awareness of him.

"But I don't see," she interrupted, "how marrying the offspring of various Henrys entitled the d'Angoux to put a rose on their shield."

As his gaze moved from the vivid blue of her eyes to the wide curve of her mouth, Rand suddenly forgot everything he had been about to say. He had never imagined being so hungry, so starved for the assuagement of a woman's flesh, so needful of her caress, her sweetness. It took a massive effort to collect his thoughts and continue.

"The rose was won in battle. In the fifteenth century, Philippe d'Anjou defeated two powerful families in the struggle for the right to rule Brittany. And if that alone didn't give him the right to take the rose as a symbol of royalty, he took to wife a sixteen-year-old maiden soon after the battle was over. An English bride—her name was Rosemonde. The English Rose, they called her, and it was said that he valued her above all else."

Rosalie hastily took her eyes away from him as the carriage edged carefully past the gate and started up the long drive to the château.

"What is the Berkeley coat-of-arms?" she asked.

"A shield, a wolf, and a birch tree. That's why Randall is such a common name in the Berkeley family, given to every firstborn son. It means shield-wolf . . . a shield that makes the warrior who carries it invincible in battle." Even though Rosalie's head was turned away from him, she could feel his eyes upon her as he said softly, "Hence the Berkeleys are usually certain of getting what they fight for."

"Until their overconfidence leads to defeat," Rosalie said stubbornly. Each tiny hair on the back of her neck quivered as he laughed, the sound delicious, masculine, warm.

"Hasn't happened in centuries."

The Château d'Angoux was unquestionably one of

the loveliest structures she had ever seen. The oldest part of it was a castle, complete with bulky, steadfast towers and rigid walls. Then, rising out of the stone and stability of the castle was the more modern part of the château, designed in a Gothic style of dainty elegance, complete with crenellation, cone-topped towers, and finely arched windows. The whole of it perched among miles of gardens and wooded forests, tiny ponds and a profusion of roses, azaleas, rhododendrons, and chrysanthemums.

"Oh, how beautiful it is," Rosalie said, and Rand's mouth twisted sardonically.

"The only monument the d'Angoux family has to offer to its name. There are no more men to carry on the line."

"It's so full of . . ." Grace? Romance? Rosalie searched dreamily for the exact words to use.

"Self-conscious grandeur," Rand suggested, and she gave him a withering look before returning her attention to the gorgeous spectacle of the château. The gravel drive passed through two more sets of gates, then wound artfully by small ponds and clusters of trees before taking a more direct route toward the château. All of the land surrounding the structure was carefully tended, the trees and flowers so well-balanced and harmoniously placed that it betrayed a history of meticulous landscaping and refurbishing. Rosalie began to see what Rand had meant by describing the estate as self-conscious, for it did indeed seem to stand in awareness of its own magnificence. Underneath the leafy fronds and the careful ornamentation it was evident that the château had once been a fortress, a tough, impenetrable giant, and the resilient strength of it still remained, although its edges had been softened by whimsical decoration.

The entrance to the château was dignified and grand, framed by half-columns that edged a wide

portico. Four wings branched off from the central
building. Strange, how the classical Roman style of it
matched the Gothic tone of the rest of the structure. It
could have easily been a jarring combination of styles,
yet something, perhaps its simplicity, blended all into a
harmonious whole. The carriage stopped and Rosalie
felt a quick flutter of nervousness intrude on her
curiosity. So many new places, so many new things she
had seen since meeting Rand, whereas before, her life
had been the same year in and year out. Mireille took it
all in with apparent ease, for her life had been nothing
but constant change.

"It looks very quiet for such a big château," Mireille
remarked.

Rand nodded briefly before unfolding his arm from
behind Rosalie. "Right now we have only a small staff,"
he replied, opening the carriage door before an approaching footman could reach them. "But in the
village there are a number of people who know the
ways of the house . . . reserve forces, so to speak. We'll
need a few of them while we're here." Then he smiled
at her, adding, "unless you would prefer to help with
the cooking and dusting?"

"If my cooking will please you and *mademoiselle,* then
so be it," Mireille said, her fatalistic shrug indicating
that the possibility of her cooking pleasing either one
of them was highly doubtful. Rosalie giggled, her eyes
twinkling as she regarded the pair of them.

"Don't tease her, Rand," she reproved, and he
closed his mouth in obedient silence, the golden hazel
eyes gleaming with a peculiar light as he threw her one
last glance. Then he swung agilely out of the carriage
to speak with the driver of the hired vehicle.

"His temper is improving," Rosalie observed in a
whisper.

"He is happy that you are better," Mireille said
wisely.

"Do you really think so? Sometimes it doesn't seem as if . . ." Under the scrutiny of those bright chocolate-hued eyes, Rosalie didn't finish her sentence, wondering exactly how much the girl understood. Surely my feelings for him must be as obvious as a beacon, she thought. Was Mireille, young as she was, someone she could trust? Her ponderings were interrupted as a middle-aged footman of gentle appearance helped them both out of the carriage, his hand steady under her weak grasp. The traveling had exhausted Rosalie, and she became irritated with herself as she realized that her strength was far too easily depleted this soon after her illness.

Feeling vaguely removed from the scene as she stepped down from the vehicle, Rosalie stood there blinking tiredly. Although Mireille was looking around in lively curiosity, she remained firmly by Rosalie's side, reminding Rand of a little watchdog as he approached the pair.

"Our arrival is unexpected," he said, offering his arm to Rosalie and leading her up the wide steps to the doorway. "It will probably take a minute or two for them to prepare the rooms."

As the front doors were opened Rosalie let out a soft, admiring exhalation, forgetting everyone around her as she took in the magnificence of the château's interior. Balustraded galleries edged the second floor, rich with tapestries and artwork, while statues of fantastical creatures perched in corners, above arches and doorways. The colors were pale and delicate: light blue, cream, lavender, mint, while thick rococo encrustations of gold glimmered on the walls and ceiling in lavishness and abundance.

"It used to be quite elegant," Rand said dryly. "Simple, restrained, tasteful. But during one of my mother's last visits here she decided to redecorate . . . again."

Rosalie nodded speechlessly, wondering how on earth anyone could live comfortably in such resplendence. The château seemed to be less of a home than a beautiful work of art. It was breathtaking to view, but how could anyone live here?

"Don't worry," Rand said, cupping a comforting hand over her elbow. "Most of the rooms are a little less overwhelming. Oh . . . this woman who is approaching—she and her husband are the caretakers of the château. Since they are both highly respected in the village, we'll hope that she'll be considered an acceptable chaperon for you. Ah, Madame Alvin?" He turned to speak to a pleasant-visaged, rotund woman, who advanced toward them with a bewilderingly rapid stream of French. Her expression was exceptionally kind if slightly worried, her neatly kept hair a silvery color of brown, her clothes and apron scented of cleanliness and starch—a clean, toasty, motherly smell that was immediately comforting. In her increasing exhaustion Rosalie could not follow most of the conversation that ensued, comprehending only a few of Rand's words. He seemed to be describing her as "my little cousin from England," explaining that she had been visiting relatives in Paris when a fever had struck, and that they were here for her to recuperate. He finished with the brief introduction, ". . . Rose, may I present Madame Alvin . . . Madame Alvin, Miss Rosalie Berkeley."

"Berk—" Rosalie began to say, stunned, and Rand smiled down at her gently, his expression brotherly as he prodded her in the side.

"Yes, I know how tired you are, *petite cousine* . . . a few minutes, and I'm certain Madame Alvin will have a room for you."

Cousin Rosalie Berkeley. It was not a role that would be easy for her to slip into.

"We have one already!" Madame Alvin said, her

sympathy and concern turning into a whirlwind of activity. "Eleazar, get the bags from outside, and do not drag those big feet! Ninette, show *mademoiselle* and her *compagne* the rooms upstairs, then fetch your sister from the village to help with the cooking. And, Jérème, the trunks outside are . . . Where is that boy? Eleazar, find him and tell him that we need his uncle to butler. . . ."

Rosalie raised her eyes to the long, limitless line of stairs that led to the second floor. Ninette, a large blond girl close to her own age, indicated that they led to the bedchambers, and Rosalie stumbled forward with feet that had turned leaden, determined to retain at least a shred or two of her independence from Rand.

"Stubborn little fool," she suddenly heard a low masculine voice next to her ear. "No doubt you intend to try the stairs without asking for any help at all. Are you planning to carry your own trunks up, as well?"

Rosalie made no reply, her face pale from the toll the journey had taken. Rand picked her up easily, his arms hooked securely beneath her back and knees. "Ah, *pauvre mademoiselle* . . ." she heard Madame Alvin exclaim, and everything passed in a rush over her head as she rested her cheek submissively against Rand's shoulder. He carried her up the stairs as the maid led the way, his breath warm against her cheek as he glanced down at her.

How strange, Rosalie mused absently, that fate had forced her to depend on Rand so much and so often . . . she who had longed for freedom and independence . . . he a man whom few trusted, who had the reputation of loathing responsibility. What impelled him to take care of her and protect her?

He carried her into a bedchamber shaded in gold and pastels, the counterpane on the small canopied bed a pale pink hue. Rosalie could do no more than cast a weary glance around the exquisite room to take in the details . . . the gilded dressing table, the ornate mirrors, the walls painted with whimsical pictures of clouds, cherubs, and dainty foliage.

"Where are you going?" she asked as the comforting folds of the bed surrounded her.

"My room is down the hall," he said, pulling the light covers over her. "Mireille is being settled in right next door. You'll feel better after you sleep for a while, love."

Bewildered by his tenderness, Rosalie found that her arms were still entwined around his neck. Slowly she released him and slid her hands under the covers, her eyes closing. She looked so absurdly helpless against the large lace-edged pillows that Rand could not resist staying with her one more minute, the mattress giving slightly as he sat by her.

"Are you going to rest also?" she asked.

"I have some things to take care of."

"What kinds of things?" she persisted, and Rand smiled.

"You don't have to worry," he said, his tone gentle. "I won't stray far from you." As he spoke, he stroked the satin tendrils of hair away from her face with a whisper-light touch, letting them curl around his fingers and then tucking them behind her ears.

"What will you be doing?" Rosalie questioned sleepily, relaxing deeply under the caress of his fingertips.

"Waiting for you to wake up, of course. And making some decisions."

"About me?" she whispered, feeling him trace the delicate line of her jaw, the vulnerable turn of her neck.

"No decisions about you," Rand replied, his voice full of low, subtle inflections that her mind was too tired to analyze. "How can I?" His thumb brushed against the pulse in her neck, then drifted to the clustered nerves near her shoulder and massaged until her muscles were soft and loose. "My dilemma is that of the miner who finds a diamond in a pile of rocks. Never having had such a possession before, he's afraid of losing it. He is besieged by questions: what kind of setting does it require . . . and how should he guard it? And how does he keep himself from becoming a miser?"

Dropping off to sleep, Rosalie barely heard his words. She wondered much later if she had felt the soft brush of his mouth against her cheek, the stroke of his breath against her skin, the sweetness of a lover's whisper in her hair. Or had it been only a dream that had stolen over her like a reluctant summer sunset?

Rosalie slept in undisturbed peace, finally wakening a few hours later when evening had already settled. Mireille was there as she opened her eyes, bustling into the room with a bed tray that contained an enticing selection of food.

"*Mademoiselle*, would you like some supper?" she entreated. As Rosalie smiled and rubbed her eyes, the girl set the tray on a gilded table. "Monsieur de Berkeley said that you would eat up here tonight," Mireille informed her, plumping up the pillows for Rosalie to lean against and rearranging the covers as she sat up. "They are so busy organizing the château . . . new people have arrived from the village, a butler, a man to clean the knives and boots, a girl to help the cook, and another to help open up more rooms."

"So you've been investigating everything?" Rosalie asked, receiving the bed tray with pleasure. "What is this?"

"*Blanc manger d'un chapon*—very good for a sick person. A capon breast milled with ground almonds, and those little things on top are pomegranate seeds."

Rosalie took a tentative bite and found it to be the most delicious dish she had ever tasted. Nestled on the gold-edged plate next to the capon was a sparse handful of mushrooms sautéed with cream and scallions, and there were also two small milk rolls, to be spread liberally with butter.

"For dessert I will bring you a strawberry cream," Mireille announced, and Rosalie laughed.

"I doubt that I'll be able to eat dessert after this."

"*Monsieur* said you must eat everything."

"Everything?" Rosalie repeated doubtfully. "I don't suppose you would—"

"*Monsieur* said I must not eat anything for you," Mireille said virtuously.

"*Monsieur* is extremely fond of dictating orders," Rosalie grumbled, thinking that Rand needed to eat just as much as she did. "I hope he had a large dinner. A very large one." The girl nodded, settling on the corner of the bed as Rosalie picked up a three-pronged fork.

"*Vraiment,* he did, after going to the stable to see the horses. The stable is made to hold forty horses, Ninette told me, and in the old days it was packed with them."

"How many now?" Rosalie questioned around a savory mouthful.

Mireille tilted her head thoughtfully. "Ah, let me think . . . only five. Monsieur de Berkeley said to Monsieur Alvin—the caretaker and gardener, who is also husband to Madame Alvin—that we need another stableboy, because he wishes to buy more horses . . . the ones in the stable now are not fast or spirited enough for him to ride."

"That sounds like him," Rosalie agreed, taking a sip of watered-down wine. "Rand's idea of riding is probably to risk his neck by racing the wind and jumping every hedge and fence in sight."

"If you wish to ride after you are better, I will accompany you," Mireille offered, and the hopefulness was so transparent in her voice that Rosalie's lips twitched.

"If you're certain you wouldn't mind——"

"Oh, no, I would not mind at all! And also," Mireille continued, apparently encouraged by Rosalie's acquiescence, "there are beautiful gardens around the château, and even a maze that Monsieur Alvin keeps clipped! If you wish, I will accompany you on afternoon walks."

"A pleasant suggestion," Rosalie agreed.

"And I will also accompany you to the fair in the village this month, which Ninette told me about. After I ask Monsieur de Berkeley for permission, of course——"

"*Monsieur* doesn't own me," Rosalie interrupted, suddenly annoyed at Mireille's assumption that Rand had the right to approve or disapprove of her activities. "We don't need his permission."

"But he is your cousin, your guardian, yes? He must be told of these things or . . . or he will become very angry with me," Mireille pointed out. Rosalie's expression softened immediately. The last thing she would wish on anyone, especially Mireille, was Rand's anger. One scowl from him was enough to chase someone's wits under the bed! "Besides, I do not think he would say no to anything *you* wanted."

"No?" Rosalie questioned, her voice dry. "Unfortunately he has very particular ideas about what he thinks I should do." And so far her attempts to manage Rand had been met with varying degrees of success. He was not an easy man to manipulate.

"*Je suis d'accord,*" Mireille said, nodding vigorously. "You are right, he is a strong-willed man." Suddenly her voice lowered to a conspiratorial whisper. "But when you smile at him, *mademoiselle*"—she lifted her tiniest finger and waggled it—"his will is no stronger than this!"

Rosalie gave a smothered laugh and broke one of the soft white milk rolls, shaking her head in dismay.

"I wonder if it was wise of Rand to pick you as my companion," she said, chuckling quietly before spearing a tiny mushroom with a three-pronged fork.

"A pair of brown geldings, an old brown match horse, a chestnut mare, and a bay," Rand listed the contents of the stable thoughtfully, the sinewy, muscular length of his legs stretched out in front of him as he lounged negligently in the frail, elaborately ornamented chair. He had come to Rosalie's bedchamber after an early-morning ride, finding her at the beginning of a leisurely paced breakfast. She was an enchanting sight, her paleness erased with the warm flush of a long sleep and recent awakening. "The bay can work up to a respectable speed, but the others are too old and well-fed to be of much use." He chuckled suddenly, his gold-tinged eyes focused on a distant memory. "I don't recall many details about the old marquis except for his love of horses. I wonder if he knows somehow that his forty-horse stable is currently being warmed by five round-sided nags who swish at flies for exercise."

Rosalie laughed, pulling apart a croissant and spreading a crumbling bit of it with fresh honey.

"You plan to augment the ranks of the d'Angoux stables soon?" she inquired.

"I'm going to visit some of the more prominent local landowners today. Perhaps there'll be a few prospects. In any event, it's customary here for the new residents of the district to pay first calls."

"Really? They're not going to make the first move and welcome us? And I thought the French were so hospitable. It makes more sense the way we do it in England, the other way around."

"I would rather that no one came to visit for a few weeks," Rand replied, stroking his lean cheek absently. The shadow of bristle made him appear darker than usual, and vaguely unscrupulous. "The reason we're here is to find some peace, not to play host to a gaggle of curious callers."

"Oh . . ." Rosalie stopped chewing in mid-thought, then forced herself to swallow. "Do you think anyone knows . . . about the gossip . . . ?"

"About the rumors concerning Brummell's daughter?" Rand clarified, and then shook his head. "You'll discover shortly that this little province is an entire world, insulated from Paris just as much as it's insulated from Japan. Local affairs are the concern here—local news, local gossip. Now, in England, you've been a gossipmonger's dream, but here . . . well, you won't make the local circuit for quite a while."

"Thank you," Rosalie said dryly. As she washed down the croissant with hot, milky coffee, her eyes brightened with a pleasant idea. "Then that means I can accompany you when you visit—"

"You can rest and relax in bed for a while longer," Rand corrected, his voice containing that autocratic note that sorely tempted her to disobey him. "And if you're feeling stronger, you can have Mireille accompany you on a tour through a wing or two of the château. There are paintings, sculptures, and amusements enough to keep you occupied for a while."

Smothering her vaguely outraged reaction to his tone of command, Rosalie contrived to keep her reply appropriately mild. Rand would not be won over by her stubbornness as quickly as sweetness.

"Will I see you for lunch?" she asked, sounding more wistful than she would have preferred. However, she

was satisfied to hear that his voice was noticeably softer
than before.

"Not today. But I'll be back in time for supper
tonight." As Rand stood up, his riding boots gleamed
with an ebony sheen in the morning light, hugging his
calves and emphasizing well-hewn thighs in a way that
any decent woman would probably ignore. As matters
were, Rosalie could not help noticing how magnificent
he was in riding clothes, how tousled and masculine he
appeared with his gold-brown hair mussed and his face
unshaven. "If you need anything, tell Mireille or Madame Alvin," he said, and Rosalie smiled at him.

"I never dreamed I'd have my own companion," she
said, licking a tiny spot of honey off her forefinger. "I
should be at home, running to fetch Elaine's morning
tea, and instead I'm lolling in an ostentatious château in
France, trying to decide how best to spend my leisure
time."

As the thick braid of sable hair trailed over her
shoulder and down to her waist, as her rich blue eyes
shone with feline contentment, Rand stared at the
appealing picture she made. Still so innocent, so serene.
He wanted to crush her slender silken body in his arms
and hold her like that for days, inhaling her scent,
hearing every breath she took and every beat of her
heart.

"You should be at home safe with your mother," he
said thickly, and Rosalie glanced up in surprise at the
change in his tone. "Deciding which color your hair
ribbon should be, which boy to dance and flirt with at
the next ball."

"I . . ." she started to say, confused by his mercurial
mood, and then she decided to smile again. "Have a
good day," she said. Her smile faltered as Rand ignored her words and left abruptly, his thick, straight
brows drawing together as he closed the door with
absolute control.

He leaned against the wall in the outside hallway as soon as the latch clicked, closing his eyes and taking a deep, even breath.

"I can't do this anymore," he muttered, his hands clenched into tight, solid fists. "God help me, I can't read your mind, Rosalie, and I don't know what you want. I'm wrapped around those little fingers, wanting to jump every time you beckon and call . . . damn, but you're hard on a man's pride."

Sometimes she was a strong woman with mettlesome spirit, sometimes she was frail and in need of his strength—her changeability was part of what fascinated Rand about her, but it also made him wary. For a while he had to establish a safer distance from Rosalie, for he was far too vulnerable to her capricious moods, and it was apparent that she needed time to think.

"I think," Mireille said, her elfin features wrinkling in concentration, "we think . . . you think . . . they think . . . he think . . ."

"He *thinks,*" Rosalie corrected, turning the pages of the English book in search of another verb to conjugate. They sat in the small sunny garden at the back of the château near the glass-paneled doors that opened from a magnificent sitting room. Chairs and cushions had been set out for them by Monsieur Alvin so that they could study outdoors in complete comfort. The breeze was warm and pleasant, permeated with the fragrance of flowers, grass, sunlight, summer. "Mireille, you are a wonder. I've never met anyone with a memory like yours. Try this one—the verb 'to be.' I am, you are, we are—"

"—they are, he are," Mireille supplied triumphantly, and Rosalie suppressed a quick urge to laugh.

"No—"

"He am?"

"He *is,*" Rosalie said, her voice colored with no small

amount of sympathy. English was not as easy to learn as French, not by half. Mireille sighed in disgust, her dark brown eyes glowing with animation.

"The English language . . . *is* like the English people: *elle n'est pas raisonable.*"

"No, it doesn't make much sense," Rosalie agreed, closing the book while smiling at her petite companion. "I think that is enough for today."

"I can do more," Mireille said stubbornly. "What is this?" she asked, picking up the nearest object within reach.

"A book," Rosalie replied.

"And this?"

"A stone. And that is a door, that is a tree . . ."

"And this?"

"A flower," Rosalie said, taking the blossom from Mireille's tiny hand and examining it reverently. She had never seen such a spectacular rose. Its petals were luxuriant and profuse, fragile and pale, shaded with yellow near the center. The stem and leaves were glossy and dark green. Its perfume was sweet, mild, intoxicating. "A very beautiful flower."

"A Gloire de Dijon rose," a new voice joined the conversation. The two women turned to see the stout form of Monsieur Alvin as he returned from pruning and clipping the flowering ivy. He was not quite so wide in girth as Madame Alvin, but his smile was just as pleasant, his eyes twinkling with the satisfaction of a man who was at ease with his life and his work. He was the general caretaker of the château in the absence of the proprietor, but his main love and talent was gardening. "Beyond the maze there is another thicket of them, shaded with pink and not yellow, and they are not as large as these. They do not have the protection of a wall, as these do. Gloire de Dijon roses need protection . . . they are strong and sturdy at the base, but their petals are delicate. They need shelter from the wind and the elements in order to grow full and beautiful."

"Yes, I understand," Mireille said, her little grin taking on a mischievous quality as she glanced at Rosalie. "Don't all of Monsieur de Berkeley's roses need protection?"

"Mireille," Rosalie said pointedly, "you are a little cat." Although she spoke in English, Rosalie knew from Mireille's widening grin that she understood the gist of the statement.

Unfortunately, as day followed day and week followed week, Mireille had much less cause than she had originally thought to tease Rosalie about Rand. The truth was, Rand was seldom with them. He was gone most of the time, overseeing matters concerning the management and upkeep of the château. There were many concerns that had been put off year after year— repairs, bills and obligations that had finally accumulated in a pile that the Alvins were not capable of dealing with. He seemed to enjoy the challenges that were presented to him, but Rosalie sensed that something was constantly bothering him. He would come in sometimes after hard, long rides, his hair and skin damp with sweat, his face taut with frustration. He refused most of the time to meet her eyes, yet his conversation and his smiles were easy, glib, automatic. His attitude toward Rosalie became less and less that of a lover, more that of the fictitious cousin. He seemed bent on erasing any lingering traces of closeness between them, never seeing her alone except for the minute or so each morning when he stopped by after riding to inquire dutifully after her health.

Each night Mireille, Rosalie, Rand, and the Alvins shared the dinner table together, for in some aspects the château was run with notable informality. But even then Rosalie could not speak to Rand about anything other than the commonplace, because after the last

course was done most of the residents of the château
retired at nine o'clock. There was never an opportunity
for her to share a private moment with him. To her
disgruntled surprise Rosalie realized eventually that he
seemed to prefer it that way! She alternated between
resenting him and wanting the special intimacy they
had once known, but to all appearances Rand did not
seem to miss their closeness. At first she was bewildered, then desperate for his attention, then dully
resigned to the fact that she was not going to get it.

Despite her dissatisfaction with personal matters,
Rosalie's health improved rapidly. In a miraculously
short time she bloomed with vigor again, a condition
she credited almost entirely to Madame Alvin's cooking. She had never eaten so well before. Everything was
fresh and carefully prepared, seasoned and garnished
with the vegetables and herbs and spices that grew in
the sprawling garden behind the château. There were
smoked ham rubbed with salt, cloves, and anise, turkey
stuffed with raspberries, fried sole and roasted meats of
every variety. Each meal was preceded by a delicious
soup, such as *potage à la Monglas*, made with truffles
and mushrooms, or *à la Crécy*, with sweet orange
carrots . . . or pumpkin soup, Rosalie's favorite because it was served in a hollowed-out glazed pumpkin.
Next came the *entremets*, a dish that was served between
courses. Usually it consisted of light, pungent concoc-
tions such as ember-roasted truffles, pineapple cream,
or tiny soufflés. Desserts were always varied and abun-
dant: Orléans pudding, a smooth custard layered with
crushed biscuits . . . apricot fritters and marzipan tarts
cunningly shaped like hearts . . . heavenly pastries
composed of layer upon layer of flaky dough filled with
delicate creams and fruits.

Rosalie noticed that Mireille was also benefiting from
the food and the extra sleep. She was becoming less an
unnaturally poised child and more a rowdy, healthy

girl, her feet barely touching the floor as she raced around the château and the grounds. Together they walked through the grounds, talking excessively and never running out of conversation material. But they never discussed Rand or the obvious fact that Rosalie longed to reawaken his former interest in her, until finally one morning Rosalie broached the subject glumly while Mireille was twisting and pinning her hair at her bedchamber dressing table.

"Mireille, it's not going to work," she said, sighing as she met the girl's eyes with her own disconsolate blue gaze. "It's useless to try to attract his attention. You might as well let my hair alone and lay out sackcloth for me to dress in. The kinds of feelings he had for me in Paris are completely gone. The way he talks to me now, the way he looks at me . . . absolutely different from then. *Dieu,* he is so damned *kind* and *brotherly* that I want to choke him!"

"Oh, *mademoiselle* . . ." Mireille said, her smile very wry as she set down the lacquer-backed brush and leaned a hip against the table. "How can it be," she asked, fixing Rosalie with a steady gaze, "that I am fifteen and you are twenty, when I am so much older than you? How can you not see what is so obvious to me and everyone else here?"

"And what exactly do you see?"

"Perhaps it is true, that love makes one blind . . . if so, I hope I never fall in love, for *vraiment,* it makes such fools of men and women! Of course *monsieur* wants you! He does not in the least think of you as a brother would . . . don't you ever turn quickly and surprise the look in his eyes? When your head is turned, *ma foie,* how he stares at you." Mireille's voice lowered, and she went to close the door. When she returned, Rosalie's head was bent.

"What more can I do?" she asked, her voice almost quivering with pained eagerness. "I hang on to every word of his, I smile at him, I touch him, and he pulls away so politely . . . he *must* know how I feel, for he is perceptive and hardly inexperienced!"

"*Mademoiselle,* I do not know what has happened between you and him. I know you a little. I know nearly nothing about him. But I can say without doubt that he is waiting for you."

"Waiting? For me to do what?" Rosalie asked blankly.

"To decide what you want from him, and what he is to you, and he will approach you only when you have made up your mind. *C'est ça.* It is very simple." A long silence reigned in the room, and slowly Rosalie lifted her eyes to Mireille's. As the girl read the doubt in Rosalie's blue gaze, she sighed and made the motion of hitting her own head with a spread palm. "Bah!" she exclaimed. "I have said too much."

"No," Rosalie said quickly, "you haven't. I need someone to help me think through this. I can't quite believe that Rand might still want me as he once did."

"I saw him in Paris," Mireille said quietly, "when he thought you might not wake up ever again. He was *fou,* and that is no exaggeration."

"*Fou?*" Rosalie repeated, frowning curiously. It was a word she had not come across before.

"Mmmmn . . ." Mireille bit her lip as she considered how to explain it. "Yes, *fou*—when things are not right in the head or the heart. When something is wrong with the thinking . . ."

"Crazy," Rosalie said, and her eyes became round as she stared at the small maid. "Rand was—"

"Yes. Completely."

"Well, I am *fou* right now. Completely. Because my heart does know what I want from him, and my head tells me all the reasons why it is wrong. Ever since I met him, my thinking and my feelings have been at cross-purposes, pushing me toward him, pulling me away from him."

"And you wonder why he is cool to you?" Mireille pointed out gently.

"Are you suggesting that he has avoided me because he's protecting himself?"

"*Mais oui.*"

"Then how do I—?"

"I am the wrong one to give advice," Mireille said, suddenly standing up and brushing at imaginary dust on her skirts. Rosalie groaned and leaned her forehead against her hands.

"The problem seems so complicated, but it's ridiculously simple. My heart wants him for forever but my mind tells me that I can't have him that long, and so it would be better not to have him at all. Isn't the solution self-evident?"

"Yes," Mireille said, and suddenly she looked haunted. It was an odd expression for the face of a little sprite to wear. Her eyes turned dark with memories of a short but complicated past, which she refused to confide in anyone. "Yes, the answer would be easy for me to choose, *mademoiselle*. Happiness blows away as easily as feathers in a strong wind. It is not solid and complete . . . it comes in little pieces. Collect them when you can. It is worthless to spite the bits and pieces that you hold because of all that you cannot have."

"I'm sorry," Rosalie whispered. "I must seem very selfish to you."

"No." Abruptly the glimmer in Mireille's eyes disappeared, and she picked up the brush to resume arranging the locks of long, gleaming hair. Abruptly she changed the subject. "I heard in the kitchen this morning that Jérème saddled one of the horses in order for Monsieur de Berkeley to visit Monsieur Lefèvre, the local tax collector. He should be back early this afternoon. If you wish, you can see him then."

"A tax collector? I thought Rand had taken care of

the unpaid taxes weeks ago, when he came here to put
the château up for sale."

"I have heard that Monsieur Lefèvre is a very bad
man, a greedy man. After Monsieur de Berkeley sold
the d'Angoux land to the tenants who worked it,
Monsieur Lefèvre raised the land taxes. But the peasants cannot afford to pay him more."

"Why would Lefèvre do that?" Rosalie wondered
aloud, frowning. "Rand told me that land taxes are
already heavier on the peasantry than on the rich
landowners. You can't squeeze blood out of a stone."

"The peasants have no voice. This far from Paris the
local men of importance can do whatever they want.
The villages are their own kingdoms. Last night a
group of peasants came to the château to ask Monsieur
de Berkeley to speak to Lefèvre on their behalf, since
he is the highest-ranking man living in the district now,
and they remember his kindness in selling the land to
them at such a low price."

"I didn't hear a thing—"

"We had already retired," Mireille said, and then
gave a smug little smile. "But I know everything that
goes on here because Madame Alvin is a talkative
woman. And what she doesn't reveal, Ninette or Eleazar tells me."

"Rand certainly didn't mention anything about it to
me," Rosalie said, folding her arms and staring at the
mirror in disgruntlement. "But then, he probably
wants me to turn my attention to some other matters
that I've put off for a long time." She felt a quake of
apprehension in her stomach, and determinedly
squelched it. "Mireille . . . after you finish my hair, I
need some time alone. I have . . . a letter to write, and
I don't know how long it will take."

The floor was littered with crumpled attempts, each
one more difficult to begin than the last. Rosalie
refused to leave her desk until the job was done. She

had never envisioned herself in such a ludicrous position. How could she write a letter asking her mother if she were indeed her mother? Would Amille be hurt by her questions, would she be angered by them? And how did she feel about the fact that Rosalie was living under a man's protection in France? *Maman . . . it is not that I have abandoned the rules of morality you tried to teach me*, Rosalie thought, wishing that she could talk to Amille face-to-face instead of writing a stilted message. *But, Maman, you never told me what to do when something else seems more important. I have not been deluded by love, or passion . . . it's just that I have begun to realize there is no happiness in safety. I have to take chances.*

When the letter was done, she folded and sealed it carefully, tucking it into a stocking bag and tying the purse to the waist of her jade-green gown. Suddenly she noticed that because of the hours spent in the sunny garden, her skin had warmed from its usual fairness to a light peach color. "Good Lord," she said, examining her face, arms, and bosom critically in the thickly ornamented mirror, "I'll get as brown as Rand if I'm not careful." The sun had also illuminated her cheeks with bright pink crescents, causing her to sigh in dismay. "Brummell's daughter," she muttered, inspecting her nose to see if it had also been reddened by the sun. "If that's what I am, I've inherited the faults and none of the perfections." Slowly she raised a slender hand to her neck, touching the place where her gold circlet had so often hung on a ribbon. An odd chill ran through her as she realized that the father she had once cursed for not being alive might be in Calais that very moment. George Brummell—George Belleau . . . if they were one and the same, then how could Amille have kept the knowledge from her? "*Maman*," Rosalie said, reaching inside the stocking purse to feel the edge of the letter with her fingertips, "how could you be the former governess to my real mother?" With a quick shiver she released the letter and went to call for Mireille.

Rosalie followed Mireille's more forthright pace into the stable with a more cautious step, for it was unfamiliar territory. The stable smelled good, of hay, horses, leather, and feed, and she peered curiously at the spacious interior. She had never seen so many horse stalls. Even with Rand's recent purchases, only a small fraction were actually occupied. Jérème, a red-haired youth of eighteen, sat on a small stool in the act of carving nameplates for the new additions to the stable. At the entrance of the two women he stood up with a start and whipped off his hat.

"Mademoiselle Berkeley," he murmured, nodding his head in a gesture of respect, and then his pale brown eyes flickered to her companion with a great deal more familiarity. ". . . *et* Mireille."

"Hello," Rosalie said, her lips tilted upward in a vaguely inquiring smile. It was apparent that something had occurred between her companion and Jérème, for Mireille pointedly ignored the boy, her little nose lifting in the air as she brushed by him.

"These are the horses Monsieur de Berkeley purchased," the maid informed Rosalie. "They are very handsome, aren't they? . . . This is Whisper, and this is Linnette. The empty place is for Diamond, a big black one that *monsieur* has taken on his visit to Monsieur Lefèvre."

"Lefèvre . . ." Jérème joined the conversation eagerly, making a pretense of spitting on the ground after the name left his lips. "The whole village hates Monsieur Lefèvre. I do not believe he will make any agreement or bargain with Monsieur de Berkeley or anyone else. Lefèvre is too—"

"Monsieur de Berkeley has had vast experience negotiating with disagreeable officials," Rosalie said reassuringly, reaching out a hand to stroke Whisper's soft muzzle.

"With respect, *mademoiselle,* not with black-hearted men who like to squeeze every franc out of a little village and fill their own pockets with it."

"He runs a large shipping enterprise and has dealt very capably with stubborn customs agents who detest English imports," Rosalie replied. "I don't think Monsieur Lefèvre will present any difficulty to him."

"I hope you're right," Jérème murmured doubtfully.

Mireille stamped her tiny foot with characteristic impatience. "Of course she's right, idiot! Anyone who has ever stepped a foot out of the village would know that a customs agent is ten times more difficult to reason with than a little nothing of a tax collector!"

Rosalie grinned at her companion's worldly-wise air and sought for a way to change the subject, since Jérème was beginning to look distinctly offended. She clicked her tongue lightly to the aging chestnut horse beside Whisper. "Who is this?" Rosalie asked, unable to make out the blunted lettering on the nameplate.

"Revenant," Jérème answered.

Rosalie chuckled.

"In English his name is Spook, Mireille. I wouldn't recommend trying to ride him until we discover how he earned it."

As Mireille began to reply, her attention was caught by a tiny movement in the corner of an unoccupied stall and she flew toward it with an exclamation of delight. "*Mademoiselle!* Oh, come here and see!"

In the stall four kittens tumbled over each other, lively bundles of gray fur that swatted and pounced at each other, then peered at the approaching visitors with bright round eyes.

"How sweet," Rosalie crooned, her eyes gleaming with pleasure. She crouched beside Mireille without hesitation, her skirts billowing on the hay-sprinkled

ground. Scooping up one of the wriggling bodies,
Rosalie stroked her fingers over the downy fur and
discovered the tenuous vibrations of a purr against her
palms. The thought suddenly occurred to her that she
was behaving with a notable lack of dignity. No lady
would squat in a stable to coo over such a discovery—
but how soft the kitten was, how trusting and fragile.
Wonderingly she fit her palm over the entirety of its
tiny head, chuckling at the miniature ears, the wispy
strands of whiskers. As she held it against her neck,
clasping the little animal in a gentle hold, it scrabbled
for a more secure position and accidentally caught at
her skin with one frail claw. Still she did not release the
purring kitten, settling it against her shoulder and
standing up as she heard the multiple thuds of approaching hoofbeats.

Framed in the wide entrance to the barn, Rand
dismounted from a huge horse that gleamed like
ebony. The horse's large, sensitive nostrils were quivering from a fast-paced ride, his great sides expanding
and contracting with deep breaths. Large, shining
hooves pawed nervously at the ground in his unwilling-
ness to stop so suddenly.

"Cool him down well, Jérème," Rand said, the low
baritone of his voice carrying even though he spoke
softly. Rosalie stared at him in absorption, hugging her
arms around herself as she drank in the sight of him. So
many times she had seen him in the most expensive
evening clothes, cool, unruffled, and perfectly handsome, yet nothing or no one could compare with him as
he looked right now, exuding unvarnished masculinity
from every pore.

The sleeves of his simple white shirt were rolled up
to just above the elbows, revealing powerfully sculptured forearms and wrists. The garment clung to him
in damp patches, especially to the flatness of his midriff

and the broad, rock-solid surface of his back. As Rand turned to hand the reins of the horse to Jérème, Rosalie's gaze skimmed admiringly over his tall, broad-shouldered form, detecting the subtle changes that had occurred in him since they had come to the château. He had gained back the weight that he had lost during her illness in Paris, regaining that muscular sturdiness that made him appear so invulnerable. Riding breeches were adhered by perspiration to the tough, strapping lines of his thighs, hips, and the lean surface of his buttocks.

The sun had infused his skin with renewed color so that it shone with a rich shade of tan. Conversely, his hair was several shades lighter, soaked liberally with the molten glitter of gold. Walking with a limber stride to a nearby well, he bent to rinse his arms, face, and neck of the effects of the long ride. Not many men possessed his type of lusty vitality, of that Rosalie was certain. She would have to be deaf, dumb, and blind not to want him. The kitten mewed in protest at her tightening grip, and hastily Rosalie let it down.

Rand walked into the stable then, drops of fresh water flying everywhere as he shook his head to get the excess out of his hair. He stopped short when he saw Rosalie standing there.

"I thought I saw someone in here," he said, his hazel eyes traveling over her slowly.

"I wanted to speak with you . . ." Rosalie began, her voice fading away as Rand frowned and walked over to her.

"You've got a scratch," he said, looking down at the thin line of red that marred the pearly smoothness of her shoulder.

"Oh, that's nothing, I don't even feel it now," she began, flinching as his hand brushed dangerously close to her breast. "It's from . . ." She found that she could barely speak as his hand settled at her waist. Rand's head lowered an inch as he bent to hear her more clearly.

"What?" he asked, his breath moist and cool from the fresh well water. His nearness was so overwhelming that Rosalie could only lift her head to stare at him mutely. They both became tense and still with anticipation, a delicious excitement burgeoning in the silence between them.

"I . . . It's nothing," Rosalie finally managed to whisper, her eyes round and as blue as sapphires, searching for what was hidden in the depths of his hazel gaze. She had never wanted him so desperately. Rand's fingers tightened at her waist. He took a shallow breath and started to say something——she would never know what, for just then he noticed the shuffling in the nearby stall.

"Mireille," Rand said wryly, and Rosalie's hand flew up to her cheek, for she had completely forgotten about her companion and the kittens. "I see you've acquired some new charges to look after," Rand commented, his eyes filled with sudden laughter.

Mireille gathered up an apronful of kittens and bobbed a curtsy to him. "*Bonjour, monsieur.* How did it go with Monsieur Lefèvre?"

"Very well. He can, on occasion, be made to see reason."

Mireille threw him a brilliant grin, her brown eyes snapping with satisfaction. "That is not his reputation, *monsieur.* You must be a remarkable opponent for him to change his mind about matters of the purse."

"I'm not surprised," Rosalie stated matter-of-factly. "It is never pleasant to be on the opposite end of a disagreement with Monsieur de Berkeley."

Rand smiled at her. Reluctantly his hand slid from her waist and he stepped away as if he were striving to place a necessary distance between them. "You wanted to talk to me?" he asked.

Rosalie nodded, fingering the top of her stocking purse. "Yes." Slowly she pulled out the letter and handed it to him. "I wanted to give this to you. Can you . . . would you mail it as soon as possible?" There was a long silence as Rand read the name and the address on the finely milled paper. His eyes rested on her thoughtfully, narrowing slightly as he read the combination of emotions that played across her delicate features. Her eyes were bright with frustrated desire, her mouth tender as she smiled tremulously. "It's time I was more honest," she whispered. "I'd like to start with this letter. And I'd like to be more straightforward with you." She wanted to say more but would not dare with Mireille there.

"Mireille," Rand said, still staring at Rosalie, "why don't you go find the kittens' mother?" His voice was husky as he added, "Take your time about it. And if Jérème starts to come back with Diamond, tell him the horse needs to be walked another ten minutes."

"*Oui, monsieur,*" Mireille murmured .dutifully, scampering out of the stable with an expression of unholy glee.

Rand smiled, his manner suddenly lazy and comfortable as he looked down at Rosalie.

"There's no need to send her away," Rosalie said, experiencing a small, unexpected measure of discomfort at the realization that she was alone with him for the first time in what seemed to be weeks. "I've said all that I intended to—"

"For what I have in mind," Rand said, pressing her backward until she was trapped in the corner of the stable, "I thought you'd prefer some privacy."

She began to stammer, flustered as he held her fast and lowered his mouth to hers. His arms went around her to shield her from the rough planking of the wall. She felt the unyielding strength of his body against hers . . . a large body that could crush hers easily, yet all his power was held in check. She opened her mouth to his, craving the taste of him, suddenly drunk with the sensation of his tongue mating with hers. Making a tiny moan of protest as he lifted his head, Rosalie wrapped her arms around his neck, standing on the tips of her toes to bury her face against the warm column of his throat. She loved him. She could not resist his touch, nor her own unconquerable desire to please him, to touch him tenderly.

"My sweet Rose," Rand whispered, then laughed breathlessly at the feel of her seeking mouth on his skin. "Wait a minute . . . don't do that. God, you're so small . . ."

He hooked his foot around a low stool and pulled it to the corner, swinging her up onto it in one easy motion. Now their eyes were at the same level. Rosalie clutched at him as she felt the tiny stool wobble.

"I'll fall," she whispered, and he shook his head slightly while sliding his arms around her back.

"Not if you hold on to me."

She stood quietly, leaning into him as she accepted the love play of his mouth. He caught at her top lip gently, then her bottom lip, tasting the corners, delving inside in a soft, knowing way that made her knees weaken. Over and over he kissed her, his kisses light and searching, his fingers threading through her hair and cradling her scalp in order to position her head. She loved being held by him. She tasted the salt of his skin and savored the flavor of him, she let her fingers wind through his wet hair, she felt the thud of his heartbeat against her breasts and thought that she would die if only to have him fill her with his own flesh just one more time. His hand slipped intimately inside the bodice of her gown, cupping a breast. As the soft peak responded to his touch by contracting against his palm, Rosalie sucked in a quick breath of much-needed air, her mind swimming in a rush of pleasure.

Suddenly aware that it was possible for someone to hear her or walk in and see them, Rosalie jerked her mouth away from his and fought to pull his hand out of her gown.

"Rand," she gasped, "what if someone comes in and sees you making love with your 'little cousin from England'?"

"It's not at all unusual for first cousins to become involved with each other," Rand said, ignoring the fluttering of her hands as he cupped her breast more possessively. "A little scandalous, perhaps—"

"And if I were your cousin," Rosalie panted, "you would have more regard for me than to do this in a stable!" As she tried one last time to remove his hand from her bodice, the stool wobbled dangerously, and she wrapped her arms more tightly around him. "Rand, I'm going to break my neck! Rand . . ." Her protests began to fade away as his lips touched hers delicately, the light pressure much more erotic than a bruising kiss could have been. "What if someone sees?" she murmured helplessly, her eyes closing. His mouth was warm and sweet as he kissed her once more, and then all Rosalie cared about was the consummate movements of his lips on hers.

"It has driven me mad to watch you these past few weeks," Rand said, his mouth sliding down to the tiny scratch on her shoulder. The feathery stroke of his tongue soothed her skin, leaving a tingling streak of dampness as he moved on to the base of her throat. "So pristine, dressed so immaculately, every hair in place . . . I've wanted to do this . . ." His hand gathered up the thin material of her skirt, then slipped underneath to find the smooth contours of her thigh, the soft roundness of her buttocks. Her thin underclothes provided no barrier to his invading hand. Impatiently he brushed them aside, intent on reaching the bare, quivering flesh underneath.

"Rand!" she gasped, her eyes flying open to cast a glance around the empty stable. The entire scene seemed slightly askew, faintly blurred. "What if someone . . . what if—?" He pressed his mouth between her breasts, his breath now touching her flesh with the heat of steam. She sighed, tilting her head back as she felt his sensitive fingers slide between her thighs in a slow, satin caress. Her entire body felt light and weightless, anchored by his possessive arms. He stroked her so softly, his fingertips measuring her responses and focusing on the tiny nerves that softened and expanded in pleasure.

"Rose, how I need you," he murmured, and as he discovered the silky dampness of her delicate flesh, Rand groaned as if in pain.

Rosalie arched against him, her face flushing as her pulse increased to a rapid pounding. "I didn't know . . . if you wanted me any longer," she said, her voice hushed, her lips parting as he stole another warm, languorous kiss from her. Exquisite sensations spilled through her, their melted richness easing the hungry dryness of need.

"Not want you?" Rand repeated softly, and his lips slid over the incredible smoothness of the skin underneath her jaw. "Little fool . . . I've told you before that you're mine. Yes, I want you . . . I want to feel you tight around me, holding me inside your body, your arms locked around my neck. I want you to look at me with a different expression in your eyes than when you look at anyone else . . . I want you to turn to me for anything you need, for comfort, for help, for pleasure—"

"I already do," she whispered, and the teasing movements of his fingers stopped as he caught his

breath, his gold-green eyes locking with hers. "Please
. . . don't stop," Rosalie panted, feeling like a rope that
had been drawn too tightly, beginning to unravel.

Rand gathered her closer, his low, hungry murmur
searing her oversensitive ears. "I won't stop, sweet . . .
I know exactly what you need."

Suddenly the passionate revelry was shredded by the
sound of a girl's scream.

"Mireille," Rosalie breathed, her desire cooling rapidly as she wondered what had happened.

In a split second Rand rearranged her clothing and
swung her down from the stool. The slumberous gleam
in his eyes had been instantly replaced by alertness, and
he cast a brief warning glance at her. "Stay here," he
said, leaving through the stable door at an easy, loping
pace.

Eleven

> Love bade me welcome; yet my soul drew back,
> Guilty of dust and sin.
> But quick-eyed Love, observing me grow slack
> From my first entrance in,
> Drew nearer to me, sweetly questioning
> If I lacked anything.
>
> —George Herbert

Mireille held a hand over her heart, the childish lines of her bosom moving rapidly up and down as she endeavored to catch her breath. Standing in front of her was a tall, rangy young man somewhere in his mid-twenties. He was dressed in well-worn clothes, a cloth sack slung over one shoulder. Mireille turned with a start as Rand approached, pasting a thin smile on her lips.

"I'm sorry, *monsieur,* it's nothing . . . this is Guillaume Germain, my brother. He startled me, that is all . . . I did not mean to be so foolish."

Rand's expression was inscrutable as he looked at the girl, for it was obvious that something was very wrong. Her eyes were filled with unshed tears, her breath short, not from surprise but from extreme anxiety. Lazily the stranger smiled, as if nothing untoward had happened, extending a hand in greeting.

"I am glad to meet you, Monsieur de Berkeley. I see my little sister is as silly as usual, jumping at shadows."

"What are you doing here?" Rand asked, calm but hardly polite as he ignored the man's outstretched hand.

"I came to find Mira. I returned to the *hôtel* in Paris after looking for work, and found only a little note explaining where she had gone. *Naturellement,* I had to discover if all was well with her . . . a little morsel like Mira, you understand, is a prime target for unscrupulous characters—"

"And knowing that, you still feel justified in leaving her alone while you disappear for weeks?" Rand inquired, his sardonic expression indicating exactly what he thought about that.

"A man must work to eat," Guillaume pointed out, shrugging lightly. He was about to continue, when suddenly his eyes fixed on an object past Rand's shoulder, and he fell into an intent silence. Turning, Rand saw that Rosalie had disobeyed his command, following him outside to see for herself what was going on. Even through his inward exasperation, Rand had to admit that she was extraordinarily lovely in that moment, her blue eyes wide with curiosity, her lips rosy and soft from his kisses, her hair escaping from its precise arrangement into wispy curls that brushed against her flawless skin.

"Mademoiselle," Mireille said hurriedly, "this is Guillaume."

"Hello," Rosalie said, coming to stand by Rand as she regarded the stranger with immediate interest. She found it strange that Mireille was looking at the new arrival with nothing resembling sisterly affection. The girl's cheeks were pale, her eyes so dark that they were almost black. Guillaume met Rosalie's gaze and smiled, his grin charming and infectious, his teeth white, his eyes sparkling. Guillaume Germain was a very attractive man and he seemed to be completely aware of this fact.

His face was carved with an exquisite attention to detail, every curve of his mouth, every filament of his eyebrows almost perfectly arranged. Like Mireille, he had eyes of the darkest, most velvety brown, and hair as black as a raven's wing. He was tall, his posture one of

languid grace, his body lean almost to the point of
thinness. He also appeared to have Mireille's happy-go-
lucky charm, for the twinkle in his eyes and the
brilliance of his smile were utterly engaging. Why was
it, then, that she could only admire his attractiveness in
a disinterested, abstract manner? Why didn't his looks
have the forceful effect on her that Rand's did?

Succumbing to a basic feminine curiosity, Rosalie
silently compared the two men. Although they were of
a similar height, there was a night-and-day difference
between them. Guillaume's agreeable face and form
did not stand a chance against Rand's physical potency.
Nothing could compare with Rand's lean, lithe body
and square shoulders, his dark gold hair and burnished
skin, hazel eyes that could dance with amusement or
gleam with moodiness. He was frustrating and arousing, and it would take a lifetime to completely understand him . . . but only with Rand did waltzing become
pure magic, only he could make her wild with passion,
only he would dare to discipline her one minute and
then tease and indulge her shamelessly the next. It
would always be Rand, she realized, no matter whom
she compared him with.

Rosalie met his eyes and saw that he had duly noted
her inspection of Guillaume. A trace of moody jealousy
flickered in his gaze, and then it was deftly concealed.

"This is not the sort of welcome I had envisioned,"
Guillaume commented to Rosalie. "I only meant to—"

"Do you usually make it a practice to wander unin-
vited around another man's land?" Rand asked bluntly.
"If so, you know to expect a less-than-enthusiastic
welcome." He glanced at Rosalie once more, and when
it became apparent that she had no sort of interest in
Guillaume, his expression became less wary.

"I rarely walk into a situation before making an
appraisal of it," the younger man replied, his gaze
direct and frank. "I did not know what sort of people

Mira was with, nor what kind of position she might be in."

"As you can see, she is content," Rand said, and Mireille nodded, her little face looking pinched. If the situation had been less serious, Rosalie would have had to smother a sudden laugh, for at the moment Mireille appeared to be anything but content. "Now that your concern has been satisfied," Rand continued, "is there anything else you would care to ask?"

"Actually, there is," Guillaume admitted. "I find it necessary to ask a favor of you."

"I thought so."

"I have spent all of my money coming here to find Mira. I have nothing to eat and no place to sleep."

"An unenviable set of circumstances."

"Is it just that a brother should suffer because of his feelings for his sister? You would surely not judge a man harshly for that. And it looks as if there are several uses around the château for another pair of hands. Your estate is impressive but its condition could be improved," Guillaume said carefully, his smile faltering as he began to see that trying to elicit Rand's sympathy was like chipping away a stone wall with a spoon.

"Your diagnosis is appreciated," Rand said, his translucent gaze flickering to Mireille to evaluate her reaction to the turn of the conversation. She appeared to be holding her breath, her expression apprehensive. "However, I have all the help I need from the village."

"The village?" Guillaume parried. "An excellent source of unskilled labor, I have no doubt. But for some of the tasks around here my talent would be more effective. In swordsman's terms, why use a pair of fists when you have the accuracy of a foil at your disposal?"

"You are skilled with a blade?" Rand inquired politely.

"I have skill with many things," Guillaume responded immediately.

"Including horses?"

"I can do anything, *monsieur.*"

Suddenly Rand's eyes flashed with brief sparks of laughter, his mouth twitching at one corner. "Apparently a common sentiment among members of your family, Germain." He looked down at Rosalie with a mocking inquiry. "What is your opinion on the matter, my disobedient little friend?"

From the undertones of his voice, Rosalie gathered that she had most definitely fallen into disfavor as a result of following him out of the stable. She chose her words cautiously, wishing she had chosen to stay where he had told her.

"Judging from your present mood, you'll do the opposite of whatever I advise," she said. "I think I'll keep silent."

"Mireille?" Rand asked, judiciously giving the girl a chance to offer an opinion, but the dark-haired maid shrugged as she stared down at the ground.

"Whatever you think, *monsieur,*" Mireille murmured.

"Then, Guillaume, provided that you have no aversion to working in the stables, you can stay. Mireille will take you to the gardens to see Monsieur Alvin . . . discuss with him the matter of your responsibilities and salary. Since he's getting on in years, I imagine you'll be required occasionally to aid him in his gardening."

"Thank you. I appreciate your kindness, *monsieur,*" Guillaume said, his smile one of relief. Mireille indicated the way to the gardens, her head still bent in a dutiful attitude. As soon as the pair had gone a good distance from them, Rosalie turned to Rand with a faintly puzzled expression.

"Isn't it strange how they—?"

"When," he interrupted, his hand clenching her upper arm in a decidedly biting grip, "are you going to start listening to what I tell you to do?"

"I always listen to you," Rosalie said, jumping slightly and making a vague effort to wriggle away from him.

"But rarely obey."

"I'm not some servant," she countered defensively, "who has to jump whenever you—"

"My sweet Rose," he said, his voice containing a mixture of weariness and distaste, his fingers dropping from her arm, "I didn't tell you to stay in the stable in order to satisfy some petty despotic fantasy. Usually I have a reason for what I do and say—in this case, your safety."

Instantly her spark of rebellion was extinguished. Rand's coolness wound around her subtly, eliciting a strong feeling of regret.

"I did not disregard your request out of spite," she offered stiffly. "I followed you impulsively."

She stood before him with a down-bent head, and Rand's hazel gaze caressed her warmly. Suddenly he wanted to pull her into his arms and tell her that there had been no harm done, that he understood her impulsiveness and she could do anything she wanted as long as it pleased her. Ruthlessly he squashed the impulse, cursing himself for letting his emotions rule his head whenever she was concerned. It was far too important to make her realize how serious the issue was. The events in Paris were never far from his thoughts, and he was determined never to let anyone hurt her again.

"I would prefer to continue allowing you complete freedom," he said gently. "But I will keep you under lock and key if I have to, until you decide to trust me."

"I trust you," she whispered. As she stared into his velvet-green eyes and felt them look into her very soul, she felt drawn to him in a way that no words could explain.

"Good." Rand let the subject drop, and swallowing hard, he turned her in the direction of the château.

"I'll walk you back. It's almost time for *déjeuner,* and I'm hungry."

Rosalie nodded and took his arm obediently, her lips having frozen together as questions, few in number but large in significance, plagued her mind. What about all that had gone on in the stable before they had been interrupted? Rand seemed to have forgotten all about it, but she certainly hadn't! Her body felt empty and tender with unfulfilled desire. Did Rand intend to pick up where they had left off at any point in the future? If he still wanted her, why didn't he make love to her? There was nothing in the world to stop him from coming to her bed at night—least of all Rosalie herself!

"The notary and the vicar both wish to call on you later this afternoon, Monsieur de Berkeley," Ninette reported dutifully, bringing calling cards to Rand on a highly polished silver tray. "Tomorrow there are also many people who wish to express their gratitude and to give you their thanks."

"Express gratitude?" Guillaume repeated, having come into the sitting room to partake of a new jug of lemonade. He had been working industriously the entire morning in the French and Chinese gardens, digging and mulching, washing porcelain figurines and cleaning the beds of colored sand that bordered the garden walks. His black hair clung damply to his head, his deep brown eyes framed with moisture-spiked black lashes. A faint trace of sun-induced color gleamed along his cheeks and the bridge of his nose, enhancing his considerable attractiveness.

As Rosalie smiled and handed him a tall glass of soothing liquid, Guillaume's smile faded. "Thank you," he said, his thriftless charm replaced by a gentleness that was unusual for him to display. Rosalie seemed to have that effect on everyone, he observed much later to

Mireille. Not only did he feel it, but he noticed that even Rand's fierce temper could be calmed with a few of her gentle words and her smile. Everyone jumped to do the smallest favor for her. It became increasingly obvious that the small community of the château revolved around her. Perhaps it had something to do with her intrinsic sweetness and the unexpected tartness that occasionally tempered her wit. Perhaps it was her beauty and the fantastically blue eyes that sometimes gleamed almost violet. Even Jean-David, the crusty old man who had come to work as the butler, seemed caught in her spell. "That one," he would say after she had passed by, "is a *sirène.*" A creature who could laugh like a child, sing like an angel, and love like a woman.

As Rosalie seated herself gracefully in an embroidered chair similar to Mireille's, she stretched out a hand to receive the stack of calling cards. Busily she thumbed through them after bestowing a gentle smile on Ninette.

"Not only the notary and the vicar," she said, flipping through the gilt-edged cards with pleasure, "but also two bankers, a physician, a score of small landowners, and a few members of the *noblesse.* And assorted wives and daughters. They want to congratulate Monsieur de Berkeley on his contribution to the maintenance of the public well-being."

"Really," Guillaume said, eyeing Rand with interest. "Pray, how did you achieve such popularity?"

"He spoke on behalf of the villagers," Rosalie said, jumping in before Rand could say a word, "to Monsieur Lefèvre, a scoundrel who had intended to raise the land taxes of the small landowners, depriving hungry people of food, taking money from those who could least afford—"

"In short," Rand interrupted laconically, smiling

reluctantly at Rosalie's enthusiastic recitation, "I'm being canonized for a ten-minute meeting with a pinch-fisted tax collector."

"And what is frustrating," Rosalie continued to Guillaume, "is that he won't tell anyone exactly what he said to Lefèvre."

"It does not bear repeating in mixed company," Rand murmured.

"Nevertheless you have made yourself extremely popular," she rejoined wickedly. "And I intend to take advantage of it by enjoying the company of our visitors."

"I don't know if you're well enough to receive callers," Rand said thoughtfully. For a split second Rosalie did not know if he was teasing or not.

"Not well enough? You of all . . ." she began, stopping abruptly as she realized what she had been about to say. *You of all people know how well I am.* Her mind flickered back to those lusty moments in the stable, her skirts pulled up to her waist . . . shaken by a rush of adrenaline, a soaring elation that could not be confined . . . the velvet bliss that had deepened after the first feverish desperation . . . the heavy languor that had filled her body, their tongues, tasting and exploring . . . the warmth of his large hand on her hip, his thumb stimulating sensitive nerves along the way to . . . *Enough!* she reprimanded herself, appalled at the path her mind had taken. A bright blush burned in her cheeks as she met his eyes. Rand stared at her intently, a slow smile pulling at his wide mouth as if he knew exactly what she was thinking. You devil, she thought in discomfort, and tried to conceal her agitation in a hasty swallow of lemonade. Guillaume watched the byplay with interest.

"I do not think *mademoiselle* would be tired by a few visitors," Mireille piped up in the silence, and Rand released Rosalie from his pinning stare as he glanced over at the young girl.

"Then, bowing to your opinion, we'll let her have a go at the company tonight," he said. "Unfortunately I can only predict that Rosalie will be bored out of her little slippers."

At this comment Rosalie directed a mild, questioning frown at him, wondering what he meant.

Mireille interrupted hurriedly, hoping to prevent an argument from brewing, for she was becoming experienced enough to read the signs. "I have heard that there are a few rumors going around the community about *mademoiselle*. They are very curious about her."

"Probably," Rosalie said, suddenly laughing in a sweet, infectious way that caused even Rand to smile, "they think Monsieur de Berkeley has a mad old crone locked in the attic."

"Or a treasure," Rand added softly, "that he means to guard quite jealously."

Her cheeks colored even deeper as she averted her gaze from him and directed her attention to the glass of lemonade.

As Rand had predicted, the endless round of callers quickly lost its novel appeal for Rosalie. Introduced to the guests as Monsieur de Berkeley's gently bred little cousin from England, she was forced according to custom to entertain the wives, daughters, and womenfolk while Rand received the men in a separate but adjacent room to discuss politics, current events, and theory.

"I think," Rosalie said grimly on the third repetition of such an evening, "that we should break tradition and all have a discussion together. Men *and* women. Like they do in Paris."

They stood alone in the receiving room, Mireille

having conveniently disappeared after the last guest had taken leave.

"This is not Paris, *petite*," Rand said, amused but sympathetic. "This is a small district in the country, where it has taken hundreds of years for the present customs to develop. I take it, then, that you don't enjoy the separation of the sexes?"

"Not when mine is so boring!"

Rand burst out into laughter, his eyes glinting. "I've never thought that, *petite*."

"Heaven help me," Rosalie continued doggedly, "after what happened in Paris, I never thought I'd want to go back there, but much more of this and I'll walk there myself. The women here are so empty-headed—all they can talk about is how to run a household, how to get the servants to do more work, what to eat for breakfast on a particularly hot day . . . and the ones who can read—do you think they would waste their time on the weekly paper, or even on something by Molière? No, they read the fashion pages, so that they can enliven the discussion with information on the new style of hats or hairstyles!"

"*Pauvre* Rose," he said, "I would invite you into our discussions gladly, but I think your presence would prove to be somewhat inhibiting. Not for me, you understand—"

"I know that," she interrupted, folding her arms across her chest and pacing across the receiving-room tiles as Rand leaned against the fireplace mantel and watched her lazily. "At least you don't mind allowing me the freedom to say what I think. But if these women are so silly that they have to be put in a separate room with their own inane conversation, they certainly wouldn't dare to contradict anything the men have to say!"

"If you're angling to be invited into the men's salon when we call upon the Huraults tomorrow afternoon,"

Rand informed her unequivocably, "your hopes are in vain. We won't be in France beyond the end of summer, so our stay is not long enough to justify the breaking of a two-hundred-year-old tradition. Therefore, as the summer continues, you can expect to become an expert on the subject of women's hats."

"Then *you* can expect," Rosalie said evenly, "that by the end of summer I will be reduced to the intelligence of a child."

Unsuccessfully Rand tried to keep a straight face. "Most men prefer their women that way," he pointed out.

"But not you," she countered, her lips suddenly curving in a smile that faintly echoed his. "Not you, Rand . . . you have a low tolerance for simpleminded people."

"You know me so well," he said, his tone gentle but somehow mocking. Rather than waste her time trying to puzzle him out, Rosalie sighed and went to the stairs.

"Good night, Rand."

"Good night," he responded, settling his broad shoulder more firmly against the wall and continuing to smile in that strange, subtly caustic way as he watched her depart.

In the days that followed, Rosalie endured the visits they received and the visits they made in return, finding gradually that although they were not intellectually stimulating, there was still enjoyment to be found in others' company. She and Rand, with Mireille and Madame Alvin faithfully in tow, attended breakfasts and private dinners, listening to occasionally competent instrument players. Sometimes there were entertaining singers to listen to, and sometimes the assemblage would all join in the music-making, raising their voices to the ceiling with a variety of results. Rand further endeared himself to the community by bringing down a wild boar on a hunting expedition with several country gentlemen, and the huge bloody tusks of the animal were admired and coveted as if they had been solid gold. He only laughed when Rosalie shuddered at Guillaume's vivid description of the hunt. Guillaume had accompanied him enthusiastically and wasted none of his inventiveness in the telling of the tale.

Rosalie had at first been mildly surprised by Rand's decision to take Guillaume along on the hunt. But after thinking on the matter she decided that a friendship between the two men was not unexpected. After all, Rand liked anyone that he could not easily intimidate, and that aside, Guillaume was eminently likable. Ready to plunge foolhardily into any situation, any adventure, Guillaume liked to make impossible boasts and live up to them. He had lived an existence as varied as it was possible for one man's life to be, having dragged Mireille on more than half of his escapades. He did not often volunteer anything more than superficial information about the things he had done and seen, nor did he allow Mireille to say much about the past. To ward against self-incrimination, he explained . . . and although it was said in a mischievous way, there was more than a touch of seriousness behind his words. Guillaume liked to live by his wits, and that failing, the sword that he kept well-polished and supple through frequent practice. Each day he engaged in a series of exercises in the garden in the early-morning hours while the ground was still half-shadowed and the day not yet begun. It so happened that this was also the time that Rand liked to ride.

Rand pulled up Diamond and sat in quiet observation one morning, his eyes narrowing in interest as he watched the flickering shadows of swordplay. Guillaume had the mark of an accomplished swordsman, one who had had little classical training but much practical experience. His knees were flexible and his movements lightning quick, a combination that had probably ensured his survival numerous times despite the poorness of his posture. Over and over he practiced guards and lunges, forming pattern after pattern as the foil flashed in the approaching sunrise. Gradually his movements slowed as he realized that he had an audience. He turned to meet Rand's eyes.

"I hope for your sake that your matches are always this uneven," Rand said, smiling slowly.

Guillaume grinned, waving the capped tip of his foil at the empty space in front of him. "Uneven is the way I prefer them, *monsieur*."

"May I offer a suggestion with the utmost respect for your considerable skills?"

"Monsieur de Berkeley," Guillaume said gravely, his eyes twinkling, "there have been and will continue to be times when my life depends on my ability with the sword. All suggestions are welcomed and accepted with the utmost gratitude. I do not like to gamble with my life . . . it is a possession valuable to myself if not to others."

"You present an unnecessarily broad target for your opponent," Rand said, dismounting and winding Diamond's reins around a fragile tree branch. "On the last combination your guard was so wide that you could have been skewered neatly after the double feint. If you angle your body more this way . . . you will change from being difficult to hit to well-nigh impossible."

"Damn," Guillaume said appreciatively, eyeing Rand with speculation. "I have only one foil to practice with, *monsieur*. But if you could lay your hands on one and would ever care to engage in a bout . . ."

"It sounds like an interesting possibility," Rand admitted. In London he was known foremost as an excellent shot, but he was a proficient enough swords-

man, having been trained in his youth and teens until
he had gained the capability to fight his way out of a
rough spot.

"I hope you will consider it," the younger man
replied sincerely. "As I indicated, the need to improve
is always a pressing one for me."

"Tell me," Rand said, a mild frown working between
his strongly marked brows, "is Mireille often exposed
to these situations in which you——?"

"Only two or three times in her life," Guillaume
replied instantly. "Only when absolutely necessary. I do
not like to expose her to brutality or violence." Slowly
he added, "Not when she was forced to see so much of
it as a little girl. Our mother was a whore, you see."
This last was said matter-of-factly, in the way that he
might have said "our mother had red hair" or "our
mother liked sweetened porridge." Rand smiled inwardly, for he had just reason to say the same thing
about Hélène Marguerite in much the same manner.
There were many different kinds of whores, only some
were far more hypocritical than others.

"We both look like her, Mira and I," Guillaume
continued, "even though our fathers were different.
She is dead now . . . caught servicing a room full of
enemy soldiers in a hideaway in 1812. It was then that I
took Mira under my protection . . . dubious as my
protection may be. I've never completely abandoned
her, though God knows she's had to learn to take care
of herself." Guillaume smiled reminiscently. "Feisty
little morsel . . . I saw her for the first time when she
was not quite twelve years old, raging in the corner
because she had been told that she would have to start
servicing customers to take up the slack that our
mother had left behind."

Rand tried to envision Mireille at twelve. If she were
this tiny and fairylike at fifteen, how could any rational
being have suggested then that she could have taken a

full-fledged man between her thighs and survived the
first night? Guillaume saw the question in his eyes and
smiled again, this time less pleasantly. "Female customers," he said. "At least that was the intention . . .
Apparently it didn't appeal to Mira."

"Outwardly she seems untouched by all of it," Rand
said, taking the foil from Guillaume and absently
testing its balance in his hand.

"Don't you believe that she doesn't remember every
shred of it," Guillaume said with certainty. "She has a
mind like a dry sponge, remembers everything, especially things you don't want her to know. Like a little
cat creeping around the corners to see what's what.
And what's worse, the older she gets, the worse her
scrapes are."

"I don't doubt it," Rand said, shaking his head
ruefully. "I don't doubt it at all."

Rosalie and Mireille had spent the morning altering
one of Rosalie's thin white cambric gowns. The weath-
er had been consistently warm and dry for the past
several days and showed every promise of continuing in
such a manner. That and the fact that Rand was gone
on a trip to Havre had caused Rosalie to sleep poorly.
Knowing that he was sleeping at the Lothaire that
night, so far away from the château . . . so far away
from *her* . . . caused a mild depression to hang over her
like a cloud. The minute he had left after brushing a
perfunctory kiss on her forehead, a large gap had been
created in her world that would not be filled until he
was back. During the days that he was gone, Rosalie
had endeavored to occupy herself by fixing her mind
on other things. After asking into the state of Mireille's
summer clothing, for the girl seemed to possess nothing lighter than a gown with elbow-length sleeves, she
had been horrified to discover the limited extent of
Mireille's wardrobe. It contained almost nothing suit-

able for a hot climate except a brown dress that was shamefully tattered.

Unfortunately, after the monumental task of forcing Mireille to accept the gift was accomplished, altering the gown appeared to be yet another mountain to climb. It was not merely a matter of shortening the hem and taking in the bodice. The entire dress had to be remade to properly fit the girl's diminutive dimensions. After hours of diligent cutting and sewing, careful fittings and many frustrated exclamations, the job was done.

They decided to go for a walk to stretch their cramped limbs. Rosalie felt no small measure of satisfaction with herself as she saw Mireille promenade carefully along the garden path, lifting the hem of the lace-and-cambric dress at every grain of colored sand that strayed in her way. She wondered how long it had been since the girl had had a new gown, but forbore to ask in deference to Mireille's privacy. As they neared a patch of Gloire de Dijon roses they heard the noises of industrious pruning and clipping. On the other side of the thicket they found Guillaume, who greeted them with a slightly crooked smile and then succumbed eagerly to their pleas to join them under the shade of a cool peach tree for an early-afternoon break. Rosalie's unease and unanswered questions concerning the strained relationship between Mireille and Guillaume had long since disappeared. The brother and sister had rapidly gained an ease together that bespoke a long and familiar acquaintance. Perhaps Mireille's first startled reaction to her brother's presence at Château d'Angoux could be explained by the mere surprise of seeing him when she had not expected him. In any case, they had become much more companionable since Guillaume had first appeared.

"Look at you . . . *mon Dieu*, what a pretty girl," Guillaume exclaimed, causing his tiny sister to flush with pleasure. "Ah, wait, Mira—seat yourself carefully, you don't want the grass to stain your gown." As Mireille seated herself inch by inch onto the ground, he spoke in a warm undertone to Rosalie. "Thank you, gracious angel. I appreciate any kindness done for Mira as if it were done for me."

"Oh, please don't thank me," Rosalie said, the delicious softness of her lips curving into a smile as she looked up at him. "I wish I had more to give her. You don't know what she's done for me." As she met his eyes, dark brown and lightened with hues of cinnabar, she suddenly became confused. In his gaze there shone a flash of hunger, adoration . . . regret, tumbled in a bewildering way. Then it was extinguished as he turned his face away, as if he were afraid of what she might see there.

"Sometimes I don't believe you're real," he murmured, smiling as if to himself. "I gave up believing in angels a long time ago, Rosalie . . . Berkeley."

She frowned at the deliberate pause, the subtle emphasis he placed on the last name. Forcing her expression to smooth itself out, she went to sit down by Mireille. Soon Guillaume began to entertain her with tales of a troupe of traveling players that he and Mireille had once joined, and Rosalie began to giggle at the ludicrous snippets of verse and dialogue that he recited. Mireille soon joined in, adroitly supplying the parts that he had forgotten over time. Soon the two women were weak with laughter, the humor made all the more piquant by Guillaume's straight face.

". . . and between acts Mira and I would provide the entertainment while they changed scenes," he said, picking up three peaches from the ground and juggling them as he continued. "Mira wore a tasty little outfit— orange, I believe it was—cut right off at the knees. Of course, considering Mira's size, that wasn't very far from the ground—" His monologue was briefly interrupted as Mireille threw a soft peach at him and he dodged it while continuing to juggle.

"That move speaks of much experience in evading projectiles," a new voice suddenly joined the conversation.

Guillaume grinned at the newcomer. "Very true, *monsieur*."

Rosalie had turned with delight at the first sound of Rand's voice, a strange relief filling her at the knowledge that he was back. She threw him an inviting smile, patting the grass beside her.

"We're being decadent, my lord. I see no reason why you shouldn't join us." Having just returned from the wearying journey to Havre, Rand obligingly let all thoughts of shipping and money slip from his mind, collapsing beside her in a graceful masculine heap. Rosalie wondered how he could seem so fresh and collected after traveling for so long. She could detect the scent of sandalwood soap on his skin and the cool white cotton of his shirt. His long legs were encased in light buff breeches and soft cuffed boots. "You're late. I thought you'd be back this morning," she murmured to him as Mireille stood up to help Guillaume with the juggling act. Rand smiled at her, the gold in his eyes mixed with gleaming fragments of jade. He leaned over as if to whisper a reply in her ear. As she bent closer to hear him, Rosalie felt his teeth catch gently at her earlobe, his tongue tracing the tip. The diaphanous caress of a breeze teased the slight dampness even after his mouth had left the spot, and she shivered as she stared at him.

Slowly she refocused her attention on the performing pair, watching as Mireille posed prettily, handing Guillaume another peach and adopting a vacuous smile as she did so. Then she tossed two more peaches deftly into the air as Guillaume juggled, so that he was manipulating six pieces of fruit. Rosalie laughed and clapped her hands in appreciation as all the peaches tumbled to the ground.

Contentedly the performers sprawled onto the grass, Mireille now childishly heedless of her dress. Rosalie allowed herself to lean against Rand, her head against his shoulder as he braced his back against the trunk of the tree.

"I am thinking of a rhyme," Mireille said drowsily, her usually high-pitched voice containing a low musical sound that was not present when she was completely awake.

"I adore rhymes," Rosalie replied, thinking that if the other two had not been present, she might have turned her nose into Rand's strong brown neck and nuzzled the warm skin hungrily . . . or perhaps she would have enticed him to kiss her.

"It is French, and I will not say it unless you translate it into English," the girl stated.

"I have translated every word I know for days," Rosalie said, sagging against Rand as if for respite. "Haven't you learned enough English yet?" She meant the remark as a joke, but Mireille took it quite seriously.

"Almost, *mademoiselle* . . . but the rhythm is not right yet. I need more—"

Rand's shoulders shook with silent amusement. Quickly he managed to recover himself enough to speak to the girl with admirable steadiness.

"Mireille. Why don't you allow Guillaume to escort you to the château? I would hate to think that that peach stain won't come out of the hem of your gown. Perhaps Madame Alvin should look at it right aw—"

"Peach stain!" Mireille exclaimed.

Suddenly she was flying down the path, chattering quickly in French. Guillaume threw Rand an ironic glance before following her at a more lethargic pace.

Rosalie turned her face into Rand's shoulder, chuckling quietly until she was certain the pair was gone. Then she raised her head and looked at him with shining eyes. "That wasn't very subtle," she said, her lungs still taut with unshed laughter.

"It is increasingly difficult for me to be subtle around you," Rand replied softly, his gold-tipped lashes lowering as his gaze narrowed.

"And for me," she whispered.

He smiled lazily and moved his head just the fraction of an inch necessary to bring their lips together, and Rosalie felt the laughter dissolve like sugar in water, spreading in cool sweetness through her veins until she was filled with a shining crystal awareness of him. Her emptiness, her separateness, slipped away like a heavy shroud. Blindly she slid a hand around his neck, trying to capture the sensations that fell over her in a gossamer cascade. His tongue dipped leisurely inside her mouth, tasting, brushing over thinly shielded nerves until she leaned against him helplessly, her body trembling.

Wrapped in a finely meshed spell, Rand felt his senses, his thoughts and awareness angle sharply toward her until she was the focus of his very existence. His hands traveled over her slender form with a new sense of discovery, each touch wondering, intimate, loving. He searched for the secrets of her body, learning things she had never known about herself, his fingertips memorizing the ways to draw out her pleasure and passion. She responded to him with a warmth that caused him to shiver in surprise. Her shy touch, the stroke of her tongue against his, and the seeking eagerness of her hands aroused Rand to a state of hot-blooded mindlessness like nothing he had ever known before.

Rosalie gasped as his hand plunged hungrily into her bodice, her heart pounding not from fear but from need. Panting, she allowed her head to fall against his shoulder as he levered her onto his lap, and then gently the round weight of her breast was lifted out of her gown. A thin moan caught in her throat as Rand bent his head to take the soft peak in his mouth. Her entire body tightened, arching at the velvet rasp and the artful circling of his tongue. Slowly Rosalie's hand fluttered to his shoulder. It was engulfed immediately in his grip, his fingers laced between hers as he tasted the sensitively molded flesh of her nipple. She discovered in breathless confusion that his lovemaking was different from what she had expected, different from what she had remembered. Rand had been her lover for only two nights in Paris. During the first evening he had kept himself under tight control, aware of her innocence and making concessions to it. The second he had been driven to claim her and he had been possessive, domineering. Now there was nothing to prove, nothing to be mindful of . . . there were only the two of them and the desire that shimmered palpably between them.

Suddenly he raised his head at a quick rush of wind through the leaves, his eyes flickering around the garden in immediate assessment. Rosalie was reminded of their scene in the stable, when they had been interrupted in the middle of a similarly intimate embrace. She knew that she couldn't bear it if he left her now. Rand looked down at her and smiled slightly, easing the gown up over her exposed breast. His eyes had deepened in color to glittering green, the skin drawn tightly over his cheekbones to show them in high relief, his wide mouth gentle, the lower lip fuller than usual. Afraid that he would deny her, Rosalie curled her fingers into the smoothness of his shirt.

"Don't pull away this time," she whispered. Tears slipped from the corners of her eyes at the thought of him leaving her empty and frustrated once more. "Not when I need you like this . . . please, I've never needed you like this."

"Love," Rand breathed, his voice low and curiously shaken, "whatever you want of me is yours. Didn't you know that?"

They remained transfixed, frozen in that dazzling moment until Rand broke the stillness by standing up and lifting her effortlessly in his arms. At first Rosalie had no awareness of where he was taking her, her sapphire gaze locked on his face as she saw only him. Then their path became twisted and intricate. She realized that he was carrying her into the maze, a design of hedges that reached to his shoulder, a labyrinth in which it would be impossible for other eyes to see or discover them.

He set her down lightly, and as Rosalie stood there her heart pattered erratically at the sight of him unfastening the cuffs of his sleeves, his hazel eyes fastened unwaveringly onto hers. She was confronted with the hard, bare wall of his torso as he let the white shirt drop to the ground. Her mouth went dry. He was beautiful. Surely no man outside the realm of fantasy could be so perfectly made . . . but he was real, and for this moment he was hers. Slowly Rosalie lifted her hands to his chest, jumping slightly at the heat of his body. Her fingertips and the delicate rasp of her nails wandered through the light, silky-rough furring of his chest, savoring the solid musculature underneath. She traced the firm, symmetrical ridges of his collarbone, then splayed her hands over leanly fleshed ribs. Rand's desire raged as he suffered under her cool, drifting touches, his arms stealing around her possessively. Then she stood on her toes, pressing her mouth to the base of his throat, and her tongue stroked over the pulse that beat so heavily underneath his skin.

"Rose," he breathed tautly as her arms wound

around his back, her hands barely meeting at his broad, square shoulders. Their loins brushed together, his hard and aching, hers tender and yielding. "Ah . . . God, Rosalie . . ."

He pressed her down to the ground onto his discarded shirt. She turned her face into the soft material, inhaling the fresh masculine scent that lingered there. Then his body descended onto hers, and she quivered in excitement as she felt the hard, demanding fullness of his manhood pressing urgently against her stomach. Rand's lips moved over the fragile surface of her neck with sensual artistry, discovering the tiny hollows behind her earlobes, the vulnerable tissues along the side of her throat. One of his hands was engaged in the task of pulling up her gown, and Rosalie crooked her legs slightly as she felt the brush of tender grass behind her knees. He moved off her partly, sliding the skirt up over her thighs and past her hips.

"Are you certain that this is . . . ?" Rosalie began tremulously, her voice fading away in sudden doubt. She felt a tiny inner shock waver through her body as she realized where they were and exactly what they were doing. Most people, she was sure, did not make love out-of-doors on the ground like savages . . . it was uncivilized. What would Rand think of her afterward for allowing him to do this when—?

"Shhh . . . don't be afraid," he was saying, his lips hot against her skin, his voice husky with desire. "Nothing between us could be wrong," he whispered, his fingers easing under her chemise. "I would never hurt you . . . ah, sweet, don't think anymore, let me love you. . . ." His words, his hands, had a peculiarly hypnotic effect on her, driving everything out except her awareness of him. His fingers combed through the curls at the juncture of her thighs, caressed her inner thighs and urged them to spread apart. Then slowly his body eased downward, and she tried uneasily to shrink away from him. "No, love," Rand murmured, his hands clasping her hips steadily. "Don't hold yourself from me . . . trust me." He caressed the hard, tense length of her legs and then shifted so that they were hooked over his shoulders. His masculinity throbbed hotly, his passion flaring as he stared down at the dainty feminine flesh. "Let me," he said hoarsely, and she relaxed slightly although her hands were clenched in agitation.

He lowered his golden head.

At the first gentle, moist touch of his mouth she cried out, reacting sharply to the quaking pleasure that seared through her body. His lips opened wider, his tongue searching the fragile, swelling nakedness. It was like a kiss, and yet not quite a kiss. Rand groaned, and the vibration of the sound sent a corresponding vibration through her body. Rosalie's senses careened wildly. Her eyes flickered open for just an instant, the image of his amber-shaded head between her thighs branded across her mind forever. Slowly his mouth moved and stroked, centering on a tiny cluster of nerves that increased in sensitivity until her limbs were stiff from pleasure. She gasped his name, suddenly drowning in painful ecstasy. Through her plummeting release the hands cupping her buttocks pulled her more closely against his mouth. His lips did not leave her until the last tremors had died into glowing embers, and only then did Rand lever his body back over hers.

Her face was moist, her translucent skin flushed with gentle color. Rosalie lifted her heavy lashes to stare at him with unfocused brilliant blue eyes. He kissed her, his mouth tinged with a sweet, musky flavor. She responded unhesitatingly, her head tilting so that their lips could fit together more intimately. Languidly her fingers moved to the fastenings of his breeches, slipping the buttons from their moorings until the garment gaped open. Rand shuddered, using his knees to spread her legs. He held his breath as he pressed into her slowly, feeling the tightness of her aroused flesh pull him deeper through her body. For a moment he was still and silent, grasping at the shreds of his control. There was no way for him to describe the sensation of possessing her, for the experience was unique. Emotion was layered with physical sensation—sex had become a matter of instinct, of feelings rather than technique. Even with all his experience, it had never been like this before. Cradling her head in one broad hand, he thrust into her, watching her eyes dilate with pleasure. Then he thrust again, more strongly this time, the action simple, monumental. As he kissed her he felt her lips tremble against his.

"Bend your knees more," he whispered. Rosalie obeyed, and gasped as she felt him push even deeper within her. Then he moved without stopping, sharply, urgently. She looked up at him, her eyes flashing like sapphires as she stared at his face, which had been carved by passion into sharp planes. Her hips lifted, her toes curled, and then Rosalie was racked with an exquisite sensation that skipped tenderly over her body, like a pebble skimming the surface of smooth water. Rand gritted his teeth, his body tight and still in the moments before he shuddered, his breath releasing gradually. As the pleasure of their joining smoothed into a slow current, they relaxed in a damp tangle, hands lazily stroking, soothing, caressing, the aftermath as exquisitely sweet as the passion that had preceded. Lazily Rand raised himself on an elbow and looked down at her with drowsy green-shaded eyes.

"It's worth going away, to be welcomed home like that," he said huskily.

She let a long moment of silence drift between them before speaking. "Rand . . . how is it going to be between us from now on?" Rosalie asked softly, her brow creasing.

He smoothed her forehead with his lips, ending with a kiss at her temple. "We've had this discussion before," he stated flatly, "and as you'll recall, it didn't end very well. Since we both appear to have conflicting ideas about the long-range status of our relationship, we'll have to take it day by day."

"But sooner or later we'll have to—"

"It can be later. Before we make any decisions, there are other loose ends to be tied up."

"I . . . Yes, I agree," Rosalie said. She had firsthand knowledge of how quickly someone's life could change, how easily fate could turn the world upside down and shake it vigorously. The only thing she could be certain of was that her life would never return to what it had once been . . . and perhaps she should be grateful for that. "But we still have an immediate problem," she pointed out.

"What's that?" he asked, a curious smile playing on his lips.

She looked at the grass stains on their rumpled clothing, on the right knee of his breeches, ground into the fabric of her dress and the material of his shirt.

"How are you going to take me back to the château like this?"

He grinned down at her as he stroked her hair away from her face. "Very stealthily, love."

Twelve

All my past life is mine no more;
The flying hours are gone,
Like transitory dreams given o'er
Whose images are kept in store
By memory alone.
—John Wilmont, Earl of Rochester

True to his word, Rand did manage to take Rosalie back to her room unseen, giving her one last, long kiss before leaving. Wondering if evidence of what had transpired was as transparent to others as she feared it must be, Rosalie was very quiet during dinner. She lifted her eyes from her plate only a few times, not daring to meet Rand's wry gaze for fear that she would spill something or choke on her food.

Exasperating man! He did not come to her bed that night. Rosalie spent two long hours glaring at the untouched door as she debated whether or not to go to his room. Finally caution won out and she reluctantly blew out the candle before falling asleep. In the morning she found a pale yellow rose near her pillow, all of its thorns removed. Holding the delicate blossom to her face, she breathed in its scent and was transported for a moment back to the garden, where the scent of roses had floated in the air as he had pressed her into the soft grass and made her his once more. In a somewhat dreamy state of mind, Rosalie spent the first part of the day with Mireille, whose company was anything but dull.

"It's right here," Mireille whispered, glancing furtively up and down the hallway.

Rosalie tried the gold dolphin-shaped door handle herself, finding that it wouldn't budge. "You're right," she said with gathering disappointment. "It's locked. But why would a portrait gallery be closed up?"

"You think it is a gallery?"

"It must be. The rooms on either side of it are filled with paintings and busts of d'Angoux ancestors." Rosalie eyed the door speculatively, nearly eaten up with curiosity. It was the only room in the entire château that she and Mireille had not explored. Meeting Mireille's eyes, she saw that the girl's rampant imagination was busy with possible explanations for why the door was locked.

"Perhaps someone was murdered in there," the small maid whispered, and Rosalie laughed softly.

"Probably it has been locked accidentally."

"Do you think we should ask Madame Alvin for the key?"

Rosalie shook her head slowly. "If it is locked on purpose she'll find some way to refuse us. And then if we were caught looking inside it, we couldn't plead ignorance."

They looked at each other and grinned, sharing the same enjoyment of a potential adventure.

"*Mademoiselle,* do you have—?"

"A hairpin? Could you do something with the lock if—?"

"*Oui* . . . but tell me if someone is coming."

Nimbly Mireille worked at the lock with a slender pin, reminding Rosalie of a squirrel foraging for nuts.

"You certainly have a variety of talents, Mira," she said, and the girl snickered.

"Living with Guillaume, one learns many things to survive, *mademoiselle.* He showed me how to do this."

It was the first time she had made any reference to her past. Rosalie tilted her head and watched her companion interestedly, her face soft with compassion. She did not know what kinds of experiences Mireille had lived through, but surely having moved from place to place would have made most people rather hard. How had the girl managed to stay so sweet and untarnished by others? It revealed an extraordinarily strong will, or perhaps Guillaume was responsible for preserving Mireille's innocence. The lock clicked quietly, and Mireille handed her back the pin with a triumphant smile. They slipped into the room like two wraiths, closing the door inaudibly.

It was indeed a portrait gallery, dark paintings covering the walls like windows filled with quaintly clothed strangers. However, one portrait was separate from the rest. It was placed between two framed mirrors. As Rosalie looked at it, she doubted that it had been necessary to direct attention to the painting in such a manner, for it would have stood out in any type of arrangement. Slowly she went to the curtains and pulled them open to let more light into the room.

"Hélène Marguerite d'Angoux," Mireille read the engraved plate on the frame, creeping closer to examine the portrait. Rosalie remained in the back of the room, her eyes round and inexplicably misty. She knew without question that this portrait was the reason why the room was locked, yet it was not clear why Rand would not simply take it down. What private memories were locked in this room with the image of this woman?

"She is beautiful," Mireille said. "Who—?"

"His mother," Rosalie replied. "Not so very beautiful, Mira." Perhaps it was her feelings for Rand that colored her impressions of the portrait. In some ways, Mireille was right: Hélène d'Angoux was physically attractive. Her face was perfectly proportioned, her lips

delicate and precisely curved in a way that reminded
Rosalie of Rand. That faintly mocking expression
around the eyes was also something familiar to her.
The eyes were not quite the same, but close. Hélène's
were perfectly green, whereas Rand's were indetermi-
nately hazel—sometimes green, sometimes golden.
They were shaped similarly, slightly narrowed at the
inner corners. It was almost eerie to see the elements of
Rand in the face of this woman. But there was much of
her classical beauty that he had not inherited, possessing instead the strong, stubborn features that Rosalie
accurately accredited to the Berkeley side of the family.

There were many things that Hélène Marguerite did
not appear to have in common with her elder son. She
did not have his wide, expressive mouth, nor did it
seem that she could have produced anything resembling his wry, flashing smile. She did not have faint
laugh lines radiating from the corners of her eyes, nor
the brilliant mixture of sun and amber in her blond
hair. There was no gentleness in her expression. Hélène Marguerite looked capable of passion, mockery,
and even anger, but not love. You hurt him when he
was vulnerable to you, Rosalie thought, and that simple
basic reaction overrode her every other impression of
his mother. She could find no sympathy in her heart
for a woman who had carelessly hurt those who loved
her. She turned away, casting the portrait a glance of
purely irrational dislike.

"Interesting," Rosalie said, her voice dry. "Unfortunately it was probably a good likeness."

"*Mademoiselle?*"

"Let's go. There are a hundred other things I'd
rather look at."

"We could go to the kitchen to see Madame Alvin,"
Mireille suggested, happily abandoning her position in
front of the portrait to open the door with care.

"Why?" Rosalie asked as the girl peered down both ends of the hallway.

"Perhaps," Mireille said, popping her head back into the room, "you would like to ask her for an English tea today?"

"An English tea? Why . . ." Rosalie paused, wondering where the girl had gotten the idea from. In France, tea was brought out only in the dire circumstance that there was no coffee to serve. Then she chuckled softly. "Is it because of the description in the book we were studying from today? Don't tell me you've never had one before."

"I have not, but if you say to Madame Alvin that you miss this custom of tea, I would be happy to join you for—"

"Of course I will," Rosalie said. The range of things that aroused Mireille's curiosity never failed to amuse and surprise her. "Let's go to the kitchen, then." They crept out of the room furtively, closing the door on the portrait of Hélène d'Angoux.

The kitchen was unusually calm, its only occupant being the solid figure of Madame Alvin. After spending the morning organizing the servants to clean the château, she sat with a cup of coffee, stirring crushed sugar in it and regretting the lack of cream to be had with it.

"The girl who comes by with the milk each morning is late," she informed the two visitors, taking a sip of the brew and sighing. "I am waiting for her . . . that girl is so slow! Talking to every man on the way, and waiting to flirt with Jérème after he cleans the stables—"

"That Jérème needs no encouragement," Mireille said, her chocolate-colored eyes dancing. "One little smile, not even a very friendly one, and he sticks like a fly in honey!"

As Madame Alvin laughed uproariously in agreement, slapping her plump knees with both hands, Rosalie cast a glance of new understanding at Mireille.

"So that's why you're so cool to him," she murmured.

"Yes," the girl replied in disgust, "but like all men, that makes him cling even more. Ah, he thinks he is a man full-grown, and he is only a year or two older than me. Conceited boy . . . he tried to kiss me the first time I visited the stable, as if I were to be had there with all the horses looking on! Can you imagine it?"

"Dreadful," Rosalie said, flushing with sudden discomfort.

Just then a knock sounded at the kitchen door and Madame Alvin bustled down from her stool with the pronouncement that it was the hapless milkmaid. After berating the girl for her worse-than-usual tardiness and sending her on her way, Madame Alvin skimmed a little cream for her coffee and set the milk on a counter. As a warm, comfortable conversation ensued, the subject of an English tea was brought up and soundly approved. Madame Alvin thought it would be an entertaining project, since she herself had never done it. They discussed the menu with increasing enthusiasm.

"In the book," Mireille said, "they had little . . . things, little . . ."

"Sandwiches," Rosalie supplied. "Cucumber and watercress, and perhaps cheese would be nice—"

"And they had gingerbread," Mireille continued, seeming very young in her excitement, "and little cakes, and sugar buns, and—"

"*Madame,*" Rosalie interrupted gently, "do not go to trouble. Whatever you wish to provide will be more than adequate. This is just so that Mira can see what it is like to have tea the way they do in England."

"Like the grand ladies," Mireille said, beaming mischievously. "I will be the *comtesse*, and Madame Alvin will be the *duchesse*, and you . . . ah, what would you be if you married Monsieur de Berkeley?"

"If I what?" Rosalie asked faintly.

"Mira!" Madame Alvin exclaimed, and proceeded to scold Mireille for having asked such a tactless question, even if it had been meant as teasing.

Rosalie colored, reflecting on the fact that marriage to Rand was fast gaining in appeal, no matter what the drawbacks. It was becoming rapidly apparent to her that if he asked her to be his wife again she would most likely accept before he could finish the sentence.

"I would be Lady Berkeley," she said gravely.

"Just like Hélène Marguerite," Mireille mused.

"*Non!*" Madame Alvin said sharply, shaking her silver-brown head for emphasis. "Not like Hélène, not at all." Mireille and Rosalie waited with baited breath for her to continue, but Madame Alvin appeared to be completely through with the subject. "Now, Mira," she inquired, "what else did the book say about English tea?"

"What do you mean, not like Hélène Marguerite?" Mireille countered.

Sighing, Madame Alvin compressed her mouth into a tight, firm line. "I should not say more."

"There are no strangers here," Mireille said persuasively. "Why would it hurt to explain to *mademoiselle* something that she is curious about?"

"There is nothing to explain," Madame Alvin replied, her eyes taking in Rosalie's absorbed expression. "You, *mademoiselle*, are not the kind of woman that Hélène was."

"You were here while she was growing up?" Rosalie asked, her serious tone contrasting sharply with Mireille's cajoling.

"Since she was born. I was here when Monsieur Robert de Berkeley came to France to court her and when they were married, and also when she brought her first son to show to the marquis. I was here during all the times that she came back here to visit. She did not like England except for London. The more time she spent there, the more she changed. I have often thought that London must be a very evil place."

"Not really," Rosalie said thoughtfully. "No more so than Paris. Parts of it are bad, I suppose . . . especially for an impressionable person. It is fast-paced and full of people who have nothing to do except amuse themselves."

"Hélène was brought up here in a very quiet way," Madame Alvin said. "In the style of the old French *noblesse*. She was very sheltered, a good girl . . . but she longed for excitement and wanted to move away from the quietness of country life. She married as soon as possible to the first man who asked—Monsieur Robert de Berkeley."

Rosalie nodded, feeling a reluctant twinge of understanding for Hélène. She knew how it felt to be stifled by monotony and to dream of change and excitement.

"But surely a husband and children, and all the activities that are involved with occupying her position should have satisfied her," Rosalie remarked. "It would have been a very busy and full life—not only would there have been hundreds of responsibilities involving her family and the community, but countless parties, *fêtes* and balls—"

"She did not like the responsibilities," Madame Alvin said, smiling with wry sadness. "But she did like the parties. I have heard that there were many scandals in London that she was involved in—I will not repeat any of the stories, for I do not know if they were true or not. But almost every two years or so she would come back to France to stay without her husband or children, and I think it was to let the gossip and troubles die down before she went back."

"And you noticed during these visits that she had changed?" Rosalie prompted, fascinated.

"Ah, *oui* . . . she began to think of no one but herself. She had the château redecorated in the latest fashion and the grounds landscaped many times, spending huge amounts of money, and worse, executing the *corvée* to do it."

Mireille clicked her tongue in appalled shock.

"What? What is a *corvée?*" Rosalie asked. "I've never heard of it before."

"That is because they no longer have the wretched custom," Mireille replied, her small face wrinkling with disgust. "A *corvée* was the right of the French nobility to command the peasants from all the neighboring villages to work for them without pay. Whenever they wanted a road built, or a garden laid out, or additions built onto the château, the nobility forced the peasants to leave the fields, even if it was in the middle of harvesttime. The food and grain would rot out in their fields as the peasants worked on the lord and lady's pretty garden."

"How awful," Rosalie murmured.

"Yes," Madame Alvin said, her voice lowering with a touch of shame. "Many people starved in the winters because of Hélène's whims. She was not a popular figure here. But the marquis, her father, would refuse her nothing." The elderly woman sighed deeply. "The unhappier Hélène Marguerite became, the more cruel she was. She finally abandoned her sons and husband, coming back here to have a child. She died in labor, and the baby along with her. My husband and I have wondered for years how her children were—I am glad to see that *monsieur* was not badly affected by all of it."

Rosalie was silent for a long moment. Not badly affected by all of it, she thought with bitter distress, wondering what Madame Alvin would say if she knew the kind of abuse that Hélène had left her sons to face.

What would she say if she knew that Rand had been a drunkard when he was only a boy and that he and his brother had survived a deplorable childhood? Rand had grown up to be a reckless hellion, while Colin, from what little she had been told, had become a fastidious dandy, a fashion plate.

"I do not think many women are good mothers," Mireille finally said, resting her chin on her hand and staring distantly at the copper pots and pans on the wall.

"Mine has been good to me," Rosalie replied, thinking of Amille and feeling an ache in her chest. "She is a very kind woman . . . and she has always despaired of the fact that I am not easily contented with what I have. She said it would lead to trouble. I think she was right."

Suddenly Madame Alvin chuckled in a jolly way, breaking the tension that seemed to have settled over them. "Mothers always like to think they are right," the older woman said.

"Yes," Rosalie agreed with a quick smile.

Rand walked into the sitting room, pausing in front of the glass-paned doors to regard the scene with warm interest. It was half-past four, and Rosalie and Mireille sat at a lace-covered table having tea. Serenely Rosalie poured the freshly brewed liquid into china cups as Mireille carefully dabbed a scone with clotted cream. The picture they presented was quaint and charming as they engaged in a language lesson, causing Rand to smile slowly. His eyes traveled over Rosalie appreciatively. She was dressed in a flowing pale blue gown, the color enhancing the blue of her eyes until they were almost painful to behold. Her hair was pulled on top of her head in a deliciously demure fashion that tempted him to sink his hands into its gleaming softness and pull it all down. She looked like a perfect lady, and there were few signs in her appearance that betrayed her lively temper and passion . . . few signs, unless one knew where to look. Gradually his gaze moved from her face and settled on the trim, neat curves of her figure and the swell of her breasts. He would have trouble keeping the men away from her in London, for hers was the kind of fresh, passionate beauty that no one could resist.

"Would you like some sugar?" Rosalie asked in slow, clear English, and Mireille wrinkled her brow before replying in the same language.

"Not only would I like some sugar . . . but I . . . would like more sandwich."

Rand laughed at Mireille's answer. "Spoken like a true Englishwoman," he said, and Rosalie looked up at him with a dazzling smile.

"We read about tea in a Jane Austen novel recently," she informed him. "Naturally it was an experience that Mireille wanted to try for herself."

"Naturally." Rand was about to say something else when they were disturbed by a minor commotion. Outside the transparent French doors, sounds of cursing and scuffling floated from the direction of the garden. Rand's eyes narrowed as Guillaume appeared with a wiry middle-aged man in tow, having twisted the stranger's arm behind his back. Although Guillaume was built on a larger scale, he was having difficulty in dragging his captive toward the château, for the man was stiff with fury. Rand twisted the door handle and sent the portal swinging open widely.

"Guillaume, what the hell is going on?" he inquired none too gently, and Guillaume's prisoner froze at the sight of him.

"Sorry, *monsieur*," Guillaume said, grabbing hold of the man's collar in order to prevent him from bolting. He was poorly dressed and appeared to be a lower-class sort, a downfallen farmer whose face was deeply lined. "I caught him stealing a bag of peaches and other articles from the garden, and was certain that you would have something to say about it."

"Indeed," Rand drawled, stepping outside to join them. Mireille and Rosalie left the tea table to draw closer, watching the men through the half-open doors.

"He also had a string of fish with him," Guillaume added, his velvety brown eyes crackling with the light of exasperation as the man struggled briefly. "Taken from d'Angoux property, I am certain."

"You must know that poaching is against the law," Rand said to the stranger, whose bony face twisted with hatred. "I am not an ungenerous man . . . I would have freely allowed you to fish or hunt on my land if you had asked for permission. However, I draw the line at being robbed."

"I am not an idiot," the man rasped. "Also not a beggar. You think any man like me would ask a d'Angoux for anything?" He was cut off as Guillaume made a sound of irritation and tightened his hold on the collar.

"*Tiens,*" Guillaume said. "Show some respect for *monsieur!*"

"I'm not a d'Angoux," Rand said.

The man laughed bitterly, staring at him with bright, feverishly excited eyes. "You cannot lie about it. My family and I have been ruined by the d'Angouxs. I would know one anywhere—it is in your eyes and face, and in your black soul! Devil's children, all of you!"

"A little melodramatic, don't you think?" Guillaume inquired, but he was ignored as Rand regarded the man thoughtfully.

"How have you been ruined?" he asked.

"I once had a comfortable home, a large family with many sons who helped me to farm, even some money to save. We lost everything because of Hélène d'Angoux and the marquis. He drained the village of everything in order to pay her bills . . . he took the peasants' grain

and charged us for storing it in his warehouse, we had
to bake our bread in his baking ovens and pay him for
it, we were taxed for everything except breathing. My
wife died of hunger because of the d'Angouxs—*that* is
the legacy you inherit, *monsieur,* and you do not have
the right to judge me for taking a handful of food from
you."

Rosalie held her breath, wanting to cry out as she saw
Rand's face whiten. He felt responsible for the sins his
family had committed, and the man's words had added
to the invisible burden of guilt that he carried on his
shoulders. It's not your fault, she wanted to tell Rand,
but held her tongue in fear of wounding his pride.

"He should not blame himself," Mireille whispered.

"He already does," Rosalie said softly, her heart
aching with sympathy.

Cool and emotionless, Rand looked over the poacher's head to Guillaume. "Let him go," he said.

As Guillaume released the man with distaste, the thin
peasant glanced at Rand with glittering eyes before
fleeing as if the devil were chasing him.

Rand turned to see Rosalie silhouetted through the
myriad of glass panes and his expression became even
more remote.

"My lord, I would like to speak with you," she said,
fighting to keep the urgency from her tone.

"Later, perhaps," he replied, sounding indifferent.
"I'm going for a ride."

Guillaume spoke then in an unusually subdued manner. "I'll saddle Diamond."

Mireille gently pulled Rosalie back to the tea table.
"I've got to talk with him," Rosalie murmured, her
emotions stirring tumultuously.

"I do not think he would listen at the moment."

"Damn," Rosalie breathed, folding her arms around
her middle and staring vacantly at the bountifully
heaped plate of scones. "Damn all of this . . . I'm not

sure what I'm going to say anyway. Oh, I wish I had asked him when he was going to get back—"

"Would you like a glass of wine, *mademoiselle?*" Mireille asked tactfully.

"Yes. And no water in it," Rosalie said, sitting down in the embroidered chair and scowling.

Rand did not return for supper. The silence around the château became so thick and tense that Guillaume finally left for the village, taking the bay. He returned around eleven o'clock, smelling of ale and tobacco, wearing a pleased expression that betrayed an hour or two spent with sociable companions.

"It is a beautiful evening," he announced, walking into the parlor with a relaxed, loose stride. "Warm and—"

"Guillaume!" Mireille exclaimed. "How can you go out to drink and flirt, knowing that *mademoiselle* is concerned about *monsieur*—"

"He is fine. I suggest that you both retire for the evening," Guillaume said, smiling as Rosalie stopped pacing across the room.

"You found him?" she demanded, her blue eyes dark and troubled.

"I happened to see him briefly. He is in one of the upper club rooms in the village—"

"Gaming?"

"And drinking," Guillaume said.

Rosalie froze.

"Oh, nothing more than the average man would have on a warm summer night in a village tavern," Guillaume hurried to assure her. "Why, I myself could not resist tippling here and there—they had this kind of brew that I've never had before . . ."

As he continued, Rosalie's brow creased deeply in worry. Guillaume had not known Rand long enough to realize that his habit was to avoid drinking, that Rand disliked any loss of his control. The incident with the

poacher had affected him badly, just as she had feared.
But she could not help feeling that it should not have
driven him to something so out of the ordinary.

"You did not speak to him?" she asked evenly, and
Guillaume shook his head. "Then there is no telling
when he will return. I believe I will retire, Mireille."

"Oui," the girl replied quietly, hovering near her
heels as they went upstairs.

Rosalie undressed and slipped into a simple white
nightgown.

As the candlelight burned steadily, she turned the
pages of a book and focused on the words without
reading them. The silence stretched and thinned,
surrounding her insidiously until she gave up all pretense of reading.

"Rand," she whispered, looking straight into the
candle flame until the edges seemed to turn violet.
"You're so proud, so independent that I hardly know
how to deal with you. You've shown me that you care
for me a certain measure, and yet you left me today
without asking for any kind of help. You've told me that
you want me—to warm your bed, to make love with
you . . . you've told me that you want me to depend on
you. I can give you all of that—but I want to give you so
much more! And unless you think of me as woman
enough to offer you comfort, I won't have you. I *will* be
more than a plaything to you." She clenched her fist as
she made the vow, her fingertips whitening.

It seemed to be hours that passed by as she waited,
until finally she heard a faint scraping noise. She slid
from the bed and padded on bare feet to her doorway.
A light flickered from the edges of a door—not Rand's
door, but the far one at the end of the hall. The
portrait gallery.

The door opened easily. Rand sat in a chair in front
of the portrait of Hélène, his long legs stretched in a
lazy masculine sprawl, the neck of a brandy bottle held

gently between his fingers. She could smell spirits from the doorway. His head turned, his hair gleaming dully in the lamplight with the movement. Silently he regarded her as if she were a stranger. So this was what Rand was like when he had had too much to drink— not engaging or boyish, but morose, quiet. His eyes were faintly glassy, his voice low and raspy.

"Get out."

He would never know how much the words had hurt. Rosalie felt the sting of them like the blow of a whip, and for several moments afterward she felt ridiculous and foolish, offering help that wasn't asked for or needed. The Rosalie Belleau of a few months ago would have fled the room immediately, faster than any startled rabbit. The uncaring look in his darkened eyes frightened her, but somehow she managed to square her shoulders and remain where she was.

"Sitting here and brooding isn't going to change a thing. And drinking certainly won't."

He made a gesture with the bottle and spoke with the patience of an adult addressing an obtuse child. "It's making me feel a hell of a lot better. So get—"

"Yes, I can see how wonderful it is for you," Rosalie interrupted acidly.

"You don't understand a thing, not nearly enough to stand there and pass judgment."

"I understand a few things about you. Including the fact that you've tried to run away from guilt for a long time," she said. "And that now you've done a turn-about and seem to prefer wallowing in it." Her voice gentled as she stared at his averted profile. "Why not try letting it go?"

"The sins of the father . . ." Rand quoted, shrugging grimly and taking another swig from the bottle. He grimaced until the fire of it eased down to his gut. "It's in the blood."

"The only thing in your blood besides a misguided

conscience is an overload of spirits." Rosalie approached him carefully as she spoke. "None of it was your fault, Rand. You aren't accountable for anything your mother or father did——"

"I know," he said, his voice suddenly raw. "But I am accountable for what *I've* done." He lowered his gaze to his hands, gripping the brandy bottle between them. "I see both of them in the things I've done," he muttered, and cast a brief glance at his mother's portrait. "Can you imagine what it's like to know that half of her is me? She was faithless and she was incapable of telling the truth, just as you are incapable of lying. She was heartless, beyond anything you could imagine. God, someone like you would never begin to understand. And then there was my father—a drunken bastard with——"

"Don't!" Rosalie interrupted, torn equally between vast anger and sympathy. "Don't say it anymore . . . don't think it anymore! I don't see her in you. I don't see your father in you." She sat on the arm of the chair and framed his face with her hands, her eyes meeting his in an electric gaze. "I've trusted you to take care of me, and you have. There are other people who need you, who depend on you. Don't sit here and be consumed by self-pity. It's not like you."

He set down the bottle and took hold of her wrists in an effort to push her away from him, but Rosalie clung to him with determination. In the fleeting struggle she slid onto his lap, and he stopped moving as her warm silk-sheathed body pressed against him.

"She's just a memory that you have to let go of. How can she have any influence on you now? This is a lovely home, a beautiful place, and with all the sunlight that pours in, don't look in the corners for shadows that aren't even there. Get rid of her, let her go."

Her last words seemed to strike something responsive in him, for Rand looked at her as if really seeing her for the first time. It seemed as if he were about to speak, and then he shook his head slightly, staring into her bright sapphire eyes.

"Why do you feel as if you have to blame yourself?" Rosalie asked in a whisper. "What is it in your past that makes you feel so guilty?"

"Rose," he said huskily, "I don't want to talk tonight. Not about the past. Go back to your room."

Her eyes searched his and her arms went confidingly around his neck. "Perhaps I am very wrong in this assumption," she said softly, "but I think that you don't want to lose me by revealing things I would not like to hear about you. But understand, you'll definitely lose me by keeping your silence. I won't let you shut me out. Tell me about the things you've done . . . Oh, Rand, they can't be that terrible."

The alcohol and the weariness seeped through him like poison, leaving him light-headed and vulnerable in a way that he had not been for years. He felt too soiled and tainted to be in the same room with Rosalie, much less hold her so closely, yet it would have taken the combined strength of a hundred men to force him to let her go. "Please, Rand," she whispered, her hands softly touching the harsh, cleanly cut line of his jaw.

The arms around her waist tightened, and then tightened more until Rosalie fell against those wide shoulders with a gasp, allowing him to hold her so tightly that she could hardly breathe. She smelled brandy and the scent of his skin, and felt him bury his face in the loose, thick mass of her hair. She heard him begin to speak, muttering words that she could barely hear, saying things that she did not understand. His hands clenched in the folds of her gown and in her hair, fingers entwining in the softness, flexing as he murmured hoarsely. Once he began talking, he could not stop. The burden of keeping it all to himself, the blots of his past, the shameful exploits in London, became too heavy to endure, and he bared his soul ruthlessly to her.

She would not have believed him capable of the things that he accused himself of; if the words had come from someone else's lips she would have thought them to be lies. He told her things that he had never shared with another living soul, secrets and admissions, fragments of stories that bordered on incoherence. Someone he had killed in a duel, a circle of friends that had been nothing better than a conspiracy of dishonor, someone's marriage he had helped to destroy. He mentioned the names of people she had read about in the London papers, and he mentioned his brother's and his parents' names. It seemed that the litany would never end.

Stroking the back of his head and neck, Rosalie comforted him with meaningless phrases. Her cheeks were hot and flushed with embarrassment from much of what he said, things so intimate that she would never have mentioned them even to Amille, ribald and bawdy confessions that degraded the ears as much as the words that were used to describe them. His arms became desperate around her, a bruising vise that she accepted willingly. Most women would have run from the room in horror, for no lady would have endured such a scene. Rosalie listened without pulling back from him, her tender clasp becoming fierce as if she sought to absorb his despair with the tightness of her grip. She had heard that the young bucks of London usually led sordid lives, seeking adventure, pressuring each other into reprehensible acts of cruelty. She did not think that Rand had been any worse than those he had kept company with, but her heart ached for his remorse and self-condemnation.

"It's all right . . . I understand," she murmured over and over again, and Rand shook his head tiredly, his eyes gleaming with liquid gold.

"God, how could you understand? You're too innocent . . . I never should have touched you."

As his outpouring faded into harsh, bitter whispers, the night matured and ripened into the deep lavender that preceded dawn. Rosalie lay quiescently in his arms, cradled against the hard, compacted muscles of his chest. Her forehead was tucked in the sloping juncture of his neck and shoulder, her fingers inserted between the buttons of his shirt to touch the warm skin underneath. Rand's chest moved evenly and steadily as he sighed quietly, feeling as if he had been battered by a storm.

"You're the only one who remembers," she whispered, finding his heartbeat with her fingertips and letting them rest on that vital pulse. "Most people can't afford to think about the past. They don't care about what's over and done with. I don't care what you've done in the past . . . you see? I'm still here. I haven't left, because I understand that you had to survive. But it's not important now, it has nothing to do with you anymore. If I can forgive you so easily, can't you forgive yourself?"

He was still for several long minutes, and she could tell without looking that his eyes were fastened on the portrait. Then he moved, gathering her more closely in his arms and standing up from the chair. Rosalie was surprised at the smoothness of the movement because she knew that his muscles had to be cramped. The muscles of his shoulders swelled under her cheek, full of latent power that mocked her frail hold on him. She clung to him wordlessly as he carried her down the hall to her bedchamber, unable to see his face. She said his name with careful quietness, but he did not reply, and then he laid her on her bed. He stared at her for a few seconds, his hazel eyes taking in every detail of her face, which had been ravaged by the lack of sleep. She did not know what to say to him any longer and so held her silence, her hands dropping reluctantly from him.

Rand lifted one of her slender hands in his and brought it to his mouth, holding it against the warmth of his lips as he looked down at her. She caught her breath, her fingers fast and tight around his. Then he left, his soft cuffed boots making no sound on the floor.

The last thing Rosalie expected to be wakened by was the distant clanging of the village bell. She tried to ignore the persistent sound and rolled over to bury her head in the pillow. Moaning, she finally lifted her head and squinted in the afternoon light that pushed past the half-open curtains. Judging from the enthusiasm with which the bell was being rung, something significant was happening in the village.

"I wonder," she mumbled, pushing the disheveled locks of sable hair out of her face and holding a hand to her head. "Either a disaster has occurred or the King of France is passing by." Sighing, she struggled from the bed and staggered over to the window to peer outside. The sunshine was brilliant and glaring, bleaching the rich greenness of the grass to a pale, white-washed hue. In the distance, toward the village, the hot blue sky appeared to be brushed with a thin, hazy film. Thinning clouds? Smoke? Rosalie frowned and left the room without thinking, instinctively heading toward Rand's room. He was not there.

"Mireille?" she called, the edge of her gown billowing out behind her as she went down the stairs. There was a minor commotion on the ground floor, people flying across the front entranceway, the door knocker rapping sharply against the portal, voices raised in fast-paced debate. Rosalie halted halfway down the curved staircase as Mireille appeared at the bottom. "What's happening? I heard the bell—"

"*Mademoiselle,* there is a fire in the village. It is spreading very quickly, and it is heading toward the shops, the main square, the church . . . they are asking all the men to come and help."

Rosalie felt a premonition that boded ill. Doubt and unease spread rapidly through her.

"How can they do anything against the fire in this dry heat?" she asked, her eyes flickering around the huge hall in search of Rand. "I've heard the Loire is several feet lower than usual—there's hardly enough water to drink, much less to put out a large—"

"Rose, what are you doing?"

Suddenly Rand, who had been passing by in the entranceway, swept past Mireille to bound up the stairs, a scowl crossing his handsome face. Rosalie remained where she was as he approached her. The white of his shirt and the light coffee shade of his strapped trousers emphasized the tawny hues of his skin and hair. She stared at him in apprehension.

"You aren't going to the village, are you?" she asked, and he hooked a steely arm around her waist to drag her up the stairs.

"What possessed you to stand there in your night-gown?" he demanded, and she fought to keep from tripping as he hauled her ruthlessly to her room. "Dammit, just standing in that little see-through costume for all the world to see—"

"I wasn't thinking," Rosalie protested, her feet moving at double pace to keep up with his stride.

"As usual."

In her worry over him, she let his comment go undebated. They reached her room, and Rand closed the door behind them. Rosalie stared at him in growing concern, her stomach clenching at the sight of him, so large and healthy and perfect. She wanted him to stay that way, and she wanted to keep him from tempting fate by placing himself in danger. The thought of him burned by fire or crushed by crumbling walls frightened her acutely.

"Please, please don't go," she said, prepared to beg shamelessly if he refused. "There are hundreds of others who can fight the fire—"

"Nothing's going to happen to me," Rand said, his voice firm and reassuring. "I'll take no risks . . . but I couldn't stay here knowing that my help might be needed. I'm a man, Rose, and only a coward would stay safe in his home when that bell is ringing."

"It's not even your village," she said, and as she met his unyielding eyes, she felt a mist of tears blur her vision. "You don't really even live here. Please stay."

"*Petite* . . ." Rand said, and his arms slid around her. Rosalie was stiff with resentment at the fact that he was refusing her, and yet she was so afraid of what might happen to him that she allowed him to pull her against his big warm body. "What if that were the château bell ringing?" he bent his head to murmur in her ear. She could tell from the sound of his voice that he was smiling as he spoke. "I don't think we would appreciate it much if every man decided to let his neighbor be the one to come and help us."

"This isn't funny!" Rosalie scolded in a muffled tone. "You said . . . you said that whatever I wanted of you was mine. I want you to stay here."

He was suddenly still. "That isn't fair, Rose," he said gravely, the amusement leaving his voice.

She knew in her heart that he was right, but that did not appease her anger and fear. "Please."

"No," he said softly, an odd glow in his eyes as he looked down at her.

Her temper blazed. "Then go! Forget everything I said, I should have bitten my tongue before asking you for anything!" She tried to pull away, and his arms tightened around her. It was ridiculously easy for him to hold her right there where he wanted her, and so Rosalie stopped struggling.

"Don't turn your face away from me," Rand said.

"Leave me alone!"

He lowered his mouth to her downturned face, nuzzling the softness of her cheek until he found the dampness of a flaring tear track with his lips.

"Go away," Rosalie choked out, but the feel of his mouth moving against her skin was more than she could bear. She became still and docile. As the silence deepened, she turned her face with a sob to meet his lips. The room around them seemed to wither away as he kissed her. Rosalie was surrounded by darkness, consumed by it, until he became the only reality that she could imagine. Aware that his mouth pressed more firmly against hers, she lifted her arms around his neck and clung tightly. She had never felt so alive, so human and vulnerable. The cool, sensual darkness filtered through her, spiraling headily, causing her to tremble at the shadowy pleasure of it. She breathed his name as he brushed gossamer kisses along her neck, and her voice seemed to come from some remote distance. Then he was unfastening her arms from around his neck, and Rosalie felt as if her body were being torn in two.

"Hold me longer," she whispered, the darkness swirling around her in an exotic mist, his masculine scent filling her nostrils and mixing intimately with the air that she breathed. "Don't leave me . . . Rand, love me."

He shivered and opened his eyes, wondering in the next hovering moment if she had meant those last two words in a physical or emotional sense. The reply he wanted to give was blocked in his throat. Rand had never spoken of love to anyone in his life, and now did not seem the right time or place. Coward, he railed at

himself, and forced his arms to loosen from Rosalie's
slender body.

"I'll come back soon," he said huskily. Her lashes
flickered upward to reveal eyes that were as dark and
blue as a troubled sea, stunning in their unrelenting
intensity of color. "Don't leave the château," he continued, giving her a little shake to make certain that the
words left a strong impression on her. "Don't set one of
your little feet outside the château, Rose, do you
understand?"

"I understand," she murmured, quivering a little as
his strong hands left her. *Rand, love me.* Thick, compressed sobs congealed in her chest, but she would not
let them out. She would not cry in front of him, she
would not beg for his love or his pity, she would not let
him guess at the extent of her fear or the reasons
behind it. She turned her back as he left the room,
keeping her back resolutely stiff.

The sky darkened as the hours passed, and as Rosalie
stared out of the sitting-room window with Mireille in
silence, they noticed a fascinating illusion. The fire in
the village became visible as night settled over the land,
and the setting sun hung over the leaping blaze. It
dropped lower and lower, until the sun seemed to pool
into the fire and fuel it with new strength. Hour after
hour the women in the château waited, for all of the
men, including Guillaume, Jérème, Eleazar, and Monsieur Alvin had gone to the village to help. Around ten
o'clock most of them decided to retire, and Rosalie
paused before the window, her blue eyes fastened
unblinking on the glow that broke the line of the
horizon. Surely half the village must have burned by
now. Mixed with her pity for those who had lost their
homes and probably some of their loved ones was the
cold fear that Rand might be hurt. He no longer struck
her as being quite as reckless as she had once considered him, but she knew that it was very likely for him to

volunteer for the riskier tasks. What if he were trapped somewhere this very second, smothering from thick smoke and thin air? What if he was being scorched by the flames that were so hot she could see their light even from this distance?

Valiantly Rosalie tried to wait patiently, waving all of the others off to bed and repeating to herself what Rand had told her. He would be incensed beyond reason if she left the château. She could picture his rage if he discovered that she had even considered disobeying him. But if she had to wait in suspense much longer, then Randall Berkeley would have to institutionalize her at Bedlam, the insane asylum north of London. She could not tolerate the buzzing anxieties that plagued her in the silence, any more than she could have held still while a swarm of flies tried to settle on her.

"Please forgive me," she whispered, closing her eyes and wrinkling her nose in agitation. She already had misgivings about her next actions. "I won't go near anyone, I won't go near the fire . . . I won't even get off the horse. I'll just go and make sure that you're all right, and then I'll come straight back. God willing, you won't even see me. And I'll never do anything like this again, I promise."

Feeling relieved at having made a decision, she blew out the candle beside her chair and turned out all of the lamps. Quietly Rosalie opened the glass-paneled door of the sitting room and slipped outside. The night air was cool as it blew against her throat, and she gathered her shawl more closely around her bare arms. Her dress was pale yellow and sleeveless, one of the simplest garments she owned. As she went into the stable and heard the nickers of the horses, Rosalie found herself exceedingly grateful for the experience she had received at Robin's Threshold, the Winthrops' country estate. Baron Winthrop had insisted that she and Elaine learn how to ride when they were young, and Rosalie silently thanked him.

"Hello, Spook," she said softly, patting the gelding's nose. "Don't be offended . . . but I'm going to take my chances with Linnette tonight."

The stars and the moon lent enough light for her to make her way through the shadowy interior of the stable, and she managed to saddle Linnette. It was perhaps inexpertly done, but at least the cinch was tight and the mare was gentle. Rosalie led the horse outside, swung herself lightly into the saddle, and hooked her knee around the pommel before urging Linnette quietly toward the village. The night air smelled of fire and burning wood the closer they came to the little community. Rosalie saw the mare's ears twitch nervously at the sounds of shouting and screaming coming from the village, and when they were close enough to hear the roar of the blaze, Linnette began to prance agitatedly.

"Pretty girl . . . don't worry," Rosalie soothed, jumping down and winding the reins around the frail branch of a small tree. They were far enough from the scene so that the mare would not be threatened by man or fire. It was easy enough for Rosalie to travel the rest of the way on foot.

The fire had a peculiarly voracious sound, and it thundered against her ears with the rush of a pounding waterfall. Rosalie's eyes darted from place to place, encountering the blackened, smoking remains of homes and shops. Sticks of furniture and burning tufts of cushions and mattress stuffings were scattered in the streets. The fire had passed through this section of the village and had been more or less beaten out, but it seemed to be growing in strength in other parts of the community. Cautiously she walked along the outskirts of the buildings, her eyes touching sympathetically on the prone figures of the wounded. How had it all started? she wondered, and moved toward the areas where the sky was brightened into gray and purple by the glow of the strongest flames.

Suddenly a woman ran down a small street screaming, and Rosalie realized with panic-induced speed that the poor creature's skirt had caught on fire. Whipping off her shawl, she ran to chase after the woman.

"Stop—I'll help you!" Rosalie cried, but the woman did not listen, and it was a mere trick of chance that she tripped on a stone and fell to the ground. Rosalie reached her in an instant, beating out the smoldering cotton with her shawl. The woman was motionless even after the fire was extinguished. It did not appear that she had been burned, for although the skirts of her dress had been destroyed, there had not been time for the flames to reach her skin.

"Are you hurt?" Rosalie asked, turning her over, and the woman stared at her vacantly. Rosalie realized that she had asked the question in English. "Oh, damn . . ." she muttered, unable in situations of duress to remember a single word of French. "Are you . . . êtes-vous . . ."

The woman burst into tears and then staggered up to move to the side of the street. Looking after her hesitantly, Rosalie gathered up her own skirts and the shawl before continuing down the street.

The church bell, now ominously silent, was silhouetted against the sky by stretching flames. The fire had not yet reached the church, but it was approaching invincibly. Rosalie murmured under her breath, hoping that the church would not be destroyed. It was the focus of the community, the center of most of the family and social activities in the village. The damage left in the wake of the fire was already of disastrous proportions, but the destruction of the church would be the worst part of the catastrophe.

She tried to get out of the way, for men were rushing

by her with sloshing buckets of water from the well and from the feeble streams that branched from the Loire. Others were beating out the fire with small rugs. A man collapsed nearby, dropping a bucket of precious water, which soaked immediately into the warm ground. His arm had been badly burned, and did not appear to have been attended to. Two or three women rushed to drag him out of the path of the men who continued to battle the fire, and Rosalie took one of his arms to help them pull him across the ground. They reached an area where several other wounded people were resting, and one of the women patted Rosalie's arm in silent gratitude before turning away to bandage yet another gory burn. Rosalie looked across the group but could detect no sight of Rand's dark gold hair, and she swallowed hard before walking away to continue her search elsewhere.

The cottages near the church were now being evacuated, the sounds of wailing children rising above the curses of the men and the roaring fire. Rosalie could not see anything resembling Rand's tall, broad-shouldered figure anywhere. Her eyes began to water and sting from the smoke, and she coughed to clear her throat of a dry, kindling itch.

She wiped her wet cheeks with the back of a hand and immediately afterward was confronted with the pitiable sight of a bawling child, who could not have been more than two or three. It was a little girl, whose hair was curly brown, her mouth nearly as wide as her face as she screamed for her mother.

"Shhh . . . little one, be quiet," Rosalie murmured, picking the child up and casting a glance around the street. No parent or relative was in sight, and she wondered what to do as the girl clung to her like a little monkey. Patting the small, cushiony back gently, Rosalie turned in indecision and ran into what felt like a solid stone wall. The child began screaming anew, this time directly into Rosalie's ear, and she squinted at whatever it was she had run into. A pair of hands clasped firmly over her shoulders, steadying her.

"Mademoiselle Rosalie? Is that you?"

The girl was removed from her arms and lowered to the ground, and Rosalie let out a relieved sigh as she recognized the handsome, soot-streaked visage above her.

"Guillaume," she said, tears coming anew to her eyes as a smoky breeze engulfed them.

His puzzled expression disappeared as he grinned at her. "I thought it was you," he said, shifting his leg slightly as the child wrapped her arms securely around his knee. "And then I thought, no, it could not be . . . not unless you had lost every bit of the good sense I previously considered you to have. . . . *Mon Dieu*, Mira didn't come with you, did she?"

"No."

"Thank heaven. Now, the next question is, whose baby is this?"

"I don't know—I hoped there would be a place where they are keeping stray children until the parents can find them."

"There is. I will relieve you of this"—he looked down ruefully at the little creature clinging to his leg—"charming burden. But even though the worst of the fire is over, it isn't safe for you to wander off alone."

"What do you mean, the worst is over? The church—"

"The fire won't reach it. They will be able to confine it to the cottages—*Dieu*, I can't really believe you're here."

"I couldn't wait at the château. I had this terrible feeling—"

"Lady angel, you aren't supposed to be here," he said, the bittersweet color of his eyes shining with subtle lights of amusement.

"I've been looking for Rand," she said. "I haven't seen him anywhere. Is he all right? Have you seen him? When and where do you think he—?"

"Slower, *jolie ange* . . . don't worry—the last time I saw him, he was helping to move the children from the vicar's cottage. He is fine."

"I don't see him—which cottage? That burning one?"

"Ah, *zut*," Guillaume said, following the direction of her trembling finger. "Oh, hell . . . yes, that one. So it has caught fire. I hope everyone is out."

Rosalie fled from him, picking up her skirts to run faster toward the blazing structure. Flames filled the windows on the second floor, making the cottage look like a multieyed demon. If Rand was in there, he was trapped in an inescapable inferno. She was paralyzed as she stood there in the light of the blaze, one hand pressed to the base of her throat. With a sound of thunder, the roof fell in, sending up a shower of sparks that danced and floated like thousands of fireflies. Rosalie started, her stomach caving inwardly, all the air leaving her lungs. Her lips moved in a soundless prayer, and then she felt her legs turn to rubber.

"Was anyone in there?" she whispered as she staggered to an old man who stood nearby, his eyes fastened on the mountain of burning rubble. "Was anyone in there?" Rosalie repeated, tugging at his sleeve, and he turned to her with empty black eyes. She backed away from him in panic, thinking that it was all an awful dream, and from then on everything changed into a succession of pictures that moved with quicksilver speed. Something hit her hard around the waist and wrapped around her so tightly that she could not make a sound . . . at the same time, a string of foul curses floated about her head, and she was turned like a rag doll as someone began to tug and beat at her gown. Dazedly Rosalie began to understand that the garment

had caught on fire, that one of the sparks must have set
the fragile material burning, and that if her rescuer
had delayed one second longer she would have been
devoured in an immediate, fatal blaze.

She was uprighted and held firmly against a hard,
tightly muscled surface, the arm that had been cutting
around her waist loosening so that a large masculine
hand could splay across her hips and press her closer.
Rosalie's face was pressed against the warm, golden
skin of a man's throat, and as she smelled the familiar
scent of it, she relaxed into trusting stillness. Her arms
lifted to clasp his broad shoulders, her upper body
leaning against his powerful chest as she listened to the
disturbed quickness of his breating.

"Rand," she said, her terror subsiding as she felt his
inexhaustible strength enfold her protectively, and the
nightmarish sickness fell away from her. After the most
blissful moment of her entire life, she pulled her head
back to look up at his face. His skin was smudged with
soot, which ringed under his topaz-colored eyes and
gave him the startling appearance of a lion. The
firelight flickered over his dark face and illuminated
the singed ends of his gold-streaked hair. He's unharmed, she thought, and stared at him with a
diamond-bright gaze.

It did not take long for her to become aware of the
fact that he was not at all happy to see her.

Thirteen

In all my being is no ripple of unrest
For I have opened unto you
The wide gates of my being
And like a tide, you have flowed into me.
— Author Unknown

"Goddammit!" Rand snarled, his grip biting as he held her away from him and kept her at arm's length to take a quick and thorough inventory of her condition. "If that dress wasn't half-burned off already, I would lift your skirts and thrash you for an hour!"

Before she could reply, he shook her roughly, and Rosalie gritted her teeth to keep them from clacking together. Then Rand was still, holding her so close that they were eye-to-eye. "I told you to stay at the château! It is dangerous for you to be here! Damn you!" She was subjected to another vigorous shaking, and Rosalie thought dazedly that her bones would start to rattle together if he didn't stop soon. She decided to throw in a word or two on her own behalf.

"I wasn't planning to get this close to the fire—" she began.

"To hell with your plans! I look around the first moment I have to rest, and I find you lit up like a candelabrum!"

Rosalie opened her mouth to answer and found herself being shaken again. Unfortunately it seemed that Rand planned to continue the pattern for a considerably long time, and she threw her arms around his neck to make him stop.

335

"Why? Why did you disobey me again?" he demanded, and she cut through the haze of his rage with a few soft words.

"Because I love you."

Rand froze, staring at her as if he did not trust his ears. His grip loosened as his fingers became lax with surprise. "You . . ." he began to repeat, and the hard edge of anger fled from his expression. It was almost more than one man could bear, to be afraid for her and infuriated with her at the same time, and then to be overcome with a wave of love so intense that he could not speak. Suddenly his mouth was on hers, his hand framing the side of her face and pressing her head against his shoulder. She parted her lips, accepting the plundering of his tongue, the blood surging fast and hot through her veins in response. It seemed that he kissed her for hours, and when he lifted his head she felt as though she was floating.

"I'm still going to thrash you," he whispered, his lips brushing against hers as he spoke. Everything around them—the fire, the crowd, the smoke—was forgotten in the wonder of momentous discovery.

"I love you," Rosalie repeated, discovering with delight that her statement elicited a new surge of warmth to gentle his expression.

His mouth twitched wryly as he contemplated her small face. "You think you've found a magic phrase to calm my temper," Rand said huskily. "I'll admit, it does much to soothe the ire . . . but I intend to keep my word, and you won't ecape completely free for having ignored my wishes."

"I was afraid that something might happen to you," she said in a small, apologetic voice. "When I saw the roof of that cottage collapse I thought that you might have been inside. I wanted to die."

He understood exactly how she felt, more than

anyone else could. His fingers played lightly at the nape
of her neck, tranquilizing the tightened nerves there.

As Rosalie allowed her head to rest against his
shoulder, Rand murmured in a soothing tone, "I know,
sweet. But have you stopped to think that all of that,
including the damage done to your gown, would have
been avoided had you listened to me before? Tonight
you've aged me another ten years, *fleur,* and at this rate
I don't have much longer to last."

"Please take me home," she whispered, drifting in
the warm pleasure she derived from the sensitive touch
of his hands. "I want to make love with you."

Rand's mouth curved in a reluctant smile, his eyes
gleaming with tiny golden lights. "God. You have a hell
of a way of ending a lecture, my love."

Rosalie sat in front of the fireplace in her bedchamber, staring absently into its vivid depths as she curled
her feet more tightly underneath her silk-clad form.
She held a lacquered brush in her hand and drew it
through her newly washed hair, brushing over and
over again until the warm length of it formed a lustrous
curtain around her shoulders and back. The wavering
light and the rhythmic motion of the hairbrush served
to calm her overwrought nerves, for it had been a
trying night. After riding home alongside Rand and
Guillaume, she had been subjected to an impassioned
lecture from Madame Alvin and reproachful glances
from Mireille. A steaming bath had followed, as well as
a thorough scrubbing to rid her hair and skin of soot
and smoke. There had been no word of good night
from Rand, an optimistic sign, for Rosalie guessed that
when all of the residents of the château retired he
might come to her room. Wistfully she tilted her head
and brushed the sable waves over one shoulder, preparing to braid them into a thick skein.

"Leave it loose."

The soft request came from the doorway, and Rosalie turned to face the visitor as the door closed with a quiet sound. Rand stood there in a wine silk robe, leaning back against the portal as he regarded her steadily. His hair was damp and freshly cropped, the singed ends shorn off to reveal a shine of pure amber. A log in the fireplace crumbled with a rustling sound, giving off a brief flash of white-gold light that played over his face and eyes with a peculiar luminescence. Rosalie caught her breath as she stared at him, knowing that something was different about him but unable to identify it. For an instant he seemed like a sleek, handsome stranger, and she was motionless as his hazel gaze swept over her. Then he smiled slowly, and she flew to him with an incoherent sound, suffused with love for him. Rand enveloped her in his arms, smiling against her hair as she stood on her toes to accommodate his height.

"I assumed you'd be asleep," he said in a muffled tone, lacing his fingers in the silky curtain of hair that provided a constant temptation to him.

"I'm not tired at all."

"I'm so glad to hear it," he replied, his smile tinged with wryness as he lowered his head to kiss her.

His mouth slanted passionately over hers, and the next thing Rosalie was aware of was that she was lying by him on the bed with no memory of how they had gotten there. He made no move yet to undress her, but his hands wandered over her with unhidden curiosity and more than a touch of possessiveness. "I love you," he whispered, and Rosalie flushed with the surge of joy that his words elicited.

"I've loved you," she replied softly, "since the first night in Paris. We were dancing, and your arms were around me . . . and suddenly I realized that I didn't want it to end." She lifted her eyes to meet his, and

Rand answered her unspoken question without hesitancy.

"That first time I left you," he said, his voice low and quiet, "when I came here to break up the d'Angoux holdings . . . I couldn't stop thinking about all that I had told you that morning. I had no idea of what had prompted me to tell you that much about my past. I was irritated by the fact that I kept thinking about you, and even more by the realization that I couldn't wait to get back to the Lothaire. My mind was filled with countless schemes to get you into bed—but as well as wanting your desire, I wanted your trust, your affection . . . things I had never asked from anyone before. I felt as if you belonged to me, and I went a little bit insane each time you denied me." The firelight shone on his golden skin with a candescent warmth, his thick lashes casting a shadow on the cleanly molded edges of his cheekbones. "You have such little hands," he murmured, lifting one of them and examining her dainty palm before pressing a kiss there. "It stunned me to realize that you held my entire world in them." Rand's thoughtful smile faded as he looked into her eyes. "Why did you refuse when I proposed to you?" he asked slowly, and Rosalie frowned, turning her face to the side. In silence she struggled to find the right words to express herself.

"Sometimes I'm overwhelmed by you," she whispered. "You're all I could ever want. But . . . we're so different. My life has been quiet, sheltered . . . and I know my own heart—"

"And you think I don't know mine?" Rand raised himself on an elbow, staring down at her intently.

"You're used to excitement, variety. I was afraid of being merely a novelty to you . . . interesting but temporary."

"Dammit, Rose," he said, his expression edged with exasperation, "a novelty? I asked you to *marry* me. If that isn't a declaration of long-lasting intentions, I don't know what is."

"You know as well as I do what marriage means to a member of the aristocracy," she said levelly. "Especially one as highborn as you. After producing a suitable heir, I had no guarantee that you wouldn't install me in the country and proceed to forget about my very existence. Considering the disparity between your disposition and mine, I thought it very likely that you would tire of me and the quiet life that—"

"A quiet life," Rand said grimly, "is something I would welcome, but I don't consider it very likely. Not when I haven't had a moment's peace since first meeting you. Somehow I can't picture our married life together descending from the level of 'tumultuous' until we're both in our seventies. Especially," he added meaningfully, "if you persist in dashing into every dangerous situation that I try to keep you out of."

"It has nothing to do with trust," Rosalie said in a rush, endeavoring to placate him. "Especially not what I did tonight. I trust you completely. Truly, I wish I could follow your requests to the letter—"

"If only," Rand said to the room at large, "the wish were supported by deed as well as sentiment."

"—but I couldn't stay here any longer. *You* wouldn't sit here and do nothing if you were afraid *I* was in danger, would you?"

It was an effective point. Rand stared at her contemplatively, his mouth twisting.

"You're going to continue using your own judgment when you decide it's necessary," he stated, one eyebrow lifting in inquiry.

"I . . . I can't behave any other way," Rosalie admitted, tracing a fingernail on the stitching of his robe and averting her gaze from his.

"What about," he inquired softly, "in an extreme

case, if I asked you to do something without questioning why?"

She looked at him directly, her voice steady and firm.

"Then I will trust you enough to do whatever you ask," she vowed. "You can depend on that. But would the reverse hold true? If I ever asked you to do something for me without questioning it, would you?"

He half-smiled, a glint of admiration lightening his hazel eyes.

"Of course, *mon coeur.*"

The pact was made. Rand's answer was heartening to Rosalie, for she began to see that he was willing to treat her as a partner, someone he would trust as well as love. Most women were not so fortunate, for most men would not tolerate the kind of debates and discussions that she engaged in with Rand. After a moment of pleasurable reflection, she dared to ask something else.

"I have always been determined," she said, "that the man I married would want me for forever . . . only me, and no other women."

"I will want you until every stone and brick of this château has crumbled into dust. You were meant for me, and I have no desire for any other woman." Rand pulled her body closer to his, his large hands molding her buttocks and pressing her to the hard, burning length of his manhood. "*This,*" he murmured huskily, "is all because of you, and of late has promised to become a permanent condition. Sweet, we could spend the rest of the night deciding on stipulations and provisions of our marriage, but since we have the rest of our lives to do that, I have an alternative to suggest."

Rosalie's temperature seemed to escalate several degrees as he shifted her hips against his. Her skin had become oversensitive and hungry for his slightest touch, her breathing shallow and fast as she struggled to accommodate an overload of messages. She wanted to be rid of the soft, clinging material of her gown, which was an unwanted barrier between her skin and his hands. She wanted to feel his hard, naked flesh against hers, for nothing in the world seemed as glorious as the multitude of differences between their bodies, rough and soft, aggressive and yielding, strong and pliant.

"Yes," she said, trapped in the brilliant color of his eyes, the indescribable mixture of hues that blended together in darkness overlaid with light. "Whatever you were going to suggest, I'll agree to it."

"Ah . . . wait," he said with a sudden chuckle, "I'd better take advantage of your mood, since I don't know when you'll be so amenable again. Put my heart at ease, *petite fleur* . . . tell me you'll agree to be my wife."

"Yes, I will," she answered breathlessly, her mouth seeking his. *"Yes."*

With a smothered groan he kissed her, his desire careening out of control. She sighed in mounting desire, pulling at the slick material of Rand's robe until the brawny lines of his shoulders emerged, and her hands splayed lovingly over the smooth-muscled expanse. The hair at the nape of his neck was much shorter than before, the newly shorn locks like thick silk against her fingertips.

Wanting him fiercely, Rosalie wrapped her arms around him and arched against the lean firmness of his body. The robe parted, and the only barrier that remained between them was the filmy layers of her gown. Impatiently she fumbled with the silken knots that held the garment in place, but desire had made her clumsy. Panting with frustration, Rosalie began to pull the sheer material upward over her thighs, aided by Rand's questing hands. He inhaled sharply as he encountered the bareness of her hips and realized that she wore nothing underneath the gown. Rosalie's slender legs parted as she lifted her hips, a gasp escaping her throat in the moment that her naked loins brushed against his. The searing heat of his masculinity pressed against the delicate cradle between her legs like a brand. She felt the warmth and power of him, the slight throbbing of his flesh that drove her wild with the need to feel him inside her, yet he held himself back, refusing to enter her.

"Why are you waiting?" she asked, her voice sounding strangely low and throaty to her own ears. She knew that Rand wanted her as much as she wanted him, for he was gasping and flushed, and he was full and heavy against her dampening flesh.

"Not like last time . . ." he muttered. "Not with your skirts bunched around your waist, as if we had no time—"

"Please, I don't care," she begged, her hair tangling over her face and neck as she writhed underneath him. "I just want you to—"

"Shhh. We have all night," he said soothingly, pulling away slightly as his fingers went to the knotted ties of her gown. Rosalie swallowed convulsively and then closed her eyes, forcing herself to be patient as he worked at the tiny silken ribbons. Her thundering heartbeat slowed a little as she waited, but it was with intense relief that she felt him undo the last of the knots and spread the gown open. The wine-colored robe and the nightgown were thrown to the floor, the edges of the garments fluttering like moth wings.

Rand looked down at Rosalie, pulling her hair away from her face and spreading it carefully over the pillow. The sable locks formed a thick, luxuriant spill, glistening with deep colors that seemed to burn within each strand. The tender paleness of her breasts gleamed with a pearly sheen in the firelight, causing Rand's breath to shorten considerably. He lifted a warm hand to the perfect curves, fitting his palm to the young, sweet flesh, stroking the peaks with the tip of his index

finger until they responded to his touch and contracted. "You're so unbelievably beautiful," he said
huskily. "When I try to remember you as you are now,
I become desperate with wanting . . . and yet the memories are poor imitations of the reality. No dream, no
thoughts, no memory could ever do justice to you." His
hand moved over her breast in one more exquisitely
textured caress before sliding down to the soft line of
her waist. "So small, so feminine," he whispered,
lowering his lips to her breast, "so sweet . . ."

She gave a thin cry as his hot, devouring mouth
covered her nipple, his tongue flickering artfully
around the excited nerves and sending sparks through
her body in a violent rainfall. She opened her thighs at
the touch of his hands, feverishly straining to lure him
closer.

"Is this your retribution for what I did tonight?" she
asked fitfully, tracing the hard, wide muscles of his
upper arms and gripping the tops of his shoulders.
"Making me wait until I die with hunger for you?"

"You'll recompense me for all I went through," he
said, his voice sounding like a lazy purr as he tasted the
smooth valley between her breasts, "by forgoing a
night of sleep. And although we'll both be exhausted
tomorrow, I promise we'll be too sated to care." His
fingertips seemed to have an acute sensitivity to the
most inflamed points of her body, wandering from
nerve to nerve and drawing incredible sensations of
pleasure up from her skin. One by one the connections
between her thoughts were severed, leaving her only
with the capability to respond to him like a mindless
creature. Rand knew exactly how to pleasure her,
stroking firmly in some places, brushing as softly as
cats' whiskers in others, muffling her pleading cries
with his kisses and showing her how to please him in
return. They drew nearer to a wavering precipice, their
bodies flexing and smoothing and gathering against

each other. Several times Rosalie waited in confusion and anticipation for him to possess her, for it was obvious that she was ready for him. Still he held back, choosing instead to tease her with sinuous caresses. After long minutes of the refined torture, Rosalie reached the limit of her endurance.

"Enough," she gasped, tired and aching with the need for relief. "I can't bear it any longer, I don't know how you can."

In response his hands grasped her hips firmly, and Rosalie realized with shock that he was turning her onto her stomach. Her breasts were flattened as she lay on the mattress, her face turned to one side as she endeavored to look at him. An odd, excited chill chased over her skin as Rand kissed the nape of her neck and nibbled lightly at the fragile hollows of her spine. Although she had never imagined it before, instinctively Rosalie sensed what he was about to do, and she quivered in nervous expectation. Rand's velvety voice teased her ears, dark and erotic whispers that filled her mind with vivid, earthy pictures. Smoothly his fingers slid between her and the mattress, splaying under her hips and lifting her upward. Her knees folded underneath her body, and she was hazily aware of the friction of his hard, lightly furred chest against her back.

"Rand?" she asked dazedly, her mind swimming as she heard the taut flow of his breathing, and then she sobbed as he thrust into her, large and potent, the sensation stringent and forceful as it rampaged through her body. His arms were braced on either side of her, and she clung to his wrists tightly, filled by his driving power until there was no separation between her flesh and his. And although his passion was violent it was also loving, for she was dimly aware that her satisfaction was paramount to him, and that every movement was designed to increase her rapture. The sensations welled inside her until she gave herself up to

them helplessly, arching against him as she was transfixed by shattering bliss. His hand reached underneath
her body to stroke her, furthering the sweet gratification as long as possible. Rosalie felt him surge inside
her hotly, and Rand pulled her hips more tightly
against his as he shuddered with the white heat of
fulfillment.

It took a long time for Rosalie to recover herself, her
mind and body drugged with a pleasant weakness that
wound around her like velvet fleece. Turning to face
Rand, she pressed her face against his shoulder and was
enclosed in his embrace, the safest haven she would
ever know. She was not aware of falling asleep, but she
knew when she opened her eyes again that hours had
passed by. Stretching and yawning, she luxuriated in
the mingled warmth of their bodies and snuggled
against Rand. As she lifted her gaze upward she saw
that he was clear-eyed and awake, and evidently had
been watching her for some time.

"It's dawn," he said, stroking the soft skin along the
side of her face with his thumb. He was fascinated by
the tumbled beauty of her, her face tinged with the
pink of the frailest seashell, her tender and well-kissed
lips, and the eyes of a blue so rich and deep that they
approached the shade of midnight. Drowsily she smiled
at him, her gaze taking on mysterious depths that
caused his heart to skip a beat. She seemed to have
some secret knowledge that pleased her greatly, and he
wondered what silent thoughts were going through her
mind.

Rosalie brushed her mouth over his heart, searching
and finding his steady pulse, her tongue touching his
skin until she sensed that his heartbeat had increased to
a faster rhythm. Raising herself up onto her elbows, she
climbed halfway onto his large body with the graceful
precision of a cat, her hands delicately placed to steady
herself as she bent her head to his throat.

"Rose . . ." he began with a husky laugh, but his amusement disappeared rapidly as she licked and nibbled at the base of his neck. Her weight, slight though it was, served to press his wide shoulders flat against the mattress, the soft peaks of her breasts brushing against his chest. In a matter of seconds his desire for her catapulted to an excruciating level. His lashes lowered as he felt the insistent, nagging desperation sweep over him in an unruly tide. He was hard and hungry for her, and his hands came up to her elbows as he prepared to pull her under him.

"No," she said, and he let go of her, momentarily surprised by the firmness of her voice. What game had she decided to play? he wondered, and his eyes narrowed as he stared at her. Bestowing a promising half-smile on him, Rosalie pulled the pillow from underneath his head and tossed the downy cushion to the floor. Completely prone, Rand gave her a measured look, his eyes full of curiosity, desire, and perhaps even a touch of frustration. He slid his hands behind his head and continued to watch her, deciding to wait a minute or two in order to discover what she intended. Rosalie resumed her slow, careful attentions, her lips wandering up to the rim of his ear and back down his neck again. She felt her own excitement increase, for it was a novel sensation to feel his powerful body so still under her ministrations, all of his strength and masculine urges held in check, leaving her free to explore him unhindered. Kissing his lips warmly, Rosalie touched her tongue to the corner of his mouth, smiling as she felt his chest rise and fall with a deep gasp. His hands came on either side of her face as he kissed her hungrily, a soft purr vibrating in his throat as her tongue slipped inside his mouth. He began to say something, but the low sound of his voice faded abruptly as he felt her fingers trace over the well-sculptured side of his waist and stroke over his abdomen. The tip of her tongue left a moist, warm trail over one flat male nipple, then the other, and suddenly Rand could not remember ever aching with such need in his life.

"I've got to have you *now*," he rasped impatiently, and Rosalie pulled away before he could reach her, turning the covers further down the bed. He was a splendorous sight, lean and perfectly made, each part of his form etched with grace and masculine vitality. Bending over him, she pressed her mouth to the taut surface of his midriff and left a downward trail of kisses along his skin, pausing at the tightly knit flesh of his abdomen and feeling him shiver as she pressed her teeth there in a small crescent. Her hair trailed over him silkily, as soft and precious as rivulets of mercury.

The tinge of passion illuminated Rand's cheekbones. His eyes were closed, his skin tightly drawn over the strong, elegant lines of his face. Suddenly Rosalie reached the object of her quest, and as her mouth and tongue tentatively caressed his throbbing masculinity, he reached a plane of sensation that he had never dreamed possible. Biting his lip, he clenched his trembling hands, a hoarse sound issuing from his throat as he felt the whispery warmth of Rosalie's wondering sigh against him. Rand's mind went blank, and he was driven so mad with desire that he barely remembered what happened afterward. He gathered her in his arms with a punishing grip, his arms as tight as steel bands around her. Rosalie gasped at his unanticipated reaction, her gentle reverie interrupted rudely as he flipped her over onto her back, his grip so tight that she could barely breathe. He ignored her indignant protests, pushing into her with one greedy shove, huge and demanding. Then Rosalie groaned, arching against him repeatedly as he rode her hard and fast. Helplessly she exploded in his arms, just before his low growl of ecstasy vibrated in her ears.

*   *   *

Clad in a demure white-and-salmon-striped gown, Rosalie sipped at the remaining coffee in her china cup. She was extremely grateful that Rand had devoured breakfast quickly and left to go riding, for she had found it difficult to face him this morning without flushing uncontrollably.

Although everyone behaved as if it were an ordinary day, she sensed that many speculative looks had been cast in her direction. She had no doubt that Guillaume and other residents of the château community had seen and reported her extraordinary behavior at the site of the fire, including the demonstrative kiss she had shared with Rand. Mireille was unexpectedly quiet, asking no questions but seeming to be very content . . . and Madame Alvin seemed to alternate between an approving tone of voice and a suspicious one. They all knew that there was much more to Rosalie's relationship with Rand than had previously been revealed— but no one was certain to what extent they were involved, or in what way. Rand's attitude was a cross between amusing and maddening. In the past hour, after coming downstairs and making some mundane remark about having a hearty night's sleep, he had treated Rosalie as if she were an indifferent acquaintance. However, every now and then he would make a double-edged comment, timing his remarks so that they invariably caused her to choke on her coffee and croissant.

After he had gone, Rosalie and Mireille finished breakfast, spreading the last of the hot rolls with fresh butter and eating them leisurely. Mireille excused herself for a few minutes, and after the girl left, Rosalie stood up from the table to walk over to the window. Guillaume passed by with an armload of dead prunings from the rosebushes. He was whistling in a carefree manner, his eyes slanting with the intimation of a smile, just as Mireille's did when she was happy.

Rosalie noticed with concern that there was a heavy white bandage swathed about his upper arm, and she went to the sitting-room doors to meet him as he walked by.

"Lady angel," he greeted her, his smile dazzling in its cheerfulness.

"I did not notice last night that you were hurt."

"You were occupied with many other thoughts, all of them more pressing than my little burn."

She refused to accept his facetious attitude, her expression retaining a touch of seriousness. "Burns are dangerous if they are not well-tended, Guillaume. Was it properly—?"

"Mira saw to it," he said with a slight shrug, taking care that he did not drop any of the clippings he held in his arms. "She is very good at such things—I have sworn many times that her touch is magic. Have you ever seen the little bundle she keeps in her room?—all kinds of foul herbs, oils, and pungent salves."

"No, I didn't know that."

"Then Monsieur de Berkeley hasn't mentioned anything about it to you?"

"No, he hasn't," Rosalie replied, wondering why Guillaume seemed so inordinately interested in her answer. "Why would he know anything about Mireille's talent at healing?"

"There is no reason why he should," Guillaume said quickly, and his dark eyes smiled into hers. "I am just making a poor effort at conversation, *mademoiselle*."

"Guillaume . . . please don't work hard today," Rosalie said. "Be very careful of your arm, and if it starts to bother you, come in right away."

"But what if *monsieur*—?"

"*Monsieur* might have been too preoccupied this morning to remember your arm, but I am certain that he wouldn't want you to exert yourself."

"You are very kind, *mademoiselle*," Guillaume said,

and his wide smile faltered as he looked into her innocent blue eyes. "The kindest woman," he added, "that I have ever met." He looked at her in a manner that made Rosalie feel flattered, bashful, and faintly uneasy.

"I have many faults," she said softly. "I'm far from being an angel, Guillaume."

He stood there in indecision, usually so facile with words, struck dumb by the sweet compassion in her face. He did not deserve even one smile from her, much less her concern, yet even knowing that did not stop him from bringing her hand to his lips and pressing a reverent kiss to her fingertips.

"You have no faults," he said, releasing her hand gently, "except that you trust too easily, *jolie ange*." With that he left her, the sun playing over him so that his hair shone like a raven's wing. Thoughtfully Rosalie walked back into the sitting room, shaking her head as she wondered if he had been trying to tell her something.

The foils flashed in the sunlight, scissoring together and then clicking apart. Guillaume's face was set in concentration as he parried Rand's smooth attack, his injured arm serving to balance his movements while the good one wielded the blade efficiently. Guillaume cursed under his breath as his triple feint was blocked, for he realized then that through a series of subtle maneuvers Rand had led him from one engagement to another with the ease of a puppeteer.

"What was that?" Rand inquired, flashing a sudden grin as he sought to find an opening in the other man's weakening defense.

"A commentary on your performance, *monsieur*. Or perhaps on my own—I am not certain which."

Rand chuckled. He enjoyed fencing with Guillaume because it presented an unusual challenge. Guillaume was not always a fair player, and whether it was from a lack of classical training or practiced cunning, he bent the rules slightly. It took a great deal of concentration to form an adequate defence to such unorthodox moves, forcing Rand to switch from automatic and reliable methods to equally inventive ones.

The exchange was halted by the appearance of Rosalie. Out of the corner of his eye Rand could see the tenseness of her body and the way she had wound her hands in the folds of her skirts. Rand held up his left hand in a commanding gesture, stilling his foil after the last block and glancing at her white face.

"Some mail has arrived," she said, her eyes dark as they fastened onto his. "A man brought it up from the village. Do you have some francs to give him—?"

"Yes," Rand interrupted, his voice deliberately calm. He knew why she was so agitated—the answer to her letter must have arrived from England. He knew also that she did not want to open Amille's letter alone. "Guillaume, we'll continue this later."

"*Certainement*," Guillaume said, his gaze traveling from one to the other of them in subtle curiosity. He took the foil from Rand and flicked the rubber cap absently, watching as the other man went into the château.

Rosalie waited in her room, sitting down on the edge of the bed and clasping her hands in her lap until Rand closed the door.

"It's from Amille," he stated bluntly, handing her one of the two letters in his hand and reserving the other for himself. "Shall I stay here while you read it?"

"Please," she murmured, her hands trembling as she broke the wax seal. "You received one also. Who . . . who sent it?"

"My brother, Colin."

"Oh." Rosalie paused, taking a deep breath and closing her eyes as she gathered her courage. The paper that she clutched in her hands held the secrets of her past, her birth, her heritage, and the information that it contained was of such importance that she was almost afraid to read it. She thought briefly of Amille writing it, and suddenly Rosalie missed her so much that she felt a physical ache inside her chest.

"Rose . . ." Rand's voice intruded on her building tension and anxiety. "What is written in that letter will not change anything. You will still be the same woman, with the same talents and strengths, and I am extremely grateful to whoever fathered you. And whether you're the daughter of Beau Brummell, Georges Belleau, or Father Christmas, I will love you just the same."

She nodded silently, bending her head over the folded parchment and opening it carefully. She spread it over her lap as she read, her eyes becoming wet with tears at the first sight of Amille's familiar handwriting.

My dearest Rosalie . . .

She turned away from Rand as she read the letter slowly, only pausing halfway through it to take the handkerchief that he handed to her wordlessly. Rand leaned against the wall and watched her, crossing his long legs and folding his arms. His eyes rested on the center of her narrow shoulders, and he stifled the urge to go over to her again, knowing that she had to face the contents of Amille's letter by herself, without intermediaries. Giving her time to absorb whatever secrets Amille had brought to light, Rand opened his own letter from Colin, scanning it and then rereading it with an odd expression on his face.

Rosalie blew her nose noisily, looking up at him with blurry vision.

"Well?" he asked softly.

"She . . ." Rosalie cleared her throat and wiped underneath her eyes with her fingers. "She wasn't my natural mother." Suddenly she half-smiled at the odd

sound of those words, and she looked upward to
contain the fresh, welling tears of emotion. Her forehead creased as she leveled a brilliant, glimmering gaze
at him. "She was Lucy Doncaster's governess. Lucy was
my real . . . I'm Lucy's daughter."

Rand nodded slightly, leaning his head back until it
rested against the wall. His eyes remained on her
intently.

"Your father?" he prompted, and Rosalie sighed in
something approaching disbelief.

"Brummell. It's all true—Amille's story corresponds
to his exactly. Something in me cannot quite compre-
hend that Beau Brummell is my father. *Brummell*," she
repeated, as if to convince herself, "the favorite of the
regent, the center of London society, the eccentric
dandy—"

"He's a man," Rand interrupted quietly, "a man, like
any other."

"According to the letter," Rosalie said, drying her
eyes before locating a certain passage, "he was the
'most handsome, shallow, and charming man Lucy had
ever met.' Amille writes that he was fond of Lucy but
that he didn't have the capability to love deeply. She
implies that he was too self-centered."

"It seems quite likely," Rand said dryly.

"And then the story becomes a little foggy," Rosalie
continued, lifting the handkerchief to blow her nose
once more. "There is a paragraph about the Earl of
Rotherham. Have you ever—?"

"No, I've never met him or heard much about him.
He is a reticent sort."

"Lucy was promised to him, but even after her affair
with Brummell had ended, she showed no inclination
to marry the earl. It says here that 'she was frightened
of Rotherham's obsession with her.' I wonder exactly
what it was that frightened her. In any event, she
conceived a child by Brummell. How strange it is

. . . that I can't think of that child being me," Rosalie said, pausing in wonder. "I suppose I'll get used to it."

"Your existence was kept a secret from outsiders?"

"Yes . . . I . . . was born in France, where Amille and Lucy went to escape from the gossip and rumors, and also from Rotherham, whose obsession with Lucy apparently hadn't decreased."

"Did he know about Lucy's baby?"

"I don't know. I don't think so." Once more Rosalie scrutinized the letter. "Amille doesn't really explain. She writes that Lucy was very frail emotionally and succumbed easily to depression after her affair with Brummell. She never really recovered from losing his love, and she killed herself a month or two after I was born. I wonder . . . I wonder what my life would have been like had she lived."

"It is possible," Rand said thoughtfully, "that she would have given Amille most of the responsibility for your care and upbringing anyway."

"She was just a child herself," Rosalie said, nodding pragmatically. "I feel . . . so sorry for her." She sighed, bending the corner of the parchment with her fingertip and letting it flick back. "After Lucy died, Amille decided to keep the child a secret. She told the Doncasters that the baby had died also, and then she took on a new name and new position, inventing a fictional husband to make her situation seem more respectable. And that is how I grew up as the daughter of the Winthrops' governess." Rosalie looked at Rand with eyes as round as saucers. "How odd chance is," she said. "If there hadn't been a fire in the theater that night and I hadn't met you, I would probably still be living with the Winthrops, never having found out any of this."

"You don't think Amille would have eventually told you?"

"It says right here: she felt there was no reason to.

She feels that only trouble will come out of the knowledge that I am Brummell's daughter, and she says near the end . . . Oh, my."

"What?"

"I didn't really read this part before. How unlike her it is. She has heard the rumors that I am staying with you, and she urges me to stay under your protection as long as possible."

"May I see the letter?" Rand asked, his tone sharpening. She handed it to him, and he scanned the last few sentences. He relaxed slightly but continued to frown. Amille had not written anything that would explain the drugging in Paris, yet it bothered him that she seemed so concerned about someone lending protection to Rosalie. "I'll be glad," he murmured, "when we are back in England. I would like to speak with Amille . . . there are a few things she will be able to explain further."

"Back in England," Rosalie echoed. Suddenly she noticed something strange about his expression, and her preoccupation with the letter and its contents disappeared to the back of her mind. She stood up from the bed, walking over to him slowly. "What's wrong?" she murmured. "The news is bad?"

"Yes," Rand said, and it tore at Rosalie's heart to see the shadowed bitterness in his hazel eyes.

"How soon do we have to go back?" she inquired, reaching out to stroke his arm.

"Two days, no longer than that."

"Rand," she asked gently, somehow already knowing the answer, "what was in your letter? What did Colin write to you?"

There was an odd look about him as he stared down at her. His face, Rosalie noticed absently, was pale underneath the tan of his skin.

"My grandfather passed away," Rand said.

She laid her head on his chest and slid her arms

around him, offering silent comfort. Rand did not shed a single tear, but he held her tightly, and something about the desperation of his grip betrayed his sense of loss. They stayed together for long minutes, swaying slightly. Finally Rosalie sensed the lessening of his grief, and it was then that she spoke with a watery sigh, her voice unsteady.

"This means that you're the Earl of Berkeley . . . *Dieu*, did I really promise to marry you?"

"It's too late to back out."

"Where did I put my handkerchief? . . . Lord, it's been a day for startling news."

Reluctantly Rand released her, finding that his pain was greatly dulled by the fact that she was there to offer as much solace as he needed. He leaned his back against the wall once more, taking pleasure in the sight of her as she hunted for the handkerchief and dried the last of her tears away.

"My grandfather badgered me incessantly about my bachelor status," Rand murmured. "My only regret is that he didn't live to see what a perfect woman I found to wed."

Rosalie suddenly chuckled. "Perfect woman?" she questioned. "With an unequaled crop of debutantes to pick from this year and scores of rich, eligible society women longing to accept your name, you chose a woman with the most singularly creative bloodlines imaginable."

"Not one word more," Rand warned, his eyes warm as he beheld her. "This is the one subject, sweet Rose, on which I won't allow you to question my taste."

She smiled and went back to him, needing suddenly to have him hold her again.

Much later, Rosalie left the letter on her writing desk and went to tell Mireille about their imminent departure. There was much organization and packing to be done. She found to her surprise when she returned to her room that evening that the letter from Amille was gone. After checking every inch of the room without a clue as to its disappearance, Rosalie went to the library in search of Rand. He sat at a mahogany table, drafting several pieces of correspondence.

"I've been thinking . . ." Rand said, blotting a letter deftly. "There is no one to whom I'd particularly like to sell the château. There have been some offers, but nothing quite suitable."

"Is there really a need to sell it right away?" Rosalie asked, filled with inner delight as she realized that he had become attached to the d'Angoux estate in the same way that she had. Rand shook his head, his mouth lifting at one corner in a lazy half-smile. "It might be enjoyable," Rosalie commented, "to come back every now and then for a spell of privacy." They exchanged a long intimate glance, which Rand finally broke with a soft inquiry.

"When you came in, you looked as though there was something you wanted to ask—"

"Oh, yes. I can't find the letter from *Maman*. I thought perhaps that you had it."

"No, I don't." Rand frowned and stood up from the table, stretching his broad shoulders and flexing his fingers. "I'll help you look for it."

They went upstairs and into Rosalie's room, a breeze catching at the door and closing it gently behind them. As Rosalie's mouth fell open with surprise, Rand located the letter underneath her desk and held it up for her to see.

"It must have been blown from the desk to the floor," he said.

"This is very odd," she replied, her forehead creasing in a perplexed manner. "I looked under the desk—I looked everywhere, and it wasn't here." She took the letter from him and gave it an accusatory glance.

"I think," Rand said, looking down at her with dancing gold-green eyes, "that you intended to lure me up to your bedchamber."

"I didn't! I—" she began in an indignant tone, and suddenly found her mouth occupied with his.

"Didn't you?" he murmured against her lips. His head moved over hers, turning so that her mouth was helpless against his invasion, and Rosalie forgot all about the letter, her arms lifting as her fingers laced through his hair.

Fourteen

Art thou gone in haste?
I'll not forsake thee;
Runn'st thou ne'er so fast,
I'll o'ertake thee:
O'er the dales, o'er the downs,
Through the green meadows,
From the fields through the towns,
To the dim shadows.

—Anon.

"Monsieur. You wished to speak to me?"

Rand looked up from the library table as Mireille came to a halt in front of him. Her features were perfectly composed as Rand stood up and motioned her toward his chair.

"Please sit down," he requested, sighing as she obeyed him timidly. She looked apprehensive, her brown eyes blinking. Half-sitting on the edge of the table, he regarded her steadily. "Things have happened very fast," he said. "I would have handled all of this differently if there had been more time to prepare. I would have preferred to talk with you before the general rumors started."

"That would not have changed anything, *monsieur*," Mireille said, her long ebony hair coming forward to conceal her face as she looked downward.

"It would have saved you a little unhappiness, perhaps. I wanted to ask you—"

"I am not unhappy," Mireille blurted out quickly. "Not at all. You and *mademoiselle* are happy, *oui?*"

"Very," Rand said. Then he grinned, his face startlingly attractive, as it was whenever he smiled. "She has accepted my proposal of marriage."

"I suspected something like that, *monsieur*."

"I'm sure you did."

"You belong together—anyone could see it."

"Mireille," Rand said with a soft chuckle, "I agree with you completely, but I would like to return to the original direction of our conversation before you side-track me further. You seem to be under the misapprehension that Rosalie and I have not included you in our plans. But we have discussed the matter and we would like for you to come to England with us as Rosalie's companion."

For once Mireille was speechless. Slowly she stood up.

"Rosalie is very fond of you," Rand continued, contemplating her silence in a thoughtful manner before his tone became even more persuasive. "We both are fond of you, and I know that you would enjoy England."

"Are you very certain you want me there?"

"My first concern is Rosalie. She is facing a new life, a new home, people she has never met before, new kinds of responsibilities. Unfortunately I will be very busy at times, and I don't want to leave her alone in a large house without knowing that there is someone there whom she trusts and has affection for. Would you come to England with us, Mireille?"

Slowly she nodded and smiled. "Yes. I will be very glad to."

"If Guillaume wishes to come with us as well, we'll find something for him to do," Rand said.

"I don't know." Mireille gave a small sigh. "He never likes to stay in one place very long. He is not happy doing the same job for more than a month or two. Please let me talk to him first."

"Then talk to him soon. I must leave tomorrow

morning on a trip to Havre to make some last-minute arrangements. I will have to know his answer before I go."

"Yes. Thank you, *monsieur.*"

"Rosalie will be very pleased that you are joining us," Rand said.

"I am so happy that she taught me some English."

He smiled suddenly. "Now you'll be able to practice it to your heart's content."

"My heart is already content," Mireille said simply, and then she left the room as quietly as a wraith.

"Please." Rosalie drew out the word slowly, sliding her arms around Rand's waist and walking her fingers up his back. Her lower lip was pursed in a beguiling pout as she looked up at him. "Say yes or I'll do something drastic."

"Drastic?" Rand questioned, grinning lazily and winding one of her stray curls around his finger. "That's a promising choice of words."

"I'll be so lonely while you're gone," she said, resting her forehead against his chest.

"You should know by now how much I hate the thought of leaving you," he replied, kissing the top of her head. They stayed like that for a long, delicious moment, clasped securely, love exchanged in the silent vow of closeness. "It's only for a few days," Rand murmured. "While you're packing everything here I'll be in Havre arranging for our passage to England and making certain that the shipping office is in good trim. I'll come back as soon as possible and we'll leave for good with Mireille and Guillaume in tow."

"Mireille and I have almost everything packed now, and I'll die of boredom without you here. *Please* say yes."

"Sweet, I don't understand why you want to go to a village fair so badly—"

"That's because you're a man. I want to see what it's like, and how the ones here are different from the ones in England . . . and everyone here is going to go, including Madame Alvin and Ninette, and Guillaume said he would stay right by Mireille and me the whole time—"

"This soon after the fire, I doubt it's going to be a spectacular—"

"Many people from other villages are going to participate. It's for such a good cause—did you know that most of the merchants are going to give a small part of their profits to help rebuild the vicar's cottage? There are going to be so many things to see and hear—"

"And buy," Rand said ruefully, beginning to relent despite his initial opposition to the idea. Rosalie lifted her face from his chest and smiled at him enchantingly. "Oh, hell," he muttered, "if Guillaume will promise to escort you—and accompany you every step of the way—I'll consider it."

"Only consider?" Rosalie's hands curved around his back and over his shoulders as she stood on her toes to press closer against him.

"Before I say yes," Rand murmured, "I want to find out what drastic measures you had concocted to persuade me."

Rosalie's smile deepened. "In the worst possible scenario," she whispered, brushing her mouth temptingly against his, "I'd intended to trade my favors for your consent."

"Then I should warn you," he replied, his blood warming rapidly as her body curved sweetly against his, "I'm in a difficult mood this morning."

"How much time do I have to win you over?"

"About an hour," he said. Her smile held a seductive promise as she pulled his head down to hers demandingly. As they kissed, he combed strong but supple

fingers through the smoothness of her hair, his thumb
lingering to trace the rim of her ear. "But at this rate,"
he added, his passion now fully roused, "I can be
persuaded in a very short amount of time. . . ."

The village fair would have been more appropriately
termed a festival. There were palpable signs of celebration and thanksgiving no matter where the eyes happened to alight. The village square was ornamented
with lanterns, fans, rich quilts, and other articles offered for sale, the merchants' stalls doing much to
disguise and camouflage the destruction left by the fire.
A cacophony of noise greeted Rosalie's ears, for bawdy
music came from several different sources and was
most often accompanied by dancing and singing. Her
stomach was reacting appreciatively to the fragrant
scents of a wide variety of food. There were *rissoles,*
savory mixtures stuffed into a crust and fried in fat, and
there were pies filled with apples and figs or sugar-
stuffed pears. Tables were loaded with large Rheims
gingerbreads, breads filled with chocolate or coffee
creams, sugared almonds, marzipans and *petits méstiers,*
sugar-and-honey wafers that dissolved in Rosalie's
mouth after each crunchy bite. Mireille was especially
fond of the caramel-glazed oranges, eating so many
that Guillaume and Rosalie began to entertain the fear
that she would make herself ill.
Rosalie was enjoying herself thoroughly, but there
were many times when she stopped to think of Rand
and his departure yesterday morning. She wished that
she could have pointed out the more entertaining
sights of the fair to him. She would have loved to see
him laugh at Mireille's gluttony, and the portly jug-
glers, and also at the spindly musicians who competed
against one another to outdo themselves in their enthusiasm. By now Rand was nearing Havre, a thought that

cheered her because the sooner he arrived there, the sooner he would return. In the meanwhile she chattered and laughed with Guillaume and Mireille as they strolled about the village square.

At midday, Guillaume glanced casually at the sky, noting its perfectly centered sun.

"Did you see the Gypsy wagon over there?" he asked, and Rosalie followed the direction of his gaze. "A fortune-teller. Has anyone ever predicted your future, *jolie ange?*"

"No," she replied, her eyes gleaming with immediate fascination. Having her fortune told appealed to Rosalie's rampant love of mystery and fantasy, which had been engendered by reading countless novels. Fortune-tellers often played a significant part in such stories, looking into the future and predicting dark, terrible and wonderful secrets that never failed to make Rosalie shiver with delight. "Guillaume, do you think it would be safe to . . . do you think we could—?"

"Anything you wish," he said, chuckling at her eagerness. A cooling breeze ruffled his shining ebony hair as he looked down at her. Rosalie smiled at him, her eyes gleaming with a vivid daylight blue. Inexplicably, Guillaume hesitated before offering her his arm. Mireille fell into step with them as they pushed through the congested square and jostling crowd.

"Monsieur de Berkeley said that *mademoiselle* should not be left alone for even one minute," Mireille said, her voice becoming higher as she sought to make herself heard above the noise.

"And so she will not be," Guillaume replied. "You and I, Mira, will go with *mademoiselle* to witness the foretelling of her destiny."

Rosalie laughed lightly. "I already know part of what she'll predict: I will be going on a long voyage, on a ship destined for a distant land—"

"You will marry a rich and handsome man," Mireille added, giggling, "and you will teach more of your language to a dark-haired girl—"

"And her dark-haired brother," Rosalie said, glancing mischievously at Guillaume. "Now you will have to learn English, Guillaume."

"I have always gotten through life very well with French, *merci*," he answered politely.

"I am certain that your French will entrance many Englishwomen," Rosalie said, "but they will not understand a word of it."

"Ahhh . . . then for the women of England, perhaps I will learn a little."

Guillaume's concession was uttered in so noble a fashion that Rosalie and Mireille could not help laughing. They neared the gaudily painted wagon, but as he placed his foot on the first tiny step leading up to the door, Guillaume stopped and frowned.

"Mira . . ." he began, and groaned in a self-disgusted manner as he made a quick search of his pockets. "Mira, do you remember where the caramel oranges are sold?"

"*Assurement,*" she said, nodding emphatically. "Why do you—?"

"I think that I dropped the money purse there. *Zut,* when I paid for the last oranges you ate, I must have mislaid it—you have quick little feet, would you run back there to see if it is still on the ground?"

"Yes, yes. But what about the fortune—?"

"I will accompany *mademoiselle* while her fortune is being told, and we will be waiting here when you return. Is this agreeable to you, *mademoiselle?*"

"Yes," Rosalie said, "but if you would prefer to wait until Mireille—"

"No, don't wait," Mireille said, shaking her head and sighing with mock impatience. "Guillaume, this is not like you." Then she smiled at him with warm affection.

"I suppose you are merely excited about leaving tomorrow for England."

"That is very true," he agreed. "Now, hurry, before some local peasant profits from my carelessness."

Mireille scampered away quickly.

Rosalie looked after her. "I hope she finds it."

"If anyone could, she will," Guillaume replied, and helped her up the rickety steps to the Gypsy wagon. Rosalie entered the shadowy interior of the vehicle cautiously, blinking in the darkness until the effects of the sunlight faded from her eyes. A small table draped with a shawl stood resolutely in the center of the enclosed space. It bore the weight of charts and maps, a crystal ball, and an unlit candle. Other articles of furniture were lodged in the sides and corners of the wagon, but they were only dim shapes. A woman sat in the corner, her hair confined by a scarf, her lips curving in a faint smile.

"Welcome."

It was too dark in there, the air still and suffocating. The fair and the sunlight seemed miles away. Rosalie felt agitation fluttering inside her body as she looked at the woman, agitation which grew until it began to throttle her. She backed up a step until she felt Guillaume's chest against her shoulder blades. Clamoring instinct told her that she was in the presence of danger, and she wanted nothing more than to leave the wagon immediately.

"Guillaume, take me out of here," she whispered. His hands moved from her narrow shoulders to her elbows in a gentle caress, and then suddenly she felt him clasp her wrists in an iron grip. In confusion, she tried to pull away, crying out as Guillaume pulled her arms behind her back and bound her wrists with a sinewy cord. "Stop it! What are you doing?" As she struggled he cuffed her lightly across the jaw, stunning her for the fraction of a minute necessary to immobi-

lize her completely. He gagged her efficiently, knotting
a handkerchief behind her head so firmly that there
was no chance of its coming undone. Then her feet
were bound, and she was trussed up like a helpless fly in
a spider's net. Guillaume picked her up easily, clucking
in reluctant sympathy as he felt her body stiff with rage
and fear, her pulse hammering.

"Easy, lady angel," he soothed, laying her down on a
thin mattress on the floor. Rosalie was vaguely aware of
the movements of the woman in the wagon, who was
busy clearing away all of the articles on the table. "You
won't be hurt. Listen to me well—no one will hurt
you." He did not look into her turbulent gaze as he
wiped the streaming tears off her cheeks. "I'm sorry,"
he whispered. "The world is not good to those like you,
is it? But angels don't belong on earth, for there are too
many poor sinners here like me and Mira and your
beloved Rand, all scrapping over what we need to
survive. I had to do this for Mira and me. We are rich
now, and I'll be able to take care of Mira far better than
you would have in England."

She made a slight sound and then closed her eyes,
refusing to look at him any longer.

"You are thinking of her," he said. "I know that you
care for her. You did not mean to be cruel to her, but
you were cruel, angel, in letting her think that she
could be more than what she is. Teaching her English,
showing her how to crook her little finger at teatime,
giving her a nice dress . . . she has begun to dream
your kind of dreams, and while they might have come
true for you, they would never for her. Do you think
any man would ever want her for something other than
a night of whoring?"

More rivulets of water slipped from beneath her
lashes, and she nodded defiantly.

"Then keep your eyes closed, *jolie ange,* for you are
blind."

He stood up and left her, pausing to murmur something to the Gypsy woman before opening the tiny door. Rosalie tried to scream as she saw the portal swing shut, but she could make no sound. Mutely she turned her head and was enclosed once more in darkness, to contend with her turbulent thoughts and her racing heart.

Mireille's steps slowed as she returned from her unrewarding search for the purse. She knew exactly where the Gypsy wagon had been, but it was gone now. It had disappeared. Her sparkling coffee eyes narrowed in sudden confusion, and she walked over to the spot where the wagon had been located. There were fresh tracks in the ground left by the metal-rimmed wheels.

"*Mademoiselle?*" she spoke aloud hesitantly. "Guillaume?"

To her vast relief, Guillaume seemed to appear out of thin air. He looked tired, and a little angry.

"I could not find the money," she told him. "I am so sorry . . . I hope there was not much in . . ." Her voice trailed off into bewildered silence as she cast a quick glance around the scene. "Where is *mademoiselle?*" she asked. He did not answer, his face turning blank and expressionless. "Where is she?" Mireille demanded, panic seizing her quickly.

"She is well. Mira, calm down or I will lose my patience—"

"I have already lost mine! Take me to her!"

"That isn't possible. Now, come with me, and I will explain what happened. I have made some arrangements, Mira, and we are going to receive lots of money, enough money for you to have whatever you—"

"I don't want money, I want to see *mademoiselle.* You've done something with her, haven't you?" Mireille stared at him, her face looking sickly as all the color left her skin. "Oh, no, Guillaume . . . why?" She began to cry, and he darted his eyes from the right to the left in order to see if anyone was watching them.

"Mira, shut up and come with me, or I promise before God that you'll never see me again."

"What good are your promises?" she sobbed, but dutifully she followed him until they were a great distance from the village square. Then he stopped to talk to her privately, cursing as he saw how red and swollen her eyes had become.

"*Merde,* don't weep anymore, Mira! This is not worth crying over, unless those are tears of happiness. We are rich, do you understand?"

"Where is she? Did you hurt her?"

"No," he said in disgust. "Do not worry over her."

Mireille could not seem to stop crying as she stared at him, although she put a small hand to her mouth and tried to keep her tears inside. She had never been afraid of her brother until now. Something inside her heart died as she realized what he had done, but some part of her still loved him, and another part grieved for him, for herself, and especially for Rosalie.

"You were the one in *monsieur's* hotel room," she whispered. "You were the one who cut him with the knife. I did not dare even think about it until now, but in my heart I was afraid it had been you."

"I only used the knife because he was trying to kill me."

"That was because you were trying to kidnap Rosalie!" she cried. "Why?"

"I have made some important contacts," Guillaume said. "Very important, Mira . . . they have influence that reaches across the Channel. It was something that they told me to do, because they knew I had been working at the hotel and that Monsieur de Berkeley was staying there as well."

"Why kidnap Rosalie? To hurt *monsieur*?"

"No, no, no . . . what you don't understand, Mira, is that they have both been lying to you since the beginning. Her name is not Rosalie Berkeley but Rosalie *Belleau*. I myself have seen proof of it, in a letter from her mother's—"

Bewildered, Mireille shook her head. "She is not *monsieur*'s cousin?"

"She is the illegitimate daughter of Beau Brummell. Rumors about it have gone all through Paris and most of England. I'm not certain why someone wants her, but whoever it is has offered a staggering amount of money for her, and now you and I have a large share of it."

"I don't want any of it!" Mireille said fiercely.

"You deserve most of it. I had no idea you were going to manage to get so close to her . . . or to Monsieur de Berkeley, for that matter. You're invaluable, Mira."

"How can you do this?" she demanded, her eyes wild. "How can you, when they have been so good to us?"

"Good to us?" Guillaume sneered. "You don't know what you're talking about. They've offered us a few crumbs of benevolence and pity. But money, Mira . . . money will feed and keep us much better than the shreds of kindness they offered us."

"I am going back to the Château d'Angoux," Mireille said in a voice that trembled with sharp emotion.

"You don't have to. We'll buy new things for you, whatever you need—"

"I am going back," she repeated, her voice hardening, "and I will wait for *monsieur*. And when he comes back, we'll find *mademoiselle* and go to England."

"Don't be such an idiot!" Guillaume snapped, his voice rough with exasperation. "Don't be a fool! It's *over*, do you understand? You will never go to England, you will never find Rosalie—"

"I will!" Mireille shrieked, and fell to the ground sobbing hopelessly. A few minutes later she repeated the words, her voice weary and defeated. "I will . . ."

"Mira, you are all I have, and I am all you have," Guillaume said softly. "That is the way it always has been and it will never change. Even if you did manage to keep Monsieur de Berkeley from killing you before you explained that this wasn't your fault . . . even if by a miracle you found Rosalie . . . they would never forgive you. Rosalie blames you now . . . she is lying on the floor of that wagon with her hands and feet tied, cursing you and me both for what has happened to her. And she'll brood about it the whole journey across the Channel, her hatred growing. And you know *monsieur* well enough to be certain that he would never forgive anyone who had helped to take his woman away from him."

"Yes," Mireille said dully, lifting her head from the ground and watching her tears sink into the dry earth. Her voice was low and suddenly steady with dark emotion. "Guillaume, will you stop this? Can you?"

"It's too late."

"Then I never want to see you again," she whispered.

"Mira . . . little Mira," he said, laughing a little at first and then looking uncertain as he realized that she meant it. "You cannot be serious . . . you are my sister, the only one I care for. This was all for you and me! You don't want to part from me—you would be alone."

"Rosalie is alone," she said, getting up from the ground and turning her head away from him. "At least my hands aren't tied."

He began to follow her as she walked away. She stopped, turning to pin Guillaume with a direct, glittering stare of hatred that caused him to freeze in disbelief and say her name pleadingly. And then she walked away, from the village, from him, from all that she had once been.

The Alvins greeted Rand at the door with pale faces. Madame Alvin's features were haggard with distress as she looked at Rand, whose hair was darkened from the late-night rain and his expression taut with foreboding.

"What's going on?" he asked curtly, and Madame Alvin wrung her hands.

"Monsieur de Berkeley, they did not return from the fair. They have disappeared, all three of them. I returned with my husband in the afternoon, and when I realized that they had not yet come back, I sent Jérème and some of the other boys to look for them. Jérème found Mireille, who gave him a note for you."

"Where is Mireille now?" Rand demanded, casting a glance around the great hall as if suspecting her to be underfoot.

"That foolish boy Jérème . . ." Monsieur Alvin spoke up, clearing his voice miserably. "He said that Mireille would not come back with him, and he did not force her to return. I sent him back yet again to get her. She is gone now too."

Rand muttered an explicit obscenity and took the tiny scrap of paper from Madame Alvin's trembling hand.

Monsieur, I did not know until it was too late. I weep for the part I have played in this, I am guilty for my actions if not my intentions. I wish I could help you, but all I know is that Guillaume was the one who wounded you in Paris and that someone has paid much money for Beau Brummell's daughter. Guillaume said that they will take *mademoiselle* across the Channel to England. I pray that you will find her and that the Lord will forgive me.

"God, Mireille . . ." Rand muttered. "Why did you run? Why?" He bent his head and turned away from the Alvins, his fingers clenching around the note. He gave a short, harsh laugh at the irony of the situation, for he had housed and fed the very man who had conspired to steal Rosalie away from him. The sound was strangled in his throat. He wondered if Rosalie was hurt or frightened. "By God, I'll kill you for this, Guillaume," he whispered. "I'll hunt you down like the scraggly fox you are." Rand had experienced complete rage before, the blinding hot emotion that raced like fire in the veins, but this went beyond that point, to a frozen state in which he could think with ice-cold clarity. Methodically, quickly, his mind sifted through a dozen possibilities and selected a course of action. Monsieur Alvin watched him uneasily, shifting from one foot to the other. Rand stood in thought for a moment longer, and then he lifted his head. "Tell Jérème to see to the horses," he said to Monsieur Alvin, who flinched at the odd, chilling look in his eyes. "I'm leaving for Calais."

Neither of the Alvins dared suggest the idea of sleep to him. The couple was almost relieved when he left, for his glacial manner and appearance had unnerved them both terribly.

Rand arrived in Calais and went straight to Brummell, knocking at the door of his apartments incessantly without hearing a response. Then he warned in a low voice of sincerity that he would break the portal in if not admitted immediately. There were quick scrabbling sounds from inside, and then the door was opened timidly. Selegue stood there in hastily thrown-together attire, his wiry figure stiffening with surprise.

"Lord Berkeley? Come in. . . . Is something amiss?"

"Brummell's daughter has been kidnapped," Rand said bluntly, striding into the room. "Because of his loose tongue. And after I find out what I need to know from him, I'm going to make certain that he never speaks again." From any other man in any other type of condition, Selegue might have considered the words to be an exaggeration of intention. However, Randall Berkeley looked completely serious, a fact which caused Brummell's valet no small amount of alarm.

"He did not mean to let the secret out," Selegue said, his voice trembling. "Having some small knowledge of Brummell, sir, you can understand what it was like for him, of all men, to discover that he had sired a daughter. A daughter who looks so much like the only woman he ever loved that he—"

"Love," Rand repeated, making the word sound like a profanity. "Comparing his kind of love with the real emotion is like measuring a glass of water against the sea. Small. Diluted. Useless. I do not hold his abandonment of the woman he loved against him, for that has little to do with me. But exchanging his daughter's safety for the sake of a few manly boasts—that I do hold against him, for his carelessness has served to take away from me the one thing that I value. Where is he?"

"He is indisposed, sir. He is lying in the next room, exhausted and near delirious."

Rand laughed dryly. It was not a cheerful sound. "A sudden illness?" he inquired. "Begun about five minutes ago, perhaps?"

"Sir, please . . . he is genuinely ill. Take a closer look at our surroundings. We have had to rely on the kindness of benevolent foreigners in order to secure the basic necessities. We have not enough coal for fire, not enough food to eat, much less the articles needed to preserve human dignity, such as soap and fresh linen." Selegue paused before adding softly, "And it all started after he let out the secret about Rosalie Bel-leau." From the way Selegue spoke, Rand knew that the valet was aware that it had all been his doing.

"I warned him," Rand replied, shrugging indiffer-ently.

"He is shrunken away to a shadow of what he was!" Selegue cried.

"Then let us hope his pride and foolish vanity have shrunk as well."

The valet was stricken by Rand's cool words. "I had figured you for a better man than this," he finally managed to say. "Have you no pity or kindness? No compassion?"

"Pity, kindness, and compassion," Rand replied slow-ly, "are the nobler elements of man's nature, serving to balance the other half—spite, cruelty, callousness. It is unfortunate"—he suddenly smiled tigerishy—"that my better half has been stolen away from me, for now I find there is nothing to check the baser part of my nature."

"What do you want?" Selegue whispered, bowing his head and clasping his trembling fingers. The sight should have moved Rand, but it did not. Something had gone dead inside him, and it would not be reawak-ened until he had Rosalie back.

"I want two lists," he said grimly. "One of every man and woman he may have told about Rosalie Belleau since I was last here. Second, an accounting of every creditor Brummell has in London, whether he owes someone a small fortune or a box of snuff."

"Yes, sir."

"And I want the lists tomorrow morning at seven o'clock, because I'm leaving for England. You'd better wake him up now and put your heads together. I don't care if that's his deathbed—I'll follow him to hell and drag him back if I have to."

"Yes, sir."

Rand turned and left without a good-bye, his mouth tightly set.

Colin Berkeley idly turned the pages of an accounting book, marking off his debts with a goose-quill pen. He sat in the library, having avoided his grandfather's empty chair in lieu of a less comfortable but far more preferable one. He did not envy the duties that lay in store for his brother, Rand, for although the money and the power were attractive, the accompanying responsibilities were not. Colin sighed, closing the book gently. A profitable night of gaming had reversed his run of bad fortune, enabling him to settle all outstanding debts, but he found none of the satisfaction that he had anticipated from the prospect of beginning his established cycle anew. He was tired of landing himself into debt and hauling himself out repeatedly. For the first time he seriously contemplated the alternatives. Wasn't there some other way for him to live? Was there any streak of respectability in him that would allow him to lead a less reprehensible life?

"A streak of respectability," he murmured, running a hand through his blond hair distractedly, a gesture quite unusual for the appearance-conscious Colin. "From which side of the family would it have come, I wonder." His emerald-green eyes were weary, his face etched with grief. He had not expected the earl's death to take such a toll on him. One corner of his mouth curled upward as he thought of his grandfather, the old sinner . . . just an older, peppery version of Colin and Rand, with a bit more common sense.

"Colin," a husky voice came from the doorway, and he jumped slightly.

"What? Oh, God, Rand it's you . . . you're back! Damn my eyes, I don't mind sayin' I'm glad you're back, but don't sneak up on someone that way . . . thought it was my conscience speakin'."

"After a twenty-four-year silence?"

Colin grinned and stood up as Rand came into the room. "Zounds, my conscience hasn't put in more than an occasional word or two, but I've never known yours to raise the roof with its volume."

Rand smiled slightly as they clasped hands briefly, and then his expression became more grave. "I had meant to get back before he finally went."

They looked at each other intently.

"It dragged on for bloody weeks," Colin replied, sitting down again with a sigh. Rand went over to the fireplace and propped an elbow against the mantel. "Though you kept him entertained till the last, Rand . . . you embroiled yourself in a nice little scandal, didn't you?"

"Did it upset him?" Rand inquired, stone-faced.

"He actually laughed about it, the old bird, and you know how he hated to laugh—said it was undignified and tried to stop, laughed some more."

"What exactly did he find so amusing?"

"He seemed to think that you took after him as far as the ladies are concerned . . . tell me, why do they find a brutish, dark-skinned bugger like you so attractive— and on top of that, how did you manage to get involved with Brummell's daughter?" Colin paused as Rand turned and walked a few steps away. "Are you going?"

"Just to the bar," Rand answered dryly, opening the decanter of brandy. "In spite of your tactless questions, I find you less annoying than usual, so we'll prolong the conversation."

"You're drinking," Colin said, his mouth hanging open. "You never drink unless you're in bad straits."

"True," Rand admitted, taking a warming swallow and closing his eyes briefly.

"You want something from me?"

Rand's eyes flickered to the window, and he stared

outside bleakly as he replied, "Rosalie Belleau has been kidnapped."

"God's nightgown, why tell me? *I* don't have her!" Colin exploded.

"She's been kidnapped because she's Brummell's daughter," Rand continued, his voice hardening slightly. "But I'm going to get her back."

"I don't know what you think I could—"

"Brummell used to belong to Watier's. That was where he gamed the most, that is the place known as the dandies' club. You frequent Watier's, and therefore you can help me get information."

"Damned if I know why I should help you, Rand."

Ignoring his younger brother's sulkiness, Rand thrust a sheet of paper toward him so insistently that Colin accepted it automatically.

"The names on the first list are already being checked out. Look at the second—those are Brummell's top creditors. Which ones would be most likely to want Brummell's daughter?"

Colin stared at him with dawning understanding and repugnance. "Oh, I see . . . you want *me* to point the accusing finger?" He snorted in amusement. "Not likely, Rand. I'm still in hot water with a few of these macaronis, enough so that—"

"Which ones?" Rand repeated, his face hard and cold.

"Why should I—?"

"Because if you don't, I'll be damned if I hand one cent of the inheritance over to you, and I'm certain you're aware that your allowance depends on my goodwill."

Colin stared at him bitterly. "Oh, this is too much . . . you'll hang that threat over my head for the rest of my life! I won't dangle from your purse strings, dear brother."

"If you help me," Rand said softly, "I'll never threaten you with it again."

"Never thought I'd see you so torn up over some little toy. Egads," Colin remarked, eyeing him with wonder, "she must be as beautiful as sin, or remarkably good in—"

"Which one?" Rand interrupted, and Colin examined the paper.

"Could be Edgehill. He still complains about Brummell quite often, mad as hell about the Beau skipping the country. Edgehill has damned funny notions of justice and such . . . I'll bet he could have taken her and considered it rightful payment. . . . Or Mountford —now, there's a funny card. He's in deep, up to his neck in debt. In and out of the club, lost his sense of humor, and looks rather desperate. Maybe he went snappy and went after her for revenge. Or it could conceivably be—"

"Then let's go. You can tell me about the rest on the way to Watier's," Rand said abruptly, nearly dragging his foppish younger brother by the collar.

He did not accompany Colin into the gaming club for two reasons. The most important was that he did not want to take the chance of his presence inhibiting any confidences that might be told to his brother. The second was that if any members of White's, his own club, suspected that he was anywhere near the archrival institution of Watier's, it could impinge his honor, cast doubts on his loyalty, and result in exile from White's. Damn the situation, Rand thought darkly, longing to get out of the carriage, go into Watier's, and knock wigs together until someone revealed something about Rosalie's whereabouts. He disliked the dandies' club, having few doubts that one of them could have taken Beau Brummell's daughter to get back at the Beau and the cowardly way he had run from his creditors. They were a spiteful lot, worse than a group of jealous women, comparing fashions and testing the workings of their puny minds against each other, preening and admiring each other and then stabbing each other in the back. In Rand's view, nothing meant much to them except money and pincurls. He rather preferred his own crowd, which at least was not hypocritical. If they were going to stab one of their own in the back, they gave advance warning.

Colin emerged from Watier's in an hour, wearing a lazy smile. He sauntered slowly to the carriage and got in, crossing his legs at the ankle and inspecting the polish on his boots.

"I'd lay money on Mountford," he said calmly. "He hasn't been in for three days, and then suddenly he appeared last night with a huge wad of cash, playin' like he was the regent himself. Someone told me that Mountford didn't crack a smile but placed bet after bet until every farthing was gone. Peterson joked to him about it, said he figured Mountford was broke, and what do you think the reply was? 'My comfort is waiting at home,' Mountford said, and left as if he didn't have a care in the world. Now, that sounds to me like he had a woman waiting for him, and I know for a fact that he isn't married—"

"Then shut up and let's go," Rand suggested tersely.

"Gad, you're sounding as uppity as the earl used to."

"I'm beginning to understand him a great deal more than I ever thought possible," Rand replied, and leaned out the window to confer with the drivers of the carriage.

Mountford did not live far from London, only a half-hour's drive or so. Rand leaned his head back during the journey there, the silence broken only by the noise of the carriage, the horses' hoofbeats, and the vaguely annoying, rasping sound of Colin buffing his nails. Rand breathed deeply of the air that blew through the open window, the heavy coolness of it filling his lungs. There was nothing like a misty English evening. The further they retreated from the city, the more delicate the atmosphere became, permeated with freshness and the unique scent of green hills and young heather. The very air of England helped to restore his hold on reality, to remind him who he was, and to impart a welcome feeling of familiarity. But at the same time it induced a faint sense of panic, for he felt so far away from Rosalie and the memories they had created in France that he began to wonder if they had been real at all. She had not been his in the scent of England or in the darkness of mist, she had been his among the scent of Gloire de Dijon roses, under the blue skies of Brittany, in the stillness of a hot summer's day. He stared sightlessly at the window, remembering, savoring, needing.

Finally the carriage wheels made crackling sounds on the gravel drive up to the Mountford estate. As they stopped, Colin looked out of his side of the carriage and gave a low whistle.

"What the deuce . . . he's worse off than I suspected," he remarked.

Rand lifted a brow inquiringly and leapt out of the vehicle, his booted feet landing softly on the ground. The estate had indeed a dilapidated appearance, a worn, weary look that spoke of months of neglect. The Palladian front needed several repairs and a good washing. There was no sign of activity around the estate.

"I heard he had dismissed most of his servants," Colin whispered, "except a valet and a cook."

Rand nodded, going up to the front door and using the knocker impatiently. His stomach was tight with apprehension. As there came no response, he tried the handle and found that the door opened easily.

"No one's here," Colin muttered. "Let's come back tomorrow."

"No. He's number one on the list." Rand walked inside and looked around curiously. There was a notable lack of ornaments and knick-knacks inside the building, a curious circumstance considering the age of the estate and the formerly conspicuous wealth of the Mountfords. The heirlooms and sundry possessions must have been sold off quietly to cover Lord Mountford's gambling debts. "No wonder he was so popular at Watier's," Rand breathed cynically. "He didn't need to bother gaming—*Dieu,* he should have just handed it out free."

Colin threw him a dirty look, understanding exactly what Rand was implying.

"*I* don't spend half the time at the club that he—" he began.

Suddenly Rand heard a faint noise from behind one of the closed doors nearby. Over the portal was etched a book, indicating that it was the library. Rand burst into the room, sending the door swinging crazily, and was confronted by the sight of Lord Mountford standing in front of a window with a revolver raised to his head. Tormented brown eyes met gold-green.

In that split second Mountford pulled the trigger.

The explosion echoed in Rand's mind with the sound of belt-strap thunder. He turned his head, a slight gasp escaping his lips as he saw what was splattered over the entire room. The most appalling aspect of Rand's memory of Lord Mountford's suicide was the emptiness inside himself. He was encased in ice, viewing the scene as dispassionately as if looking over an illustration in a book. Then he fled up the stairs, opening and slamming doors in search of any sign of Rosalie. In the last room Rand stood amid the threadbare furniture with his feet splayed apart, his hands by his sides as he bowed his head. It had been a false lead.

Mountford had never had Rosalie, he was just a poor wretch who had not been able to bear the wreck he had made of his life.

"Rose, where are you?" Rand whispered, despair settling on him like a black frost. He took a deep, heaving breath and then regained control of himself. Walking down the stairs slowly, he watched with a frozen face as Colin backed away from the library doorway.

"Oh God . . ." Colin said, wearing a revolted expression. "I've never seen anything so disgusting." He pulled out a handkerchief and wiped a suddenly clammy brow, turning a pale shade of green. "Rand, I don't want to pay calls with you anymore."

"As you wish." Rand continued down the stairs and headed toward the front door. Colin followed with alacrity.

"But . . . what are you going to do about Mountford?"

"Cross him off the list," Rand replied shortly, his emotionless tone inspiring no little awe in his younger brother as they left the Mountford estate.

With each minute that ticked by, Rand felt that his chances of finding Rosalie decreased. He knew that he would spend the rest of his life searching for her if necessary, but it was important *now* that he move quickly, think well, find the right answers . . . now, while the iron was hot and the coals were glowing. It was only on the point of exhaustion that he returned to the Berkeley mansion, sprawling on his bed in a state that more resembled unconsciousness than slumber.

The next afternoon Rand went to White's, no longer finding it the place of ease and comfort that he once had. He had erased the most obvious signs of strain about his countenance with a shave, a good scrubbing, and several cups of coffee. Immaculately dressed in a bittersweet-chocolate-colored coat, a cream vest, tan trousers, and shining Hessian boots, Rand walked through the club with an effective imitation of good-natured ease. He greeted old friends and struck up conversations with two newly accepted members of White's. When ribbed about the rumors concerning his involvement with Brummell's daughter, Rand chose to smile mysteriously while inwardly despising those who dared mention her name. Foremost in his mind was the first list Brummell and Selegue had given him, the list of those who had visited Brummell in Calais and learned of Rosalie's existence. Some of the men on that list were present at this moment, and he made it a point to talk to each one of them, asking subtly leading questions and gauging their reactions. In the midst of a deceptively lazy conversation, a bewigged waiter came up to him with a simple message.

"Beggin' pardon, sir . . . but there's a lady at the door wantin' to see you."

"A young lady?" Rand questioned, his eyes narrowing.

"I don't think so, sir."

"Then I have no interest in her," Rand replied, the unchivalrous remark causing a huge roar of laughter from his companions.

George Selwyn clapped him on the back in hearty affection. "By God, you'll never change, Berkeley!"

Rand smiled slightly, and then he glanced down at the uncertain waiter, who voiced a timid question. "Sir?"

"Hang it," Rand said, sighing and raising his eyes heavenward. "I'll go see her for a minute."

"Oh, to be so put upon . . ." George murmured, grinning as Rand left the jovial group.

Rand's smile disappeared as soon as he left them, for he was annoyed at the unknown woman's interruption. It was probably Clara Ellesmere playing at some silly game, or perhaps one of her cronies who had accepted

some sort of dare. Yet some quiet impulse prompted
him to investigate the little mystery, and he gave the
waiter a generous tip after following him to the front
door of White's. A small woman stood just outside, her
face concealed by the hood of her gray cape. One long
curl of dark hair strayed from the hood, and at the
sight of it Rand's heart started hammering madly as he
stepped outside with her. The door of White's closed,
the noise, light, and laughter fading abruptly as he
faced her.

"Who . . . ?" he began with a curiously airless whisper, and the hood fell away as she turned to him and
lifted her face to look at him. An ache of disappointment seared through Rand as he saw that the woman
was a stranger. She was probably in her middle forties,
her skin almost unlined and her eyes dark and kind.
She was too warm, too inviting to be a member of the
aristocracy, for there was no touch of pride or haughti-
ness in her face. She was, however, a woman of some
circumstance, because her elaborately arranged hair
and her well-cut clothes betrayed large expenditures of
money.

"I am so sorry to have disturbed you. You are Lord
Randall Berkeley?" she asked. Her voice was compassionate and almost motherly, and it had a curious effect
on Rand. He had never been so drawn to a stranger,
not since he had first set eyes on Rosalie. Illogical
thoughts seized hold of his mind: he felt that she knew
him, that somehow she understood him.

"Yes," he answered inaudibly, and his head moved in
a slight nod.

"I went to visit you . . . your brother said that you
would be here. I have heard of the rumor that Rosalie
is missing. I believe I can help you find her."

Rand stared at her as if hypnotized.

"Who are you?" he asked hoarsely.

"Lord Berkeley . . . I am Amille Courtois Belleau."

"She . . . she talked about you to me very often," he managed to say, his eyes fastened onto her as if he were afraid that she would dissolve into the air. Just the fact that Amille was standing there before him, that she was real, made Rand feel that he had come closer to finding Rosalie.

"She wrote a letter to me from France, asking about her parents," Amille replied, taking a step closer to him as if sensing his fear that she would slip away. Her gaze locked steadily with his, searching and sympathetic. "She wrote about you and how things were between you, and that is why I took the liberty of—"

"I am glad you did," Rand interrupted. "I must talk with you right away. Would you care to return to my—?"

"I think," Amille said slowly, "that perhaps we should go to my terrace house. If our conversation is to be useful, Lord Berkeley, it must be conducted in a frank manner, and there I will be assured of no prying eyes or ears."

"If it will not make you uncomfortable for you to be seen . . ." Rand started to say, and then he paused in surprise. "Your terrace house, Madame Belleau? But are you not the governess of Baron Winthrop's—?"

"No," Amille said, slipping her hand through his arm and inclining her head toward a gilded carriage drawn by two chestnuts. She gave him a small smile, looking very French. "Not any longer," she said. "My carriage is waiting. Why don't you come with me, and I will have you brought back here when we are done talking. I do not live far from here." He nodded mutely, and when they were seated and safely enclosed in the vehicle, Amille continued. "Rosalie told you of the night we were separated. The opera fire—"

"Yes."

"I assume you met her shortly after that. She did not tell me in the letter what happened after that, nor do I wish to know anything about it, but obviously some set of circumstances caused the two of you to go to France together."

"Yes," Rand said in a low voice, his lashes flickering down to conceal the expression in his eyes.

"After being unable to find her, I returned to Winthrop House, hoping that Rosalie had found her way back there on her own. She had not. Baroness Winthrop is not an understanding woman, nor a particularly kind one, and the next morning she discovered Rosalie's absence. The baroness felt that if I had raised my daughter with what she called 'moral leniency,' then perhaps I had done similarly by Elaine Winthrop, her daughter. I was dismissed that morning."

"I am sorry."

"I am not," Amille replied, suddenly smiling. "The dismissal brought about a long-awaited change in my life, one that has brought me much contentment. What the baroness did not know, and what Rosalie does not know, is that for years I have been the mistress of Baron Winthrop. We have had such an understanding for a long time, and for many years the baron has wanted to establish me in a residence of my own. I insisted on keeping our relationship secret, however, because I wanted a respectable childhood for Rosalie. The education, the horses, the rudiments of a fine upbringing, were all things I wanted her to have. I intended to allow my relationship with the baron a freer rein once Rosalie was married or old enough to understand—"

"She'll understand."

Amille smiled at him. "I know that now."

In unspoken agreement they avoided discussing the most urgent questions until they reached the privacy of Amille's terrace house. It was a most luxuriously furnished residence, replete with tasteful silkwood furniture, rich carpeting and upholstering, beautiful embroideries, and delicate china. Amille handed her cape to a plump, cheerful-looking girl as they walked in.

"Martha, would you bring us some tea in half an hour," she requested softly, and seated herself gracefully on a mint-green velvet sofa. The girl cast Rand an admiring glance before leaving. "A former employee of the Winthrops," Amille commented, casting Rand a mischievous smile. The quality of her smile and not the actual shape of it reminded him of Rosalie, and he stared at her absorbedly. "I have lured many of the best ones, including the cook, to work for me . . . with promises of better salaries and kind treatment. Now," Amille said companionably, "I will have more than enough time to tell you what you need to know, all before Martha returns with the tea."

Rand nodded cautiously, sitting down in a nearby armchair.

"The story," Amille mused, pursing her lips slightly, "need not be long or complex. I will tell you the facts, and I will elaborate on whatever points you wish to be made clearer. I was the governess to Lucy Doncaster. Although Rosalie favors her in appearance, she does not in temperament. Rosalie is far stronger, more intelligent, and more confident than Lucy could have ever imagined being. Lucy was a sweet girl, however, and I was fond of her. I still do not understand why she was able to attract men so strongly—perhaps it was her helplessness. The fact is that many men were completely obsessed with her . . . especially the Earl of Rotherham. He and she were promised to wed, and all might have ended well had it not been for the interference of a vain, handsome boy who took a fancy to Lucy."

"Beau Brummell," Rand said grimly.

"Yes. Lucy returned his feelings a hundredfold, for although Brummell was merely fond of her, Lucy loved him so deeply that she never recovered from it. Despite my best efforts to prevent them from seeing each other, Lucy conceived a child by him. It was at this time that Brummell, unaware of her . . . condition, lost the edge of his desire for Lucy and fell in love with another young woman. And after her another, and after that one yet another, each one used to add a layer to the shell of his ego. Lucy was consumed by heartsickness and depression, swearing that she did not want to live any longer. Her family was unaware that she was going to have a child. I persuaded them to let me accompany Lucy on a trip to France, telling them that she was suffering from a nervous condition and needed new scenery. My family in France is quite respectable, and the Doncasters were satisfied with our declared intention to stay with my relatives.''

"And did you in fact stay with them?"

"Yes, with my parents, who were sworn to secrecy about Lucy's baby. They have since passed away with the secret still intact. I had planned to leave the child with them until we could find someone to adopt it.''

"A tidy plan," Rand said, casting an admiring glance at her.

"I thought so," Amille admitted wryly. "But not only did I underestimate the depth of Lucy's love for Brummell, I underestimated the Earl of Rotherham's obsession with her. He was incensed at the postponement of their marriage and consumed by his passion for Lucy. Somehow he discovered where we were and went to France. After going to the market one day, I came back to my parents' cottage to find him there, staring like a madman at Lucy, who was at that time eight months pregnant. He said many things to her, Lord Berkeley, dreadful things which made a girl as fragile and sheltered as Lucy scream and cry. And then, before rushing out of the cottage and back to England, he made it clear that he still wanted her, that he was still going to marry Lucy, if only to punish her and the child for what they had made him suffer. He felt that he had been betrayed . . . no, profaned, and he swore he would satisfy his need for vengeance. The dread this created, on top of her anguish over Brummell's desertion, caused Lucy to go a little mad, and shortly after Rosalie was born, Lucy climbed upon the parapet of the Quai d'Augustins and threw herself into the Seine."

"And you decided to keep Rosalie."

Amille smiled. "I loved her from the first time I saw her. To protect her I took a new name and pretended to be a respectable widow. I have never regretted keeping her because she has brought me as much joy as a daughter could give to a mother."

Rand was suddenly still, his body stiffening as the realization hit him. "God. I've been asking the wrong question," he said huskily. "Over and over again: why would someone want Brummell's daughter. *Brummell's* daughter!"

"That is right, Lord Berkeley," Amille said, and her eyes were shadowed with a peculiar combination of emotions. "I have been afraid of it ever since the rumors and articles began about Rosalie's identity and her involvement with you in France. Rosalie has not been kidnapped because she is the daughter of George Brummell. She has been kidnapped because she is the daughter of Lucy Doncaster."

Fifteen

Only joy, now here you are,
Fit to hear and ease my care;
Let my whispering voice obtain
Sweet reward for sharpest pain,
Take me to thee, and thee to me . . .
—Sir Philip Sidney

The door was bolted.

Rosalie swore at the discovery, throwing down the hairpin clutched between her fingers. Angry, frustrated tears threatened to spill from her eyes but she held them back as she paced from one end of the overelaborate room to the other. After working at the lock for hours and finally hearing the blessed click that had signified freedom, she had found that the door still would not open. There were no windows, no tools that would aid her in escaping, no fireplace . . . in short, there was no way out except for that door. The fact that the room was luxurious did not comfort her, for it was still a prison. The embroidery, fancywork, filigree, posies and bouquets, ruffles, and rosettes did little except to irritate her. This room had none of the well-organized flamboyance of the Château d'Angoux; instead it possessed a cluttery English prettiness that threatened to suffocate her.

A lit oil lamp perched on one of the small tables by the frilly bed; a basket of perfect fruit posed on the other. Rosalie walked over and selected an apple, biting into it cautiously. The fruit was firm and sweet, and she chewed it slowly as she reflected upon the events of the past three days. Ever since Guillaume had left her in the Gypsy wagon she had been bound or locked up, transported from place to place by a succession of strangers, who had not mistreated her but had not spoken a word about her eventual fate. Escape was always made impossible, for her abduction had been conducted with care and an obvious amount of fore-thought. Part of the journey had been by ship. Even though they had landed at night and she had been blindfolded, Rosalie had recognized the scents of the English docks, English air, and the sounds of English voices. It was slightly comforting to know that she had been brought back here instead of transported to some foreign country where the language and the people were unfamiliar to her.

Judging from the somber stillness of her surround-ings, Rosalie guessed that she was in a house located deep in the countryside: no traffic, no horses, whistles, or voices. Occasionally she would hear the scuffling sounds of servants' feet just outside her door, but it was evident that they had been told to ignore her stubborn pounding and her shouted demands.

"Cowards," she gritted between her teeth, throwing the half-finished apple into the nearest receptacle and resuming her pacing. "All of you are cowards. At least have the courage to face me and tell me why it is I'm being held against my will!" Her voice rose in helpless fury as she directed it toward the bolted door. "I don't know if it's night or day! I can't breathe in here! I have no books, no papers—damn you all, I'm sick of wait-ing!"

Silence.

"I'm going to go mad," Rosalie whispered, pressing her hands against her temples and taking a few deep breaths to calm herself. Unbuttoning the front of her high-necked lavender dress, she lay down on the bed and stared up at the ceiling, liquid pooling in her eyes until she closed them and tried to occupy her mind with sane, sensible thoughts. She wondered where Rand was, and if he was as distraught as she, and if he had caught Guillaume and made him confess where she had been taken. He will find me, she told herself. He will take England and France apart until he finds me.

She did not doubt his love for her, nor his strength and persistence. Rosalie even managed to smile as she thought of him in a rage . . . although the sight was awe-inspiring, a small part of her was always excited by his anger, for the intensity and wildness of it reminded her of his passion. Then she thought of him laughing, his teeth white against his copper skin, eyes glowing, his amber hair shining with layers of gold and brown. She remembered him as he told her that he loved her . . . how wonderfully gentle his mouth would become, how strange and compelling the mixture of colors in his hazel eyes was. Sighing, Rosalie found that her body had relaxed in temporary peace, her nerves now tranquil. "Neither you nor I will let anyone part us," she murmured, dragging her fingers back and forth across a neighboring pillow. "You are my life, and separated from you I am nothing. Bring me back to life, Rand." Rosalie turned her cheek into the pillow and slept, immersing herself in more thoughts of him.

The lamp was low as she struggled to wake from comforting dreams, but a brilliant flood of light entered the room. The door was open, she realized, and she snapped into wakefulness. The light was from a massive chandelier in the main hall beyond this room. Rosalie shot up from the bed, freezing in place as the door was closed again.

"Turn up the lamp, please," a gruff male voice requested, and with trembling hands she complied, nearly burning her fingers on the hot glass. The darkness was banished to the extreme corners of the bedroom, lamplight filling the air with a sultry white-yellow glow.

The man in the room was easily twice her age, his face pale-skinned, his hair startlingly dark in contrast and frosted with charcoal gray. He was a large man with a spare, fit physique, dressed in expensive, fashionable clothes and a formal white cravat. His features were vaguely saturnine, his nose thin, his brows thick and black, his mouth slender and dark in color. What frightened Rosalie was not his build or his features but the expression in his eyes. They were black and gleaming, like two onyx stones. His gaze traveled over every inch of her, widening with bewilderment and then with a hunger that caused a deep recoiling inside Rosalie's midriff.

"Lucy," he said, his voice corrugated with emotion.

She regarded him with wide eyes, her lungs expanding and contracting deeply, her skin gleaming like pale satin in the light. Lifting the back of a slender hand to her perspiring forehead, Rosalie brushed away the collecting dampness there, still watching him with a trapped, hypnotized gaze.

"I'm . . . I'm not Lucy," she said.

He shook his head slowly. "No. You're her daughter."

"Yes." She would have started inching toward the closed door, but he was still standing there, staring at her as if about to devour her. "I've been locked up, tied and gagged for days," she said, her voice strengthening into tautness. "Why have you done this to me? Who are you?"

"I am sorry about that, Miss Doncaster."

"That's not my name," Rosalie said sharply. "I am Rosalie Bel—"

"It doesn't matter what your name is," he interrupted, moving a few steps closer to her. She shrank

away from him, moving to the wall as she avoided the
bed. "Lucy belonged to me, and you're her daughter.
And you belong to me."

"Lucy . . . belonged to you?" she repeated in a whisper, her face mirroring her confusion. What did he
mean? He was far too young to be Lucy's father. "Are
you . . . a Doncaster?"

He snorted at the idea, shaking his dark, gray-frosted
head. "I am the Earl of Rotherham."

Rosalie could feel her face fade to a sickly hue. "I
don't understand," she managed to say. "She never
belonged to you. She was in love with George
Brummell—"

"Be silent!" he exploded, and his face went through a
terrifying contortion before he regained control of
himself. Rosalie quivered but kept her gaze fastened
unflinchingly on his, and slowly his mouth curved
upward in a thin smile. "So fearless, are you?" he
questioned.

"Was my mother afraid of you?"

"Had she been faithful, there would have been no
reason for her to fear me. I loved your mother very
much. She was the most beautiful woman I'd ever seen.
I loved everything about her with a passion that no one
could understand, certainly not your coward of a
father. I loved her shyness, her serenity, her soft skin,
and her long hair . . ." He reached out to a lock of
Rosalie's hair and kept it in his hand, fondling it with
his white, slender fingers. "Your hair is even longer
than hers was. And you have her eyes . . . did you know
that?"

Rosalie shook her head jerkily.

"Doncaster blue," Rotherham continued. "Only the
Doncasters have eyes that color . . . dark blue, almost
violet."

"Oh," Rosalie breathed in surprise. "I thought they
were from—"

"You thought that since *his* are blue that your eyes were his," Rotherham finished for her, and he gathered another lock of her hair in his hand. "No. Not at all. Brummell's eyes are not so bright as yours, not so passionate and expressive."

"Say whatever you like about him," Rosalie said, her skin crawling as she saw him wind her hair through his fingers. He was planning to bed her, she realized, and the thought turned her stomach. A picture appeared in her mind for a fleeting instant, of his white hands running over her body. Her lips twisted in a trembling half-smile as she continued. "Nothing will change the fact that he is my father and that Lucy chose him over you."

Rotherham swore at her. His hands pressed on either side of her head, framing her face in a tight vise. Ineffectually Rosalie tried to bolt away, gasping as his body pressed hers against the wall. He was aroused, and she felt the straining shape of him against her abdomen. As she let out a disgusted sob and tried to pull his wrists away, he jerked her hair tighter. Her eyes were slitted from the pressure of his hands near her face.

"Why don't you scream?" he asked, his thin mouth so close that she could feel his breath on her cheek.

"Would it do any good?" she whispered. "No. I will not scream, because you wish me to be afraid of you, and I am not. I am merely revolted by you, just as my mother was."

"You are a whore, just as your mother was," Rotherham spat, bringing his body so tightly against hers that she expected to hear her bones crack. "I know all about your affair with Berkeley—everyone knows about it. But now you're my whore, and I will have you for all the times that I wanted Lucy and could not have her."

"You're insane! I am not my mother!" she cried hoarsely.

"You are—you're part of her," he contradicted, and his eyes closed as he moved his pelvis against her. "You feel like her. By God, you feel like Lucy." He groaned and pressed his mouth to hers, seeming not to notice that her teeth were tightly clenched. "I've looked for you ever since I lost Lucy," he muttered. "I've known about you all these years, ever since I saw her in France, swollen with you. Little whore, her belly full with Brummell's bastard when she was promised to me!" He kissed her neck and muttered Lucy's name again, his coarse hair brushing against her cheek. Suddenly Rosalie could not stand it any longer and screamed, trying to strike him. He caught her wrists easily, his grip so tight that her fingers went numb.

"You'd bloody well better enjoy this," she said thickly, barely recognizing her own voice. "Because you'll pay for it with your life, and if I don't find a way to kill you first, someone else will."

"You mean your lover," Rotherham said, his fingers delving into the valley between her breasts. "You will never see him again. You will never lie with him again. And if you ever escape from me, I'll have him killed within an hour of your disappearance."

"No!"

She fought him in blind panic, squirming away from his engorged manhood and managing to wrench one hand away from his grip. Flailing at him in a desperate attempt for freedom, Rosalie managed to strike him in the throat. Immediately her other hand was released as he choked for air. Running to the door, she scrabbled at the knob and sobbed in gratitude as it opened. She could hear him behind her, his heavy footsteps seeming to thunder in her ears. A silent scream echoed through her insides, and she ran like a mad, wild creature, into the cavernous main hall and toward the endless slope of steps that led to the front door. The scene was a mere

blur before her eyes, the paralyzed figures of a manservant and a maid barely impinged on her mind as she
passed by them. Rosalie half-fell, half-ran down the
steps, her thoughts in a tumbling whirl as instinct took
over her body, forcing her feet to move faster and
pumping adrenaline through her veins. Halfway down
the stairs she fell on the landing, her palms hitting the
hard marble with a loud smack. Every bone in her body
was jarred. Behind her, the sound of Rotherham's
boots came closer. With a harsh breath Rosalie picked
herself up and prepared to run down the remaining
stairs, when suddenly a dark shape obstructed her path.
Helplessly she collided with it, her feet slipping on the
marble. In a fraction of a second she knew that she was
going to fall and die. No one could survive a tumble
down those hard, gleaming steps.

Shocked, she felt herself being snatched from the
fall, pulled upright and held lightly, securely against a
hard body. Dumbly she quivered and remained there,
gripping her rescuer's coat lapels in a desperate bid for
protection.

"Rosalie. Be still, my love, and don't tremble so." She
heard Rand's voice, and uncomprehendingly she
looked up at him. "Have you been hurt?" His hazel eyes
moved over her face in careful assessment.

Collecting her wits in a fumbling attempt, Rosalie
stared up at him with dilated eyes. "Rotherham
. . . Guillaume . . ." she stuttered, trying to tell him
everything in a confused flurry.

He cut her off by placing a forefinger on her lips. "I
understand."

He was so calm, so wonderfully calm and strong.
Rosalie hid her white face against his coat. Rand looked
up at Rotherham, who was only a few feet above them
on the stairs.

"My greatest pleasure," Rand said to him evenly,

"would be to kill you with my bare hands. If you have a preference for any other method, I'll be glad to oblige you."

Equally controlled, Rotherham cast him a slight smile. "Are you competent with a straight saber?"

"I am considered to be."

"By your fledgling contemporaries?" Rotherham questioned. "Or merely by yourself?"

"Why, both."

"The weapons are downstairs in the first room. If you care to follow me . . ."

"Of course," Rand said politely, a frosty, feral gleam in his topaz-shaded eyes. He shrugged out of his coat and handed it to Rosalie, who clutched the garment in a death hold. The saber, she thought numbly, was probably the best weapon for them to duel with, for it would ensure that the contest of abilities would be finished quickly. It possessed a blade of triangular section, wickedly sharp on the front edge. Requiring strength as well as skill, it weighed more than a pound and tired the forearm easily.

Fear-stricken about what might happen, she wanted to beg Rand to take her away from here and forget about Rotherham, yet she knew that he would have refused her. She did not speak to him, biting her lower lip as he walked down the steps after Rotherham. Rand paused and turned back to her with a mocking, "Hold the railing as you come down." Rosalie nodded, meeting his quick glance and abruptly seeing all that she had missed before. In his eyes burned a stark blend of love, pain, and fury, but he dared not relinquish his control or he could not accomplish what he had to do.

Both men had removed their coats but not their boots, each seeming to be satisfied with the handicap as long as the other was equally encumbered. Afraid of being a distraction to Rand, Rosalie stayed almost out of sight, remaining at the bottom of the stairs to catch what glimpses were available through the open doorway.

"A good piece," Rand commented after pulling a saber off the wall.

"You will not need to use it long. I'll cut you down before you know what has happened," Rotherham said, his onyx eyes piercing. "After twenty years I will not lose her again. She was intended for me."

"My God, are you well in the head?" Rand inquired, the course of his blood increasing with rage. "What delusions do you suffer from?"

"You don't know a thing, you insolent pup." Rotherham sneered. "*She* understands well enough, although you don't."

"Understands what?"

"That she rightfully belongs to me. She will pay for being the same whore that her mother was—"

"Your conversation is tiresome," Rand interrupted with a snarl. "As well as irrational."

They lifted the heavy weapons in salute, the briefness of the gesture a studied insult on both parts. Rosalie held her breath as the engagement began, the sabers clashing edge to edge. They fought with cutting strokes and strangely swift attacks launched immediately after the parry. It was a type of swordplay different from anything she had ever seen before, for the mock battles staged in the plays she had attended were conducted with the light scratching, maneuvering, and delicate offense of the foil. There was nothing light or delicate about the real-life duel she watched so intently: it was direct, simple, and acute.

Rand discovered immediately after the fight had begun that his opponent was well-experienced at saber fencing, and he held Rotherham at a distance while sizing up the situation. Rotherham guarded all of his lines well, his technique strong and his lunge impressive. They were both tall men, which made agility essential in defending against each other's long reach. Rotherham's advantage was experience. He had obviously practiced the saber riposte until it was second nature, able to deliver an instantaneous reply to each attack. Rand had to rely not on practice but on instinct, forcing himself to subdue his emotions and concentrate on trusting his own reflexes.

All of his recent fencing experience with Guillaume now became a disadvantage—dueling with foils was a different art from sabers. This was quickly apparent as he engaged Rotherham in *quarte*, a technique which Rand had used so successfully in besting Guillaume. It was not well-suited to the saber. The blade of Rotherham's weapon bit into his unprotected arm, causing Rand to inhale sharply with pain. Any more damage done to his forearm and he would become disabled.

"Competent?" Rotherham sneered. "That you are, but nothing more."

Rosalie sat down abruptly on the stairs as she saw the scarlet blossom on Rand's white shirt sleeve, her legs unable to support the rest of her body. The blades flashed like streaks of lightning, swinging through the air and meeting with sharp, whipping sounds.

Rand's concentration became complete as the engagement wore on. He forgot about his arm, his anger, everything but the mathematical precision of the strokes of the sabers. Feint. Parry, riposte. Low *tierce* to protect the flank. Low *quarte* to protect the stomach. The attacks became faster, the fight quickening until the only defense was to redouble the attacks.

It seemed to Rosalie that they fought for hours. She saw every detail of what was happening as if it had been slowed to a snail's pace, yet there was nothing she could do to help Rand. She could only watch, her hands clenched around the stair railing until her knuckles were white from the pressure. Her life was suspended on the outcome of the duel, just as Rand's was.

After two feints and *tierce* yet again, Rand interrupted Rotherham's attack with a single lunge. The
saber sank deeply through Rotherham's flesh, ending
his life with startling promptness. He dropped to the
floor without a sound, his body thudding gently onto
the flat surface.

Slowly Rosalie stood up and went to the doorway,
stopping a foot away from Rand. His thick lashes
lowered as he looked away from her and dropped the
saber. His chest rose and fell rapidly, his body retaining
the tensed, charged energy of the fight. Then silently
he stared at her, his face expressionless as he sought for
some word, some action that would help to banish the
icy control he had built around himself. Intuitively
Rosalie pressed her body against his rigid muscles,
curving to him and sliding her arms around his waist.

"I love you," she murmured, clinging to him. "I
knew you would find me . . . Oh, your arm, Rand . . ."
As her warmth and soft whisperings gradually slipped
under his guard, Rand wrapped his arms around her,
burying his face in her hair. A faint, incoherent sound
left his throat and he pulled her tighter.

He was whole again.

Rosalie stirred in her husband's arms, her skin
pinkened with pleasure, her eyes half-closed with feline
contentment. For the first time they had made love as
husband and wife, and although the experience was as
lusty and breathtaking as ever, a new element had been
added. Now they were joined by God and ceremony as
well as love, and henceforth the world would never look
upon either of them as a single entity.

She was sorry that Amille would never know this
particular kind of completeness with Baron Winthrop,
yet in spite of that, Amille seemed to be happier than
Rosalie had ever known her to be. The two women had
spent a long time together the day before, talking

about all that had happened and recognizing that although they were not related by blood, they were nevertheless mother and daughter. Smiling in contentment, Rosalie turned her attention back to Rand.

"*Maman* once told me that a woman's duty was to give man pleasure," Rosalie said, her silken legs entwined with his pleasantly rough ones. "But she never told me that he returned the obligation."

Rand chuckled, lifting his mouth from her tingling skin and looking at her with an intimate glow in his eyes.

"I must admit, before meeting you I never expected to find such pleasure in the marriage bed."

"Why is it," Rosalie wondered thoughtfully, "that a man is supposed to find fulfillment only in the arms of his mistress and not his wife?"

"Because unlike me, the average man does not marry his mistress."

As he had expected, the taunt roused her ire. Uttering mock threats of revenge, Rosalie slammed a pillow over his mischievous face and shrieked with laughter as Rand rolled on top of her to keep her still. They engaged in such play for long, enjoyable moments until the tickling and cavorting changed into inquiring strokes and unrestrained caresses. Rosalie felt the irresistible magic of his lovemaking saturate her senses. She returned his kisses eagerly, still unable to believe that he was hers and that he wanted her with the same insatiable hunger that consumed her. Boldly he possessed her, his shoulders rising above hers in flexing power. Rosalie sighed in pleasure, her arms encircling his neck. She loved this moment above all others, when she knew that she was his entire world and that his every thought, his every sensation, centered upon her alone.

After their passion was sated they talked with uninhibited freedom, sharing their thoughts.

"Do you suppose," Rosalie asked quietly, "that we'll ever see Mireille again?"

"It depends," Rand replied, shrugging. "If she's still with Guillaume, I'd say it was likely."

"Why? Are you still planning to look for Guillaume?"

"At this moment I have men scouring England and France for any sign of him."

"I don't care about him. But I would like for Mireille to be found." Rosalie was quiet for several minutes after that, until Rand kissed her forehead and voiced a gentle question.

"What are you thinking about?"

"Brummell," Rosalie answered hesitantly. "I wonder how often he thinks about me . . . or Lucy."

"He probably tries not to," Rand replied. "And I'll wager that it haunts him every day." Rosalie nodded wistfully, laying her head on his chest and drawing from his steady comfort.

They were quiet and content in each other's embrace until the sun began to rise, its gentle light shining through the luminous mist of dawn. My first day as his wife, Rosalie thought, and her eyes glittered with sudden tears of bliss. Rand took his contemplative gaze from the window and looked down at her, understanding her with the acute perception that love brings. They smiled at each other, and then their lips met in a passionate kiss.

"Rose . . ." Rand breathed against her mouth. "No more adventures for a while."

"None, I promise."

"A year's respite is all I ask. Now that we're married, we'll set up a household, have a child, go to an occasional ball—"

"Yes, my dearest love," Rosalie agreed, smiling secretly to herself.

Somehow she knew that adventures would find them anyway.

In the spirit of romantic
passion and rousing adventure,
we invite you to read
this thrilling excerpt from

To
Love A
Rogue

by
Valerie Sherwood

A deliciously sexy historical
novel, with a heroine who is
as much a rogue as the
men who pursue her

Coming in October, 1987
from ONYX

Philip mumbled something and pressed a kiss on a trembling nipple before he rose and began to dress. Lorraine could hardly see him in the darkness but she began to dress as well—in her other dress. There was not much difference between them to be sure—both were russet, both were worn, but at least this one, while much mended, did not have a bad rip in it. She wished she had something better to wear, for both these homespun gowns represented her status as a bound girl and they were part of all the unhappiness she was leaving behind her.

"Wait here until I've cleared the door," he murmured. "Then after a moment you can come down."

She waited quietly for several minutes, then crept over and peered down into the dim empty room below. It was almost daylight, and as she moved to lower herself, she realized that the ladder was gone. Philip must have thoughtlessly removed it.

Then it struck her with shock: Philip meant to leave without her! He was not going to subject her to the dangers of his escape—he was going to run for it alone! Oh, no, he must not!

She lowered herself through the hole in the low ceiling and dropped catlike to the hard-packed earthen floor below.

i

Before her the inn door stood open, and to her surprise, Oddsbud came through it carrying an armload of wood for the fire. She had not known Oddsbud was up, and wondered fearfully if he had seen Philip. But his words were for her.

"Lorraine!" he exclaimed. "Up already?" He gave her a surprised look, for Lorraine usually had to be roused by much calling and pounding on the ceiling.

"I . . ." she choked, no good explanation coming to her.

At a noise behind him, Oddsbud's attention was diverted. But Lorraine's eyes dilated as, through the doorway behind him, young Bob swaggered in wearing the stranger's blue coat. The tavernkeeper, standing stock still with the load of firewood clutched in his beefy arms, stared at those silver buttons, those dark blue velvet cuffs. "Where did you get that coat?" he whispered hoarsely. "Don't tell me there was murder done here last night?"

Bob shrugged and laughed. "Of course not," he scoffed. "I diced the fellow for it and won. Like the fit?"

"It hangs on you. That fellow's shoulders were inches wider," said Oddsbud, eyeing the sky blue coat in alarm. He added slowly, "'Tis folly for you to wear it, Bob, for many saw him wearing it last night."

Bob laughed again. He had a pleased and reckless air about him, and he went over and sat down.

"Bring me a tankard of ale, old fuss-box and stop your whining. No harm's been done that will overset you!"

Shaking his head, Oddsbud turned to Lorraine. "Bring the lad his ale."

Lorraine hesitated. She wanted to run after her dearest Philip, but wouldn't that give away the fact that he'd been here? she asked herself guiltily. She'd done enough to him already! As she stood uncertainly, through the door erupted a frightening sight.

A man with a bloodied dark head and a torn cambric shirt stained with mud, his gray eyes bloodshot and blazing like seven devils in his white face, burst through the door and was upon Bob before he could even rise from his seat. The man's hard fist smashed into Bob's surprised and frightened mouth, bloodying his nose and sending him back hard against the wall. A blow from the left and one from the right rocked Bob's head from side to side.

"And now," the man said in a low deadly voice, "I'll relieve you of that coat, you thieving swine. And if you so much as crease it when you take it off, you'll get a ball between your ribs!"

Terrified, Bob saw that he was looking down the barrel of a large pistol held in a very steady hand. "I only borrowed the coat," he choked, his dazed eyes staring in fascination at the pistol. "You'd not yet come to and I thought you'd not miss it for a while. I meant to bring it back!"

There was a growl of disbelief from the man before him. Lorraine and Oddsbud stood transfixed.

Bob was sweating now, and terror shone in his eyes. "I didn't mean to hit you so hard with that stick of wood last night."

"Came at me from behind, you did, while your friend took a shot at me!"

Bob swallowed. "Philip never even pointed his gun at you—he fired up into the trees!" He struggled out of the coat as he spoke. "'Twas but a game. We were only funning—"

"Fun!" Cameron roared as he reached over with a rough hand and, seizing young Bob by his shirt, shook him so hard his teeth rattled in his head. "I heard your fancy friend and that clod in buckskins planning outside how they would start a fight and lure the girl out—and make her think Buckskins was dead to gain her sympathy

—and then into the woods with her so Satin Coat could bed her! And now I've no doubt I was the 'corpse' that was used to hoodwink her!''

Lorraine's eyes grew wide with comprehension and horror. She felt the strength leave her limbs and almost crumpled to the floor.

"Does a wager mean so much to you rustics that you would jump a man from behind?" Cameron snatched his coat and stuck his gun back in his belt. "By God, I'll teach you manners!" Raile roared. In fury, he drew back his arm and delivered such a blow as sent the quaking young man across the room to end up stretched senseless over a table.

"A good job, that," said the tavernkeeper in a pleased voice. He studied Bob's fallen form admiringly. "And something I've often yearned to do myself."

"A . . . wager? Did you say a wager?" asked Lorraine in a voice that shook.

"Aye, the satin-coated dandy planned to bed you by a ruse." Raile swung around to see her swaying, white-faced, against the doorjamb, her hemp-pale hair a tumbled mass, her face such a picture of woe that it wrenched his heart. "And from the look of you, I see he managed it."

Lorraine nodded in misery. Her slight form seemed to shrink as she leaned against the doorway staring out into the morning mist where Philip had gone—without her. She was fighting for control, but her body felt spent and used. Her lips moved tremulously as she fought back tears.

"If you'll but point out where the tall laddie is, I'll punish him for you, lass," Raile added grimly.

Lorraine opened her mouth to answer him but no sound came out. The weight of the world seemed suddenly to have fallen onto her slender shoulders, and had the very ground dropped away from beneath her feet at that moment, she would have taken no notice.

Swallowing, she moistened her lips and tried again to answer the stranger.

"He is gone," she mumbled. She peered outside, feeling numb. "I suppose he must have gone home. He told me he must fly for he had killed you. That as you fought you had pulled out a pistol and he had whipped out his own and shot you, unthinking. I felt—I felt it was my fault . . . that he had killed you out of jealousy over me and would most likely die for it." She covered her white face with her hands and rocked in silent misery.

"So he played on your tender sympathies," muttered Raile in disgust.

"Fool of a wench!" Oddsbud turned from admiring Bob's fallen form and spat. "Ye must have known young Philip's been courting Lavinia Todd down Providence way?"

Lorraine hadn't known, and a spasmodic shudder went through her body.

Raile swung a bloodshot gaze toward Oddsbud, who fell silent—till he thought of business. "You're forgetting!" he cried indignantly. "You can't leave! You owe me for last night's ale and supper!"

The tavernkeeper's sharp voice brought Raile's lowering attention onto him again. "'Tis pay you want, is it, landlord? For letting your patrons be set upon in your establishment and half-killed and left out in the trees by your woodpile to die? Well, here's for the ale and the supper!" He threw a coin on the table so hard it bounced off and rolled across the hard-packed earthen floor, turned contemptuously, and went out, brushing by Lorraine, who sagged in the doorway.

He untied his horse and mounted, a stern figure in his sky-blue coat and muddied boots and trousers.

As he wheeled about, prepared to make off into the morning mist, he caught sight again of the girl, trembling with wordless grief in the doorway.

"Ride with me and I'll take you out of here, Lorraine," he said evenly. "You've only to climb up, and we're off."

Lorraine dropped her hands and looked up, caught a wavering vision through her tears of a tall grim man astride a big brown horse.

Ride with me!

He offered her escape! And how could she stay here and face them, all those men, Oddsbud's patrons, with their sly grins, their catcalls, their covert pinches, their guffaws, and see the knowledge writ plain across their smirking faces that Philip—Philip whom she'd loved with all her heart and had believed loved her too—had bedded her, not for love, *but on a wager!*

Oh God, she could not face Philip!

Lorraine gave no thought to the future. At that moment she cared not if the tall man on the big brown horse were the devil himself. He had offered her escape and she would take it! Without a word she ran toward him and he swung her up before him on the saddle.

"Ho there!" roared the landlord, erupting wrathfully after them out of the tavern. "You can't take the wench with you! Lorraine's indentured to me for another year!"

The Scot, who cared not overmuch for the law, had nevertheless a fine feeling for liberty—his own and others'. His sinewy arm was locked about the girl's slender waist and he felt the swift thud of her heart, felt her young breasts bounce as she started fearfully at the tavernkeeper's wrathful cry.

"I've just loosed her bonds!" Raile wheeled his big horse about, sending Oddsbud scurrying back. "She'll have a taste of freedom with me!"

"I'll have the law on you!" shouted Oddsbud, shaking his fat fist but staying well back from the armed stranger.

"Be damned to your laws!" Raile called back over his shoulder. "I'm taking the girl with me—for shame that you'd hold a woman's body in bondage!" He nudged his horse with his knee and they were off in the morning mist.

"After them, Oddsbud!" cried his wife, who had come out in time to hear this last exchange of words.

Irresolutely Oddsbud turned to go inside for his musket. Then he paused to look after the wild pair, flying down the road on a fast horse. The last he saw of them was the girl's pale hair streaming in the wind and Raile's broad shoulders as they disappeared from view.

"Hurry!" bawled his wife, shaking him frantically by the shoulder. "Can't you see they're getting away, you fool?"

Oddsbud shook her off. Some tattered shreds of gallantry were still left in him. In his heart he felt reluctant admiration for the durable stranger who had after all been struck down at Oddsbud's establishment and left for dead.